"You're tense." He stated it, rather than asking.

She swallowed. He'd picked up on her feelings and there was no use in hiding them. "I'm…a little nervous, yes."

He stopped short of the doorway, turning to look at her. "You know, Jazmin, we don't have to do anything tonight, if you're not sure."

"It's not that." She looked away from his intense gaze. "I want you, Savion. Probably more than I'd care to admit."

He placed his free hand on her shoulder. "Jazmin, you can feel free to tell me whatever you think I need to know and keep the rest to yourself. I'm not here to pressure you into anything. Not talking, or kissing, and certainly not making love."

She shifted her gaze back up to meet his, seeing the sincerity in his eyes.

"I want to make love to you tonight, Jazmin. But if you're not ready, for any reason, I will wait." He gave her shoulder a gentle squeeze before dropping his hand away.

She exhaled. "Let's go inside."

Kianna Alexander, like any good Southern belle, wears many hats: loving wife, doting mama, advice-dispensing sister and gabbing girlfriend. She's a voracious reader, an amateur seamstress and occasional painter in oils. Chocolate, American history, sweet tea and Idris Elba are a few of her favorite things. A native of the Tar Heel state, Kianna still lives there with her husband, two kids and a collection of well-loved vintage '80s Barbie dolls. You can keep up with Kianna's releases and appearances by signing up for her mailing list at www.authorkiannaalexander.com/sign-up.

Books by Kianna Alexander

Harlequin Kimani Romance

This Tender Melody
Every Beat of My Heart
A Sultry Love Song
Tempo of Love
A Love Like This
A San Diego Romance
Love for All Time
Forever with You

Visit the Author Page at Harlequin.com for more titles.

KIANNA ALEXANDER
and
JOY AVERY

Forever with You &
The Sweet Taste of Seduction

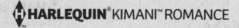

HARLEQUIN® KIMANI™ ROMANCE

ISBN-13: 978-1-335-00585-4

Forever with You & The Sweet Taste of Seduction

Copyright © 2019 by Harlequin Books S.A.

The publisher acknowledges the copyright holders of the individual works as follows:

Forever with You
Copyright © 2019 by Eboni Manning

"Numb, Discovery, Distinguished"
Copyright © 2019 by Erica D. Wade. Used with permission.

The Sweet Taste of Seduction
Copyright © 2019 by Joy Avery

PLEASE RECYCLE · THIS PRODUCT IS RECYCLABLE

Recycling programs for this product may not exist in your area.

HARLEQUIN

www.Harlequin.com

Printed in U.S.A.

CONTENTS

FOREVER WITH YOU 7
Kianna Alexander

THE SWEET TASTE OF SEDUCTION 205
Joy Avery

In loving memory of my sweet, funny
and fashionable aunt.

Gwendolyn Denise Mckinnon
1957–2017

Acknowledgments

As always, a shout-out to my Destin Divas,
the best squad a girl could ask for.
Thanks to Kaia Alderson-Tyson, my brainstorming
and crit partner. Thanks to my street team,
and thanks to all my readers, no matter how long
you've been reading my work.

FOREVER WITH YOU

Kianna Alexander

Dear Reader,

Thank you so much for picking up a copy of *Forever with You*. I hope you'll enjoy Savion and Jazmin's love story. Savion, the eldest and most serious of the Monroe family, has had good reason to be that way. He's been hiding a secret from his friends and family, one that may change the way they perceive him. Read on to find out how he and Jazmin navigate that bumpy terrain together.

This will be my last Sapphire Shores book with Kimani Romance, but who knows? If you, the reader, want to see more Sapphire Shores books, reach out to me on social media or by email. I love hearing from you!

All the best,

Kianna

Chapter 1

Jazmin Boyd sidestepped between the clothes-laden circular racks inside of Driven to Distraction, her eyes scanning the selections for just the right piece. The interior of the boutique reflected the exterior; the rose-gold paint job on the facade continued inside, where the plush pink Victorian-inspired furniture, crystal chandeliers and polished teak floors accented the space. The boutique, easily the most exclusive apparel store on the small island of Sapphire Shores, North Carolina, was the obvious choice for finding the right dress for the social event of the spring season.

She reached into a section of metallic cocktail dresses and was still rifling through it when Sierra Dandridge-Monroe, her closest friend, appeared beside her. Holding up a teal, sequined halter dress, Sierra released a squeal of excitement. "Girl, isn't this cute? I think this is it. I need to try it on."

Jazmin gave her friend a sidelong glance. "Isn't that dress a little short for a fortieth anniversary party? I'm thinking this crowd is going to skew a little older."

Sierra shrugged. "I'm already married to Cam. I'm not trying to impress anybody but him." She held the dress against herself and twirled. "Besides, older doesn't necessarily mean more conservative. Cam's parents certainly aren't, and it's their party."

"Okay, I'll give you that." She returned her attention to the rack, moving each hanger aside and inspecting each individual piece.

Behind her, Sierra quietly asked, "Still trying to cover it up, huh?"

Her hand went to her neck, her fingertips grazing over the hardened skin beneath her top. She nodded.

"You know, I've noticed a change in you since you've been here on the island, working on the show." Sierra's hand came to rest on her shoulder. "You're a lot calmer and happier here."

"That's true." Sierra was as insightful as ever, and Jazmin would be the first to admit that she'd been far more relaxed since her arrival on the island. *But I'm still not ready to let people see my scar.*

"You know, it's already getting pretty hot and humid around these parts. And as the summer wears on, it's gonna become pretty hard to cover up, the way you have been doing." Sierra gave her shoulder a squeeze before letting her hand drop. "I don't want you bursting into flames, Jaz."

She giggled, loving the way her friend could infuse

a bit of humor into an uncomfortable moment. "I appreciate your concern, Sierra. But I'm just not there yet." She slid another outfit to the left and stopped, looking at the dress she'd just uncovered. Picking the hanger off the rack, she raised the garment in front of her. The lavender dress, woven through with shimmery silver threads, had long, sheer sleeves. The high, regal neckline appealed to her, since she'd come to favor this style over the last few years for both elegance and coverage. "This looks very promising."

"Wow, Jaz. It's gorgeous." Sierra reached out and stroked her fingertips over the soft fabric. "Let's try these on. Remember, we still have to get accessories. And I want to get back to my husband before it gets dark out."

She shook her head as they headed toward the back of the store to make use of the fitting rooms.

Inside the quiet cocoon of the changing room, Jazmin slipped out of her jeans and T-shirt and into the dress. Looking in the full-length mirror, she smiled. The color of the dress made her skin tone pop, and she loved the fit—close, but not too tight. She unlocked the door, stepped out and waited in the mirrored common area for Sierra to appear in her dress.

When Sierra finally emerged in the hot little teal number, Jazmin instantly remarked, "Yeah. That's the one."

Sierra grinned, revolving and checking all the angles in the mirrors. "Yeah, you're right." She paused then, looking her over. "And you have got to buy that one, Jaz. It's perfect for you."

Regarding her reflection, she had to agree. It covered everything she wanted to be hidden from sight, but didn't obscure the figure she worked so hard to maintain. "I agree. Looks like we're ready to move on to the accessorizing phase."

Still dressed in their new finds, the two women circled the boutique, trying on jewelry and more. Sierra bought a pair of gold hoop earrings encrusted with crystals, as well as a pair of pumps nearly the same shade as her dress.

"I've got a pair of silver shoes that will work with this dress." Jazmin selected a pair of dangling crystal-chandelier earrings, a few sterling silver bangles and a silver clip for her hair. After they'd gotten back into their street clothes, they piled their purchases on the counter and pulled out their wallets.

Carrie, the boutique's owner, smiled as she rang them up. "It's so great to have you shopping with us again, Mrs. Monroe. My daughters and I are really looking forward to season two. It's starting to film again soon, isn't it?"

"In the next week or so," Sierra answered as she handed over her credit card.

Watching the exchange, Jazmin was once again thankful for her behind-the-scenes role on *The Shores*. As time passed, and the show became more popular, she watched Sierra go through more and more of these fan encounters. Sierra was a natural at this, so she was always gracious and poised while being pelted with questions and comments from eager viewers. Jazmin knew that if she had to deal with that level of attention, it would quickly start to grate on her nerves.

"You know, it's really my girl Jazmin you should

thank," Sierra commented, gesturing toward her. "She's in charge of postproduction, so the finished product you see on television is the result of her hard work."

Jazmin smiled as Carrie's attention swung her way. "Well, when your rough material is already so high-quality, it's not so hard to do." She gave Sierra a playful jab in the shoulder, then stepped up for her turn to pay for her items.

Carrie handed Sierra her bag. "Well, I appreciate both of you for your hard work. My daughters are seventeen and twenty, and we rarely agree on anything these days. But we can all sit and watch *The Shores* together." She used her price gun to scan the tags. "And it's nice to know that you're actually friends and not just coworkers."

"What can I say? I'm a lucky girl." Jazmin winked in Sierra's direction.

By the time the two of them left with their purchases, it was well past six. The sun was moving toward the horizon, but there would be another good hour of sunlight before darkness settled over the island. The cool, refreshing breeze coming off the Atlantic wafted by, lifting the loose ends of Jazmin's hair and making her sigh with delight.

"Do you wanna go for dinner? Or are you rushing home to your man?" Gripping the handle of her bag in one hand, she used her other one to gently pinch Sierra's shoulder.

"Ow!" She twisted her lips in a mock frown. "See, that type of abuse is why I'm taking my butt home."

Jazmin rolled her eyes. "As if there was any doubt. I'm gonna hit Della's on the way in. I'm starved."

"Okay. See you at the party, boo." Sierra reached out and pulled her into a hug. "Text me when you get home, Jaz."

"Sure thing." She gave Sierra a squeeze, then her friend waved and walked to her car, got in and drove away.

After she left, Jazmin tucked her bag into her trunk, then strolled down the sidewalk toward the deli.

Savion Monroe eased into the chair behind his desk with a sigh. Being able to shut himself in his office and decompress, after what had been a very long day, gave him immense relief.

He'd spent the better part of the day in meetings with the rest of the staff of Monroe Holdings, Incorporated. As the chief executive officer, he was responsible for final approval for all MHI's projects. The day-to-day management of all the existing properties held by the company, which owned 63 percent of the land and buildings on the island, would be enough to keep him busy. However, MHI was in the final stages of planning the most important project they had ever tackled: the Mary Ellen Monroe Memory Park. The green space, meant to memorialize Savion's paternal grandmother, had finally gotten all the necessary approvals and permits to move forward. His father, Carver, was overseeing a memory garden containing a bust of his mother that would serve as the centerpiece of the grounds.

I'm going to do this right. Not just to honor Grandma, but to make my father proud. He worked hard to keep the business successful, just as his father had done before retiring. Savion understood that even as the eldest Monroe child, he wasn't necessarily entitled to the CEO role. He'd earned it by showing his father a strong work ethic and a commitment to the family real-estate empire. Working side by side with his two younger siblings could be stressful at times, but he loved knowing that he was an integral part of the family legacy.

He grabbed his leather-bound daybook, opened it and placed it on the desk in front of him. The book measured five-by-eight inches, and the brown leather had started to crack around the edges, showing how aged and well-loved it was. It was his single most valued possession, and he never went anywhere without it. At night, he laid it on his nightstand while he slept, in case he awakened in the wee hours and needed to make note of something. When he drove, it rested in the center console of his SUV. Wherever he went, it was either in his hand or tucked beneath his arm. Because of its size, most people assumed it was a planner, a place where he kept track of his appointments and responsibilities. He'd migrated his schedule to a cloud-based app ages ago, along with the rest of tech-savvy society, but he'd kept the book, knowing that people's perception of it as an ordinary planner would work in his favor.

And no one, under any circumstances, was allowed to touch it. His brother and sister often teased him about his "unnatural attachment" to the book, but they knew better than to try him, so they left it alone. He made sure that every new employee knew never to mess with it, should he ever mistakenly leave it lying around. While he couldn't imagine ever being careless with

the book, he considered his hands-off decree an extra
insurance policy for keeping his writings private. He
wouldn't know what he'd do if someone were to open
it and peruse the contents.

Picking up the pencil resting in an elastic loop on
the inside of the leather cover, he flipped to a blank
page and started jotting down his thoughts.

He'd written three and a half lines when he heard
someone knocking on his office door. With a groan,
he tucked the pencil back into the loop, then closed the
notebook and the cover. "Come in."

The door swung open and Hadley strolled in.
Dressed in a dark skirt and white blouse with the blue-
and-green MHI logo on the front, she carried a small
stack of folders. Looking at his desk, she said, "Sorry.
I didn't mean to interrupt your planning period. I can
come back later if you want."

He shook his head. "It's already after five. I'm going
home soon, so go ahead and say what you need to say."

She chuckled while stifling a yawn. "We both know
you'll be here a while, but okay." She came to the desk,
taking the seat across from him, and opened one of the
folders. "I came to let you in on the last-minute preparations for Mom and Dad's party."

He frowned. "I thought everything was taken care
of."

"It is, for the most part. But one of the interns
screwed up two of the payments, and I've gotta get
that straightened out." She blew out a breath, as if exasperated. "They paid the caterer the money due to the
deejay, and vice versa. Now the deejay owes us a re-
fund and we still have a balance with the caterer. It's

a bit of a mess." She yawned again, her eyes closing briefly then popping open again.

"Sheesh." He leaned back in his chair. "The party's in two days. Do you have enough time to straighten it out?"

"Yes, if you let me have tomorrow off. That way I can go do this in person."

His brow hitched. "You're telling me you need the whole day off to do those two things?"

"It's not just that." She glanced down at a page in her folder. "Remember, the company is coming over to set up the tent tomorrow, too, and I'm also overseeing the decorations, the people installing the dance floor, making sure we have enough fans and that the electrical hookups are in place—"

He put up his hand. "Okay, okay. Stop rattling off items on the list. Considering all that, yes, you can take the day off."

"Great. Oh, and you know Cam's off tomorrow, too, right?"

He rolled his eyes. "Damn it. I forgot." He watched his sister close the folder and stand. "What is he doing? Because I know he's not helping with the party. He hates planning things like that."

"You're right, he's not helping me. He's taking Sierra to Wilmington to see the battleship. Apparently, after all this time here, she's never been on it."

"Fantastic," he groused. The USS *North Carolina*, a World War II–era battleship docked on the seaport in downtown Wilmington, was one of the most popular tourist destinations in the area. The most decorated American battleship of the Second World War, the old

BB-55 had seen combat in every significant American naval offensive in the Pacific theater. "I'm gonna guess he booked a special VIP tour, right?"

She nodded. "Of course. You know Cam. He never does anything by half measures." She walked over to the door, leaned against it and yawned again.

Feeling his brow furrow, he asked, "Sis, are you okay? You seem tired." Studying her face, he noted that she also looked a little pale.

She waved him off. "I'm fine, just a little wiped. Guess I should have had that second cup of coffee."

He wasn't sure if he believed that, but he wasn't about to rile up his baby sister. *I'm too tired to deal with her if she gets snappy.* "You know, you're hardly ever here since you married Devon. And it's more of the same with Cam since he and Sierra got hitched. Am I the only one around here who cares about keeping MHI in the black?"

She rolled her eyes. "Savion, you already know we care about the family business just as much as you do. The only reason you're here all the time is that you insist on avoiding romantic involvement."

"You two already fell into the 'love trap.' I can't be falling in, too. Somebody has to be the responsible one."

"Whatever. You can do both, you know." She stood in the door frame, poised to walk out. "And let me assure you, it's no trap. It's the best, most enriching part of my life." With that said, she and her folder disappeared.

Left alone in his office, Savion contemplated his sister's words for a moment, then pushed aside his thoughts and faced down the work still to be done.

Chapter 2

Jazmin reclined in the plush padded folding chair, a filled flute of champagne in her hand. The atmosphere beneath the big white tent set up on the Monroes' sprawling property was as festive as tonight's occasion called for. Sitting next to her, Sierra drank from her own glass of prosecco. "Can you believe Carver and Viola have been married forty years?"

She shook her head. "It's really something. Especially since Mrs. Monroe only looks about forty-five herself." She looked over to the head table and saw the happy couple seated at the center. While they were surrounded by their children and close family members, it was obvious that Viola and Carver only had eyes for one another. *Maybe it's the glow of love that keeps her looking so young.*

Sierra's voice broke into her thoughts. "Campbell

can be a handful sometimes. But we're in it for the long haul. One day, you'll be coming to our fortieth anniversary party."

"I'll be sure to put it in my datebook," Jazmin chided, elbowing Sierra playfully. The sound of a fork striking glass caught Jazmin's attention. Her gaze swung back to the head table, just in time to see Savion, the eldest Monroe child, climb to his feet. Conversation died down, and the hired disc jockey stopped spinning records as everyone present looked toward the front table. Savion's tall, solid frame, draped in an expensive-looking tailored tuxedo, commanded attention. The tux, a deep shade of blue, was complemented by his crisp jet-black shirt and blue-and-gold striped tie. The dark pools of his eyes shimmered in the candlelit glow inside the tent. His strong jaw and goateed chin made him look like the perfect combination of refinement and ruggedness. His deep voice filled the tent. "I'd like to thank you all for coming out tonight, to celebrate my parents' milestone anniversary. Forty years of love and commitment is no small feat, especially in today's world. It seems marriage has fallen out of fashion, and folks change spouses as carelessly as they change clothes. I'm grateful to my mother and father for the example they have shown my siblings and me, and for the stable, loving upbringing they gave us."

Jazmin felt a tear slip down her cheek as the profundity of his words struck her.

Savion lifted his glass into the air, and everyone followed suit. "I'd like to raise a toast. To my father and mother, who have shown us all how beautiful love can be. Congratulations."

"Salud." Jazmin took a sip from her glass, then set it on the table to join in the rousing applause that went up as Carver leaned over and tenderly kissed his wife of four decades. A sigh escaped Jazmin as she watched the exchange. As everyone took their seats, the band began to play the classic jazz standard "In a Sentimental Mood." Carver stood, gallantly offering his hand to Viola, then led her to the dance floor set up between the head table and the rest of the tables.

Jazmin pressed her hand to her chest, watching as the couple of the hour swirled around the dance floor, their bodies pressed close together. Mrs. Monroe looked resplendent in her floor-grazing gold charmeuse gown, and her husband's dark tuxedo, gold bow tie and vest made their attire as perfectly complementary as they were to each other.

Sierra sighed. "Look at them. They're so dang sweet together it makes my teeth hurt."

Campbell appeared next to the table, wearing his signature smile. "Sierra, come dance with me, baby."

"I thought you were supposed to be sitting at the head table?" Sierra made the remark with a cocked eyebrow.

"I am. But I'm not about to miss an opportunity to dance with my beautiful wife."

Sierra stood and took his hand. Glancing Jazmin's way, she said, "I'll be back, girl."

Jazmin waved her off. "Go on, dance with your man. I'll be fine."

After the newlyweds wandered off, Jazmin settled back in her chair, nursing the remains of her champagne. She let her gaze sweep around the tent, to the couples taking the dance floor and the folks hanging around at the tables and by the buffet. This was her second time at a Monroe family shindig, the first having been Campbell and Sierra's London wedding last fall. She had to admit, they knew how to throw a classy affair.

Thinking of the wedding brought up memories of dancing with Savion. He'd been sure on his feet as he guided her around the floor, and she could clearly recall how he'd smelled of rich amber and fir, and the way he'd kept her laughing with his dry wit. He was fine. The kind of fine that made a woman want to throw both caution and her panties to the wind. She didn't want to dwell on that too long, lest the glass of champagne already in her system make her abandon her better judgment. So, she turned her mind elsewhere.

She'd been on the island of Sapphire Shores for a little over a year now, working as postproduction manager on *The Shores*, the popular television drama filmed on location here. Showrunner Devon Granger, whom she'd known for years in Los Angeles, had pulled her in on the project, and she truly enjoyed it. Working with the cast and crew had been mostly pleasant, save for a few bumps here and there. The only thing she didn't like about her gig with the show was the slow pace of life on the island. Being a city girl, born and bred in LA, made the quiet calm of the island seem a bit maddening at times. Still, because she loved the work she did here, she did her best to embrace the island, its residents and all its quirks.

When she thought about it, the call from Devon had come at just the right time. As much as she loved LA, she'd needed to get away from there, needed to get a fresh start, far away from where things had gone off the rails for her. And after she'd secured her position on the production team, the first suggestion she'd made was to let her good friend Sierra read for the lead role. Mindful of the happiness of the occasion, she pushed away those thoughts. Today wasn't about dwelling on the darkness she'd left behind in the City of Angels. Today was about celebrating a love that had lasted four decades and was still going strong.

She noticed Savion standing at one end of the head table, talking to a man she didn't recognize, but whose features bore similarities to Carver's. The way they conversed conveyed a certain familiarity, another factor that made Jazmin think the two of them might be related. Whoever the other man was, he and Savion seemed to be having a serious conversation. Jazmin also noticed that every few words, one of them would gesture in her direction. After the third time, Jazmin could feel her brow creasing. They seemed to be talking about her, but she couldn't imagine why they'd be doing that, or what they might be saying. *What's going on over there?* It appeared she would soon get her answer because, a few moments later, Savion started striding toward her, his gaze locked on her face.

After making his toast celebrating his parents' union, Savion left his seat and moved toward the end of the head table, intending to grab a dessert from the buffet. He was waylaid when his cousin Troy stepped into his path. "What's up, Savion?"

He could feel the smile stretching his lips. "If it ain't

troublemaking Troy. I haven't seen you in forever. How you been?" The two shared a quick embrace.

"I'm doing okay. And you're right, it's been way too long since I came to see my East Coast fam."

Savion gave his cousin a playful punch in the shoulder. "You're damn right. What's it been, five or six years?"

Troy shrugged. "To be honest, I don't even remember. But, of course, I wasn't gonna miss Uncle Carver and Aunt Viola's milestone anniversary."

"How's Uncle Wardell?"

"You know Pops. He's salty as ever." Troy laughed. "But as long as I make sure to keep him supplied with cigars, he does all right."

He didn't have to ask why Wardell wasn't present— he hated weddings, anniversaries and anything associated with what he referred to as the "farce known as love." His uncle's brief marriage to his aunt Frieda had been strained at best and disastrous at worst. The West Coast Monroes were known for drama, at least up until Frieda had split, finally giving Wardell grounds for divorce. "What have you been up to?"

"Ranching, mainly. Worked on a couple different spreads out west, mainly between Santa Fe and Durango." He ran a hand over his hair. "I've stayed pretty close to home because I love it out there, ya know?"

"I get it. You've always been a fan of wide-open spaces." He'd visited the area twice in the last few years, and he could see why Troy loved the plains so much. To call the area "scenic" would constitute a gross understatement.

"I'd ask what you've been up to, but I already know.

Still working in the office, doing your CEO thing. I see you, cousin. Go ahead and take over the world."

Savion shook his head, stepping back to look at Troy's black suit, white shirt and gold tie. "You clean up all right, Troy."

"Thanks." Troy made a show of tugging his lapels. "You look pretty clean yourself. So tell me, Savion. What's been happening around here?"

He chuckled. "Man, it would take all day to tell you what's happened since the last time you visited."

"Good thing I'm staying a few weeks. You, Hadley and Cam will have plenty of time to catch me up." Troy winked.

"I was headed to the dessert table. You wanna join me?"

Troy shook his head. "Watching my sugar intake. Plus, let's be honest, Savion. The only sweet thing you've got your eye on is that one over there." Troy made a sly gesture over Savion's shoulder.

Savion already knew to whom Troy was referring. He glanced in that direction, his eyes falling on Jazmin Boyd. She worked in the production department on *The Shores*, and she'd danced with him at Cam's wedding last fall.

Today, she wore a shimmery purple cocktail dress that just grazed her knees. The high neck and sheer sleeves covered her shoulders and arms, but the hem did nothing to hide the expanse of her long brown legs, which attracted his attention. Her upswept hair, light makeup and dazzling earrings completed her elegant look.

Troy snapped his fingers. "See? You've been checking her out all evening. Do you know her?"

Savion sighed, annoyed that his cousin had so easily picked up on his interest. "I know her, but just barely. Her name is Jazmin and she works on Devon's television show."

Troy elbowed him. "Go talk to her! You've been sweating her all night. Might as well go make a move, playa."

Savion rolled his eyes. His cousin was known to be a shoot-from-the-hip type of guy, so he wasn't surprised by Troy's words. "What about you, Troy? Is there anyone special in your life?"

"Nah, man. And don't be trying to change the subject." Troy gestured toward Jazmin again. "You go get your lady, and I'm about to catch up with the rest of the fam."

Savion drew a deep breath, turned and walked toward Jazmin. Their eyes met and held as he approached. She stood from her seat as he entered her space. "Savion. How are you?"

"I'm fine, Jazmin. And you?"

"Doing well." She glanced down, the dark fan of her lashes fluttering. "It's…nice to see you again."

"Believe me. The pleasure is mine." At that moment, he felt the words of a verse bloom inside his mind. She was walking inspiration for the words that flowed from his pen.

The DJ segued into a slow cut by Ro James, and Savion saw the window of opportunity opening. "Jazmin, would you honor me with a dance?"

She gave him a soft smile. "Sure."

He took her hand and eased her out onto the dance floor. Pulling her close enough to get a comfortable hold on her waist, yet leaving a respectable distance between them, he began to guide her as he swayed along with the pace of the music. She smiled, moving a little closer to him until their bodies touched. That was fine by him. Having her so near made his temperature climb a few notches. But as long as it was her decision to close the distance, he was down.

Holding her near as they danced together felt much more natural than he had expected. She seemed to fit perfectly into his arms, as if she'd been formed to be held by only him. He looked down into her eyes, and she met his gaze.

"Savion." His name left her lips with a breathy sigh.

"Yes?"

"Either I've had too much champagne, or you're having an effect on me."

Intrigued by this development, he asked, "What makes you say that?"

"I…want you to kiss me."

He cocked an eyebrow. "Do you?"

She nodded.

"And you're sure about that?"

Another nod. "Yes."

"You don't have to ask twice." So, he leaned down and placed a gentle peck on her lips. They were yielding and sweet, and she tasted of strawberries. He purposely kept the contact brief, aware of the prying eyes of his family and friends all around them. Besides, in case it really was the champagne talking, he wanted to err on the side of caution. When he drew back, he immediately missed the softness of her lips.

She smiled. "I enjoyed that. Probably a little more than I'd like to admit."

The song came to an end, and they took a step apart, giving each other space. Still, nothing could break the attraction that crackled between them like an electric current.

The sound of a loud whistle caught Savion's attention, and he turned to see his cousin Troy signaling to him, a broad grin on his face.

"Who is that?" She posed the question in a voice laced with humor and curiosity.

Rolling his eyes, he turned back to Jazmin. "That's my cousin Troy. My only cousin on my Dad's side. Ignore him."

She laughed. "If you say so."

"Savion! Come over here!" It was Hadley, wildly gesturing to him from the other side of the tent. "We're taking pictures."

"Duty calls." Savion stepped back again, taking a moment to kiss Jazmin's hand in parting. "Thank you for the dance."

She blushed. "You're welcome."

After that, he reluctantly walked away, knowing that if he didn't, his sister would only call him again, and louder.

But even as he moved away from Jazmin, he couldn't deny the pull of her presence, which lingered around him like the sweet fragrance of her perfume.

Chapter 3

With a tall cup of iced coffee in hand, Jazmin sat at the long table in the studio conference room. She knew she shouldn't be drinking coffee past 4:00 p.m., but she'd been dragging since lunch and desperately needed a boost. The caffeine flowing through her system gave her just enough of a buzz to keep her from resting her head on the table for an impromptu nap.

All around her sat the showrunners and the principle cast members. The actors were doing table reads of their scripts for the first episode, which was due to begin filming in a few days, and the showrunners were there to observe.

Aaron Tarlton, the show's director, sat silently at one end of the table, while executive producer and showrunner Devon Granger occupied the seat at the opposite end. Jazmin sat to Devon's right, along with head

writers Kris and Amelia. The actors sat on the left side
of the table.

Sierra, who played the main character, Karen Drake,
turned to Grayson Richardson, the gray-eyed, caramel-
skinned heartthrob who played Karen's love interest,
Xander Lasalle, and delivered her line with the same
passion she did when on camera.

Boy, she's really selling it. What an actress. Jazmin
loved to watch her friend at work, and seeing Sierra
give Grayson a deep, longing look, she was once again
amazed by her talent.

Grayson, known to be something of a goofball despite his reputation as a sex symbol, read his lines in
the same manner. Every bit of energy Sierra gave him,
he returned to her. He even clutched Sierra's hand as
he spoke of his character's devotion to Karen.

Cast newcomer Zola Revere, who'd been recently
placed in the role of Xander's long-lost half sister, Phaedra Lasalle, was another story. Zola, a tall, willowy
twenty-two-year-old with bountiful coils of dark hair
and skin the color of almonds, was the youngest person
in the cast. There were a few interns still in their teens,
but none of the actors on the show were near her age.

Jazmin assumed Zola's awareness of her relative
youth contributed to her shyness. Having seen Zola acting in a short-lived drama from last year, *River's Edge*,
she knew the young sister had talent. She'd do fine at
The Shores, as soon as she found her voice.

As the other two actors turned toward Zola, she delivered her line in a rushed whisper.

"Hold on," Amelia said, leaning forward. "Can you
run that last line again, Zola?"

Zola did as she was asked, but without raising the volume very much.

"Hold on, hold on." Aaron put up his hand. "Zola, we need to be able to hear you. Deliver your lines loudly enough so we can hear you. If you keep doing what you're doing now, even the mics won't be able to pick up what you're saying."

"Buck up, kid," quipped Grayson. "We're all rooting for you to do well here."

Around the table, everyone added their words of encouragement.

Jazmin watched Zola's face light up. They started the read again, and this time, she delivered her line with the appropriate gusto.

"Xander, you know our father would never approve of what you're doing!" Zola stabbed an accusatory finger in the air, in Grayson's direction.

Grayson smiled. "Now we're cooking with grease."

Watching as the rest of the reading progressed without any problems, Jazmin drained her iced coffee while she jotted notes in the small pink notebook on the table in front of her. Devon always asked the crew members present at the table reads to write down their thoughts on things, including the general direction of the show, character arcs and specific lines of dialogue. She liked the new direction the writers had come up with for the second season, and she thought the viewers would like it, as well. With any luck, season two would be just as popular as season one.

After the table read ended, most of the people present cleared out of the conference room. Aaron remained, along with Sierra, Devon and Jazmin. While the men talked shop, Sierra gestured to her. "Jaz. Let's go in the hallway."

Tossing her empty cup into the trash can, she followed her friend out of the room.

In the corridor, Sierra pulled out her phone. "I wanted to show you some of the snaps from London that I haven't shown you yet."

Moving closer to her friend, she looked at the screen. "Oh, are these from filming the movie?" Sierra's main reason for being in London last fall was to film her first romantic comedy, *Her London Love.* There were photos of Sierra with her leading man, in the fitted dress she'd worn for her fictional nuptials, and plenty of random images of the sets, her cast mates and the crew at work.

"Some are, and some are from the real wedding and honeymoon." She scrolled to a photo of her and Campbell, dressed in their wedding finery.

Jazmin couldn't help smiling as she viewed the image. The happy couple was locked in an embrace, their lips pressed together, with a fantastic aerial view of London as the backdrop. "You guys are so cute."

Sierra winked. "Thanks, girl. I really want to go back. Between the wedding and the filming, we never got to see Big Ben. I'm also hoping to get out of the city, take in some of the English countryside."

She leaned back against the wall. "I feel you on that. I'd really like to go to Stratford-upon-Avon one day."

"Really? I never pegged you for a Shakespeare fan."

"Yeah, I'm down with Will Shakes. He had a real way with words. You might say he was an early insult comic."

Sierra's expression conveyed her surprise.

"If you don't believe me, look up 'Shakespearean insults' on the internet someday."

Sierra chuckled. "Maybe I will, Jaz." She tucked her phone into the pocket of her black blazer.

Aaron left the conference room then, squeezing out between the two women. "Excuse me, ladies. I'll see y'all tomorrow."

"Bye, Aaron." Jazmin moved aside as the director passed, watching him disappear down the hall.

Devon came out then, his phone in hand. "Hadley just texted me some of the pictures she took when we were in Tahiti last month. She got a lot of good ones, especially of the beach and the sunsets."

Both women leaned in to see, but Jazmin knew she was the only one holding back an exasperated sigh. The images of her boss and his wife, frolicking in the azure blue water, or the beautiful sunsets over the island, were enough to turn her green with envy.

"Wow. Looks like you two had a great time." Sierra gave Devon's shoulder a squeeze.

"We really did." He put away his phone.

For whatever reason, both Sierra and Devon suddenly looked Jazmin's way.

She shrugged, then stated drily, "I could show you pictures of my potted ficus. I named her Fiona, after our dearly departed character from season one."

Sierra's lips pursed, but Devon immediately started laughing.

"Really, Jaz?" Sierra folded her arms over her chest in mock offense.

Jazmin shrugged again. "You know I love you both,

and I'm happy you're happy. But you make a girl's life seem awfully empty."

By now, Devon was headed down the hall, still chuckling. "I'll see y'all later. And Jaz, give my regards to 'Fiona.'"

Sierra stayed behind. "Jaz, are you okay?"

She laughed. "Girl, I'm fine. I was just teasing you two. You're easy targets, ya know?"

Her brow crinkled. "Jaz..."

"I'm cool, okay? You're as bad as Mama." She started walking toward her office. "I'll see you later, girl. I'm about to starve."

Savion walked into Sweet Temptations with one thing on his mind: the sugary deliciousness of one of Carmen's key lime cheesecakes. Ever since the bakery had opened four months back, he'd been coming here once or twice a week to satisfy his sweet tooth. And while he occasionally indulged in one of owner Carmen Delacroix's other treats, like double fudge cookies or maple peanut-butter blondies, the made-from-scratch key lime cheesecake was his absolute favorite way to treat himself after a stressful day.

Carmen, stationed on a stool behind the counter with an issue of *Real Simple* magazine in hand, looked up when he entered. "Hey, Savion. How are you, boo?"

He smiled back, knowing it was Carmen's way to call everyone who entered her door by some endearment. "I'll be doing a lot better once I get my cheesecake." He made a beeline for the counter, peering into the glass case and letting his gaze sweep over her offerings. Seeing the single, generous slice of cheesecake sitting there, in front of a porcelain plate heaped with cookies, broadened his grin.

"You're in luck. I've only got one slice of key lime left for the day."

"Well, box it up for me, please." He rubbed his hands together, his taste buds already anticipating the flavor of the rich dessert. "It's been hell at work and I really need this pick-me-up."

"You got it." Carmen set aside her magazine and hopped down from the stool. As she turned to grab a box from the stack she kept on a shelf in the prep area, the bell over the door tinkled, indicating the entry of another customer.

He turned in time to see Jazmin stepping over the threshold. A group of four people entered behind her, but by the time the door swung shut again, she looked his way.

Their eyes met, and they silently assessed each other for a few moments. She wore a white button-down blouse with a pair of dark slacks that hugged the curves of her shapely hips. The silver belt circling her waist matched the buckle of the low-heeled loafers on her feet. Her hair was up in a bun on top of her head, but a few tendrils had fallen to frame her beautiful brown face.

Looking at her made it hard to think. He blinked a few times, trying to restart his brain.

"Hi, Savion." Her soft-spoken words beckoned him back to reality.

"Hi, Jazmin. Nice to see you again."

"Likewise." She swallowed, her eyes darting to the display case. "Oh, good. There's one left." She moved toward the counter.

"I see you have a sweet tooth, too. Looks like we have that in common."

She gave him a small, uncertain smile. "So we do."

Carmen cleared her throat then. "I've gotta go to the back for a box. I'm out of the size I need for the cheesecake." She started toward the kitchen. "Be right back."

"Take your time." He rested his elbow on the case, leaning on it and doing his best to look casual despite the way his heart raced whenever Jazmin was near. When he looked her way again, he found her brow furrowed.

"Did she say she's boxing up a cheesecake for you?"

"Yes."

"What kind?"

"Key lime."

Her expression morphed into a full-on frown. "Let me guess. You just bought the last piece, right?"

He watched her for a moment, then spoke. "I did. And by the look on your face, that's what you came for."

She nodded. "I know it's terrible for me, being so heavy and rich. But I don't smoke, and rarely ever drink. A girl's got to have at least one vice, and mine is cheesecake."

"You've taken a fancy to Carmen's cheesecakes? I'll bet you had some really great ones out west."

She shook her head. "Nothing that came close to the ones I buy here."

Carmen returned then with the pastel yellow box, emblazoned with the store's logo—a drawing of a smiling cupcake. Placing it on the counter, she wrapped the cheesecake in parchment paper, then slipped it inside. Closing it, she said, "Come on down to the register and I'll ring you up."

Jazmin's hand shot up. "By any chance do you have

any more key lime cheesecake stashed away in the back?"

Carmen shook her head. "Sorry, honey. This is my last one. I only make four a day. Can't stand the thought of one of my creations spoiling before it's bought and enjoyed."

"Thanks, anyway, Carmen." Her face a mask of disappointment, Jazmin clutched the strap of her handbag and turned toward the door.

I can't let her leave here with that long face. "Wait." He reached out, his fingertips grazing her arm before she could walk away.

"What is it?"

"Listen, it looks like your day was just as rough as mine. And as much as I'd like to eat that entire slice by myself, it's probably not the healthiest thing to do."

She tilted her head to the side. "What are you getting at, Savion?"

"Why don't we share it? It'll be my treat."

She appeared to think it over.

One of the other ladies waiting in line huffed aloud and made a show of crossing her arms over her chest and tapping her foot.

Savion looked from the woman's tight face back to Jazmin, hoping she'd make up her mind before Miss In A Hurry's head exploded.

Finally, Jazmin asked, "Where would we eat it?" The bakery, while unmatched in service and offerings, was a small place with no seating. "I know you don't expect me to come to your place."

He chuckled. "Of course not. I'm a gentleman to the core, so I propose a neutral territory."

"Like where?"

"Are you saying yes?"

She sighed. "Yes."

"One sec." He reached for his wallet, paid Carmen for the slice of cheesecake and took the box from her. "Come with me." With his hand resting lightly on her arm, he led her outside into the cool evening breeze.

On the sidewalk in front of the bakery, she stopped and eyed him. "Okay, so where are we going to eat the cheesecake?"

He looked out toward the water. "Weather's nice. Why don't we sit on one of the benches down at Richardson Point?"

A few beats passed before she said, "Sounds good. Tell you what. I'll run down to the Bean Bonanza and grab us two coffees, then I'll meet you there."

He smiled. "Bet."

"So, what would you like?"

His lips curled into a mischievous smile.

Her cheeks colored, and she looked away. "I should rephrase that."

"If you must."

She took another deep swallow, like the one she'd taken earlier. "How do you take your coffee?"

"Tall, dark and sweet. Just like you." He winked.

She stared at him, and he thought he saw heat dancing behind her gaze.

A moment later, she mumbled, "Um, I'll see you there."

He tried to hide his amusement as he watched her scurry off but had little success.

Chapter 4

When Jazmin got out of her car at Richardson Point, she scanned the four benches near the beach access entrance. It didn't take her long to spot Savion, sitting on the farthest bench from the parking lot. She recognized the dark blue button-down he'd been wearing, and she licked her lips when she noted the way the shirt hugged his broad shoulders from behind.

Get it together, girl. Stop gawking and get over there. Her hankering for the cheesecake compelled her forward. Holding a small plastic bag and gripping the tray bearing the coffees, she walked around the edge of the lot, taking the beach access point until it led her to the sandy strip bordering the Atlantic.

As she approached, she could see him jotting in a leather-bound book spread open on his lap. When she reached him, he looked up and snapped the book closed. With a smile, he patted the bench next to him. "Have a seat."

His reaction to her approach made her curious about what he'd been writing in the book, but she didn't know him well enough to be prying into his personal business. Sitting down, she placed the tray holding the coffees on the bench between them. With a man as sexy as Savion, she needed the distance.

"I got the guy behind the counter at the coffee shop to hook me up with a couple plates, forks and a plastic knife." She held up the plastic bag.

"Thanks, but I was just gonna dig into the cheesecake with my hands."

She stared at him, but his face gave away nothing. "Excuse me?"

He started to laugh, a low, hearty sound originating in his diaphragm. "I'm kidding, of course. Thanks for getting the accoutrements."

She shook her head. "You're just full of shenanigans, aren't you?"

He shrugged. "Sometimes. But I'm very serious when the occasion calls for it." He held her gaze for a few long, silent moments.

She reached for her coffee and took a swig, hoping the warm liquid would wash away her nervousness. Just when she felt she might squirm under his scrutiny, he broke the silence.

"Hand over the knife." He flipped open the box holding the cheesecake and held out his hand. "Not sure how well I'll be able to cut this with a plastic knife, but I'll do my best."

She pulled out the knife and handed it to him. While

he worked the flimsy plastic through the thick filling, she took out the plates and forks.

He scooped up the two misshapen slices and served them both. Then he raised his coffee cup in her direction. "Here's to new friendship, forged over cheesecake."

She raised her cup in kind, smiling. "Hear, hear."

They ate in companionable silence, with the small paper plates resting on their laps. Unsure of what to say to her handsome companion, she kept her eyes trained on the water. The crystal blue water, rising and pushing toward the shore in a show of frothy white beauty, mesmerized her. The sound of the waves set her mind at ease, giving her a much-needed rest from worrying about the bevy of tasks she still had to complete for the show's second season.

After they'd polished off their portions of the delectable dessert, they stuffed the plates inside the plastic bag. Breaking the companionable silence, he said, "How did you come by your love of key lime cheesecake?"

She smiled. "By chance. I love cheesecake, always have. I used to always get the chocolate swirl, or the strawberry one. A few months back, Carmen suggested I try the key lime, and I've been hooked ever since."

He chuckled. "Carmen's kind of a sweets pusher, isn't she?"

"Never thought of it that way, but I guess she is." She giggled. "What about you? Why do you love it?"

A broad grin spread over his face. "I got it honest. My grandma, Mary Ellen, made the best key lime pies and cheesecakes you could ever put in your face. Nobody can make it like she did, but Carmen's is the closest approximation I could find."

"I see." She loved the way he looked when he smiled. It made his deep brown eyes sparkle, put a little dimple in his cheeks and made his goatee-accented lips look even more enticing.

"Considering my grandma passed away when I was nine, and I can still remember the taste of her baking, that should tell you how special it was." He paused. "How special *she* was."

She sensed that he wanted to share his memories, and that flattered her. "Tell me about her. What was she like?"

His smile remained but became more subdued. "She was a real pistol. Only about five feet tall, weighed maybe a hundred and ten pounds, but people knew not to cross her. She only wore pants, never dresses or skirts, and she loved to fish. But she also loved her garden—she'd plant zucchini, tomatoes, cucumber, spinach, you name it. And she had the best azalea bushes on the island, hands down. After she passed, Dad had all of them transferred onto his property."

"She sounds like quite a character."

"You'd better believe it." He leaned back against the bench. "She was the one who taught me and Cam how to fish. Hadley was too small back then, but Dad taught her when she was old enough. He promised Grandma he would, when she…" His voice trailed off. The look in his eyes said he was reliving an old, yet very real pain.

She touched his hand gently but didn't press him to go on.

He drew a deep breath, then spoke again. "You know, you're really easy to talk to."

She offered a soft smile. "I try."

"It was Gram's land that started MHI. When she passed, she left it to Dad. He bootstrapped it, hustled, gathered investors and started developing the land. Once he started turning a profit, he bought more land. Now we own more than sixty percent of land and buildings on the island."

She noticed the pride in his voice. "It's quite an impressive legacy."

"I know, and we want to honor that. That's why Dad is doing the memory park in her honor." He laced his large fingers together, then stretched his arms overhead. "It's the most important project I've ever done, and that's what has me so stressed I was ready to dive face-first into that cheesecake."

She giggled. "Is it really that bad?"

He shrugged. "I guess not. Maybe I'm blowing it out of proportion or being too hard on myself. But I can't screw up on this. We all owe our success to Gram. Plus, I can't disappoint my dad that way, you know?"

She nodded. "I get it." In a way, she felt similarly about giving her parents the grandchildren they wanted so much.

"Cam and Hadley say I'm our parents' favorite, and that's probably true. What they don't realize is how much pressure that puts on me to live up to the title." He tossed her a wry look. "Anyway, I've talked enough. What's your story, Jazmin?"

She inhaled a deep draw of the refreshing salt air. "Let's see. I was born and raised in Los Angeles.

Leimert Park, to be exact, and my parents still live there. I loved hearing about your grandmother. I never knew any of my grandparents."

"Really?"

She nodded. "My parents were older when they had me. Mom was thirty-eight and Pop was forty-one. All four of my grandparents were gone before I was two."

He looked thoughtful. "Wow."

"Anyway, my parents were pretty lax in the discipline department. They were 'free-range' parents, I guess. Gave me way too much freedom, no curfew, let me do basically whatever I wanted as long as I was open with them. Pop used to joke that they were too old and tired to chase after me and punish me, so they just let me find my own way."

"Wow. That way of parenting doesn't really fly here in the South."

"So I'm told. Hadley said the same thing."

"How do you feel about being raised that way?"

She thought about it for a moment. "I don't really know. I never felt unloved or anything like that, and they took care of my every need. I guess all that freedom forced me to develop good judgment earlier than most kids."

"Makes sense." He smiled. "How is production going on the set?"

"We're working on redoing the title sequence and the end credits. The network execs wanted something fresh for season two."

"I'm sure you'll deliver on that."

"You're pretty good company, Mr. Monroe." She

elbowed him playfully in the arm, figuring it would barely register against the firm muscle there.

"I'm glad you think so. Because I feel the same way about you, Ms. Boyd."

And as the sun touched the horizon, she moved the drink tray and scooted closer to him. In any other case, she would be rushing home to prepare for the next day. But sitting there with him, she felt more content and at peace than she had in a very long time.

Savion checked his watch as he made his way across the parking lot at Shoreside Grocery Friday evening. He'd wanted to go home after another long day at the office, but since there was nothing in his fridge but baking soda and some milk of questionable freshness, he'd swung by the store after leaving MHI.

He'd parked a good distance away from the store, choosing a space that had some shade from one of the magnolia trees planted alongside the lot. He loosened his top button, and he could swear he saw steam come out. It was an unseasonably hot and humid May day, heralding a scorching hot Carolina summer ahead.

The sky was an endless, cloudless blue, the sun a bright yellow orb radiating light and heat on the island. The air was as thick and warm as an afghan, and as he speed-walked through the lot, he anticipated the cool blast of air-conditioning that would greet him once he crossed the threshold of the store.

The promise of relief from the heat propelled him forward, until he saw Jazmin strolling down the sidewalk. Even with the large, round lenses of the sunglasses concealing most of her face, he knew it was her.

She was coming from the opposite direction, around the side of the store, as if she'd parked over there. She wore a summery beige dress that barely grazed the tops of her bronze thighs, and her hair was swept up in a ponytail atop her head.

He stopped at the edge of the walk.

As she approached, she stopped, as well. She raised her sunglasses and perched them on her head, her eyes locking with his. "Savion…hi."

"Hi, Jazmin. Good to see you again." That was a gross understatement. Seeing her was such a pleasant surprise, it almost made him forget how hot it was.

"Looks like we're both shopping today." She started walking again, headed toward the store's main entrance.

He fell into step behind her. "Yep. I hate shopping, but it was either come to buy food or eat baking soda for dinner."

She chuckled. "That bad, huh?"

"Absolutely." The automatic doors parted, and he sighed as the cold air hit him, offering respite from the oppressive heat. Still following her, he clapped his hands. "Ah. Thank God for air-conditioning."

She turned his way and opened her mouth to reply as they stepped onto the rubber mat at the door.

In the next heartbeat, a shower of confetti rained down on them. It seemed to be coming from all directions, and she covered her eyes while he blew out some of the brightly colored paper that had gone into his mouth.

"Congratulations, you two!" A man in a bright red suit, holding a microphone, stepped into their path. "You're the lucky winners of the Summer Love Sweepstakes!" Several other people joined the man, including a cameraperson from the local news station, and uniformed members of the store's staff.

"Wait a minute," Jazmin began, gesturing toward Savion. "He and I are—"

"Going on an all-expenses-paid weekend retreat to the beautiful, exclusive new Water's Edge Inn in Wilmington! This new bed-and-breakfast hasn't even opened yet, and you'll be its very first guests! Aren't you excited about your romantic getaway?"

His brow furrowing, he said, "Listen, I don't think you understand—"

"But that's not all," the man continued, looking at the camera and gesturing toward Savion and the bewildered Jazmin. "Our lucky couple will also receive VIP tickets with backstage passes to the sold-out Brian McKnight concert at Thalian Hall Center for the Performing Arts."

Her eyes widened. "Did you say Brian McKnight? As in, *the Brian McKnight*?"

Mr. Red Suit nodded. "Yes, ma'am, that's what I said. And it's all yours for being Shoreside Grocery's lucky hundredth customer today! Anything you'd like to say to the folks watching at home?"

Savion glanced her way.

She stepped closer to him. "Sidebar."

He leaned down until her lips were next to his ear. "Go ahead."

"I know this sounds crazy, but I've been trying to see Brian McKnight in concert since forever. So, is there any way you could just go along with this?"

He blinked a few times. "Are you sure about this?"

She nodded. "You heard the man. The show is sold out and this is the only way I'm getting in."

He felt his lips tilt into a smile. "If it means that much to you…"

She placed a hand on his forearm and gave it a gentle squeeze. "Believe me. It does."

"Then yes. I'm down." He tried not to read too much into the situation. After all, she was simply going along with this so she could indulge her fangirl fantasy of meeting one of the best R&B singers to ever stand in front of a mic. Wasn't she?

She smiled, then turned back to the guy in the loud suit. "I'd like to say that Savion and I feel so lucky to have won the giveaway."

"Excellent!" Mr. Red Suit grinned and patted them both on the shoulder. Gesturing to another man wearing a suit in a much more muted color, he said, "This is Nathan Wesley, owner of the Water's Edge Inn. Just head on over to the customer-service desk, and he'll go into the details."

Savion fought off his shock as she reached over and grabbed him by the hand.

"Come on, honey. Let's go find out what we need to do next." A syrupy sweet smile accompanied the remark.

He grinned back at her. "Whatever you say, baby."

Her expression changed, and for a moment, he thought she might be annoyed that he'd called her a pet name. But the look disappeared as quickly as it had shown up. He let her lead him by the hand toward the customer-service desk, wondering all the way what he'd just gotten himself into. *I hope she's not mad. After all, I was just following her lead.*

They spent the next thirty minutes signing paperwork with the owner of the inn and posing for pictures being taken by a reporter from the *Sapphire Shores Dispatch*. She seemed a bit stiff as he placed his arms around her waist for a photograph, but she smiled nonetheless. Noticing her hesitance, he put a bit of distance between them. The last thing he wanted to do was make her uncomfortable, and he made a mental note to talk to her about it once the hubbub died down.

By the time the camera crew, the inn owner and Mr. Red Suit left the store, he could feel the tension rolling off her like the heat outside reflected off the road. She made a beeline for the door, and he followed her.

Outside on the sidewalk, he caught up with her just before she rounded the corner. "Jazmin, what's wrong? Did I do or say anything that made you uncomfortable?"

She stopped. Turning back to face him, she shook her head. "I just came in for a few things. Instead, I got a camera crew. I mean, I got swept up in the moment—winning those Brian McKnight tickets. But it was all a bit much, you know?"

"I get it. This whole thing caught me off guard, too. But I just wanted to be sure it wasn't something I did that made you run off."

She shook her head again. "No. Actually, I feel pretty comfortable with you."

He watched her expression, noting the panic that crossed her face. "I'm guessing you didn't mean to say that aloud."

"Nope. But there it is."

He smiled. "I'm glad you said it." Knowing that she felt comfortable in his presence pleased him in ways he wouldn't have expected. "So, how are we going to work this thing?"

She shrugged. "I'll take next Friday off work. We'll go up to the inn, check in, go to the show, then hang out and chill. Then we'll come home on Sunday."

"And does this weekend indicate any…shall we say, evolution of our relationship?"

She folded her arms over her ample chest. "Savion, what relationship are you referring to?"

He watched her for a few silent moments before speaking again. "Are you denying the attraction between us?"

Her lovely face flushed, and she looked down as if analyzing her bejeweled sandals. "Well, no."

He reached out, touched her hand. "Jazmin, I would never, ever do anything to make you uncomfortable. This weekend excursion to the mainland will be under your control, in every aspect."

She looked up then and stared into his eyes. "Really?"

"Absolutely. Still, there's something you should know."

"What's that?"

"You may think you know what you want now." He squeezed her hand. "But that may change once we're alone together. Just know that I'll respect your wishes, whatever they may be."

Her mouth dropped open. The look in her eyes seemed to communicate a mixture of shock and…desire. A few beats passed before she blinked several times and snapped her mouth shut. Turning on her heel, she started for the lot.

He called after her. "Aren't you going to do your shopping?"

"It can wait," she called back, without looking his way.

Chuckling, he turned and went back into the soothing embrace of the air-conditioned store.

Chapter 5

The next day found Jazmin at home. Grateful for a day off amid planning season two of the show, she'd decided to use the day to catch up on some of her housework. Entering her laundry room, she eyed the pile of laundry and sighed. Her town house in The Glenn was comfortable and spacious, and the neighborhood had plenty of amenities. One of the services the staff provided was laundry, complete with fluff-and-fold, but she couldn't abide by the idea of a stranger touching her underthings. So, she bent down, taking a few moments to separate out her whites, then started a load in the front-loading washer. Padding barefoot down the stairs, she stifled a yawn.

As noon neared, she made herself a quick lunch of chicken salad, lettuce and tomato on a croissant. Pairing it with a bottle of water and a small bag of plain potato chips, she took her plate into the living room and sat down on the sofa. She grabbed the remote and flipped on the large, wall-mounted flat-screen television across from her.

The default setting meant the television was always on News 10, the local station, whenever it was turned on. The noon report was just getting started, so she set down the remote on the couch cushion beside her. *I guess I'll see what's happening on the island.* She placed the plate on her lap, then lifted her sandwich and took a bite.

The anchorwoman looked into the camera, with the trademark expression worn by newscasters all over the world that said she was "serious, yet approachable." "Welcome to News Ten's noon report, your source for everything newsworthy for the barrier islands. I'm Rory Nash. For our top story today, we take you to Sapphire Shores, where a grocery run led to a run of good luck for two local residents."

Mouth full of buttery croissant and zesty chicken salad, Jazmin paused midchew. "Oh, no."

Sure enough, footage of yesterday's confetti-filled ambush at the supermarket appeared onscreen. She'd just been dashing in for some milk and a few other essentials. She hadn't expected to run into Savion on the sidewalk, and that had thrown her a bit. She felt her pulse quicken whenever he was near. He was a well-built man, charming and handsome in a way that made it hard for her to breathe when he entered her personal space.

It would have been rude to walk into his path and not speak, and she'd been in the South long enough to know the expectation of politeness outweighed most other things. So, she'd spoken, striking up a short conversation with him. And when he'd opened his mouth, releasing that deep baritone, thick with his Carolina drawl, she'd been mesmerized. He could have been reciting the alphabet and she would have been riveted by every single letter.

Because she'd been so busy talking to and drooling over Savion, she hadn't been paying attention as she entered the store. That had left her open to be caught completely off guard by the whole sweepstakes thing. Looking at the footage now, she could see the guy with the "confetti cannon" had been standing right in the middle of the produce section. *Had I actually been paying attention, there's no way I would have missed that guy.*

She watched the rest of the brief report in dismay, shaking her head at the wide-eyed, bewildered expression on her face. *I look like I'm having a bad reaction to something, and now that crazy-eyed face is plastered all over the damn TV.* She sighed. There was nothing to be done about it now. *At least I finally get to see Brian McKnight in concert.*

She tried not to think about the rest of the prize. She'd be alone, with the fine-as-wine Savion Monroe, in a room at a romantic inn for an entire weekend. And while she knew logically that she didn't have the time or the patience for a relationship right now, logic rarely ruled in cases like this. The attraction between them was real, way more real than she'd like to admit. And because of the way he made her feel, there was really no predicting how the weekend would go.

The ringing of her cell phone snatched her out of her thoughts. Reaching to the teak coffee table in front of her, she picked up the device and answered it. "Hello?"

"Hey, honey bun. How are you?"

She smiled. "Hey, Mom. How are things going?"

Azalea Boyd laughed, the sound light and airy. "Fine, fine. Your father is out on the golf course right now, and I'm just lounging around the house. Got a whole stack of magazines here I want to catch up on reading." She yawned. "What are you up to today?"

"Catching up on chores. I've got a mountain of laundry to do, and I'm going to give the whole place a good cleaning and dusting. Once the filming of the show's second season really kicks off, I'll be working really long days, and probably some weekends, as well."

"Oh, yeah. I remember you telling me about that. What's going on in the studio?"

She gave her mother a brief, layman's-term explanation of what was happening. "Right now, we're in preparation mode. The crew is redecorating existing sets and building new ones, setting up for on-location filming, testing equipment. The writers are, well, writing, and the cast is running their lines. Other than that, it's just making sure the equipment in the production suite is in working order and training an intern."

"Sounds like you've got a lot going on at work, honey bun. Is there anything going on in your social life?"

"You mean, other than hanging out with Sierra?" She chuckled. "Mom, we both know I don't have a social life. I'm too busy with work."

Azalea's displeasure was evident in her voice. "Honey bun, we've talked about this."

"Mom, I just have so many goals and plans. There are so many accomplishments I want to make in the world of television production. I want to break down barriers for the young black women coming up behind me, you know?"

"I know, baby. But you can't cuddle up to your accomplishments and broken barriers at night." She sighed. "I'm not trying to meddle in your life, I promise. Your father and I just want the best for you."

"I know, Mom. I know. And I love you both for caring so much about me."

"Breaking down barriers is wonderful. And if that's all you want out of life, I'd say keep doing what you're doing." Azalea paused. "But we both know you want more."

"After everything that happened, I don't know what I want anymore." She didn't get specific. Her mother would know what she was referring to, without her having to dredge up that old pain. Drawing a deep breath, she made her move to change the subject. "There is one thing I want. Why don't you and Pop move closer to the East Coast? Even when *The Shores* is over, I'm probably not going to come back to California, at least not to live."

"Nice segue, honey bun." Azalea chuckled. "And let me remind you, I need some serious motivation at my age to pick up and move to the other side of the country. A grandchild would do nicely."

She rolled her eyes, grateful her mother couldn't see

her. "And on that note, I'm going to get back to cleaning. Talk to you later, Mom. I love you."

"Love you, too."

She disconnected the call, glancing at her half-eaten sandwich.

Suddenly, I'm a little short on appetite.

After covering her plate in plastic wrap, she set it in the fridge and trudged back upstairs with her cleaning caddy.

"Son, did you hear me?"

Savion snapped himself out of looking out the window at the sky. "Sorry, Dad. What did you say?"

On the other end of the phone line, Carver chuckled. "I wish you'd quit daydreaming while I'm talking to you. I said, your mother and I are on our way to the airport. Time to celebrate this anniversary properly."

"Great, Dad. You and Mom have a great time in Europe." His parents had been planning their getaway to Portugal and Spain for months now, and he thought it was a wonderful way for them to celebrate forty years of wedded bliss. "How long is it gonna take to get there?"

"Let's see. Our flight from RDU takes us to Philly, that's about ninety minutes. Then it's overnight, seven and half hours from Philly to Madrid." He blew out a breath. "Longer than I've ever been on a plane, and I can't say I'm looking forward to it. But we're going first class, so it should be comfortable."

"Hopefully."

"Even if it isn't, I couldn't deny your mother this trip. She's wanted to go for so long, and after everything she's given me, and all she's meant to me, how could I say no?"

Savion felt his heart squeeze in his chest. His parents had set quite an example for him when it came to healthy romantic love. He had deep admiration for the way they cared for each other. "Tell Mom I love her."

"Love you, too, baby!" Viola shouted her reply in the background.

"You're on speakerphone, son. I'm just making sure I have everything I need in my bag. Can't be holding the phone and doing that."

Savion laughed. "Okay, Dad. Was there something else you need? I don't want to hold you two lovebirds up from getting to the airport."

"Yes. There is one more thing. Are you going to make sure the final inspections and permits are done for the memory park?"

He inhaled deeply, touching his fingertips to his temples. "Yes, Dad. I've got it covered."

"I'm sure I don't have to tell you how important this is, Savion. It's the most important project this company has ever taken on. It's about this family's legacy."

"Trust me, Dad. I'm well aware of the significance of the memory park."

Carver cleared his throat. "I trust you, son. I just don't want you to get distracted by your upcoming 'rendezvous.'"

Shock hit him for a moment, followed by realization. He cringed. "So, you know about that, huh?"

"Sure I do. It was all over the news, son. Everybody on the island knows that you're going to the mainland for a romantic weekend with that pretty producer from the television show."

He let his forehead drop against the cool glass pane of his dining-room window. "Dad, please don't make a big deal of this. I'm just doing Jazmin a favor."

"Oh, is that what it's called nowadays?" The humor in Carver's voice was apparent.

He sighed. "Good one, Dad. But I'm telling the truth. Jazmin said she's been trying to get to a Brian McKnight show for ages, and she wasn't about to turn down tickets with VIP passes. So, I agreed to go along with this 'romantic getaway' thing so she can get her fangirl on."

"Is that so."

"Yes."

Carver made a grumbling sound deep in his throat, the sound he made whenever he thought someone was trying to sell him beachfront property in Kansas.

"Come on, Dad. Don't hit me with the untruth grumble."

"Are you going to sit there and tell me you're not attracted to Jazmin? As if I don't know any better?"

"I didn't say that." He wasn't about to lie to his father. Despite being over thirty-five, he knew his father would still go upside his head, if he felt it was necessary. But his refusal to be dishonest with his dad had less to do with fear of reprisal, and more to do with the respect he had for him. "I'm just laying out what she and I discussed."

"I'm glad you had sense enough not to deny it. I watched you dance with her at Cam's wedding, and again at the party. Heck, even the way you were looking at her in some of those photos they showed on the television gives it away."

"You've made your point, Dad." *Am I really so transparent to others?* He didn't want the whole world to know his feelings, at least not until he and Jazmin could come to some sort of understanding. "I know what you're thinking. But I don't have any plans on starting anything up with her. We're just going on this trip as friends."

"Be sure you keep it that way. Proximity can give you all kinds of ideas if you know what I'm saying."

He cringed again. *I can think of a hundred other things I'd rather talk to my father about than my sex life.* "Yes, Dad. I know what you're saying." *He's reminding me of the playboy days of my youth, as if I've forgotten.* Once upon a time, the coed dorms at North Carolina State had been like a playground for him. Now, though, he was well past that revolving-door-dating stage—time and experience had shown him the folly of that enterprise.

"Let me get out of here. Don't want to miss the flight. Keep the ship afloat while I'm gone, Savion. I'm counting on you."

"Aye, aye, Cap'n," he said in his best pirate impersonation.

"I'll message you when we get to Madrid. I love you, son."

"Love you, too, Dad."

After he disconnected the call, he stood by the window for a few moments more. If his father's statement was correct, he and Jazmin's little getaway was probably already the talk of the island. He could imagine the diners at Della's and the ladies under the dryers at the hair salon, all discussing what might happen between the two of them while they were away. He hated the feeling of being grist for the gossip mill, but such were the perils of life in a small community.

Running a hand over his hair, he went to the couch and plopped down on the soft cushion. Then he picked up his leather-bound book and flipped his notebook to a blank page. Grabbing the pencil from the loop, he began to write.

> In creation
> I discovered in discovery
> I learned in learning
> I established Me in me

As he wrote, releasing his feelings and perceptions onto the page, he felt some of the tension in his body slipping away.

> I found a light
> In this light I found her
> in her I found We
> And We give love a name—Life

Ever since he'd first laid eyes on Jazmin, she'd become a muse for him. Whenever he was around her, the words seemed to compose themselves. It was all he could do to tuck them away in a corner of his mind until he could be alone to commit them to paper. With all the inspiration she provided, he knew he'd be flush with content for weeks.

His writings were a private indulgence of his innate creativity; his notebook, a secret sanctuary from the realities of his daily life.

Once he felt he'd gotten it all out of his head, he tucked away the pencil and closed the leather cover.

Chapter 6

Sunday, Jazmin crawled out of bed just after eight. Rubbing her bleary eyes, she squinted against the sunlight as she dragged herself to the bathroom. Once she'd gotten some coffee in her system, she returned to her bedroom to get dressed for her morning workout. Donning her compression shorts, a blue workout T-shirt and her favorite walking sneakers, she pulled her hair up into a high ponytail to keep it out of her face. Once she was ready, she grabbed her water bottle, purse and keys and left her town house.

During the short drive to the Magnolia Health and Fitness Complex, she hummed along to the eighties music playing on the satellite radio in her compact sedan. It was a beautiful day on the island, with wispy white clouds accenting a sun-filled blue sky. Letting down the front windows, she enjoyed the feel of the cool morning breeze caressing her face as she drove.

After she'd parked her car in the lot, she got out and crossed the grassy field that stood between the fitness complex's main building and the outdoor walking track. She'd been coming here for a while and knew the layout of the place. There was the building that housed two workout rooms filled with modern equipment, male and female locker rooms with hot tubs and steam rooms, space for group fitness classes, and a juice bar. Outside and to the right of the building was the soccer field, which was surrounded by the walking track she used. Behind the building, there were tennis and basketball courts, two of each, as well as an area designated for sand volleyball.

There wasn't anyone else out there, at least in her line of vision, and that pleased her. That meant she could keep her own counsel and focus on her walk, without being roped into a conversation with an overly friendly local.

Solitude wasn't the only reason she came to the track so early. As she stepped onto the springy, recycled-tire surface of the track, she drew a deep breath to kick up her energy. Early morning was also the only time of day she could walk outdoors this time of year. She'd learned the hard way last summer that the combination of oppressive heat and overwhelming humidity made outdoor activities unbearable past noon.

Plugging her headphones into the audio jack on her phone, she started up her favorite classic-soul workout playlist and popped the buds into her ears. Within a few moments, she'd set her pace to the rousing beat of Curtis Mayfield's "Move On Up."

She usually aimed to do eight laps around the track, which would give her about two miles of brisk walking. Though she sometimes jogged, she wasn't a runner, so she kept her focus on even pacing rather than speed. The beat of the music kept her moving around the track in time.

Rounding the corner for her third lap, an image of Savion popped into her mind. She could see the strong lines of his handsome face, the way his cheeks dimpled when he smiled. She could hear his deep voice in her ear. She could almost smell the scent of his cologne on the breeze. He smelled of fir and bergamot—earthy and masculine.

There were so many things about him that intrigued her. The way he walked, the way he exuded such confidence. The way he took his day planner with him everywhere.

She crinkled her nose about that one. He struck her as a savvy guy, full of charm, charisma and self-assurance. So why was he still carrying around a paper planner, and guarding it so furiously? That day at the beach, he'd tucked it away the moment she'd gotten close. Who was that protective of their planner? *Unless it's not a planner.* Maybe there was something else inside that leather cover.

She laughed inwardly. *Whatever is inside that leather cover is the least of my worries right now.*

In many ways, she was still processing their upcoming trip to the mainland. She'd acted impetuously in a stressful moment, but that was understandable. Who walked into a grocery store expecting to be the center of attention? From the moment the first volley of confetti had hit her in the face, she'd been gobsmacked. She considered herself a laid-back person, and all the attention had put her in an awkward place. Even so, she wasn't going to pass up tickets to that show. Her decision to accept the prize had been driven by her desire to finally see Brian McKnight in concert.

Or were there other desires at play?

She missed a step and tripped, but managed to readjust before she went crashing down on the track's surface. Continuing her walk, she cringed, wondering if she'd been motivated by something deeper, something she didn't care to admit. Yes, her love for all things Brian McKnight was very real. But she couldn't seem to shake her growing attraction to Savion, either. Was there some part of her subconscious mind that wanted to go on the trip, just to be alone with him?

What is it about him that gets me so distracted? She shook her head, but shaking off thoughts of him was going to take more than that. So, she picked up her pace to a comfortable, but quick jog.

Running from one side of the court to the other, Savion swung his tennis racket. He managed to swat the air as the Day-Glo yellow ball sailed right past him, smacking into the fence with a metallic thud. Groaning, he jogged to retrieve it and tossed it back to Troy, who was stationed on the other side of the net.

"Wow, Savion. Your game is garbage today."

He frowned at his cousin. "Thanks for pointing that out, but I assure you, I knew it."

Troy shrugged. "You know I'm not one to clown you…too much, but I didn't come all the way from New Mexico to visit my family for this, man. Your body's here, but I don't know where the hell your head's at."

"Just serve the ball," he groused, crouching and holding his racket in the ready position.

Troy chuckled. "All right. Miss this shot and it's all over for you, cousin." He winked.

Savion rolled his eyes but said nothing.

Troy tossed the ball into the air, then delivered a smack with his racket that sent the electric-yellow sphere flying. Savion darted to the rear right corner of his side of the court, extending his arm to try to return the serve. He could see the ball getting close to the racket's surface, so he flicked his wrist.

The ball knicked off the edge of the racket and hit the ground, bouncing as it rolled past his foot.

Savion tossed his racket to the court's bright green surface. "I'm done, Troy."

"I'll say." Troy jogged past him to retrieve the ball. Entering his space, he pointed at the racket. "I'm just gonna grab a water and turn the ball basket in at the desk…if that's okay."

"Why are you even asking?"

"Because you look ready to spit fire."

Savion sighed. "Go ahead and return the equipment. I'll wait for you on the bench."

"Bet. Be back in a flash." With the ball-basket hand, Troy opened the gate and walked across the grounds to the main building of the fitness complex.

Alone on the court, Savion ran a hand over his face. *Troy was right—my game was absolute trash today.* He couldn't recall ever losing to Troy in tennis. Hell, this wasn't even Troy's best sport—he was much better at baseball. Today, though, his concentration had been shot from the beginning. That lack of focus had led to probably the lousiest game of tennis he'd ever played.

He walked off the court, exiting through the gate and heading for the benches lined up in the grassy area just beyond it. The benches sat on a slight hill, facing away from the road to allow a view of the rest of the outdoor sports area, as well as the thick line of towering pine and spruce trees that bordered the complex's property. Sitting down on the wooden slats, he kept his gaze on the tree line.

Troy returned with two bottles of water and sat down next to him. "Thought you could use this." He handed him one of the bottles.

"Thanks." He cracked it open and took a long draw. The cold liquid refreshed his parched throat.

"So, you gonna tell me why you're so distracted today?" Troy turned up his own bottle for a deep swig, draining half of the contents. "You've never let me whup you at tennis like that before."

He reached for the small towel he'd left draped over the back of the bench, wiped the sweat from his brow. "You're right. If my head was in the game, I'd have dragged you up and down the court."

"You're probably right, but it doesn't answer the question at hand, does it?" Troy fixed him with a questioning look.

He blew out a breath. "It's Jazmin, okay? I can't stop thinking about her."

"The girl from the anniversary party? Or, should I

say, the one you're going on that trip to the mainland with?"

He rolled his eyes. *Is there anyone on the island who doesn't know about that damn prize?* "You saw her, didn't you? That's no girl, that's a woman."

"Very true, cousin." He whistled. "She is fine."

A pang of jealousy clenched his gut, but he held his tongue. He had no real ties to Jazmin, and therefore no right to yell at his cousin for noticing how attractive she was.

Troy must have noticed his expression because he scooted farther down the bench. "Don't punch me, Savion. I'm not trying to get with her, I would never do you like that. But you look like you could use some advice."

"I don't know." He shrugged. "I'm going on this trip with her, but I don't really feel like I know her well enough, know what I mean?"

Troy appeared surprised. "Never thought I'd hear Savion Monroe, the international playa, say something like that."

He chuckled despite his mood. "I'm reformed, Troy. This isn't college. It's real out here, and I'm too grown to be chasing skirts and playing games." He stopped short of saying his next thought aloud. *Maybe it's time to build something real, something that will last.*

Looking thoughtful for a moment, Troy asked, "Why don't you ask her out on a date? You know, before you go to the mainland together? That way, you can get to know her a little better before the trip."

He scratched his chin, thinking back to their time on the beach, sharing the key lime cheesecake. She'd talked a little about her upbringing, and he'd revealed way more than he'd expected about his memories of Gram Mary Ellen. Still, what he'd heard from her had only increased his curiosity about her past. "I probably should do that. Might make things less awkward on the drive inland."

"Then do it." Troy finished the rest of his water, then crushed the bottle in his fist.

"I will. The next time I see her." He hadn't gotten her phone number, and though he could probably have asked Sierra, he thought that might be too invasive. *Aside from that, I'm a grown man. I don't need my sister-in-law to be the go-between for me.*

"Gimme your bottle. I'll toss it in the recycling bin." Troy stood and held out his hand.

After draining the last of the water, he handed over the bottle. Troy walked away, and he went back to watching the tree line.

A moment later, Troy called, "Hey, isn't that Jazmin over there? On the track?"

Turning to glance over his shoulder, he saw her. Even though she was rounding a curve and facing away from him, he recognized the curly mop of her hair, piled into a ponytail. He also recognized her stride; it was feminine, but purposeful. "Well, damn."

Troy chuckled as he made his way back to the bench. "Time to pay the piper, cousin."

Wiping around his hairline to make sure he'd gotten as much sweat and grime off as possible, he tossed the towel on the bench and stood. Strolling up the hill, he approached the track. Rather than going up to her, and possibly killing her workout vibe, he waited near the right side of the track for her to pass him.

When she came his way, she snatched out her earbuds and stopped, but continued walking in place near him. "Savion. Good morning. Looks like we have all the same habits, huh? Seems we're always running into each other."

"I have no complaints." He winked.

A soft smile lifted her lips.

"Listen, I know you're exercising, and I don't want to waste your time. Would you consider going out with me? I think we should spend some time talking, you know, getting to know each other, before the trip. What do you say?"

Her smile brightened. "I say yes."

Chapter 7

Jazmin entered the doors at Burgers Galore Monday evening, taking a moment to look around. She checked every corner in her line of sight but didn't see Savion anywhere.

It had been open for a couple of months now, but this was the first time she'd been inside. She'd been wanting to try the food here for a while, so when Savion had invited her to dinner yesterday, this seemed the perfect place to suggest. It was a casual setting, ideal for what she considered to be an easygoing meal. She'd chosen her outfit to reflect the nature of the evening, donning a pair of khaki shorts, a flowing yellow top with fluttery sleeves and a pair of shimmery gold sandals. The gold, seashell-shaped studs in her ears were her only jewelry, and she'd secured her hair away from her face with a thin yellow headband.

She stopped on the giant map of the world painted on the floor, waiting her turn at the hostess desk behind an elderly couple. She looked down for a moment and saw she was standing in the middle of the Pacific Ocean. She smiled. *This is the only way I'll ever be able to do that.* When she approached the desk, she cleared her throat. "I'm here to meet Savion Monroe, but I don't think he's here yet…"

The hostess, clad in a white shirt, blue jeans and a red apron, smiled. "He's here, miss. Follow me."

Jazmin followed her around the desk, into the dining room, then through a swinging door into a smaller room, probably set aside for parties and private gatherings. There, near the front of the room, where the windows faced out on the parking lot, sat Savion. He stood and smiled, showing off his perfect teeth as she approached the table. Dressed in a light blue polo shirt and dark blue slacks with brown loafers, he appeared both attractive and comfortable. She noted the way the fit of the shirt showed off the muscles of his torso, and the way the slacks lightly gripped his powerful thighs. Swallowing, she came to stand by him.

As the hostess walked away, leaving them alone, he grasped her hand and lifted it to his lips. Brushing his mouth against the back of her hand, he said. "Hi, Jazmin. You look lovely."

"Thank you." *You don't look so bad yourself.* She could feel the heat rushing to her cheeks, and to her belly.

He walked around the table and pulled out her chair. "Please. Have a seat."

She did, and as he returned to his seat, she caught a

wonderful view of his firm-looking backside. If she'd been a more brazen woman, or at least if they'd known each other longer, she might have given it a squeeze. But, circumstances being as they were, she kept her hands to herself. *Easy, girl. Don't let yourself get carried away.*

He slid a menu across the table to her. "I'm kind of surprised you chose this place for a first date."

"Just another one of my quirks, I guess." She shrugged. "I love burgers. To me, there's nothing better than a burger, when it's done right."

"Really? Because you could have easily asked me to take you anywhere on the island, and I would have made it happen."

She watched him, feeling the impact of his charm already. "I appreciate that. But I'm perfectly content here." She picked up the menu, evaluating her choices.

"Since you're a burger lover, you picked the right place. They have a great selection here."

She glanced up then, looked at all the maps, compasses and images of world landmarks painted on the walls. "I love the theme of this place—travel the world between two buns. It's a little corny, but still inspired." Her attention went back to the menu, where she looked over the selections themed for different countries or regions. "This Italian burger with prosciutto, mozzarella and fontina is really looking good to me."

He nodded as he pored over his own menu. "I've tried that one, it's really good. I think I might try the Greek burger this time."

She read the description on her menu. "'A freshly

ground lamb patty topped with grilled zucchini, red onion, sliced kalamata olives and feta cheese.' Wow."

He chuckled. "I'll let you know how it is."

Once the waiter had come and taken their order for burgers and a shared basket of hand-cut fries, they were alone again. She noticed him watching her, and suddenly felt parched. Reaching for the filled glass of ice water on her side of the table, she took a long sip.

"So, Jazmin. Let's get into this. I'm looking forward to learning more about you, so we don't go to Wilmington as strangers."

"Where should I start?" She honestly didn't know. What did he want to know most? How much would be too much? She knew of only one topic she didn't want to discuss, and she planned on keeping that under her hat.

"Let's start small and simple. For instance, I'm guessing your favorite food is burgers. So, what's your favorite color?"

She laughed, tugging on the end of her sleeve. "Oddly enough, it's yellow. What's yours?"

He smiled.

"Don't tell me it's blue."

"Yep."

She laughed again. "Look at us." She shook her head. "Let's see. My favorite music is classic soul and R and B, and you already know Brian McKnight is my favorite artist. What do you like to listen to?"

"I like classic soul, too, but I love funk. You know, Earth, Wind and Fire. The Gap Band. Dazz. D Train. But my favorite is probably the Isley Brothers."

She smiled. "I see you've got good taste. 'Voyage to Atlantis' is a classic."

"Agreed. But Brian's had some cuts, too. 'You Should Be Mine' still jams to this day." He sat back in his chair, rubbing his fingertips over his chin. "Yeah, I can see why ladies love the brotha so much. He's definitely got the chops."

She noted how he didn't feel the need to hate on Brian, as other men in her past had. "Okay, I've got a question. What's your middle name?"

He cringed. "You go first. Mine's pretty stodgy."

"Mine is Carmen, after my parents' favorite opera." She sipped from her water glass. "So now you see why I was so quick to take a recommendation from our favorite baker."

"I see. Well, my middle name is…" He stopped speaking in midsentence, his gaze going beyond her. "Saved by the bell."

"Only temporarily." She turned and saw the waiter approaching with a tray loaded down with their food. The tantalizing aroma awakened her stomach, and it growled in anticipation.

Once they had their plates in front of them, he reached for his burger, ready to dig in.

She cleared her throat to get his attention. "Hold on. I told you my middle name, now I want to know yours."

He frowned.

"It can't be that bad."

He sighed with resignation. "It's Fitzgerald, after my mom's brother."

She tilted her head to the side. "See? It's not that

bad. True, it seems a little serious for you, at least from what I know of you so far."

He appeared surprised. "Really? What makes you say that?"

"I see you as charming, and intelligent. You're laid-back, but also intense, in your own way." She popped a fry into her mouth. "You strike me as the kind of man who approaches things calmly, but who won't rest until he gets what he wants." It wasn't until after she'd said the words aloud that she realized all the ways they could be perceived.

A smile that could only be described as mischievous crossed over his face. "Your perceptions are correct, Jazmin. I'm impressed at how insightful you are."

She stuffed another fry into her mouth before she said something else that would lead to trouble. *What is it about him that makes me want to get into trouble?*

"I'm enjoying this, getting to know you. And I have to say, the more time I spend with you, the more attractive I find you."

She offered a soft smile but said nothing.

While they ate, they continued to converse about various topics. By the time the plates were cleared away, she felt relaxed, as if she was dining with an old friend.

"So, let me put this out there." He wiped his hands on a napkin, crushed it and tossed it on the table. "I've never been serious about anyone. Not really."

She blinked several times, wondering how they'd gotten on this topic. "And why is that?"

"My parents call me 'flighty and indecisive,' and my siblings call me a player. The truth is, I'm neither. I'm just very discerning. I don't like to waste time pursuing something that I don't see real potential in." He locked her with an intense gaze. "You are another matter altogether."

She felt her pulse quicken under his scrutiny.

"What about you, Jazmin? Have you ever been seriously involved?"

The comfort she'd settled into over the course of the meal began to melt away. She closed her eyes, feeling her chest tighten under the weight of those dark memories. "Trust me, Savion. No good will come from dredging up my romantic past."

"It's all right, Jazmin."

Hearing his voice, she opened her eyes again and found him still watching her. His expression had changed, softened.

"I didn't mean to be pushy. The last thing I want to do is make you uncomfortable." He reached across the table, clasping hands with her. "You can tell me whenever you feel ready, and not a moment before, okay?"

Enjoying the warmth of his skin against her own, she nodded. "Thank you." The knots of tension inside her body loosened, and she realized his sincere concern for her feelings. Something shifted inside her at that moment. And as much as she told herself that she didn't have time for romantic entanglements, she wondered if there was any real way to stop what was happening between them.

Savion held on to Jazmin's hands, feeling the trembling subside. He hadn't expected her to react that way to his question about her past. Now that he knew his query had made her uncomfortable, he kicked himself inwardly. *I shouldn't have asked her that. What was I thinking?* While his own past had been filled with frivolous encounters with the opposite sex, that didn't mean she'd had similar experiences.

"I'm okay, Savion. You can stop looking so concerned." A soft smile tilted her lips.

He chuckled. "Good to know. Now, what can you tell me about the exciting world of television production?"

One expertly arched eyebrow rose. "Seriously? You want to talk about work?"

He shrugged. "It might be boring to you, but remember, I don't know the first thing about what goes on behind the scenes at a TV show."

She opened her mouth, but before she could say anything, the waiter appeared again, this time with their dessert. He released her hands, and they moved to free up the tabletop.

"Here's the cheesecake with key lime ice cream you ordered, sir." The waiter placed down the two plates, as well as two gleaming silver spoons.

"Thank you." Savion picked up his spoon. "I hope you don't mind that I ordered dessert ahead. They didn't have key lime cheesecake, but I thought this would be the next best thing."

Her smile brightened. "I don't mind at all. It looks delicious." She picked up her spoon and scooped up a small piece of cheesecake and a dollop of the ice cream.

When she brought it to her lips and slid the spoon into her mouth, she made a sound indicative of pleasure. "It's just as good as it looks."

His groin tightened. *I wonder if the same is true about you, Jazmin Boyd.* "I'm glad you like it."

A few bites in, she seemed to remember their conversation. "Sorry, what was I gonna say?"

He laughed. "You were going to tell me about all the exciting parts of your job."

"I don't know if any of what I do is necessarily 'exciting,' but I'll tell you about it. Basically, my team and I are the last people to interact with and make changes to the show footage before it goes to the network to be aired. We're responsible for taking all that raw footage and turning it into something cohesive, appealing and screen-ready."

"I see. You said something about the opening and closing sequences when we were on the beach." He polished off the last of his dessert. "How's that going?"

She looked surprised. "You remember me saying that?"

"Of course. I always remember the important things."

Her cheeks darkened, and she looked away for a moment, then continued. "We've got the opening sequence done, and it's approved by the higher-ups. But we're still going back and forth over that closing sequence. It just needs a few more tweaks."

"How long do you have to get it done?"

She twirled a lock of glossy hair around her index finger. "Three weeks at most. The sooner, the better." She finished the last bite of her cheesecake and set down her spoon. "What about you? How's the project going with the park?"

He leaned back in his chair. "We're in that limbo stage between planning and execution. Everything is tied up right now until we get the last few permits from the state and the town commissioner. I can't submit the local request until the state approval comes in, so..." He shrugged. "For now, it's the waiting game."

"When do you hope to break ground?"

"By June first. That way we can have everything in place and properly protected before the peak of hurricane season." He hated to even think of Gram's memory park being damaged or flooded during a storm, but with the island being where it was, the team had been forced to make contingency plans. "We're doing as much as we can to keep the whole place intact should a bad storm hit—that's all by design. Dad insisted on it and wouldn't even entertain landscaping plans that didn't offer that kind of protection."

She nodded. "I think that's a smart approach. It's pretty similar to the way buildings are constructed in California, to protect them from collapse during an earthquake. Gotta work with what you're given."

He blew out a breath. "I don't know about you, but I need this vacation."

She giggled. "I'm with you on that. This whole thing came out of nowhere, but in a way, I'm glad it happened. I haven't taken any vacation days the whole time I've been working at the studio, and I need a doggone break!" She leaned back in her chair, fanning herself with her hand. "Our jobs aren't physically taxing but making decisions all the time can be exhausting."

"You're preaching to the choir, for real." He'd always been in the position of power at MHI, but now, with his siblings constantly distracted with their young marriages, he'd taken on even more of the decision-making around the office. "I hope your team is more focused than mine is right now. Both my siblings are newly wed."

She nodded. "They're pretty amazing, actually. Hard workers, great attention to detail."

He scoffed. "Don't rub it in my face. Hadley used to be superefficient before she and Devon married. And Cam, well, he never did all that much work even when he was single."

She laughed then, a deep belly laugh. "Is it that bad?"

"Yes, unfortunately." Even through his frustration, her amusement was contagious, and he found himself smiling. "I don't know what I'm going to do with those two. They're lucky I love them so much."

When she finally stopped laughing, she commented, "I guess I should pack. Although I don't know what to wear to the concert." She tapped her chin with her index finger. "I just hope my crappy luggage will hold up for one more trip. I'm not going to have time to replace it before we leave."

He tucked away that little tidbit of information. "I don't think you'll need to pack much, it's just a weekend."

"Yes, but a woman has to travel with a lot more stuff than a man."

He cocked an eyebrow. "I think that's by choice, Jazmin."

"You say that now. But trust me, you don't wanna see me without my beauty preparations."

He disagreed but didn't say so aloud. He would be honored to see her when she first awakened in the morning, to see the sun illuminating her bare, unadorned skin.

Once the dessert plates were cleared away, he paid the check.

She yawned. "Excuse me. The bed is calling my name."

"Happens to the best of us after a meal like that." He stood and stretched before offering his hand. "Let me walk you to your car."

She grabbed her purse and slung it over her shoulder, accepting his hand.

They walked out of the restaurant and into the warm night air. Strolling slowly down the sidewalk toward where she'd parked, he watched the moonlight play over her soft features. There was no denying her physical beauty. But he sensed an even more radiant beauty inside her, and it called to him like a siren's song wooing a sailor in the night.

By the time they stopped near the front of her car, he could ignore the call no longer. With his free hand, he grazed his fingertips over her jawline. Feeling her tremble beneath his caress, he said softly, "I want to kiss you, Jazmin. Can I?"

Staring up into his eyes, she nodded. "Yes, Savion."

He lowered his lips to hers, giving a series of gentle presses. Her mouth was much sweeter than the dessert they'd enjoyed together. She pressed her body against his, and his arms instinctively wrapped around her. He swept his tongue over her bottom lip, then dipped into the cavern of her mouth. He enjoyed her for a few long moments, then pulled back, mindful of where they were.

She sighed softly. Straightening, she spoke. "Good night, Savion."

"Good night." Reluctantly, he released her.

She smiled, then fished her keys out of her purse.

He stood on the sidewalk and watched as she climbed into her car, started the engine and drove away.

Chapter 8

Jazmin slid her chair up to the workstation console, exhaling deeply. Picking up the mug of coffee she'd sat on the drop leaf to keep it away from the equipment, she took a sip as she waited for the computers to boot up. She'd been the first person to arrive at the postproduction suite today, and she'd only stayed in her office long enough to fire up her personal coffeemaker and brew her first cup. Now, as she neared the bottom of that mug and contemplated a second to fight off the midweek blahs, she thought back to her date with Savion two nights ago.

He'd been a perfect gentleman in every way, yet she'd felt passion building inside her like well-tended fire. Hearing him speak about his life so openly, along with his willingness to be frank about his romantic past, had left her even more intrigued with the charming real-estate executive. And when he'd kissed her, she'd felt enough fireworks to put any big city Fourth of July display to shame. *And here I am, on the verge of going on a romantic getaway with him.* After all this time spent carefully avoiding romantic involvement, it seemed there was no way she could avoid what was happening between them.

As she set down her empty mug, she could hear voices and footsteps in the corridor outside the suite, heralding the arrival of the rest of her team. All five video monitors were booted up and displaying the time—five minutes past eight. She smiled, loving the fact that her small but dedicated team always came in a bit before their eight-thirty work call whenever they were in a pinch. She never had to ask them to come early or stay late; they simply did what was necessary to complete the work.

The voices grew louder, and she turned her chair to face the door as her team filed into the suite. First in line, as always, was Randolph Diggs, her video producer. Tall and tan with piercing blue eyes and spiky light brown hair graying at the temples, he wore his typical uniform of a pastel polo shirt, khaki pants and brown loafers. At fifty-nine, he'd been in the television industry for more than twenty-five years and had experienced the many changes in professional production firsthand. His experience and insight were invaluable.

Trailing behind Randolph was Drea White, the youngest member of the team. Fair-skinned with wavy dark hair and brown eyes, she'd just celebrated her nineteenth birthday. Before coming to intern for the show, she'd completed an associate's degree in general studies at Coastal Carolina Community College.

Trisha Dewitt, the sound producer, entered a few steps behind Drea. Brown-skinned with hazel eyes and coiled tendrils of blond, highlighted hair framing her face, she smiled at Jazmin as she entered. The twenty-six-year-old was a no-nonsense girl from the Atlanta area. She brought a sense of balance and professionalism to the team.

"Morning, boss lady." Randolph tucked his lunch bag into the drawer of his desk. The three desks for the team members were located across from the monitors and the console and separated by fabric-covered partitions.

"Morning, everybody." Jazmin stood, stretching as she watched everyone put their things away in their designated areas. "We're going to do our best to wrap up the closing sequence today. We're on a tight deadline, and at this point, we're pushing it."

"Have the writers sent us any new treatments?" Trisha slid her chair over to her spot at the console.

She nodded. "Yes, but thankfully there are only two versions this time. We should be able to wrap this up today, barring any disastrous occurrences."

"Great." Randolph flexed his fingers as he pulled up his seat to the section of the console centered beneath the monitors. "If they've finally narrowed it down to two, one of these has got to be the winner."

"We can only hope." Drea, stationed at her desk, opened the case to the touchpad she used for minor editing tweaks. Setting it and the stylus on the desk, she said, "Let's get this party started."

Jazmin chuckled. "You all go ahead. I need a second cup of coffee. Anybody else want some?"

Trisha scoffed. "You know I never touch the stuff."

"Had mine on the way in," Randolph offered while playing his hands over the dials and switches.

Drea shook her head. "Trying to cut back on caffeine."

"Suit yourselves." Mug in hand, Jazmin strolled into her private office and fired up her single-cup coffee machine. When she returned to the suite, it was quiet save for the clicking and tapping sounds of everyone at work. Trisha had donned the headset she wore to pick up every nuance of the show's sound effects, background noise and soundtrack. The headset essentially drowned out the outside world, so no one attempted to engage Trisha in conversation when she wore it. Drea was busy sketching something on the touchpad and looked very engrossed in the task.

Randolph, however, went about his job with a different approach. Leaning back in his chair, he read over the treatments that the writers had sent over that were displayed on the center monitor. "Are we going to make both versions and let them choose?"

"That's our best bet." She sat down next to him, returning her mug to the same spot it had occupied before. "Do you think it's feasible to get it done today?"

He nodded. "Sure thing." He switched to another monitor. "You know, when I first started out in postproduction, everything was done manually. We had to transfer the film to video, use an edit decision list with time stamps and codes to splice the clips together, then take everything to the color-grading room to make it look pretty for TV." He chuckled. "Now, everything's digitized. What used to take an entire team of maybe eight or ten people can now be done by a team as small as this. Even smaller, depending on the software and equipment they use."

She loved listening to Randolph's nostalgic tales of television production in the nineties. That was a world that seemed almost foreign to her but still intrigued her because of her love for the profession. "I've got a lot of respect for the folks who came before me. They had to do it the hard way." She thought for a moment. "Randolph, you've been doing this approximately forever, right?"

He grinned. "Sounds about right."

"Let me ask you something. Do you know how to program a VCR? There's an old one in storage at my parents' place, and they can't remember how to do it."

He whistled. "Sorry, Jazmin. Way above my pay grade."

She shook her head, laughing. "You were my last best hope, Randolph."

A bell tone sounded, indicating an intercom call from the front desk. "Ms. Boyd?"

"Yes, Darcy?"

"There's a package at the desk for you. Courier just left it."

She felt her brow furrow. *I wasn't expecting any deliveries.* Even though she loved to indulge in a bit of online shopping, she rarely ever had things delivered to the studio. "Thanks, Darcy. I'll send someone for it." She turned to Drea as the intercom turned off. "Can you run down and get that for me, please?"

Drea nodded. "No problem. Do you need anything else from there while I'm gone?"

Randolph stifled a yawn. "If there are any donuts

in the main break room, you can bring a few of those back. That is, if your hands aren't too full."

"Got it." Drea disappeared into the corridor.

Jazmin was standing over the console, studying the monitor as Randolph built out the footage to fit the first treatment, when Drea returned. Balancing a large cardboard box in one arm, and holding a folded paper bag in her free hand, she asked, "Where do you want this thing?"

"Dang, it looks heavy." Jazmin marveled at the size of the box.

Drea shook her head. "Not heavy, just big. Where do you want it?"

"Just set it on my desk."

Drea did, then returned to the suite and handed off the paper bag to Randolph. "No donuts, but they did have bear claws."

"Score." He unfolded the bag and looked inside. "Thanks, Drea."

Offering a crisp salute, Drea returned to her desk.

Jazmin kept working for the next couple of hours, consulting with her team as they toiled on the first treatment. By the time the lunch hour neared, her curiosity got the better of her. "I'll be back in a bit." Leaving the suite, she entered her office and closed the door. The packing label indicated that it had been shipped from a boutique in Raleigh. *I haven't even heard of this place, so I know I didn't order this.* The label gave no indication as to who had sent it. Using a pair of scissors from the cup on her desk, she cut the tape and opened the flaps on the large box. Before dealing with the paper-wrapped item inside, she took out the invoice and read it. Her eyes widened when she saw the item name and price, and widened more when she read the bottom portion, labeled Note from Purchaser.

Jazmin,
You deserve something nice to travel with. I hope you like it.
Best, Savion

Setting aside the invoice, she opened the layers of glittery gold paper to reveal an overnight bag. Lifting it out, she marveled at the fine leather craftsmanship. It was dyed a sunny shade of yellow, with the handles and shoulder strap a soft shade of light brown, and high polished brass zippers and hardware.

A smile spread over her face. *This is gorgeous! How thoughtful of him.* Savion had really been listening to her and had taken the initiative to solve a small annoyance that had been plaguing her.

Tucking the bag back into the box, she sighed contentedly and returned to the suite.

Thursday afternoon, Savion walked into MHI's conference room just after 3:00 p.m. Seated around him were the other staffers: Campbell, office assistant Lisa, and the two interns, Max and Yancey.

Taking his seat at the head of the table, he laid his notebook and a loaded manila folder across his lap. He looked to his brother at his right. Campbell was busy scrolling on his phone. "Cam, where's Hadley?"

He shrugged. "Home, I guess. She left right after lunch. Said something she ate didn't agree with her."

Awesome. This is just what I need right now. He exhaled and ran a hand over his face. "Will she be back tomorrow?"

Campbell shrugged again. "I don't know. I'll text her and ask, though."

"Let me know what she says." He laid the folder on the table and opened it. "In any case, we need to get started."

Lisa, sitting to his left with her open laptop, gave him a brief nod. She was excellent at transcription and kept very thorough meeting notes.

Campbell's phone dinged. "She says she'll probably be in late if she comes in tomorrow. Depends on how she feels."

Savion held back his sigh. "We need to tie up a few loose ends on the memory-park project so that construction can get started on time. We've finally received our state approval, so now, we're moving on to gaining approval at the local level."

Placing his phone face down on the table, Campbell asked, "What do we need to be doing?"

"I'm going to hand-deliver the state-approval paperwork myself to the council office, so we can get the ball rolling there. I'll be out of the office tomorrow and Monday—"

"We know. For your 'romantic getaway.'" Yancey made a goofy, doe-eyed face.

He sighed. Having graduated from high school at fifteen and community college at seventeen, Yancey was a prodigy. She was eighteen now, but situations like this pointed to her lack of maturity. "As I was saying,

I'll need you all to be especially vigilant and efficient in my absence."

"By doing what, exactly?" Max was known around the office for his straightforwardness.

"The inspector from the council may drop by while I'm gone. If so, give them the tour of the land. Also, make sure to follow up with the contractor on Monday. He should have gotten a copy of council approval by then, and we'll need to start finalizing the schedule, so we can set up a groundbreaking ceremony."

"I've got it, bro. Between the four of us, we've got it covered. Even if Hadley's still under the weather." Campbell stifled a yawn. "Stop worrying so much."

He stared at his brother. "I'm sure I don't have to reiterate how important the memory-park project is…"

Campbell groaned. "No, you don't. I remember Gram, Savion. I loved her, too, and I'm not going to screw this up."

Surprised, yet pleased by Campbell's promise, Savion nodded. "That's good to know, Cam. Okay everyone. Remember that the everyday operations still have to be handled. Make sure the clients in our properties have the best possible experience and handle any problems that come up promptly."

Everyone around the table answered affirmatively.

Satisfied, he stood. "You're released. I'm going to be leaving early today to drop off the paperwork. If you have any problems, Cam's your man." He slapped his brother on the shoulder as Cam and the others left.

Lingering in the empty conference room for a few moments, he opened his leather-covered book and started to write.

If you would only trust me
The journey we could take
Put your hand in my hand and take this journey
with me
I understand the road we must take
Allow me to lead you, but know I understand
you travel from afar
You may have met many but not me
Allow me to explore the depths of your mind,
dive into the pools of your thoughts
Allow me to listen to your heartbeat
Share your stories, feel your pains and your
glories…

With Jazmin lingering in his mind, he closed the book and walked out into the hallway. When he passed through the lobby, headed toward his office, the main entrance door swung open. He swiveled his head and saw Jazmin standing there. She wore a pair of fitted white capri pants and a pink three-quarter-sleeve top. Her skin and the dark ringlets of her hair shimmered in the afternoon sunlight filtering through the glass. Stopping, he blinked a few times. *Is she really here? Or am I just thinking about her that hard?*

She smiled. "Hi, Savion."

Clearing his throat, he smiled back. "Jazmin. It's good to see you. I hope you're not having any problems at the town house."

She shook her head as she walked toward him. "No, everything is fine at the town house. I actually came to see you." The sweet, feminine fragrance of her perfume reached him a few beats before she entered his personal space.

A short giggle came from the direction of the reception desk. He cut his eyes briefly at Lisa, who'd returned to her post there after the meeting. Lisa had the decency to try to appear busy.

His eyes raked over her form, and for the first time, he noticed the gift bag in her hand. "I'm flattered."

She raised the bag, handing it to him. "I wanted to thank you in person for the overnight bag. It was very thoughtful of you to get it for me, and it shows you were listening to me when we went out the other night."

Knowing Lisa's prying eyes were on them, but not caring, he placed a hand on Jazmin's waist. "I always listen when there's something important being said."

"I see." She gave him a sultry wink. "So, here's a little token of my appreciation."

Taking the bag, he reached inside and pulled out a brown leather portfolio cover. It was finely made and lacked any embellishment except for his initials engraved in the cover in an Old English–style font.

"It's for your datebook. I noticed the one you have is a little ratty, so I thought you could use it." She paused. "I hope it's the right size."

He nodded, still admiring the craftsmanship. "It's perfect. Thank you, Jazmin."

"You're welcome." She leaned up and placed a soft kiss on his jawline.

Warmth radiated from the spot her lips had touched, spreading throughout his body. "I was going to call you about our travel plans. Are you okay with me driving us up to Wilmington? It's not that long of a drive, a couple of hours at most."

"Sure. What time do you want to leave?"

"I'll pick you up around noon, if that works for you."

"It does." She eased away from him. "I need to finish packing, so I'll see you tomorrow."

He nodded. "See you then." His eyes followed the tempting sway of her hips until she was out of the building and out of sight.

After she was gone, he turned to Lisa. "Entertaining enough for you?"

"Definitely, Mr. Monroe."

Shaking his head, he went to his office and closed the door behind him.

Chapter 9

Jazmin studied the contents of her overnight bag for what seemed like the hundredth time. She wanted to make sure she had everything—especially all the accessories for the outfit she'd chosen to wear to the Brian McKnight concert. *Can't be looking busted when I meet my favorite singer.*

A few days ago, she'd been nervous about what might happen between her and Savion while they were alone together. Now, though, something had changed inside of her. She genuinely looked forward to everything the weekend would bring. She was a grown woman with needs, and if she decided to let him fulfill those needs, what was the harm in that? Not every encounter had to lead to a long-term relationship. She planned on enjoying her time with him to the fullest.

I'm sure we're both mature enough to handle whatever might happen.

She checked her phone, which was lying on the bed next to the bag, for the time. *Six minutes to noon. Savion will be here any minute.* She mentally ran through a list of her essentials, while rifling through everything she'd put in her bag. Finally satisfied, she zipped it closed.

Walking to the full-length mirror on the outside of her closet door, she did a quick turn to make sure she looked presentable. She'd chosen a pair of dark blue capri leggings and a yellow tunic with long, flowing bell sleeves, choosing to balance comfort and style for the road trip. Based on Savion's estimate of their travel, she would have plenty of time to settle into the inn and change clothes before they had to be at the venue for the show.

Satisfied with her appearance, she tossed the straps of both her overnight bag and her purse over her shoulder and carried her things downstairs. As she descended the steps, she heard a knock on her front door. A smile came to her lips. *He's here.*

She walked over to the front door and opened it, and was greeted by six feet two inches of bronze masculinity. He was dressed in a pair of gray cargo shorts, a closely fitted black T-shirt and a pair of black sneakers. The shirt clung to the powerful muscles of his chest and arms, while the shorts revealed his strong, defined legs.

Her tongue darted out before she could stop it, sweeping over her lower lip. "Hi, Savion."

He winked. "Ready to go?"

She nodded. "Just let me lock up."

"Cool." He took hold of the straps of her purse and overnight bag. "I'll take these to the car."

She watched him stride toward his SUV, marveling at the way he walked. Each step exuded confidence, and she admitted to herself that he was pleasant on the eyes whether he was going or coming. Fishing her key chain out, she locked the door and returned the keys to her pocket. That done, she went to the car.

He stepped in front of her, opening the passenger-side door.

Ducking beneath his arm, she grabbed her purse off the seat, climbed in and buckled up. Before long they were underway.

As he drove, he glanced her way. "I thought you might be hungry, so I'm going to stop by Della's for some food to go. We can eat on the ferry ride to Southport."

"Sounds good."

"What would you like?" He turned onto the road where Tracemore Plaza was located.

Like most cast and crew members of *The Shores,* she'd pretty much memorized Della's menu. "Grab me a number-five lunch special with plain chips and lemonade, please." She unzipped her purse, taking out her wallet.

He shook his head. "I've got you covered, Jazmin."

She put her wallet away. "Thanks."

They pulled into the lot, and Savion went in to grab their food. He returned with two paper sacks about fifteen minutes later and handed one to her along with her drink. "Here you go."

"Thank you." She set the bag on the floorboard and settled in for the short ride to the ferry stop.

Later, as they stood on the ferry together, Savion tapped her on the shoulder. "Let's find a seat so we can eat."

Before she could answer, her stomach growled loudly. She chuckled. "I think we'd better."

She followed him around the deck, passing other passengers of all ages, until they came to an empty bench. There they sat side by side with their lunches.

"I can't believe I'm finally going to see Brian McKnight in concert." She made the comment between sips of lemonade.

He chuckled. "I'm just happy I could help you live the dream." He crunched on a chip. "How long have you been into his music?"

"Since the early nineties. The first time I heard him sing was on Vanessa Williams's album, *The Comfort Zone*. He was a guest on it for a song called 'You Gotta Go.' Been hooked on his voice ever since."

He nodded, looking thoughtful. "You've been rocking with him for a long time. Never let it be said that you aren't a loyal fan."

"What about you? You said you love the Isley Brothers. Ever seen them perform live?"

He shook his head. "Nah. I've been to a few really good shows over the years, though. Babyface, Guy and New Edition were probably the best shows I've ever seen."

"You've got good taste."

Conversation flowed easily between them, and she alternated between watching his face and watching the scenery as the ferry moved over the blue surface of the inlet. It was a beautiful blue-skied day, the warm breeze wafting over her like a whisper. Being with him like this made her feel so content, so at peace, she wondered what the rest of the weekend would bring.

By the time they drove off the ferry in Southport, she found herself stifling yawn after yawn. "Man. The good food and the warm sunshine has gotten to me."

He laughed. "We've got a good forty-five minutes or more on the road, depending on traffic. If you're sleepy, go ahead and take a nap. I won't be upset."

"I appreciate that." No sooner than the words left her lips, her heavy eyelids closed.

It wasn't until she felt tapping against her shoulder that she awakened. She looked at Savion's amused face, blinking several times against the sunlight.

"We're here." He cut the engine, taking the keys from the ignition. "I'd ask you if you had a good nap, but based on the sounds you were making, I think I already know the answer." With a wink, he slipped out of the seat.

Mortified, she clamped a hand over her mouth. She tended to talk and moan in her sleep, a fact relayed to her by her roommates and friends ever since college. Reflecting on her torrid dream made her cheeks feel like they were on fire. He probably thought she'd been dreaming of doing various naughty things to Brian McKnight. In reality, she'd been dreaming of doing naughty things to Savion. *Crap! I know better than to fall asleep around other people. Sierra's still teasing me from an incident years ago.* When he opened the passenger-side door, she stepped out with her purse in hand. "Sorry. Guess I should have had that second cup of coffee this morning."

"Don't worry about it. Cam talks in his sleep, too, and the stuff he says is way worse. Trust me." He stepped back so she could get by, then closed the door. Gesturing to his armload of luggage, he said, "I've already got your bags. Let's go check in."

During their short walk to the front door, she marveled at the beauty of Water's Edge Inn. The main building was a stately looking Victorian-style house, complete with a wide sitting porch outfitted with wooden rockers. The soft yellow siding, black shutters and white gingerbread trim gave the place a quaint, welcoming look. The grounds were gorgeous as well, with the colorful wildflowers planted around the house giving way to a rolling lawn of verdant green grass.

As they climbed the five steps to the porch, a man stepped out the front door. She recognized him as the owner of the inn—he'd been there the day she'd won the prize—but she couldn't recall his name.

"Mr. Monroe, Ms. Boyd. Welcome to the Water's Edge Inn. I'm Nathan Wesley—we met at the supermarket."

She nodded. "Yes, I remember. It's nice to see you again, Mr. Wesley."

He shook her hand. "Please, call me Nathan." He shook hands with Savion, as well. "My wife, Eartha, is waiting inside. Won't you come in?"

She entered, with Savion and Nathan following close behind. At the desk, they met Eartha Wesley. The petite brunette with a round face and kind brown eyes was chatty, as was her husband. Check-in took less than five minutes, but politely extracting themselves from the Wesleys' company took twenty minutes more.

When Jazmin thought she couldn't take another minute of pleasant chatter, Eartha smiled her way. "Nathan, look at us. We're keeping these lovebirds from going up to their room."

Usually, Jazmin would have corrected anyone referring to her and Savion as a couple, but she wanted to make sure she had time to get ready for the concert, so she didn't protest.

Nathan slapped his hands on the desk. "Dang it, Eartha, you're right." He gestured toward the stairs. "You two can go on upstairs to room two-oh-one. If you need anything at all, just give us a holler."

By the time they made it upstairs, it was after four. The room, decorated in shades of blue, green and yellow, featured a bevy of rich mahogany furniture. The centerpiece of the space was the elegant four-poster bed, dressed in a thick comforter and several fluffy throw pillows. To the left of the bed, there were two upholstered chairs sitting on either side of a round, polished table. The was also a love seat and a short-legged coffee table. Ceramic vases of fresh, vibrant flowers and paintings depicting the various seaside scenes complemented the furnishings.

That night, as Savion escorted Jazmin to their seats in the front row of the Thalian Hall Center for the Performing Arts, he could feel the excitement rolling off her body. She looked gorgeous in the fitted royal blue dress, with its high neckline and bell sleeves, and a pair of matching pumps. He didn't know why she insisted on covering her neck and shoulders, but other than that, he had no complaints about her attire.

The packed house made for a bit of difficulty reaching the front row, but after circumventing the crowd and the security guards stationed around the space, they finally claimed their seats.

"Wow." She placed her handbag beneath the chair, her gaze focused ahead. "We have an amazing view of the stage from here."

"Yeah, it's pretty sweet." He gave her shoulder a playful jab. "If Brian exhales deeply, we should be able to feel it from here."

She giggled. "You're a mess, Savion."

He winked.

"Seriously, though. Thanks for going along with this whole thing, and for bringing me here. I really appreciate it."

He shrugged. "I'd never stand between a woman like you and something she truly wants."

She smiled brightly in response to his comment, and he felt his heart squeeze in his chest. Knowing he'd made her smile like that did something to him, something he couldn't quite name. Whatever it was, it felt like getting a victory, like he scored a triple-double on the court.

Once the show got underway, he watched her reactions. The crowd was on their feet by the time Brian finished his opening number, the classic ballad "One Last Cry." As Brian moved seamlessly through his catalog of hits, holding the crowd captive with his voice, Savion had to admit he was enjoying the show. *Vocally, Brian is in top form. And what a showman. The women in here are basically eating out of his hand.* Jazmin knew every word to every song, and sang along loudly, like the true fan she was. She appeared to be on the verge of tears during "Crazy Love," and Savion could only shake his head. Her exuberance was both touching and contagious, and before he knew it, he was singing along to the songs he knew.

Listening to the lyrics, Savion felt a certain kinship with Mr. McKnight. After all, love songs were basically poems set to music, not very different from some of the writings in his own leather-bound book. Savion didn't have a singing bone in his body, but he did feel he had a romantic streak. It had been ages since he'd indulged his inner romantic, though. None of the women he'd encountered recently had seemed right.

Until now. He looked to his right, watched Jazmin singing and swaying in time with the music. She was totally caught up in the moment, with the emotions evoked by Brian's words radiating from her face. All other cares had fallen away, and she was sold out for the here and now. She glowed.

It's beautiful.

She's beautiful.

Brian closed the show with "Back at One," and when he hit the last note, the crowd erupted during several minutes of an enthusiastic standing ovation. Savion joined in, noting Jazmin alternating between clapping and dabbing at her eyes. He could tell she'd experienced something profound, and he was happy he got to be a part of it.

After the show ended and most of the crowd filed out of the venue, Savion stood with Jazmin in the VIP line. Noticing how shaky she seemed on her feet, he tapped her on the shoulder. "Are you gonna be all right? Your knees are knockin,' as my Gram used to say."

She released a nervous titter. "I'll be fine… I hope. I just can't believe I get to meet him."

"You work in television. I know this isn't your first time meeting a celebrity."

She shook her head. "Of course not. But this isn't any old famous person—this is Brian McKnight."

He smiled, finding her enthusiasm endearing.

As their turn in line approached, she hung back, so he walked up to Brian and stuck out his hand. After greeting them, the singer asked who he should make the autograph out to.

Savion gave Jazmin's name, spelling it for the singer. After Brian signed, he offered to pose for a selfie, but Savion pulled Jazmin forward. She was still hanging back, too shy to move. "Come on, Jaz. He doesn't bite…"

She edged closer to Brian, her voice trembling as she spoke. "Oh, Mr. McKnight, it's so nice to meet you. I've been listening to your music since forever and I just love you."

Savion chuckled as she gushed over her favorite singer. This was too cute.

After he gave Jazmin her signed poster, Brian reached out his arm to Jazmin to draw her closer but stopped short. He glanced Savion's way, as if seeking his approval.

Feeling his brow furrow, Savion turned the gesture over in his mind for a moment before realization hit him. *He thinks we're together.* Rather than correct the music legend, Savion simply gave a dismissive wave. "Go right ahead, man." He stood back and watched as Brian hugged Jazmin. She released a tiny squeal of delight, then posed for the selfie with the singer and Savion, whom she insisted should join them.

Later, as they walked out of the concert hall toward his SUV, she chattered nonstop about the evening. He had the poster safely rolled up and tucked beneath his arm, and as they walked, she reached out and grabbed his hand, never stopping the flow of words streaming out of her mouth.

"I can't believe he hugged me. I mean, I just can't!"

"It happened. I saw it." He shook his head but felt the smile tugging his lips.

"This was easily the best show I've ever been to. After all these years, he can still hit those notes. Amazing."

"It was impressive, I gotta admit." He stepped off the sidewalk, leading her around to the passenger side of his SUV.

"And he's just so nice. And so humble! I mean, he's a legend, and it's so nice to know he's not full of himself. If he'd have been a jerk, I would've…"

He leaned over and kissed her on the lips.

She looked up at him, her eyes wide.

Was that surprise? Or outrage? What was she thinking?

Not wanting to wait, in case he'd offended her, he took a step back. "I'm sorry, Jazmin. I shouldn't have done that without asking you. Seeing you this happy and excited just got to me, and I…"

She blinked a few times but said nothing.

He sighed. "Anyway, that's no excuse. I want you to know that you don't owe me anything. We aren't going to do anything that makes you uncomfortable."

As the last word faded, she leaned up and kissed him. Her lips parted, her tongue sliding over his lower lip, and he felt electric heat shoot through his bloodstream. She wrapped her arms around his neck as his palms came to rest on her waist. He turned her slightly, her back coming to rest against the body of his vehicle, and leaned into the kiss. Their tongues mated and mingled for several long moments.

He pulled back, knowing that if they kept this up, he'd abandon all his good sense and home training.

She blew out a breath. Her hand slipped around to caress his jaw. "Savion, you've been a perfect gentleman, and I know I don't owe you anything." She paused.

His breaths came hard and fast as he waited.

"But I want to give myself to you."

He stared into the dark pools of her eyes. "Are you sure?"

She nodded. "Very."

He moved her aside, opening the passenger-side door. "Then what the hell are we doing standing out here?"

Chapter 10

Walking hand in hand with Savion on the garden path that led to the side entrance of the inn, Jazmin glanced over at him. His features were softened by the moonlight, but the desire in his eyes was as plain as the silver orb in the night sky.

Their eyes met briefly, then she looked away. Emotions and logic were warring inside her, and neither seemed to have the upper hand. Her body craved him; the craving was unlike any she'd ever felt before. Yet as much as she yearned to feel everything he had to offer, a flicker of fear made her hesitant.

How will I explain my scar? If he sees it, he'll want to know what it is and how it got there. What if he's repulsed by the sight of it? The thoughts raced through her mind and her hand constricted around his.

"You're tense." He stated it, rather than asking.

She swallowed. He'd picked up on her feelings and there was no use in hiding them. "I'm…a little nervous, yes."

He stopped short of the doorway, turning to look at her. "You know, Jazmin, we don't have to do anything tonight, if you're not sure."

"It's not that." She looked away from his intense gaze. "I want you, Savion. Probably more than I'd care to admit."

He placed his free hand on her shoulder. "Jazmin, you can feel free to tell me whatever you think I need to know and keep the rest to yourself. I'm not here to pressure you into anything. Not talking, or kissing, and certainly not making love."

She shifted her gaze back up to meet his, seeing the sincerity in his eyes.

"I want to make love to you tonight, Jazmin. But if you're not ready, for any reason, I will wait." He gave her shoulder a gentle squeeze before dropping his hand away.

She exhaled. "Let's go inside."

They entered, then traversed the dimly lit interior of the inn until they made it upstairs to their room. There, he opened the door and stood back as she walked through, then followed her.

She kicked off her shoes, tossed her purse onto one of the upholstered armchairs. She walked to the glass doors that led out to the small balcony and stood in the circle of moonlight on the carpet. While she looked out at the night sky, she noticed Savion, sitting on the edge of the bed.

A small smile touched her lips. *He's showing respect by keeping his distance.* She admired that about him. The desire flowing between them was so thick and so electric it practically glowed, yet he was holding back until she felt comfortable enough to take things further.

"Savion." She glanced over her shoulder, calling his name softly.

He stood, silhouetted in the darkness of the room. "Yes?"

"Come here, please."

She felt him enter her space a moment later. Having him near her only made the charge in the air stronger. She closed her eyes. "Hold me."

He obliged, stepping behind her and wrapping his strong arms around her waist.

A sigh escaped her. His arms felt safe, warm. His embrace felt like home.

She turned in his arms and his lips crashed down against hers. Swept up in the magic of the kiss, she slipped her arms around his neck and leaned into him. She wanted this, wanted every inch of her body to touch every inch of his. He responded by deepening the kiss, his tongue thrusting into her mouth.

When she finally pulled back, a bit breathless, she found him watching her with glistening eyes.

"Will you let me make love to you, Jazmin?"

"Yes, Savion." She pressed herself against him. "Yes."

The kissing began again, only this time, they both knew where the road would lead. Her hands swept over his muscled shoulders and down his arms, as his large palms caressed her back, hips and thighs before coming to rest on her behind. When he gave her a little squeeze there, a yelp of pleasure left her lips.

He stepped back, stripping off his button-down shirt and the sleeveless undershirt beneath.

She drew in a sharp breath at the sight of him. His glorious body that begged to be touched. She closed the distance between them and placed her hands on his chest, moving them over the muscled hardness. When she slid the flats of her thumbs over his nipples, he emitted a low, rumbling growl.

Smiling down at her, he wove his fingers into her hair. "I will return the favor." He placed a fleeting kiss against her lips before gently turning her.

Her breathing hitched when she felt him grasp the zipper pull at the back of her dress. He dragged it down with aching slowness, and her heart raced as he spread the open halves. Bending, he placed a series of kisses on the exposed skin along the curve of her back, and her knees buckled.

He steadied her and stood, pushing the dress over her shoulders and down her arms. The garment fell away, pooling around her feet.

She held her breath, waiting.

A moment later, he grazed his fingertips over the long scar that started near the base of her neck and went over her right shoulder, extending halfway to her elbow. "What is this, Jazmin?"

Her heart stopped. It was the question she'd known was coming but hadn't wanted to hear.

Crossing one arm over her chest, she bolted for the balcony door. Throwing it open, she ignored the sound of his voice calling her name and rushed out into the balmy night. She knew there was no one else around for miles, and right now, out here felt much safer than being inside with him and his question. The tears began then, falling down her cheeks like rain. She hugged herself, wrapping her arms around her torso, and let the pain have its way.

She felt him behind her but didn't turn or acknowledge his presence.

"I'm not going to press you about this, or about anything. Curiosity got the better of me for a moment, that's all." He placed his hands on her shoulders, offering a gentle caress. "You don't have to answer me. You can tell me when you're ready, and not a moment sooner."

Drawing a deep breath, she sniffled, then used her hands to wipe her face. "I'm sorry. I didn't expect to react like this."

"Don't apologize." He used the pad of his thumb to wipe away her tears.

"I know it's ugly to look at. That's why I keep it covered."

His expression changed from sympathy to confusion. "Are you kidding? There isn't anything about you that could ever be ugly to me, Jazmin."

Having seen the scar in the mirror these past two years, she would beg to differ. Still, she gave him a teary smile. "That's really sweet of you to say."

"It's also the truth." He cupped her face with his large hand. "You don't even know how beautiful you are, do you?"

She blinked, taken aback by the earnest sincerity of his words.

"Jazmin Carmen Boyd, you are the most beautiful thing I've ever seen. And I would very much like to show you how I feel if you'll let me."

Something inside her shifted, and the change was

palpable. The tears stopped, replaced by a sense of wonder and admiration for the man standing before her.

She didn't know where this would lead, didn't know what the future held. Then again, no one knew those things. What she did know was that he'd shown himself sincere, caring and respectful. Whatever was happening between them begged to be explored fully, and she wasn't going to keep denying herself the pleasure he promised.

She stroked his jawline. "Let's go back inside, Savion."

He grinned. "Yes, ma'am."

She screeched softly in surprise as he scooped her up, tossed her over his shoulder and carried her through the open doors.

Inside the shadowy room, Savion slowly finished undressing Jazmin. He took his time, stopping to kiss and caress each newly bared inch of her golden skin. The sounds of her soft moans and their breathing were accompanied only by the song of insects flowing in with the breeze through the open balcony doors.

He lay her down on the bed and stood back for a moment to admire her. The sight of her, naked and bathed in moonlight, made his blood race.

Words flowed through his mind, narratives pouring to describe her lush beauty. She was gorgeous enough to fuel his dreams and fill his notebook pages for years to come.

He plucked the condom from his back pocket. Stripping away his trousers and boxers, he tossed them over the armchair in the corner. He was hard and ready; the sight of her had been enough to arouse him. He covered himself, then joined her on the bed. She sat up, facing him. He rested his back against the headboard, pulling her into his lap.

They spent a few hot moments kissing and caressing each other. He wove his fingers into the dark riches of her hair while her hands gripped his shoulders. When she broke the kiss, she looked into his eyes and purred like a contented tigress.

He groaned low in his throat. He'd thought he couldn't be any more turned on, and she'd already proven him wrong. He had a feeling that trend would continue well into the night.

She kneeled up, straddling his hips. He pulled her close, so he could sample the dark tips of her breasts. Drawing one nipple, and then the other, between his lips, he enjoyed the soft cries she gave as he suckled her. His hands on her waist held her in place, giving her no means of escape from his hungry mouth.

Her hips began to rock, and he could feel himself getting closer and closer to the place he most wanted to be. He let her take the lead and kept up his attention to her breasts while she moved on top of him. Suddenly she shifted back, and he felt the tip of his dick at her opening. She shifted forward again, and as he slid inside her, he saw her bite her lip.

Her body wrapped around him with a warmth and tightness that threatened to push him over the edge. He held fast, determined to enjoy this ride with her for as long as possible. So he took his focus off the hot pleasure she generated in his lower regions, and instead concentrated on touching her. He caressed her face, her shoulders, her breasts and her stomach, then eased his hands around to give her ass a gentle squeeze.

She purred again, increasing her pace a bit. With each rise and fall of her body, a moan slipped from her lips. The sights, the sounds and the feel of her were threatening his very sanity but he held on to what little control he had left.

She changed her ride then, grinding her hips, working her body against him in sensuous circles, and he growled. Gripping her hips, he thrust up and met her movements with motions of his own. Fire shot through his blood, his insides felt molten-hot and fluid, as if he was melting, too.

"Savion!" She shouted his name in the darkness, her body flexing and contracting around his.

That did it. Moments later, he trembled as his release shot through him.

In the aftermath, he held her close to him, listening to the sounds of their heavy breathing. The still open doors allowed the night breezes in, and he felt the cool air moving over his sweat-dampened skin. "Jazmin, you're incredible."

She rested her head against his shoulder. "You're not so bad yourself."

He chuckled, reveling in the feeling of holding her. What she didn't know was that he hadn't just been talking about her lovemaking. It was so much more than that. Everything about her seemed to call to him. It was as if he'd been missing a piece all his life, without even knowing it, until he'd found her. She filled a void in him he hadn't known he possessed.

And now that he'd found her, he never wanted to be without her again.

Chapter 11

Jazmin tried to open her eyes but couldn't because her face was smashed into the soft feather pillow. Turning her head slightly, she managed to squint against the sunlight filtering into the room. Shifting around until she was on her back, she sat up, stifled a yawn and looked around the room.

Her gaze landed on Savion. Wearing a pair of blue striped pajama bottoms, he was seated at the table a few feet away, scrolling through his phone. In front of him was a covered tray.

She yawned again, then smiled as memories of his lovemaking rose to the surface of her mind. *What a night.*

He looked up from his phone, his expression conveying his contentment. "Good morning, sleepyhead."

The sheet fell away, revealing her nudity as she

reached up and stretched her arms above her head. "Morning."

He winked. "The view from here is amazing." He looked pointedly at her chest.

Feeling the familiar warmth creeping into her face, she grabbed the sheets and wrapped them around her torso. "I see you're chipper this morning."

"After what we did last night, how else would I be?"

She giggled. *He's got a point there.* "What time is it?"

"A little after ten."

"I must have really been tired. I don't usually sleep this late."

He gave her a knowing look. "I kind of figured. That's why I tried to be quiet, I didn't want to disturb you."

Her stomach grumbled. Hoping he hadn't heard it, she gestured to the tray. "What's in there?"

He lifted the lid and showed her. "Continental breakfast. There are some croissants, fresh fruit and coffee. I didn't know how long you'd be asleep, or what you'd want."

She crawled out of bed, and while he watched, she picked up the button-down he'd been wearing the day before and slipped into it. Closing the buttons, she walked toward the bathroom. "Just let me wash my hands." Moments later she came to the table.

"We can always order a hot breakfast if you prefer. We're the only ones here, so the service is pretty fast."

"This is a good start. I don't want anything heavy just yet." She sat in the chair across from him.

"How do you take your coffee?" He grabbed the handle of the white ceramic carafe and retrieved a matching mug from the tray.

"It's complicated. If you pour it for me, I'll dress it up."

"Whatever the lady wants." He filled the mug and passed it to her.

Dipping into the small, covered containers on the tray, she added a little cream and sugar to her coffee. Once it passed the color and taste test, she took a long sip. "Mmm. Good coffee."

"I'm glad you approve." He grabbed a plate and passed it to her, then took one for himself. "Let's eat."

They filled their plates with the offerings. She chose two croissants, green grapes and bright red strawberries. While they ate, they bantered.

"What a show, huh? I gotta say, I can see why you were so excited to see Brian in concert."

She nodded, swallowing a mouthful of tangy fruit. "All my girls who had seen him raved about his performances. My expectations were high, and he definitely delivered."

"What about me?"

She paused, confused by his question. "What do you mean?"

"I mean, I don't know what you expected of me for our first night together. But did I deliver?"

His forwardness caught her off guard. She coughed, then took a sip of her coffee to ease the tightness in her throat. "You shoot from the hip, I see."

He shrugged. "That's me."

Setting aside her mug, she reached for his hand. "To be honest, I never thought we would even reach a physical level, so I didn't have any expectations. But I will say you were very, very impressive, Savion." She gave his hand a gentle squeeze before releasing it.

"That's good to know." The self-satisfied smile on his face spoke louder than his words.

When they'd finished eating, he gathered all the dishes onto the tray and set it in the hallway outside their room. She watched him walk, captivated by the muscles working beneath his burnished skin. Returning to the table, he sat down and gestured for her to sit on his lap.

Her brow hitched.

He patted his legs. "I promise not to bite unless you request it."

Shaking her head, she stood. "What are you up to, Savion?"

He smiled. "Right now, I just want to hold you."

Slowly, she padded over to his chair and let him draw her onto his lap. The thin fabric of the pajama bottoms wasn't much of a barrier between her bottom and the luscious thickness of his manhood. So she shifted around a bit to get comfortable, or as close to it as she could manage.

When she stilled, he undid the top button of the shirt, baring part of her neck.

She stiffened. "What are you doing?"

"Shh." He opened the second button, pushing the shirt away to bare her right shoulder.

Knowing the scar was visible, and probably looked even less attractive in the daylight, she wriggled. "Savion…"

He stilled her by placing his large hand on her stomach. "Jazmin, listen to me, baby. I don't know where or how you got this." He traced his index finger along the part of the scar that peeked above the garment. "It doesn't matter to me, because I know you'll tell me when you're ready. But there's something I need you to understand."

She closed her eyes as he retraced the scar. His touch made her feel both peaceful and exhilarated. "What's that?"

"You are absolutely gorgeous… Wonderful… Perfect…in every way." He punctuated each descriptor with a warm kiss along the column of her neck. "I don't ever want to hear you say the word *ugly* when you're talking about yourself again, understood?"

"Yes," she replied breathlessly.

"Do you promise?" He flicked his tongue over her earlobe, then dragged it down the sensitive skin at the edge of her jawline.

She bit her lip to keep the moan from spilling out.

Another lick followed this time, down the side of her throat. Reaching the base, he suckled the area where her throat met her shoulder. "Well?"

"No… I mean yes…" She felt confused and aroused, but arousal won out. "Whatever you want me to say, so you'll make love to me."

Before she could draw another breath, he was on his feet, with her still in his arms. He carried her back to the bed, put her down and stripped away his shirt to reveal her nudity. His hands caressed and teased her sensitive skin, his lips kissed and nibbled each peak and valley of her body. Soon her entire being burned with ecstasy, and she could do nothing to stop the flood of soft moans escaping her lips.

He left her for a moment, to discard his pants and sheathe himself with protection. When he returned, the mattress gave as he climbed into bed with her.

He hovered above her, centering his hardness between her thighs. And as he slipped inside, joining their bodies, he growled into her ear.

Even in the haze of passion, she heard his words as clear as day.

"I love you, Jazmin."

Before she could respond, the first orgasm swept her away.

Savion sat on the balcony Sunday morning, with an open copy of *USA TODAY* in his hands. Wearing only a white terry robe and his shorts, he'd come out to enjoy the mild weather. The day had dawned gray and overcast, and the temperature hovered in the low seventies. The breeze rustling the pages of his paper felt good against his skin.

On the other side of the small wrought-iron table from him, Jazmin reclined in the second chair. She also wore one of the inn's fluffy robes over her lush nudity. She flipped through the pages of a fashion magazine, occasionally reaching for the bottle of water she'd placed on the table.

He couldn't remember the last time he'd felt such contentment. The rolling green lawn of the inn, punctuated by three large gardens bursting with colorful blooms and a man-made lake, provided a beautiful, relaxing feast for the eyes. The inn was located so far off the beaten path that traffic noise and city commotion couldn't be heard. Only the wind and the sound of the birds and insects encroached on the near silence.

A sudden, insistent buzzing sound drew his attention.

He looked to his left and saw Jazmin pluck her phone from the hip pocket of her robe. She looked at the screen, and from what he could tell, she was reading a message from someone. After a few moments of studying the display, she used her thumbs to tap out what he assumed to be a reply, then pocketed the device again.

She glanced his way, offering a quick smile before turning her attention back to the magazine.

He mirrored her expression, then went back to reading the world news section of the paper.

The buzzing started again.

This time, he kept his eyes on the news, but in his periphery, he could see her silently reading and responding. He drew in a breath. *I wonder who she's talking to.* She hadn't exactly been open about her past, at least not in terms of relationships outside of her family. Doing his best to shake off his curiosity, he kept reading.

The text alerts sounded four more times over the next ten minutes, and each time the buzzing cut through the silence, he did his best to ignore it. *It's not my business. She's an adult, she can talk to whoever she wants.*

That was what the logical part of him said. But the illogical part, the part of him that had blurted out the truth of his feelings during a moment of passion the night before, said other things.

What if she's talking to another man? He wondered why his mind jumped straight to that conclusion. It seemed too early in the relationship—or whatever it was they had—to be feeling jealous.

Can I really get upset with her? Are we even in a relationship now that we've slept together, or is this just a temporary arrangement?

Holding the paper at an angle that would hide his reaction, he silently cursed as she answered the sixth text message from whoever was blowing up her phone.

Or at least he thought it was silent.

A moment later, she asked, "Savion, did you say something?"

He cringed. *Damn, I'm caught.* Lowering the paper so they could see each other, he shook his head. "Nothing important."

One of her perfectly groomed eyebrows rose an inch. "For some reason, I don't believe that."

He didn't respond. Instead, he watched her, waiting to see if she'd volunteer any information about whom she'd been conversing with.

She took a deep breath, setting aside her magazine. "I hope you don't think it's rude of me to be texting when we're spending time together, because my work will force me to do that from time to time."

He shook his head. "No. Is work texting you now, while you're on vacation?"

"No. It's my mom." She sighed. "If I don't respond immediately to her messages, she starts coming up with scenarios involving me lying in a ditch somewhere."

"Your mom does that, too, huh?" He chuckled. "If Viola Monroe hasn't heard from one of her children in seventy-two hours, she's calling the sheriff and forming a search party."

She giggled, a light tinkling sound that melted away some of the tension in his body. "Well, anyway, she wanted to know how the concert was."

Surprise made him lean forward in his chair. "So she knows where we are?"

She made a funny face. "Not exactly."

"Now, I'm confused." What did she mean by that?

"My parents know I'm here. They know I got a ticket to see Brian McKnight, they just don't know all the details." She looked away, as if embarrassed.

He thought about what she'd said for a moment before it dawned on him. "Oh. So they don't know you're with me." He didn't know why that bothered him so much, but it irked him nonetheless.

She nodded. "Right. It was so much easier that way."

He sat back in the chair, feeling a bit deflated. She'd essentially hidden him from her parents, erasing him from their so-called "romantic getaway" in favor of letting them think she'd traveled to Wilmington alone.

As if sensing the change in his mood, she said, "Wait, Savion. I just figured out how this must sound to you, and trust me, it's not that way."

He folded his paper and set it aside. "It's fine, Jazmin. Technically, I didn't tell my parents, either—they saw it on the local news."

"In any case, I didn't tell my mom I'm here with a man because she's been harping on me for years to give her some grandchildren. I'm sure you remember me telling you that my parents are older than most of my friends' parents, so there's a sense of urgency for them."

"I can understand that." His parents were healthy and youthful and would probably live another fifty years, but that didn't stop them from leaning on their children for grandkids. He could imagine the pressure was much heavier in Jazmin's case since her parents were already over seventy. Luckily, one positive aspect of his younger siblings' recent marriages was that the pressure to produce a Monroe heir had been shifted to them.

"If I'd told her we were here together, I kid you not, she'd be naming the grandchildren right now."

He laughed. "Our moms should really meet. Sounds like they have a lot in common." Oddly enough, though, he could easily envision Jazmin as his wife, and mother to a few little darlings of their own. He'd never thought of any of his previous partners that way. But when he looked into her eyes, he could see a future far different, and far more fulfilling than any he'd ever imagined for himself.

"Good. Then you're not mad?"

He shook his head. "Nah. Could have been worse." *Crap.* He hadn't meant to say that last part out loud.

She tilted her head to one side, studying his face. "What do you mean by that?"

"Nothing." He leaned back in the wicker chair, gazing out at the lake, watching the light play over the shimmering surface.

She snapped her fingers. "Aha! You thought I was talking to a man, didn't you?"

He shook his head but didn't make eye contact. "I never said that."

"You didn't have to! Your face said it for you." She grinned. "You thought I was talking to another man, and you were jealous!"

He groaned, then crinkled his mouth into a frown. "Don't tease me about this, Jazmin."

She got up, walked over to his chair and stood in front of him. Her positioning essentially forced him to look at her.

They watched each other silently for a few beats.

Then she sat down on his lap, her expression of amusement softening into something much more affectionate. "I heard what you said last night, Savion."

He waited for what she would say next, bracing for the sting of her telling him for the millionth time that she didn't need romance in her life right now.

She draped her arms loosely around his neck. "I didn't have time to respond before my, um…" She chewed her lip. "Before pleasure got the better of me. But I just wanted you to know—" she looked deep into his eyes "—I love you, too, Savion."

Hearing those words pass her lips made his heart thud in his chest. Drawing her down to his kiss, he savored the taste of her and the feeling of holding her close to his heart.

Chapter 12

Monday afternoon, Jazmin watched the passing scenery as Savion drove them off the grounds of the Water's Edge Inn. Inside, she reflected on what had turned out to be one of the most eventful weekends of her life. She'd expected to enjoy her long-awaited meeting with Brian McKnight. What she had not expected, though, were the passionate interludes she'd shared with Savion.

She glanced over at him, admiring his profile as he kept his attention focused on the road. The line of his jaw, dotted with shadowy stubble, made him look even sexier than usual.

As if reading her mind, he reached up to run his fingertips over his chin below his goatee. "Can't believe I forgot my razor. I must be looking pretty shaggy right now."

"A little." She chuckled. "But don't worry, it looks good."

He smiled. "I'm glad you like it. I'm going to have to at least trim it before I go back to the office, though."

They lapsed into silence again, and she wondered what he was thinking. Was he analyzing the state of their relationship the way she was? *Do men even do that?* After a few long moments, her curiosity demanded satisfaction, so she asked, "What are we now, Savion?"

He shrugged. "I know we're in love. Not sure it needs a label beyond that."

She turned over his words in her mind and could see the truth in them. Still, it nagged at her that she hadn't been completely forthcoming with him about her past. Drawing a deep breath, she braced herself for all the possible reactions to what she had to say. "I want to tell you how I got my scar."

"I'm listening."

"Five years ago, I met a man named Dresden. He was handsome, charismatic and something of a bad boy. Played drums in a funk band, and we met at a show. He just had this presence that really grabbed my attention. We dated about six months before I moved into his place." She paused, gauging his reaction. She'd heard how folks in the Bible Belt judged people for what they referred to as "living in sin," and she wanted to see if he was one of the judgmental ones.

His expression didn't change. After she was silent for a few minutes, he said, "Go on."

"We were together almost three years, and a lot of it was good. But when he was playing gigs, he drank. And when he drank too much—" She sighed, feeling the sadness rise until she was unable to finish the sentence.

"It's okay, Jazmin." His deep voice encouraged her, reassured her.

"Dres came home one night, drunker than I'd ever seen him. I don't know, maybe he'd had more than just alcohol. Anyway, he accused me of cheating, and he started screaming at me. I told him repeatedly that I'd been faithful, but he didn't believe me." She could see the tightness in Savion's jaw, an indication that he didn't like where this story was going. Neither did she, but she felt she had to get it off her chest. "He chased me into his music room and grabbed a letter opener off his desk." Tears filled her eyes. "I was terrified. He pinned me to the wall and used the tip of the letter opener to cut me. Told me no man would want me once I was scarred."

"How did you get away from him?" His tone held a quiet urgency.

"There was a plaque he'd gotten from the lead singer of the band on the wall. It was really big, so I got one arm free, snatched it off the wall and smacked him over the head with it. When he passed out, I took my purse and keys and left." She wiped away the tears spilling down her face. "I went to the police to press charges, then to the hospital. I never went back there. I left clothes, personal items, but I've never set foot in that place again."

"And what happened to this asshole?"

She sniffled, buoyed by the knowledge of his protectiveness. "He did six months in county jail for misdemeanor assault. Right around the time he was due to get out, I got the call from Devon to work on the show. I came to North Carolina and haven't looked back."

"That was quite an ordeal you just described. And I'm happy you felt comfortable enough to tell me about it."

She took a deep breath, finally feeling the tears subside. "You're very easy to talk to."

"It just burns me up that this jerk is roaming free. He'd better hope we never cross paths."

She smiled. "I can't say I hate the idea of you giving Dres a swift kick in the rear end."

He frowned. "Did he ever hit you before that? Ever make you feel unsafe?"

She shrugged. "He'd never taken it that far."

"He was definitely a monster for behaving like that. Do you know why you stayed with him for so long?"

She narrowed her eyes, because his tone was a bit accusatory. "I've thought that plenty of times. But I can't go back and change my actions." She wanted to say more but kept quiet. If she went down this path with him, her emotions would get the better of her, and she'd end up cursing him out.

"I'm sorry, I didn't mean to say it that way." He sounded contrite. "You know I would never treat you that way, don't you?"

She nodded, because she trusted him in a way she'd never trusted another man. Though his statement about her staying too long had been hurtful, it wasn't enough to erase her feelings for him. She couldn't really explain it; a gut feeling told her that her body and her heart were safe with him.

"If I ever pulled some mess like that, Cam and Pop would take me out on the fishing boat just to throw me overboard." He shook his head. "As they should, because no man has any right to treat a woman that way."

She smiled but didn't say anything in response. Now that she'd told him the story behind her scar, relief washed through her. Being honest with him had felt good, at least up until he'd decided to question her good sense. Had his opinion of her changed? And did she really want to be involved with someone who was so quick to lay the blame at her feet?

At least he'd apologized. She shifted her gaze back to the passing scenery, resolved not to dwell on the matter.

By the time the lunch hour rolled around on Tuesday, Savion was ready to call it quits for the day. He'd arrived to work that morning to find the office in the midst of a crisis, one he'd been trying to rectify for the last few hours.

At a quarter past noon, he sat behind his desk, on the phone with the representative from the council. "Ma'am, can you repeat what you just said?"

"Yes, sir. I said, when you brought in your paperwork last week for the permit you requested, the signature page was missing. The form was turned in toward the end of the business day, so no one noticed the error until Friday. A clerk reached out to your office but was told you were unavailable."

"I was on vacation, but the signature page was here on my desk."

"Well, our clerk spoke to someone named Max, who said he didn't have access to your office because there was no one present with a key."

He rubbed his open palm down his face. "Okay, ma'am. So, what would I need to do to get this straightened out?"

"We still have all the rest of the pages of the form, so if you can bring the signature page into the office by three o'clock, we'll get you squared away."

"Great."

"But remember, sir. The filing will still take forty-eight hours to process. That I won't be able to issue you an official permit until late Thursday afternoon, at the earliest."

"Thank you." He hung up the phone briefly and took a deep breath to calm his nerves, then picked it up again. This time he dialed Caruso and Sons, the contractor assigned to the memory-park project.

"Al Caruso speaking."

"Hey, Al, it's Savion Monroe, again."

"What did you find out, Mr. Monroe?"

"The council can issue us a permit by late Thursday. So, when could we break ground?"

There was the sound of muffled conversation and typing on the line for a few moments before Al answered. "My office manager says next Monday is the soonest we can start. Not this coming week, the next one."

Savion cursed under his breath. "That's the absolute soonest?"

"Yes. When the permit didn't come in yesterday, we knew the memory park would be delayed, so we put our workers on other jobs. A few of them went back to the mainland. Sorry, man, that's the best I can do."

He sighed. "Can y'all swing a ceremony on Friday?

You don't need the whole crew for that, just the folks from the front office."

"I don't see why not. We've already got the ribbon and the giant scissors." Al chuckled.

He realized that was the foreman's attempt at a joke, but in his current mood, the humor was lost on him. "Okay. I'll let my father know there's been a slight change of plans."

"Make sure you remind him of the project-delay fee, as well. It's one and a half percent of the final project costs, before taxes."

He stifled a groan. "Thanks, Al. I'll be sure to let him know. Have a good day." He placed the receiver in the cradle and sat back in his chair. He groaned aloud, wondering how he could have let himself make such a stupid mistake. He looked at the signature page, resting on the corner of his desk. *I must have dropped it there and not realized it.* He'd been in such a hurry to go home and get ready for his romantic getaway that he'd lost focus.

I was so busy thinking about Jazmin that I did the one thing I promised myself I wouldn't do—I let my father down. His parents were due back this week from their anniversary trip, and he knew his father wouldn't be pleased to learn that the groundbreaking had to be delayed. If they were building somewhere inland, the one-week delay probably wouldn't be that big of a deal. But since they were on an island, racing against time to prepare an outdoor site for hurricane season, that week of lost time could potentially prove disastrous.

He stared up at the ceiling for a few moments, hoping his Gram's spirit would guide him to get the job done, the right way. He pushed back from the desk. If he wanted to avoid further delays to the memory-park project, he needed to get the signature page downtown. He tucked the page into a folder, got his keys and started toward the door.

He'd crossed the lobby and stepped outside when his phone buzzed with a text from Jazmin. He slipped the phone from his pocket and read it.

Wanna come by the studio?

He smiled, despite his bad mood, and fired off a reply. Will text you when I'm done with work.

The part of him that loved her wanted to see her again.

The part of him that wanted the memory-park project to succeed wondered if there really was room in his life for a relationship.

It was happening to him, just like it had happened to his brother and sister. He'd fallen into the love trap. Despite all his efforts to avoid getting involved with anyone, he'd managed to fall in love with Jazmin. And he'd fallen hard. His feelings for her ran deep, and no matter how much he wanted to, he couldn't simply dismiss them or pretend they didn't exist.

Climbing into his car, he tucked the phone away. Right now, he needed to focus on correcting his careless mistake. He was determined to make the best of this situation, and everything else would simply have to wait.

Chapter 13

Jazmin was in the lobby of the studio that evening, leaning against the reception desk. She scrolled through her social-media feeds, occasionally looking out through the front windows of the building. Most people had cleared out of the place a couple of hours ago, including the rest of the postproduction staff. Other than the janitor and the security guard stationed at the gate, there wasn't anyone else present on studio property. She'd already let the guard know she was expecting a visitor, and to let him through once he showed his identification.

When she saw Savion's car pull up in the lot, she went to the glass door and turned the lock, so he could enter. He appeared at the door moments later, and she let him in. He wore a pair of dark denim jeans, a red polo and blue sneakers. His casual dress did nothing to detract from his good looks—at this point, she'd concluded he'd look good in a potato sack.

She noticed the leather planner tucked beneath his left arm, and it pleased her to see that he'd started using the cover she'd given him.

As they walked down the corridor toward the postproduction suite, he asked, "Are you sure it's all right for us to be prowling around here this late?"

"It's only eight thirty. Besides, we're not prowling. I'm giving you a private tour of the postprod area." She opened the door to the suite and gestured him inside. "What's going on with that memory-park project?"

"We've hit a little snag, but we'll get back on track."

She sensed there was more to that story, but he didn't elaborate, and she didn't want to pry.

He moved to the center of the room, his gaze sweeping over the space. He pointed at the consoles. "That's a complicated-looking setup."

"Lucky for me, I've got a very talented staff." She spent a few moments naming some of the instruments on the panel and giving a brief explanation of their functions. "I hope I'm not boring you or being too technical."

He shook his head, though he didn't look terribly excited, either. "Whatever happened with the closing sequence? Is it done yet?"

She shook her head. "Unfortunately, no. We were given two treatments and we completed both before I left. The showrunners chose while I was gone, but they still feel the sequence is lacking something. So, we're still tweaking."

"You'll figure it out. I have every confidence in you."

"Thanks. I feel the same way about my team. Without postproduction and the work performed by my staff on this equipment, *The Shores* wouldn't be the great show so many people know and love."

"So, this is where the magic happens?"

She giggled. "You could say that. The footage we get from next door is pretty raw, and we have to make it look presentable for television."

His brow hitched. "Next door?"

She pointed at the frosted glass wall between her office and the video-editing console. "The set is just on the other side of this wall. There's a door in my office that leads over there."

"Can I see it?"

She sensed the change in his energy, telling her that his true interest lay in touring the set. "Sure, if you want." Leading him through her office to the door she'd referred to, she flipped the switch to turn on the lights.

As light filled the cavernous space, she saw his eyes widen.

"Wow. I didn't realize how huge this place is." He started walking, stopping in the center of the set that acted as the living room of Sierra's character, Karen Drake. "It doesn't look this big from outside."

"People say that all the time." She giggled as she moved toward one of the dolly-mounted cameras. "Ready to make your television debut?" She flipped the switch on the side, and a red light indicated the camera was on.

He laughed, standing in front of Karen's coffee table. "What should I do?"

"Just play along," she teased. "Do something entertaining."

He appeared to be thinking it over. "In that case, I can only think of one thing to do." To her surprise, he grabbed the planner from beneath his arm and flipped it open.

She scoffed. "Don't tell me you're going to read your appointments out loud."

His smile was mischievous. "So that's what you think is in here? Huh." He flipped through the pages, stopping on one. "Tell me what you think of this, Jazmin."

She listened, keeping the camera trained on him.

A breath later, she realized he was reciting…a poem.

For I am the beholder, I wish you could see the beauty I see

For I am Not the Hunter preying up his prey, for hurt and pain I shall never bring

For I am Not your Judge, but I will honor you

For I am the King praying I met my Queen

As you stand before me your very essence intoxicates me

All I see is

The intelligence of your mind

The sincerity of your eyes

The strength in your hips

The grace in your stride

Even the lightning bolt that runs down the side of your body

Lets me know you weathered your own share of storms

All I want is to be your Peace

When he'd finished, she switched off the camera and slowly walked toward him. "Savion, I had no idea you had that kind of talent."

As she neared him, he grabbed her hand. "No one else knows. I've never shared my poetry with anyone, until now."

A shiver ran through her body, and her heart squeezed inside her chest. "I'm honored." She felt truly special, knowing he'd shared something so private with her. "Your poem is amazing."

"So is my muse." His gaze met hers. "I've never been so inspired as I have these past few weeks."

Heat pooled in her core as their eyes locked. *The lightning bolt that runs down the side of your body... he was talking about my scar.* He'd taken the mark that had brought her shame and described it in such a lyrical, beautiful way. In an awe-filled voice, she repeated, "Amazing..."

She leaned up for his kiss and savored the feeling of his lips and his embrace for as long as she could stand it. When she pulled away, breathless and dazed, she said, "We need to get out of here."

"What's the rush?"

She traced her fingertip along his jawline. "Well, for one thing, Karen's sofa is just a prop. If we make love on it, or any of the furniture in here, it will break."

He gave her a wicked smile. "In that case, let's go."

Hand in hand, they dashed toward her office. On the way out, she flipped the switch again, plunging the fictional world of *The Shores* into darkness.

Savion awoke to the sounds of someone shuffling around in his bedroom. Rolling over in bed, he noticed he was alone. His eyes scanned the room in the soft pre-dawn light until he saw Jazmin. She stood near the foot of the bed and he could tell she was getting dressed.

"Going somewhere?"

She stopped moving, looked his way. "Sorry, I was trying not to wake you."

He stifled a yawn. "No worries."

"Anyway, I've got to be at the studio at seven this morning for meetings, and I still need to run home for a shower and fresh clothes."

He let his head drop back against the softness of the pillow.

She sat down on the end of the bed and started putting on her shoes. Her phone rang, the sound cutting through the silence. Reaching into her pocket, she slipped it out and answered. "Hello? Oh, good morning, Sierra. Thanks for the wake-up call, but I'm up."

He shifted onto his side, knowing it would be intrusive to stare at her while she was on the phone.

"No, I'm still at home, but I'm up and getting ready. Uh-huh. Okay, I'll be there by six forty-five or so. See you then."

He cringed. *Again, with that?* She never seemed to want anyone in her life to know when she was with him. He rubbed his hand over his eyes, shifting his position again to watch her.

She'd put her phone away and gotten into her shoes, and was on her feet. She came around to his side of the bed and leaned down to peck him on the cheek. "I've gotta go."

He caught hold of her hand. "Wait, Jazmin."

She sat down on the edge of the bed. "What is it?"

He drew in a breath. "Why did you tell Sierra you were at home?"

She shrugged. "That's where I'm headed."

"Yeah, but it's not where you are right now." He gestured around. "You're in my house, in my bedroom. You've been here since last night when you willingly came here to make love to me. Remember?"

She pursed her lips. "I remember. How could I forget when you're so spectacular?"

The comment stroked his ego but didn't solve the issue at hand. "I appreciate that, but if I'm so great, why are you keeping me a secret? I thought we were past that?"

She exhaled, ran a finger through her loose, dark curls. "Savion, I love you, you know that."

"I love you, too, baby."

Her lips turned up into a soft smile before she continued. "But I'm a private person. I'm not interested in being the subject of water-cooler gossip at the studio."

He sat up, wanted to be at eye level with her. "I can understand that. But do your parents know we're seeing each other? They aren't going to contribute to that."

She nibbled her bottom lip. "No. But we already talked about that. I don't want to get them started on the grandkid thing again."

He sighed.

Her expression changed then, and she tapped the center of his chest with her index finger. "Wait a minute. You've been hounding me about not telling people about us. Have you told your siblings? Your parents? Your friends?"

He leaned back against his oak headboard. "Troy

knows." That was more due to his cousin's percep-
tiveness than anything else, but he didn't want to tell
her that.

"One person. Your cousin from the West." She threw
her hands up. "See? We're pretty much even."

He ran his open palm over his face. The sun now
peeked over the horizon, changing and brightening the
light flowing through the window. He gazed out at the
fence separating his backyard from the wooded area
bordering his property, realizing he didn't know what
else to say. She was right. "I don't mean to make such a
big deal about it. I just don't know what I'm doing here.
Remember, I've never been serious about a woman before. I don't know the protocol."

She stood, stretching her arms above her head.
"There isn't any protocol. We're supposed to just do
what works for both of us." She leaned in, cupped his
jaw and pressed her lips against his. "This whole thing
is still new. Let's just take it one step at a time, okay?"

"Deal." He patted her behind as she walked away.

"I'll call you later." She strolled out of the room.

He listened to her footsteps as she went down the
hall, through the living room and out the front door.

Alone in the quiet of his room, he thought about
the exchange they'd had. Part of him thought she was
right. They shouldn't rush things. Yet another part of
him, the part harboring such an intense love and desire for her, wanted to tell everyone they knew that
they were together.

She made a good point. *I haven't really been telling people, either.* He wanted her to acknowledge his
presence in her life to the people that were close to her.

He couldn't say why, but he wanted her to do it first. Could it be because none of his previous girlfriends had ever introduced him to their family and friends? He'd never really cared about such things in his relationships before. That was yet another sign of how serious his feelings were for Jazmin.

He grabbed his phone from the nightstand and checked the time. *It's just past six.* He climbed out of bed and headed for the shower. He usually got to the MHI office around eight thirty, but with things being as they were with the memory park, he thought he could stand to go in early.

When he arrived at the office just after eight, he was surprised to find his father sitting behind his desk.

Carver's face was set in a serious expression, his tone somber as he spoke. "Morning, son."

Stepping farther into the office, Savion shut the door behind him. "Good morning, Pop. How was Europe?"

"Wonderful. Your mother and I had a great time." He reclined in the chair. "We were plumb worn-out, though, so decided to cut our trip a little short."

"Glad to hear it."

"That's not why I'm here, though."

Taking the seat across from his father, Savion had a flashback to years ago, when this had been Carver's office and he'd been a newbie, fresh out of college. Back then, his father had seemed so impressive and imposing. Now, he seemed much more of the latter. "I know why you're here, Pop. And I'm sorry things didn't go as planned."

His father chuckled. "I can see you're appropriately

contrite. You do know the project-delay fee is coming out of your salary, right?"

He nodded. "That's fair."

Carver leaned forward over the desk. "Anyway, I didn't come here to lecture you about that, either."

Savion felt his brow furrow. "I'm confused, Pop."

He chuckled again. "I know you are. That's why you made such a silly mistake."

Though he hadn't seen his siblings yet, Savion knew it was a safe guess that Cam had been the one to spill the beans on what he'd done. "Cam never did get over that middle-child syndrome, did he?"

"No, but that's not important. What's important is that if you were so distracted with Ms. Boyd that you flubbed this project, the most crucial one I've ever assigned you, that means something."

He drew in a breath, shifting in his seat. Here was his opportunity to tell someone how much he cared about Jazmin, and he'd be damned if he wasn't going to take it. "I love her, Pop."

"I know that." Carver rested his elbows on the desk, lacing his fingertips together. "The question is, what are you going to do about it?"

Chapter 14

"Jazmin?"

Looking up from the weekly entertainment magazine spread open on her desk, Jazmin saw Drea standing in the door between her office and the production suite. "Yes?"

"We just got some new footage from next door."

"Visual sent over another clip? How long is it?"

She shrugged. "Less than two minutes. Randolph said it just showed up on the video server, in a new file inside the closing-sequence folder."

"Maybe it was a glitch that caused it not to be included last time."

"Or maybe they made file updates?"

She scratched her chin. "Okay. Well, if they want us to add it, go ahead and let Randolph do his thing."

"I'll tell him." Drea shut the office door as she left.

Jazmin looked back down toward her magazine. She'd been trying to read the feature teasing the second season of *The Shores* for the better part of an hour, but she found it impossible to concentrate. As long as she'd been sitting there, staring at the words on the page, the only takeaway she had was from the first paragraph—the show would need to deliver in a big way to top the ratings and buzz it received during its first season. The whole team, cast and crew included, knew there was a lot riding on this season.

With a sigh, she stuck a sticky note on the edge of the page to mark her spot and shut the magazine. There was no use in torturing herself any longer when she knew her concentration was shot.

And what's bothering me? She scoffed. A man. After two and a half years of enjoying a drama-free, single existence, she'd traded that in for a man, one she hadn't heard from in the last two days. Savion hadn't bothered to call or text her since she'd left his house early Wednesday morning. She'd been giving him his space since he seemed upset that day. Now she was beginning to get annoyed.

Should I have told my parents about him? Should I have told Sierra? At this point, if she was to inform them of her involvement with Savion, she didn't even know what she would say. She knew one thing—she loved him. But what would that mean going forward? She had no idea. All the time she'd spent outside of the dating pool had left her a bit rusty in this regard.

"Knock, knock." Sierra swung open the office door.

Jazmin jumped. "Damn, girl. Why didn't you text me that you were coming over here?"

"I did. I texted you like four times. Check your phone, sis." She pointed to the phone, lying faceup on the edge of the desk.

Jazmin noted the flashing notification light and grimaced. "Sorry. You know I keep it on vibrate during the day and I guess I didn't hear it."

Shaking her head, Sierra settled onto the edge of the desk. "We both know that thing vibrates hard enough to rattle this desk, so you must be distracted." She pointed to the magazine. "Don't tell me it's *Entertainment Weekly* that's got your face cracked like that. Because if it is, you need to cancel that subscription."

She shook her head. "I was reading the article about the show, but that's not it."

Sierra studied her face for a few silent moments. Then she snapped her fingers. "It's man trouble."

Jazmin groaned.

"It's Savion!" Sierra slapped the edge of the desk. "It makes perfect sense. Cam says his brother has been impossible ever since you two got back from Wilmington. How was that, by the way?"

Her mind went back to the trip. "The concert was amazing, and Brian…"

Sierra rolled her eyes. "C'mon, Sierra, you know that's not what I meant. It's Brian McKnight, it's not like it wasn't gonna be a good show. I mean, what happened with you and Savion? Did y'all…you know?"

She looked away.

"Oh!" Sierra giggled. "So that's what happened. Cam says Savion's concentration at work is garbage."

Mine is, too. But she didn't say that aloud.

"You're in love with him, aren't you!"

Jazmin frowned. "Girl, keep your voice down. This office isn't exactly soundproof, and there's no reason my team should know my business."

Sierra giggled but complied. Her voice much softer, she said, "Have you told him how you feel?"

She nodded. "And he feels the same. I just don't know what to do with that."

Shaking her head, Sierra stood. "Love can be complex, but it doesn't have to be. You two need to have a real conversation about where this thing between you is going."

"I agree." She laced her fingers together, stretching her arms over the surface of the desk. "I'm not sure how to approach it, though."

"Why don't you just invite him to the cast party tomorrow night? The atmosphere will be super laid-back. Then after the party, you two can go grab a coffee or something and hash this out." She turned toward the door. "I've gotta get back on set. But think about what I said, girl." She disappeared out the office door, leaving it open.

Jazmin mulled over her friend's advice for a few moments. The party, celebrating the completion of filming of the show's first episode, could potentially provide a festive backdrop to break the ice between them. Grabbing her phone, she fired off a text to Savion.

Sorry for the short notice, she began.

Drea poked her head in the door again. "The footage is incorporated. Do you want to take a look at it?"

She shook her head. "I'm out of ideas. Just submit the rough cut for the party tomorrow."

"You're sure?"

"Yes. We've been at this forever. It's possible the

showrunners will love it, and if not, maybe the cast and the rest of the crew will have some helpful input."

"Okay. I'll deliver it to the executive suite."

After Drea left, she finished her text.

...but why don't you swing by the cast party tomorrow at 8?

Sending the text, she relaxed back in her chair and pocketed her phone, telling herself she wasn't going to sit and stare at the screen, waiting for him to reply.

She stood and walked out of the office, through the postproduction suite to the main corridor. "I'm going for a snack. I'll bring back some donuts or something from the lounge."

Randolph tossed up his hand. "Thanks, boss lady."

Trisha, wearing her headphones, didn't look up. Drea offered a nod.

She was walking down the corridor when her phone buzzed on her hip. She snatched it out of her pocket to check it and sighed when she saw a message from her mother.

Ethel Charles next door just had her fourth grandchild. It's a girl.

She could read the subtext, the words her mother hadn't said. Other women her age were enjoying multiple grandchildren, and Jazmin hadn't even given her one. Groaning, she tucked away the phone and headed for the lounge.

Now I really need a donut.

* * *

Seated at the dinner table in his parents' house, Savion forked up some of his mother's lemon-dill salmon and ate it, savoring the flavor. He hadn't been feeling his most social, but he couldn't turn down his parents' dinner invitation. It wasn't just the lure of his mother's cooking that had brought him, though. He wanted to hear all about their weeklong trip.

Viola and Carver occupied the ends of the table, while Hadley sat across from him. Campbell sat to his immediate right, leaving three empty seats around the large table.

"Too bad Sierra and Devon couldn't get away from the set tonight." Campbell popped a roasted potato into his mouth. "They are really missing out."

Viola smiled. "Nonsense. There's plenty of extra for you to take home when you leave."

"You're the best, Mom." Campbell threw two thumbs up in their mother's direction.

Hadley covered a yawn with her hand. "Yeah, Mom. Dinner is great."

Carver looked her way. "Hadley, have you been sleeping? You look tired."

"I am." Hadley stifled another yawn. "All I want to do is sleep lately."

Viola looked at Carver, and Savion noticed the sparkle in his mother's eyes. To his surprise, she said nothing.

"So, Mom, Dad, tell us about your trip." Hadley crunched on a forkful of salad as she watched her parents with an expression of eager anticipation. *That's the most alert she's looked all night.* Savion sipped from his glass of iced tea.

"It was wonderful," Carver began. "Three days in Madrid, three days in Lisbon—"

"And four glorious days in Barcelona." Viola finished the sentence, her gaze locked on her husband's face. "We saw such beautiful sights. The cathedrals. The Royal Palace of Madrid. Plaza Mayor."

"Remember the view from Vasco da Gama Tower in Lisbon?" Carver wiped his mouth with a napkin. "There we were, on the observation deck, five hundred feet above the city. You could see for miles around. Remind me to show you kids the pictures after dinner."

Viola snapped her fingers. "The view was amazing. But my favorite place in Lisbon was Rua Garrett. The shops, the museums, the scenery. It was breathtaking."

"As much as you love to shop, I'm not surprised that was your favorite," Carver quipped.

Cam asked, "What was your favorite part of the trip, Dad?"

Carver scratched his chin for a moment. Then he stood, walked slowly to where his wife sat and placed his hands on her shoulder. "Honestly? Being with your mother was the best part."

Savion smiled, as did his brother and sister. He could see the blush coloring his mother's cheeks.

"When we were in Barcelona, we went down to the coast, to this little place called Sitges. And I held Vi's hand and walked with her along the Mediterranean as the sun was setting. And when I looked at my bride, I realized I still feel the same passion for her I felt when

I married her forty years ago." He leaned down, and kissed Viola's cheek. "I realized how blessed I am."

Viola looked up to her husband with tear-filled eyes and an affectionate smile. "The feeling is mutual, Carver."

The room fell quiet as the children watched their parents bask in each other's love.

Savion knew that his parents had something rare and beautiful, and it made him happy to see the way they appreciated each other. He'd never thought he could have something like that for himself. Jazmin was the first woman to come into his life and make him wonder if he could have it, even long for it.

A sob broke the silence.

All eyes turned to Hadley, who dabbed at her eyes with one of Viola's cloth napkins. Realizing everyone was looking at her, Hadley said, "This is just too sweet!" Moments later, she ran from the table, still in tears.

Cam snorted. "She seems a little bit emotional."

Carver looked at his sons, then back to his wife. "Well, well, well."

Crumpling his napkin, Cam stood and stretched. "I'm stuffed. Couldn't eat another bite." He started gathering the empty plates.

"Make sure you pack up something for my daughter-in-law," Viola instructed as Cam walked past her, carrying the stack of dishes from the table to the kitchen. "Who knows if she's eating well, working all those long hours at the studio."

Carver sat down in the empty seat next to his wife. Viola said, "I'm really looking forward to this party tomorrow. I can't wait to see what they've got in store for the second season." She'd been watching the show since the first episode, and since Cam and Sierra had married, she loved being able to brag to her friends about her famous daughter-in-law.

Carver nodded. "It should be fun. But at ten, we're leaving." He chuckled. "I'm old, and I need my sleep."

So, they're both going to the party. He knew his brother and sister would be there, due to their spouses' involvement with the show. Savion thought about the text he'd gotten from Jazmin, the one inviting him to the party. The one he still hadn't answered. If he stayed home, he'd literally be the only Monroe missing from the gathering.

Viola asked, "You're going, aren't you, Savion?"

He shrugged. "Haven't decided yet."

Carver frowned. "Are you avoiding Jazmin?"

"Wow, Pop. Just ask him flat out then." Campbell returned to the room at that moment with a foil-wrapped plate, retaking his seat. He set the packet on the table in front of him. "You gotta be delicate with Savion, you know he's uptight."

Savion rolled his eyes. "Shut up, Cam."

"I'm not wrong, though." Cam leaned back in his chair, crossing his arms over his chest. "Just come to the party, man. Don't be the odd one out."

"Your brother's right. Whatever's going on between you and Jazmin, that's even more reason you should be there."

"I know she invited you."

Savion cut his eyes at Campbell.

"Don't be looking at me like that. You know my wife is her closest friend here, so she told me."

Viola interjected. "Don't be rude, Savion. If she invited you and you don't have any good excuse not to go, then you should go."

Savion sighed. "Fine."

"I hope you'll show up at the party with a little more enthusiasm than that," Carver remarked. "After all, if she's already got your heart in her handbag, there's nothing you can do but give in, son."

He shook his head. His father was probably right, but that didn't mean he had to like it.

Chapter 15

Saturday night, Jazmin stood by the drink station set up inside the main studio space, her glass of punch in hand. It was a little after eight and the celebration had just gotten started. The crew had put in an entire day's work, breaking down and moving the sets off the floor of the studio and storing them away.

Looking around now, she noted how different the studio space appeared in its current configuration. Ten round tables, all set with six chairs each, had been brought in, along with two long rectangular tables that served as the buffet. Della's had catered the event, and as Jazmin looked over the assortment of sandwiches, finger foods and desserts, she knew this would be the night for cheating on her usually healthful eating. The drink station next to her was a large square table, staffed by an intern responsible for serving champagne from several bottles, and the bright red punch from two large crystal bowls.

Glancing around, she searched the assemblage for Savion. He'd finally accepted her invitation to come to the party this morning, but she wondered if he'd changed his mind. She drew a couple of deep, cleansing breaths as she headed for the buffet table. *It's still early. Chill out, girl.*

Della, stationed between the tables stuffed with food, smiled as she approached. "What's the matter, honey? You look like you lost your kitten."

She plastered on a smile. "Just nervous about the season. We put in a lot of work and we want it to be well-received, you know what I mean?"

"I know that's not what's got you looking like that, but okay." She reached over, grabbing a plate. "Listen, honey. You like chicken salad?"

She nodded.

"Good." Della placed a split croissant on the plate and layered one side with chicken salad, lettuce and tomato before assembling it. "Here. A little bit of my famous chicken salad will turn that frown upside down." She handed over the plate. "That and dealing with whatever man who's got your face screwed up." She winked.

She could only chuckle in response as she accepted the plate. "Thanks, Della." She moved on down the table, adding a few fresh strawberries, a mini quiche and a delectable-looking slice of Carmen's double-chocolate cake. Her plate filled, she wandered over to an empty table and sat down.

While she ate, she watched the scene around her.

Her colleagues were mingling, eating, having a great time. Under any other circumstances, she'd be doing the same. This thing with Savion had her so off-kilter, she didn't know what to do with herself. Sierra was right about one thing—they needed to come to an understanding about this relationship. She was ready to commit and be exclusive, but could a playboy like Savion ever be persuaded to get off the dating merry-go-round and get serious with her? His declarations of love were very sweet, and she trusted that his feelings were real. But would that be enough?

As she finished up her food and walked over to toss her trash, Savion walked in. She nearly dropped everything when she saw him. He was dressed in all black—button-down shirt, slacks and loafers with a gold-chain accent at the toe. He stood in the doorway, one large hand in his hip pocket, surveying the room.

Prickles danced down her spine. *He's looking for me.* She quickly dumped her trash and made a beeline in his direction.

His eyes met hers as she approached. "Jazmin. I was looking for you."

She smiled "Hi. I'm glad you could make it. Sorry for the short notice."

"No biggie." He gestured toward the crowd. "Did I miss anything?"

She shook her head. "Devon's going to make a speech, and so is a network exec who flew down from New York, but that hasn't happened yet."

"Cool." He moved closer to her. "When this party is over…"

"I know. We need to talk."

He nodded, then walked over to the drink station.

"Aren't you going to eat something?"

He shook his head. "Not yet. Had a big dinner—Mom's leftovers."

Once they each had a glass of champagne, they returned to the table she'd been sitting at.

The sound of someone tapping a glass with a fork echoed through the space. She turned to see Devon standing in the center of the tables.

"Time for the speeches," Savion remarked.

"I want to thank everyone for coming out tonight." Devon glanced around the room as he spoke. "We have so much to celebrate here at *The Shores*. There's our talented cast, including the newest member, Ms. Zola Revere." He gestured toward Zola, who stood from her seat and graciously accepted the applause that followed. "I want to thank Zola and all our cast members for sharing their gifts with us, and with our audience. Stand up, y'all."

Jazmin looked around and saw Sierra, Grayson and the other actors stand, and she joined in applauding them.

Devon continued once the clapping died down. "We also have our amazing crew, whose hard work makes our show the best it can be. Writers, producers, visuals, tech, equipment operators—everyone who works here is so valuable to what we do. So, if you work on the show, in any capacity, stand up so we can applaud you."

Doing as her boss demanded, Jazmin stood along with her coworkers. Savion looked directly at her as he clapped, and she felt another tingle shoot down her spine.

"So, again, thank you for coming out to help us kick this season off right." Devon raised his glass. "Here's to a brilliant season." Everyone raised their glasses in a toast, and as Jazmin sipped from hers, she noticed Savion watching her silently. *What is he thinking right now?*

Before she could ask, Devon introduced the network executive who was to speak next. She did her level best to listen to the man as he droned on about advertising revenue from the show, ratings numbers and all manner of boring corporate speak. With Savion sitting across from her, regarding her as if he was undressing her in his mind, it was near impossible to focus. She settled for just keeping her gaze on the speaker, though that didn't lessen the impact of Savion's attention.

The man from the network finally wrapped up his speech, and she clapped along with everyone else, mostly out of relief that he was done talking.

"Okay, now it's time to see the end result of all this collective effort." Devon walked over to the projection screen that took up most of the south wall. "Here's the first episode of season two of *The Shores*." He made a hand gesture, signaling the boy in the visuals booth to start the projector, then took his seat.

Jazmin looked at the screen as the opening sequence she and her team created started to play. *It looks great onscreen. I hope the closing sequence looks just as good.*

Sipping from his glass of champagne, Savion watched the episode playing before them. Sierra, being a principle character, got a lot of screen time. He found himself amused and impressed with the antics of his sister-in-law's onscreen persona.

He kept his focus on the screen, occasionally glancing toward Jazmin. She sat across from him at the small table, wearing an expression that conveyed her interest in the show. He assumed it was her first time viewing the episode as well, and he could understand her wanting to see how it had turned out.

I guess they finally got those sequences right. He thought the opening sequence had definitely improved over the season-one version. He considered telling her that, but seeing how into the show she was, he decided it could wait until later. After the party ended, he could give his opinion on the closing sequence, as well.

The plot of the episode revolved around tying up the departure of Fiona Lasalle and introducing her long-lost half sister, Phaedra, in her place. As a resident of the island and someone who knew so many people at the studio, Savion knew that Mia Hopkins, the actress who portrayed Fiona, had been fired for her off-screen bad behavior. On the show, however, the writers had come up with an ingenious explanation for her absence. He watched the scene unfold, almost wishing he'd grabbed some popcorn from the food table.

"Who are you?" Xander demanded of the woman on his doorstep.

"Your other half sister, Phaedra." She pushed past him into the house. "Another child of our playboy father, Terrence LaSalle."

"That I can believe. I see you inherited Dad's boldness." Xander closed the door behind her. "But why are you here?"

"To tell you of the sad demise of our sister, Fiona." Phaedra's lips trembled. "I'm afraid she won't be back."

Xander made a fist. "I tried to stop her from going on that trek to climb Mount Everest, but she wouldn't listen."

Phaedra walked over and touched his shoulder. "I hear she made it to the top. But she couldn't make it back down."

Somber, dramatic music queued up as the scene changed, and Savion could only shake his head. During the first season, Fiona, an enthusiastic outdoorswoman, had casually mentioned such an excursion. If only Mia had known that line would be used to kill off her character. He also loved that the writers had decided to keep the subtle, yet campy humor that had made the show such a hit.

The drama continued as the episode explored the lives of the other residents of the fictional world of *The Shores*, and he felt drawn into the various storylines in a way he hadn't during the first season. He could tell the writers had put forth extra effort with the script and storyline, and the actors were delivering stellar performances. All in all, he thought Devon should be very proud of the hard work of everyone involved and planned to tell him that later.

As the episode continued, he got up to get popcorn and returned to his seat with the paper bag. Offering some to Jazmin, he watched as she scooted her chair closer to his. They shared the snack as they watched the show together, and he mused on what life would be like with her as his one and only. Would they spend nights like this together at his place, curled up on the sofa watching a movie and trading war stories about the crazy things that happened at their jobs? Or would she even open up enough for them to enjoy things like that?

He understood that she'd been hurt by some jerk who didn't value her. Obviously, the asshole didn't realize what he had. Jazmin was beautiful, intelligent and capable. He wanted something more with her, something special. But he also didn't want to end up paying for another man's mistakes.

He looked over at the table where his parents were sitting with Cam and Sierra. Hadley and Devon were at a table up front. Even Troy had come and was leaning against a wall by the door, enjoying the show while he sipped from a glass of punch. Troy's jeans and cowboy boots stood out among the party wear of the others in attendance, but that was typical of his Western-raised cousin. With the whole Monroe family present, he felt even more compelled to figure things out with Jazmin.

As if reading his thoughts, his father looked in his direction. Meeting his eyes, Carver gave his son a curt nod.

Savion sighed. *The episode is almost over. We'll go somewhere and deal with this as soon as it's done.*

The last scene of the episode was at a memorial service for Fiona. The characters, standing around a large portrait of Fiona, each tossed a rose into a small wooden box. As the box was shut, the image froze and the credits began to roll.

Enthusiastic applause filled the room, and he joined in but kept watching so he could see the entire closing sequence. Since Jazmin and her team had gone through so much trouble pulling it together, he was curious about the result.

Still images of the cast members flipped by, providing a backdrop for the credits. Near the end, though, a video appeared as the name of the production company rolled by.

Savion's mouth dropped open when he realized what was onscreen.

That's me.

As he watched in shock, he saw himself delivering the lines of the poem he'd recited to Jazmin that night in the studio.

I didn't even know she was recording me!

He swiveled to look at her and found her mouth agape, as well. "I... What... How did that get into the sequence?"

He stood. He had no intention of listening to whatever lame excuse she had for this betrayal. "I'm not buying that for a second. You recorded me and didn't even tell me."

"I didn't mean to save the footage and..."

He was already moving toward the exit.

Chapter 16

Jazmin trailed a few steps behind Savion as he strode out of the main studio and into the corridor. "Savion, wait a minute."

He ignored her.

She called his name again, inwardly cursing the high-heeled shoes that were now slowing her down.

He didn't stop, didn't look back. "No. I don't want to hear it."

"Please!" She picked up her pace and caught up to him, grabbing the back of his shirt.

He stopped then, turning blazing eyes on her. "Fine. Say what you have to say, and when you finish, I'm out."

"I don't know how the footage got into the sequence, but I'll make sure they take it out."

"Oh, really." He folded his arms over his chest. "You

don't know how it got included, but you didn't think it was necessary to tell me you were filming me."

"You're right, I shouldn't have done that."

"You're damn straight. Now everyone has seen me reciting my work, and now you want to say what you shouldn't have done. How could you expose me like this?"

She blew out a breath. "You can't think I did this on purpose."

"I can, and I do." His expression remained serious.

"Savion. Listen to me. Yes, I recorded you. I thought you knew the camera was on that night. But I never saved the footage, and I never intended for it to be used."

"Obviously you didn't delete it."

"Don't you remember what happened that night?" She tried to get closer to him, but he took a step back. "We left to make love and I was distracted. We were both distracted."

"Sure, we were. But only one of us did something dishonest."

She looked down at her shoes, her entire being racked with guilt.

He shook his head. "How can I believe you, Jazmin? You told me yourself that you and your team couldn't come up with a good end sequence. That something was missing. I guess you finally figured out what it was."

Tears gathered in her eyes. "I'm so sorry, Savion. Please believe me."

He turned away from her. "I've never shared my poetry with anyone. Never. I wanted to protect my art from the outside world. After all these years, I finally felt safe enough to share it with someone. And you turn around and expose my entire private world to everyone I know, just like that." He started walking once more. "I don't ever want to see you again."

She started walking, too, but when he looked back at her, with the hurt burning in his eyes, she halted her steps.

"I trusted you, Jazmin. Now I see what a terrible mistake that was." He shook his head, then turned and left. Moments later, she heard the heavy metal door that led to the parking lot creak open, then slam shut.

Leaning her back against the wall, she put her face in her hands and let the tears flow.

Motoring down Shoreside Boulevard, Savion cursed aloud.

How could I have trusted her? I should never have told her about my poetry.

He'd gone more than twenty years keeping his writing a secret from everyone, and that had worked out just fine. Now, when he'd finally felt safe enough with someone to share his work, it had backfired spectacularly. He couldn't even articulate the betrayal, the embarrassment he'd felt when he saw himself spread across that huge screen, reading his private thoughts in front of a very public gathering.

He sighed. Anger and hurt warred inside him, and he needed to get somewhere he could clear his mind. He knew of only one place to go, but he'd need to stop by his house first.

When he pulled into his driveway a short time later,

he climbed out of his SUV and went inside. In the bedroom, he changed into a pair of cargo shorts and a brush cotton T-shirt, along with a pair of sturdy sneakers. Tucking his phone into a pocket of the shorts, he searched through his closet for a duffel bag. Then, he tossed a few sets of comfortable clothes and a few other essentials into the bag. As he zipped it up and went into his den to grab his other supplies, his phone vibrated against his hip.

She'd better not be calling me. Slipping the device out of his pocket, he checked the screen. Swiping, he answered the call. "What's up, Troy?"

"What's going on with you, man? I saw you storm out of the party a little while ago."

"It's complicated."

"I bet. I don't know how much you know about the acoustics at the studio, but we could hear you two arguing in the hallway."

He sighed, pressing his fingertips to his temple. "Is there a reason you called, Troy?"

"I just wanted to make sure you were all right."

"I appreciate that."

"I never would have pegged you as a poetic soul, Savion. But I'm impressed with your work."

He gritted his teeth at yet another reminder of the way Jazmin had violated his trust. "That's good to know, but I don't want to talk about that."

"So, what are you going to do, now that the secret is out?"

He sighed. "Nothing. I mean, what can I do? As of right now, I'm getting my rods and supplies together to go out on my boat and leave all this foolishness behind."

"For real? Care for some company?"

His brow hitched. "You want to go out on the water with me?"

"I'm not about to let you go out there alone, not in such a foul mood."

"Troy, are you serious? You don't even like going to the beach." He couldn't imagine a scenario where his cousin would enjoy spending time on the open water.

"True. But that should tell you how much I love ya, fam." He chuckled. "I'm willing to suffer through it, just so you won't be out there, staring at the water and looking sad, all by your lonesome."

Despite his aforementioned "foul mood," Savion could feel his tension lessening a bit. "I hate to admit it, but I could probably use the company." He pulled his favorite rod from the rack in his den closet, setting it next to his tackle box. "Listen. Can you meet me at Sanderson Point Pier in thirty minutes?"

"Yeah. I'm already at your parents' house. All I have to do is change."

"You need to pack a couple of clean outfits. None of that boots-and-jeans stuff, either. I'm talking sweats and shorts, comfortable, nonslip footwear. And bring a jacket and a hat—it gets cool out there."

"Aye, aye, Captain."

He groaned at his cousin's corny joke. "Do you want to fish with me? If so, I'll bring an extra rod for you."

"If I'm going out on the boat with you, I might as well give it a shot. Don't know if I'll be any good at it, though."

He reached into the closet to grab another rod, slipping it into the long vinyl zippered case with his. "Don't worry about it. I'll give you a quick lesson once we're out on the water."

"Sounds like a plan. See you at the pier." Troy disconnected the call.

Pocketing his phone, Savion gathered his duffel, the tackle box and the rod case. Hauling everything outside to the car, he tucked it into the back of his SUV and shut the hatch. His passion for fishing was the main reason he owned such a large sport utility vehicle—it allowed him the space to transport his rods and gear back and forth to the pier.

He returned to the house once more, to fill his soft-sided cooler with drinks, snacks and sandwich fixings. He typically spent two, at most three days out on the water, since he had comfortable sleeping quarters in the hold. His boat, a gift he'd purchased himself on his thirty-fifth birthday, was named the *Queen of Zamunda*, a reference to his favorite film.

He'd been working so hard lately, it had been months since he'd taken out the *Queen*. Tonight, he planned to rectify that.

He tossed the cooler into the passenger seat along with his journal, then started the engine. He backed out of the driveway, and drove off toward the pier.

Chapter 17

Seated in a pedicure chair at Crowned by Curls Monday afternoon, Jazmin eased her head back against the leather upholstery. The droning of hair dryers and a dozen unrelated conversations going on around her were mere background noise to the soundtrack of guilt playing in her head.

I really screwed things up with Savion. She wished her feelings for him were something she could turn off as easily as Izzy, the nail tech, flipped the switch that controlled the massage function of her chair.

"Jazmin?"

She snapped back to reality at the sound of her name being called. "Huh?"

Izzy chuckled. "I said, lift your foot, honey. I can't get at your heel."

"Oh, sorry." She moved her foot.

"Girl, you are super pitiful right now."

Jazmin swiveled her head to her right, to where Sierra sat in the next pedicure chair. "You know, you could have left me at home, instead of dragging me out here. You knew I'd be terrible company."

Sierra pursed her lips. "And that's exactly why I did drag you out. What kind of friend would I be to just leave you there alone, looking all miserable?"

She shrugged. "A bad one, I guess."

"A terrible one. And how in the world do you zone out like that when somebody's touching your feet? I'm way too ticklish for that." She snorted as the nail tech worked a pumice stone over the outer edge of her right foot. "See?"

"Normally I wouldn't have zoned out. But I have so much on my mind."

"I know, Jaz. And trust me, I understand that you're in pain. But there's no reason you have to look as crappy as you feel."

"She's right," Izzy interjected while filing Jazmin's toenails. "My grandmother had a saying. 'Thank the Lord I don't look like what I've been through.'"

Sierra snapped and nodded in Izzy's direction. "Thank you, Izzy. See, Jaz? Izzy gets it." She leaned toward Jazmin's chair. "That's why we're getting pedicures, manicures and fresh hairdos. It's all on me and I'm not taking no for an answer."

Jazmin couldn't help smiling at her friend's generosity, despite her sadness. "Thanks, Sierra. I really appreciate you doing this for me, even if I am bad company."

"I'm here for you, girl."

She sighed, shifting around in the chair to get into

the ideal position to enjoy the vibrating massage function. "Good. Tell me what to do about Savion."

"Well, let's see. From what I overheard when you two were arguing in the hallway..."

Jazmin's eyes widened. "You heard all that?"

Sierra nodded. "I think everybody did. When y'all rushed out, the room got really quiet. You didn't close the door behind you, and the next thing we heard was you two arguing. Now I see why the boom operators are such sticklers for keeping the doors closed when we're filming."

She sank down in the chair, wishing the buttery leather would swallow her up. "Damn. That makes this whole mess even more embarrassing."

"Anyway, he trusted you enough to share his poetry with you, and now that the footage was shown to everybody at the party, he feels betrayed. Does that sound about right?"

"Yes, that's basically it."

"Meanwhile, let's talk about that poem." Sierra took a sip from the bottle of water next to her chair. "It was beautiful. He wrote that about you?"

A familiar warmth filled her cheeks, and she nodded.

"Honey, if he's got that kind of romantic soul, you've got to make things right with him." Sierra tapped her chin with the tip of her index finger. "First of all, tell me how this all happened."

She briefly recounted the night she'd given Savion a tour of the postproduction suite and the main studio floor. "It's true, I didn't tell him I was filming him. I thought he knew. But I never saved the footage, so I didn't think it would be a big deal."

"Help me out here. Remember, I'm an actress, and I don't really know the technical side of things. Why is it important that you didn't save the footage?"

She thought for a moment on how to explain the situation in the simplest fashion. "Everything is digital now, so video files and still images are saved to the camera's memory during filming. In the past, the visuals department manually uploaded files to the studio server to be processed by postproduction. Any file left on the camera after twenty-four hours that hadn't been uploaded by the team would be deleted automatically."

"Okay, so, if I'm following you, you assumed the footage would be deleted, right?" Sierra watched her intently, awaiting an answer.

"Right. So, I was just as shocked as everybody else to see the footage on the screen." She blew out a breath. "I wanted to get to the bottom of how this happened in the first place. So, I called Devon. He's the showrunner and the studio head, so he knows everything that happens around there."

"What did Devon say?"

"He said they just got a software upgrade for the cameras. Now, instead of manual uploads, all footage taken by the cameras is uploaded automatically to the studio's server, in real time. Then it shows up in the postproduction's department server." She wrung her hands. "Basically, the footage was being uploaded as I filmed it, only I didn't know it."

Sierra's eyes widened. "Well, damn."

"You're telling me. What makes it so bad is, Drea

came to my office and told me new footage had been sent over, but I was too distracted to check it. I just told my team to send in the rough cut of the closing sequence, hoping it would either be just right, or the cast and crew would submit ideas on how to improve it." She shook her head. "Instead, I got myself into a huge mess."

Sierra appeared sympathetic. "It was an honest mistake, Jaz. There was no way you could have known about the upgrade."

"I know. But that doesn't make me feel any better about things."

"Are you still taking feedback on the sequence?"

She shrugged. "Sure. What did you think of it?"

"I loved it. It's perfect." Sierra smiled. "And there's no way you could have known this, but everybody else loved it, too."

"Really?" Jazmin wanted to believe her, as it was the only bit of good news she'd gotten in the last couple of days.

"Yes, really. People were raving about it. And I'm not the only one who thinks Savion is a gifted poet." Sierra touched her arm. "Once you get things straight with him, you should really encourage him to publish his work."

She laughed bitterly. "You mean *if* I can get things straight with him."

Sierra waved her off. "Look, let me give you some advice. You need to make things right with him, and you are fully capable of doing so."

"How? He doesn't even want to talk to me after this royal screwup."

"Have you tried calling him?"

She nodded. "And texting him. And emailing him. I've done everything except send up smoke signals."

"What, no telegraph wire?"

Jazmin rolled her eyes. "Been watching *Dr. Quinn, Medicine Woman* again, Sierra?"

She giggled. "All jokes aside, though, I can find out where he is. Remember, he is my brother-in-law."

"Fine. You locate him, and I'll talk to him."

Pulling out her phone, Sierra tapped the screen a few times, then started thumb typing. "I'm gonna hold you to that."

"Who are you texting?"

"Don't worry about it. Just know I'm gonna find out where he is."

She sighed. "All right. Let's say you can find him and he'll see me. What am I supposed to say to him?"

"You owe him an honest apology and an honest conversation. Lay it all out on the table, just like you explained it to me. Let him decide if he can trust you again."

"What if he can't? Or won't?"

She held her hands up. "At least you will have tried. Accept his decision."

Drawing a deep breath, Jazmin nodded. Sierra hadn't told her what she wanted to hear, but she had given her the sage advice she needed.

If she got the opportunity to speak with Savion, she would do her level best to make him understand what had happened.

Around sunset Monday evening, Savion had the *Queen of Zamunda* anchored about thirty miles offshore. Standing by the port bow, he held the handle of his rod, waiting for a bite. He and Troy had been on the water about thirty-six hours now, and his onboard cooler held the eight fish they'd caught in that time.

The *Queen*, a Yellowfin 42 Offshore model boat, was a showpiece as well as a functional fishing vessel. It boasted a powerful quad outboard motor that helped her glide over the water as smoothly as a hot knife through butter. She was forty feet long, aristo blue thanks to her custom paint job and had a fully lined lower berth featuring two six-foot-six-inch bunks, and a shower and bathroom facilities. He'd purchased the boat because it allowed for both short fishing trips and longer overnight excursions in total comfort.

Troy appeared at the top of the steps then, having just returned from the berth. "How's it going up here?"

"Okay. Haven't had any bites in the last little while, so I might just reel it in." He glanced back at his cousin, who flopped down on the upholstered bench behind him. "Did you figure out how to flush the head yet?"

Troy rolled his eyes. "You mean the toilet? Yeah, I got it." He rubbed his palms up and down his bare arms. "Damn, it's cold!"

"I told you to bring a jacket." He chuckled. "Landlubber."

"Whatever, man. I gotta say, though. Your boat is pretty friggin' sweet. I know it had to set you back a pretty penny."

He nodded, his gaze still on the rolling surface of the water. "Yes, she was costly. But totally worth it, as you can see."

"Yeah. Never thought I'd be able to take a shower on a damn boat."

"You should come to visit us here on the East Coast more often, Troy. You'll learn a thing or two."

"Word." Troy shifted on the seat. "You know we're running out of food, right? I just drank the last beer."

Savion shrugged. "We'll be good for another night, I think."

"Nah, man." Troy shook his head. "It's like you said. I'm a 'landlubber.' You've had me out here plenty long enough and I'm not staying out here another night."

"Why not? You got a pressing engagement on shore?"

He frowned. "Savion, stop tripping. If you wanna stay out here another night, you gonna have to run me to the pier so I can drive myself back to Aunt Vi and Uncle Carver's house."

"Really? I thought you said I shouldn't be out here alone?" Savion gave up on catching anything else and started turning his reel to bring his line in. "How are you gonna abandon me like that?"

"Oh, please. We both know the catch you really want is on the island. So, when are we going back?"

"I don't know." Savion stared out over the water, as he'd been doing since they'd left shore, but seeing only Jazmin's face. His heart ached at the thought of her, but he couldn't just toss his feelings for her out with the trash. Still, he didn't want to see her, not yet. It was times like this that he resented how small and close-knit the island's community was. *I don't want to risk running into her, because that will only remind me of her betrayal.*

Troy asked, "Why did we even come out here? Are you hiding from her?"

"No." He was absolutely hiding from her. But he wasn't about to tell Troy that.

"Then why fishing? You could have gone anywhere you wanted. Hell, you could have gotten on a plane, you're grown."

Savion shrugged. "Dad brought us fishing a lot as kids. Cam and Hadley don't really do it very often anymore. But when Cam's upset, he still watches *Bassmasters*. I'm a man of action. So instead of watching other folks fish, I do it."

"Okay, then let's go back, Mr. Action." Troy stood, pacing the deck. "I'm a cowboy, not a sailor. Get me back on dry land or it's gonna be a problem, cousin."

Savion shook his head. "All right, all right. Anything to stop your complaining." Moving to the console, he raised the anchor and turned the boat back toward land.

As he guided his vessel over the sparkling surface of the water, he wondered what awaited him when he returned to shore. He'd taken a personal day off work to allow him some extra time on the water. He'd have four days to prepare for the ribbon-cutting ceremony at the memory park, which was thankfully back on track now. No one had called the satellite phone on the boat since he'd been gone, which meant there hadn't been any serious emergencies. Once they got closer to shore and cell-phone signals got stronger, he'd probably get a whole heap of text messages and email alerts, but he'd deal with those once he was back home.

Troy came to stand behind him, giving him a playful slap on the shoulder. "Buck up, Captain. You'll get your damsel back."

Shaking his head, Savion focused on getting his goofy cousin back to his beloved dry ground.

Chapter 18

Early Tuesday morning, Jazmin pulled her car into a parking space at the health complex and cut the engine. She got out of the car and walked toward the track, looking around to see where her walking partners were.

She spotted Hadley and Sierra sitting on a bench by the track. Heading over, she planned to say good morning. But when she got closer to them, she could tell something was wrong. "Hey, what's going on?"

Sierra, who had her arm draped around Hadley's shoulders, said, "Girl, I don't know. But Hadley's a mess."

Hadley, her face pale and drawn, looked up at Jazmin. "I'm so nauseous. And my head is pounding."

Jazmin cringed, taking a giant step back. "When did this happen?"

Sierra shrugged. "A few minutes ago, when we got

out of the car. She rode with me, and she was fine when we were driving over."

"It's that smell," Hadley whined. "Don't y'all smell it? It's awful!"

Confused, Jazmin sniffed the air. "I don't smell anything."

"I don't, either." Sierra followed suit and took a deep breath. "Except…freshly cut grass."

Jazmin looked down at her shoes, saw the clippings clinging to the pink suede. The grass had recently been cut, but what did that have to do with how Hadley felt? "Allergies, maybe?"

Sierra shrugged. "I don't know. Anyway, I'm taking her to urgent care. Whatever's going on with her, she needs to get checked out."

Jazmin nodded. "I'll follow you over there."

They helped the ailing Hadley into the passenger seat of Sierra's car, then she climbed in and drove off, with Jazmin following close behind. The two cars made it to Stinger Urgent Care in less than fifteen minutes. As they walked to the lobby, Jazmin put in a quick call to the studio and asked to be put through to the suite. "Postproduction department, Randolph speaking."

"Hey, Randolph, it's Jazmin."

"What's going on, boss lady?"

"I'm going to be in late this morning. I'm at the urgent care with a friend. Can you all hold things down until I can get there?"

"Sure thing."

She ended the call with him as she and Sierra took seats in the empty lobby. While Hadley walked over to the reception desk, Jazmin asked, "Did you let Devon know we're here?"

Sierra nodded. "Yes. I also told him we'd take care of her. He was about to leave the studio and drive over here."

"He's a good husband." Knowing Devon was so concerned about his wife made her smile.

"Shouldn't take long for her to get seen. After all, there's nobody else here."

Sure enough, a nurse escorted Hadley through the door to the interior of the clinic a few minutes later.

Sierra turned her attention back to Jazmin. "So, any progress with Savion?"

She shook her head. "No."

"Come on, now." Sierra frowned. "Didn't I get the intel for you on where he was, just like I promised I would?"

"Yes, yes, I know. He took his fishing boat out for a few days."

"And that's why he wasn't answering your calls and texts. There's no real signal out on the open water."

She looked at her hands in her lap, not wanting to look at her friend's perturbed face.

"He's back on land now, Jazmin. So, you really don't have any excuse for not reaching out to him again."

"Sierra, I told you. I don't know what to say to him."

She rolled her eyes. "Girl, are you really sitting here in public, wearing a tank top and telling me you don't know what to say to him? Really?"

Bewildered, she asked, "What does this have to do with my workout clothes?"

"You don't even realize it, do you?"

Still confused, she tilted her head to the right. "Apparently not, Sierra."

"Look, you've been covering up your scar for two whole years. You were never seen in public with the scar visible. Remember when we were out, buying dresses for my in-laws' anniversary party? You passed up at least half a dozen gorgeous dresses because they would have shown that damn scar." She tapped her index finger against the center of Jazmin's forehead. "Hello. Girl, look at you now. Showing it without any shame whatsoever."

Jazmin glanced down at her shoulder. She hadn't really thought about it, but now that Sierra had pointed it out... "You're right. I wasn't even thinking about it when I got dressed this morning."

"It's not just today. The dress you wore to the cast party was a halter. As a matter of fact, you've changed the way you dress ever since..." She stared up at the ceiling as if thinking about it.

"Ever since I got back from that trip I took with Savion."

She snapped her fingers. "Bingo. Now, what does that tell you?"

Thinking back to that night at the inn, she recalled the way he'd kissed along her scar, all while telling her how beautiful and perfect she was. Then he'd made love to her, with the breeze blowing and the moonlight shining on the bed. That night, he'd laid claim to her soul as well as her body.

"I'm not gonna ask for the play-by-play, not while we're in public, anyway. But whatever happened between you two was profound." She touched her shoulder. "He helped you break through your shame. Shame you shouldn't have carried. No woman should carry."

Jazmin opened her mouth to say something but stopped when she saw Hadley being escorted back to the lobby by a nurse. Hadley's eyes were wide, and she looked a bit shaky on her feet as she held a small square of paper in one hand.

She and Sierra got up and walked over to Hadley.

Sierra grabbed her free hand. "Girl, are you okay? You look like they gave you shock therapy or something."

Hadley shook her head.

Jazmin asked, "Did they say what's wrong with you? What's that in your hand?"

Still wide-eyed, Hadley held up the paper. "It's…a prescription for…vitamins."

"Okay, I'll take you to get it filled," Sierra offered. "But if you don't tell us what's wrong I'm gonna burst."

Hadley stammered, "I'm—I'm…pregnant."

Stunned silence fell among the three women for a moment.

Then Sierra squealed, "I'm gonna be an auntie!"

"Wow." Jazmin giggled. "Congratulations, Hadley."

The two women hugged their poor shocked friend, then escorted her out to the car, laughing and talking the whole way.

"What's on your mind, son?"

Savion glanced at his father for a moment, before returning his gaze to the rolling green lawn behind his parents' home. "Nothing, Pop."

Shifting on his lounge chair, Carver gave him a censuring look. "Savion Fitzgerald Monroe. You're my oldest child, so you've been with me and Vi the longest. And I know you know better than to sit on my patio and tell me a lie."

He blew out a breath. "How about this? Tell me what you think about the memory-park project, then I'll tell you what I'm thinking about."

Carver shrugged. "Fair enough. You know, despite your little mistake, things are settling out with the park. Everything is in place for the ribbon-cutting ceremony in a few days."

"That's good to know. And, again, Pop, I'm sorry I was so careless."

Carver waved him off. "It's not a big deal. Actually, this worked out better than I intended."

He looked his father's way. "How?"

"If we stick to the plan from here on out, the park should open on a very special date. August sixteenth."

For the first time this week, Savion felt a genuine smile tugging at his lips. "Gram's birthday."

"Right. I was so focused on getting it open in June before hurricane season kicked off, I didn't even think of holding off until her birthday. Sure, we'll miss some of the summer tourist crowd, but there's always next summer, isn't there?"

"Certainly. The Mary Ellen Monroe Memory Park will be around for a long, long time." He sat back in his own lounger, reclining against the cushioned backrest. "Now, tell me what's bothering you. You still haven't spoken to Jazmin, I'm guessing."

He shook his head. "No. She tried to contact me

over the weekend while I was out on the boat, but she hasn't reached out recently."

"And what's stopping you from reaching out to her?"

"Pop, I don't want to deal with her right now."

Carver frowned. "Why? Because you love her, and you're scared of where that could lead?"

He stared at his father, amazed at his keen perception. "Pop, I can't do this with her right now."

"What is it, exactly, that you can't do?"

"Be with her. Don't you see?" He sat up again, suddenly feeling antsy. "My workload at the office has tripled since Cam and Hadley got married. I'm the last one in the office who can fully focus on keeping MHI in the black. If I pursue this thing with Jazmin, then what happens to the family business? You worked so hard to build it, Pop."

Carver cleared his throat. "We."

"Huh?"

"*We* worked so hard to build MHI. We, as in, your mother and I." He leaned forward. "Stop using work as an excuse to avoid relationships, boy."

"But, Pop, I—"

"No, listen, son. Here's what you need to understand. MHI would not be the successful business it is today without your mother. It's not just about having her by my side, acting as my partner in the business. It's about having her as my partner in *life*."

Savion scratched his chin. "I've never thought about that. But you and Mom are different."

"How? You can't go through life pushing people away in some misguided quest for success." Carver stood, walked over to his son and sat down next to him. "The family company is one of my proudest accomplishments. But do you know the greatest thing I've ever done?"

"What is it?"

"Marry your mother. Without her, none of what I have would be possible. She supported me in business, and her love gave me the drive and motivation to work hard. She made our house a home and protected my heart from a cruel world. And she gave me you, Campbell and Hadley." He touched Savion's shoulder. "You may think MHI is my legacy. My true legacy lies in you and your siblings."

Savion watched his father quietly, not knowing what to say.

"Do you love her, Savion?"

He nodded. "Yes. I do, Pop." Regardless of the fight they'd had, his love for her was his truth. It had settled deep down in his soul and there was no going back.

"The love of a good woman, the right woman, can push you to levels of greatness you never thought possible." He squeezed his shoulder. "I'm not telling you what to do, son, because you're an adult. But you'd better think twice before you throw this opportunity away."

Carver got up then and headed for the back door. "I'm going in. It's getting too hot out here for an old man." He opened the sliding door, but paused. "Are you coming?"

Savion shook his head. "Not just yet."

With a nod, Carver disappeared into the house, sliding the door shut behind him.

Lying back on the lounger, he stared up at the endless blue sky. In less than two hours, it would turn to darkness. But for now, the puffy clouds moved by, passing over the island and momentarily dimming the sunlight.

His father's words replayed in his head. *The love of a good woman, the right woman, can push you to levels of greatness you never thought possible.* Could Jazmin be the one? They were each bringing their own separate issues to this relationship. Could they overcome those things and build a life together? And most of all, could he trust her? He had far more questions than answers.

Still, what they shared deserved at least a fighting chance. He resolved to hear her out if she reached out to him again. The least he could do was try, and they could see where things ended up.

Chapter 19

Don't chicken out.

You can do this.

Drawing a deep breath, Jazmin raised her hand, folded her fingers and knocked on Savion's door. It was Wednesday evening, and she knew he was home since she'd just parked in the driveway behind his SUV.

I've cut off his escape route. Now he'll have to listen to me. She giggled at her own little joke, even as her frayed nerves threatened to make her cry. Mindful of the conversation she'd had with Sierra, she'd chosen her outfit carefully. Cutoff denim shorts, jeweled sandals and a fuchsia tube top. The top, a relic from the recesses of her closet, was the perfect thing to wear tonight.

She knocked again, this time with a little more force. Just in case he hadn't heard the first time.

Legs shaking, palms sweating, she waited.

Finally, she heard his deep voice call out from the other side of the door. "Who is it?"

"Jazmin."

There was a shuffling sound, then a few clicks as he unlocked the door.

When he swung it open, all the air left her body in a whoosh. He was dressed in a pair of light gray sweatpants but was barefoot and shirtless. He had a small white towel draped over his left shoulder. The rippling muscles of his upper body were slick with moisture. A strong, masculine scent emanated from him, a mixture of citrus, pine and something subtly smoky.

Is that sweat? She licked her lips, then swallowed. "Hi."

His expression flat, he responded in kind.

Her mind started to play through several scenarios of what he might have been doing, but she shook off those thoughts as best she could. "Am I...interrupting?"

He shook his head. "Not really. Just finished working out."

She could imagine him, lying on his back on a weight bench, his powerful arms flexing as he lifted and lowered a heavy barbell. "Oh, okay." She shifted her weight nervously from left to right. "Listen, would you mind if I come in? I really think we need to talk."

His expression softened. It wasn't quite a smile, but it was a definite improvement. "Come on in." He moved aside, allowing her entry.

Once she'd stepped onto the gleaming hardwood floor and into his living room, he shut the door behind her.

She glanced around his home, taking in the African-inspired art, deep blue walls and minimalist decor. The last time she'd been here, she'd not been looking at the furnishings. "Your home is lovely."

"Thanks." He gestured to the bright white contemporary sofa. "Have a seat."

She did, never taking her eyes off him.

He toweled himself off, then tossed the cloth back over his shoulder before sitting in the matching armchair across from her. "So, you wanted to talk. I'm listening."

She drew a deep breath, choosing her words carefully. "Savion, I can't begin to tell you how sorry I am about what happened. I swear to you, I never intended for your poetry to be inserted into the show."

He nodded but said nothing.

She continued her explanation by giving him the basics, just as she'd told it to Sierra. "So, at the time I was filming you, I didn't know the footage was being uploaded." She laced her fingers together, placed her hands on her lap. "Regardless of that, I should never have filmed you without your explicit permission. It was a stupid whim, and I'm so sorry for doing that."

He stroked his chin yet remained silent.

"Look at me, Savion. Look at what I'm wearing." She gestured to the tube top. "I've been hiding my scar for so long because it reminded me of what I endured. It made me feel unattractive and ashamed. Then you came along. You saw my biggest flaw and called it beauty. Hell, you even wrote about it. And I realized, I don't have to be ashamed anymore. Because *I* have nothing to be ashamed of."

"You got all that from me?"

She nodded. "Yes, Savion, I did. And not only am I done hiding my scar, I'm ready to do something proactive. No more running from my past. I'm going to start a foundation for battered women, do some speaking engagements." She shrugged. "I have no idea how to go about any of this, but I'm willing to do the work of finding out. Maybe my story can help someone else find their healing."

A ghost of a smile crossed his face. "That's great to hear. I applaud you for getting to that place of positivity, Jazmin. And I can forgive you for your mistakes." His tone was calm, even. "I just need to know you understand how this has affected me."

She placed her hand over her heart. "I don't, but I'm willing to listen. What I do know is that I underestimated the intimacy of the situation. At first, I didn't know you were about to recite a poem. But I should have shut the camera off the minute I knew."

His expression changed then, as if he was impressed by something she'd said. "Intimacy. Now you're starting to see where I'm coming from." He stood, started to pace as he spoke. "The reason I never shared my poetry with anyone is that I consider my writing to be extremely personal. My poems contain so many of my innermost thoughts, dreams..." He paused, locked eyes with her. "Even my fantasies."

She inhaled sharply, feeling the weight of his gaze as if he'd touched her.

He started pacing again. "That's why it hurt me so much to have my writing put on public display. For me, reading my work to you was an act of complete intimacy. I was sharing my mind and soul with you, just like we shared our bodies when we made love."

She felt tears gathering in her eyes. "Savion, your words were so potent, so beautiful. I was moved. And knowing that you wrote about me makes me feel beyond special."

He came to the sofa, sat down next to her. "You've been a muse to me since the first time I saw you, Jazmin. It was a little over a year ago when the studio first opened. I was running on the beach early one morning, down by Richardson Point. Some of the crew had gathered on the beach, I guess to talk about filming. You were all standing by the pier. When I ran past and saw you talking to Devon, I was so distracted by you, I missed a step and nearly busted my ass."

She laughed as the tears streamed down her face. "Did you write about that incident?"

He nodded. "I sure did. If you're good, I might let you read it someday."

Hope glimmered inside her. "Does this mean you forgive me, Savion?"

He used his thumbs to brush away her tears. "Yes, Jazmin. I love you too much to let you go. It's taken me some time, and some lecturing from my father, but I've finally realized how much I need you in my life."

She released a sob, but this one was fueled by joy instead of sadness.

He pulled her against him, holding her tight against his chest.

When the tears subsided enough for her to speak, she whispered, "I love you, too. So, so much."

After spending a few long moments savoring the feeling of having her in his arms again, Savion released Jazmin and sat back a bit.

She looked at him with smiling, damp eyes. "What is it, Savion?"

He scratched his chin, feeling the desire rise within him. "You know, before you showed up, I was on my way to take a shower."

Passion gleaming in her eyes, she took the bait. "Care for some company?"

He brushed his fingertips over her jawline. "Hell yes."

He stood, and moments later, she squealed as he tossed her over his shoulder and carried her down the hallway toward his master suite. Inside his bedroom, he took his time kissing and caressing her out of her clothing. By the time she was naked, she was trembling.

"Are you cold?"

She shook her head. "No. But I'm very, very hot for you, Savion Monroe."

He grinned. "That's just what I wanted to hear, baby." He stripped off his sweatpants and boxers.

Her gaze shifted down, then back up to meet his eyes as her tongue darted out and slid over her lower lip.

Taking her hand, he led her into his bathroom. The shower stall, enclosed in glass on three sides, had been custom-built after he purchased the house. It was large enough for several people; even though he showered alone, his height meant he needed space. There were three showerheads—one on the left, one on the right and a huge rainfall one mounted above the shower stall.

After opening the door, he stepped inside and started the flow of water from the two lower heads. He beckoned her with his curled finger, holding the door open. "Come here and test the water."

She stepped inside the stall with him and he let the door close. Running her hand under the water, she nodded. "It's perfect."

He turned on the rainfall head, stepped beneath the rush of water and pulled her close to him. With the steam swirling around them, he kissed her. She slipped her arms around his neck while he wove his fingers into her soaked curls. Water cascaded down his face and body, and as the kiss deepened, his desire for her only grew.

Stepping aside from the flow, he watched her. She stood before him trembling, still partially beneath the center showerhead. For the moment, he simply enjoyed the sight of the water cascading down her body, flowing over all the parts of her he wanted to please.

He leaned down, working the tip of his tongue over her nipples. She twisted and purred as he held on to her waist, keeping her near, so he could savor the dark points. Moving lower, he placed soft kisses on the plane of her belly, continuing his journey down her body until he kneeled on the tiled floor.

He moved his hand over her bottom, then beneath her thigh. Using his other hand to steady her, he lifted her leg and placed it over his shoulder. A growl left his lips as he leaned into her and buried his face between her thighs.

Her legs buckled, but he kept her stable as he worked his tongue over her most sensitive flesh. She was sweet and fragrant with desire, and as he moved his fingertips to her opening, he could feel the warm, slippery evidence of her need. Her hips undulated in tiny circular motions that expressed her ecstasy, and her soft cries rose above the sound of the water, reverberating off the walls of the shower. He kissed her there, over and over, before swirling his tongue around her hard little clit.

She came then, her hips thrusting forward as her back arched, and he held on to her wet, slick hips to make sure she wouldn't slip to the floor as she rode out her climax.

He stood again, and she fell into his arms, leaning up for his kiss. As their lips touched, their hands toured each other's bodies. While he caressed her skin, the water aiding his exploration, he knew he could never get enough of her, not even if they made love for an eternity.

She drew back from him, looking up to him with passion-hooded eyes. "Now, Savion. Please."

He knew what she was begging for and he wouldn't deny her any longer. He lifted her up, and she wrapped her legs around his waist as he pressed her back against the shower wall. Adjusting his hips between her open thighs, he probed her with his hardness, eliciting a sharp inhale. Tilting his hips back, then forward, he pushed the tip of his dick inside her.

Her tightness made him growl, and after lingering a few seconds, he eased himself deeper, deeper still until he was fully engulfed in her feminine warmth. A long, low moan escaped her lips as he filled her. And when he began to stroke her, his hands squeezing her ass as he moved inside her, she evaporated into a series of high-pitched cries.

Steam enveloped the entire stall as he made love to her. His body begged for release and he kept a tenuous hold on his crisis, wanting to see her climb the heights of passion first.

"Mine," he groaned, thrusting deeper.

"Yes" was her strangled reply.

He kept going, picking up the pace, hoping to brand his name across her very soul. Her cries rose an octave as he moved her away from the wall. Still gripping her hips, he pounded into her, raising and lowering her to meet his thrusts.

She screamed, the sound splitting the silence, and he felt her body pulsing around him moments before his orgasm tore through him. His legs buckled, and he barely managed to snatch one hand from beneath her in time to slap his palm against the wall for balance.

She clung to him in the ensuing silence, her slick body pressed against his. He savored the moment, feeling his heart swell with a love so strong, he could barely breathe.

Chapter 20

As Thursday dawned, Jazmin opened her sleepy eyes in the dim light. Blinking a few times, she came to full awareness of the heavy, muscular arm draped over her naked hips. The realization of what had happened made her smile. She was in Savion's bed, and best of all, in his heart.

She didn't dare roll over, because she didn't want to wake him. His soft snores ruffled the silence, and she snuggled down in the sheets, content to enjoy the feeling of his embrace.

The practical side of her intruded on her contentment as she wondered what time it was. Filming of the rest of season two was happening at the studio, which left little work for her in postproduction. Still, there was the matter of correcting the closing sequence, and of doing research into starting her nonprofit foundation.

She yawned, smothering it with her hand. *Maybe I'll just go in late today.*

He stirred then, groaning as he came awake. "Good morning."

"Good morning." She leaned in for his kiss. "How'd you sleep?"

"Pretty good, considering how little sleep I actually got." He reached around her, slapped her ass playfully.

"We've gotta get up, you know. Got to work, be adults and all that."

"Oh, I have some very adult things I want to do to you, right here in this bed." A wicked gleam sparkled in his dark eyes.

She teased, "Didn't you get enough last night?" He'd made love to her four times before they'd finally fallen asleep.

He shook his head. "Never. I can never get enough of you, baby." He shifted, moving his body against her until she could feel the hard evidence of his sentiment pressing into her stomach.

She licked her lips, unable to resist the lure of him. She rolled over onto her back, then slipped her hands beneath the sheets to draw him on top of her.

Later, after yet another satisfying session of love-making, she rolled away from him and grabbed her phone from his nightstand. "Okay. We really have to get up now. It's after eight."

He sighed. "I guess you're right. I would take a day off, but with the ribbon cutting being tomorrow, I'll be needed around the office."

She sat up, then swung her legs over the side of the bed and stood up. "I never know what's going to happen in the production suite. So, I should probably go in, too."

"Since we're both late, at least let me make you a little something to eat."

"Sounds nice."

They both took quick, separate showers, then dressed and met in the kitchen. Savion, in his uniform of dark blue button-down and black slacks, made a pot of coffee while he scrambled a few eggs. Adding toast and a handful of strawberries, he set the two plates down on the table. "Voilà."

"Thank you. It looks great."

"What time are you going in?"

"Ten. That's about as early as I can manage, considering…" She gave him a look.

"I know. I told Cam I'd be in by ten thirty."

She forked up some of the eggs. "About your poetry, Savion."

"What about it?" He watched her over his steaming mug of coffee.

"Have you ever thought about getting it published?"

He looked thoughtful for a moment, then shook his head. "I never thought about that. To me, my writing is more of a hobby."

"I heard that people at the party were really impressed with your poem."

His brow hitched. "Who told you that?"

"Sierra. She said everyone was talking about it, and one person even cried."

He scratched his chin. "You know, Troy went out on the boat with me, and he said essentially the same thing."

"See? Your words have the power to move people, Savion. Why wouldn't you want to share that gift with the world?"

He was quiet for a little while. "I'll think about it."

"That's all I ask." She finished her food. "Well, that, and for you to help me out with this nonprofit I want to start."

He set down his mug. "What would you want me to do?"

"I'm not sure yet. I'd definitely want you to travel with me when I go places to speak, though."

He nodded. "Whatever you need, baby. We'll make it work."

She smiled, coming around to his side of the table. Easing into his lap, she put her arms around his neck. "So, we're really going to do this thing, huh?"

He squeezed her close. "We sure as hell are. And we're gonna rock it 'til the wheels fall off, as they say."

"I love you, Savion."

He brushed his lips against hers. "I love you more."

At the ribbon-cutting the next day, Savion couldn't wait until the ceremony was over. He'd seen Jazmin arrive right before the event began, dressed in a bare-shouldered yellow sundress that showed off her sweet curves and bronze shoulders. He nodded to her, a smile pulling up his face.

"I see you took my advice," his father said from the chair next to him on the dais set up before a ribboned entrance to the work site and a small tent for refreshments. "Everything all right now?"

"Right as rain," Savion said, then stood and went to the podium for opening remarks.

The short but moving ceremony went off without a hitch, and after the speeches, the ribbon cutting itself and the handshakes with dignitaries, Savion rushed to find Jazmin. She was sipping a glass of punch when he approached, and she put it down on the table to greet him.

But he did more than say hello. He swept her into an intense hug, planting a kiss on her lips that she eagerly returned.

"Nice to see you, too," she teased.

"No more hiding in the shadows. I want everyone to know we're together."

"So do I," she said, and he noticed her winking at Sierra, who stood nearby. "In fact, I've told my parents I want to FaceTime with them in an hour, to share some great news." She looked him in the eye. "You available?"

He grinned, the warmth of his love cascading through his body.

"For you, baby, I'm available...forever."

Midsummer

The cool breeze flowing over the Appalachian Mountains touched Savion's face, and he inhaled deeply. Up here, the air was so fresh and invigorating, he wondered how he even functioned closer to sea level.

He stood on the balcony of his cabin high above the rest of the world, draped in a thick cotton robe. Looking out over the tops of the towering green pines, he felt a sense of peace wash over him.

Jazmin appeared behind him then, slipping her arms around his waist and leaning her head against his back. "I can't believe we just ran off and eloped. Your parents are going to freak out, big-time."

He shrugged. "They were so wrapped up in planning Hadley's baby shower and getting ready for a grandchild, it was easy to slip away." He chuckled. "Hell, they might not even have noticed we're gone yet. It's only been a day and a half."

"Still. I would never have expected I'd do something like this."

He turned around to face her. She wore a robe just like his, and he knew she had nothing on beneath it. Drawing her into his arms, he teased a fingertip over her full lips. "That's why I'm in your life. Adventure."

She laughed. "If you say so."

"You say my parents are going to be mad. What about yours?"

"Are you kidding me? You met my parents. They're so desperate for a grandchild, this won't even register for them. When I call them up and tell them we got married, they'll just start asking when the baby is coming."

He leaned down, placing a kiss against the fragrant hollow of her neck. "In that case, we'd better get busy making that baby. Can't keep them waiting."

She sighed, melting against him. "Savion."

He kneeled and placed a soft kiss against her knee.

Her lips formed an O shape, but only a tiny squeaking sound came out.

"Hmm?" He continued to nibble on her knee as he worked the belt of her robe free and slipped it down her shoulders.

She caught it. "What are you doing? We can't do… that…out here!"

He chuckled. "Baby, there aren't any other cabins for miles. There's no one out here to see you naked… or hear you scream."

She released her grip on the robe, letting it pool on the balcony's wooden floor. Admiring her gorgeous nudity in the sunlight, he ran his palms over her hardened nipples and savored the moan she gave in response.

"I know we're on the mountaintop," he said softly. "But let's see if we can't get you a little bit higher, baby."

And soon, her cries of pleasure were echoing in the silence of the forest.

* * * * *

Ray could feel Delanie's angry gaze burning into his back as he walked away, leaving her seething over his words. Now she knew how it felt to be dismissed. It had probably been a first for her.

To be honest, he was surprised she hadn't pounced on him. By the expression on her lovely face, she'd definitely wanted to draw blood. So *fiery*, Ray thought, laughing to himself.

Apparently, it had dawned on Delanie that she needed him far more than he needed her. Actually, that statement wasn't 100 percent accurate. For a brief moment, he'd needed to kiss her. Especially when she'd glided the tip of her tongue over that suckable bottom lip of hers.

Yep, in that moment, he'd definitely needed her far more. And something told him she'd needed—or wanted—a little bit of him, too.

Joy Avery works as a customer service assistant. By night, the North Carolina native travels to imaginary worlds, creating characters whose romantic journeys invariably end happily-ever-after.

Since she was a young girl growing up in Garner, Joy knew she wanted to write. Stumbling onto romance novels, she discovered her passion for love stories; instantly, she knew these were the type of stories she wanted to pen.

Joy is married with one child. When not writing, she enjoys reading, cake decorating, pretending to expertly play the piano, driving her husband insane and playing with her two dogs.

Books by Joy Avery

Harlequin Kimani Romance

In the Market for Love
Soaring on Love
Campaign for His Heart
The Sweet Taste of Seduction

Visit the Author Page
at Harlequin.com for more titles.

THE SWEET TASTE OF SEDUCTION

Joy Avery

Dedicated to the dream.

Acknowledgments

To everyone who has supported me on this glorious journey, I acknowledge you with love!

Dear Reader,

As always, thank you for taking this ride of love with me. Whether this is your first #joyaveryromance experience or your tenth, I appreciate you and your support. I hope you enjoy Delanie and Ray's romantic journey.

Ray is by far one of my most beloved characters. The way he adores the women in his life is captivating. You will fall in love with him and that Stetson hat. I can't wait for you to meet both Delanie and Ray and venture with them as they both travel a path of rediscovery, finding each other along the way.

I love hearing from readers. Visit me on the web at www.joyavery.com. And be sure to connect with me via the social media links.

Until next time, happy reading!

Love, light and laughter,

Joy

www.Facebook.com/AuthorJoyAvery
www.Twitter.com/AuthorJoyAvery

Stay in the know: http://eepurl.com/KkLkL

Chapter 1

Every time Delanie Atwater thought about the fact she'd inherited a vineyard—a freaking vineyard— her stomach knotted, churned, did cartwheels while her nerves kicked into overdrive. There were so many things she could have done with her divorce settlement. Purchased a home in Belize, an oceanfront cottage in Turks and Caicos—a bed-and-breakfast in New England, even. Yet, here she was in small-town North Carolina with ambitions of turning a dormant vineyard into a thriving business.

Southern Charms Winery. No, that wasn't it. She'd struggled with the perfect name since she'd learned her uncle had left her and her brother this property. Bryan, her non-adventurous younger brother, wanted nothing to do with the place and had allowed her to buy him out. Now that she thought about it, maybe she should have sold, too. But no, she wouldn't sell. Something about this new venture, this new chapter in her life felt...right. This was a challenge and a fresh start rolled up into one big adventure-sized burrito, and she was ready to take a bite.

You can do this, Delanie. You can do anything you put your mind to.

Reciting the words her mother had spoken to her often as a child still mostly calmed her at thirty-four. But a hidden degree of anxiousness lingered. And being stuck in this traffic jam for the past twenty minutes wasn't helping.

Delanie craned her neck in an attempt to see around the beat-up, rusty pickup in front of her. "What in the heck is the holdup?" There shouldn't be a traffic jam in a one-horse town. *Her* one-horse town. *Her* new home. "Welcome to Vine Ridge," she mumbled, then fell back against the plush leather seat of her S-Class Mercedes.

Maybe she should at least see how much she could get for the place? *No.* Her uncle had clearly wanted the property to stay in the family. What other reason would he have for willing it to family members he hadn't seen in decades? Even though she barely knew her uncle, he was family, and family meant everything to her. She would honor his unstated wishes. The declaration revamped an emergence of nerves. Closing her eyes, she rested a hand on her forehead. "A freaking vineyard? I own a freaking vineyard."

But hadn't this been a dream of hers since she was a young girl? Ever since watching the Keanu Reeves movie *A Walk in the Clouds*, she reminded herself with a smile. Too bad the only thing she knew about wine was how to drink it. Yep, she was nuts. But was being nuts all that bad? She'd needed a change. And going from sane to nuts might just be the transformation she needed.

Giving this a long hard thought, she still had to question herself. *What are you thinking, Delanie Claire Atwater?*

Ha! The answer to that was easy. Getting as far away from California—and her no-good ex-husband—as she could. Delanie opened her eyes and swept them from left to right, feeling as if she'd been dropped into an episode of *The Andy Griffith Show*. Instead of Mayberry, it was Vine Ridge. Yep, she'd gotten pretty damn far, all right.

Why couldn't she have inherited stock, or something else that wouldn't require soil tests, irrigation systems, marketing plans, applying for licenses, forming an entity… The list of to-do's went on and on. How would she do it all when she couldn't even do something as simple as coming up with a name for the place? It all made her head spin.

The one thing that helped her to keep focus was the fact that she knew her mother would want her to do this. *Legacy.* Her mother's sweet voice played in her head as if the woman were speaking from the space right beside her. For kicks, Delanie glanced over at the empty peanut butter–colored leather seat. "I know you're guiding me, Momma. And I'm going to do my best to make you proud."

Doubt crept in again, when her ex's wounding words replaced her mother's. *The only thing you'll ever be good at is being my wife.* "You're wrong, Cordell," she mumbled. "I'm so much more."

She lifted the plastic water bottle from the cup holder and shook it as if doing so would cause it to miraculously refill itself. *Great.* Not only did she have to sit here for only God knew how much longer, she would dehydrate while doing so.

Could this day actually get any worse?

Frustrated, she slammed a hand into the horn. "Go, already." She doubted her efforts would yield any results, but it sure had felt good. So good, in fact, she did it again, and again, and again, punctuating each firm press with an affirmation.

"I don't need you, Cordell Atwater!"

Honk.

"I don't need any man!"

Honk.

"I can do anything I—"

She stopped abruptly when the driver's side door of the pickup in front of her opened. A denim-clad leg was the first thing she saw. A beat later, she caught sight of the rest of the body it belonged to. *Oh.* Tall. Easily over six feet. And toned. Like a visit to the gym was part of his daily routine. And chocolate. Exquisite, high-quality milk chocolate, not the bargain bin stuff.

Delanie's lips parted slightly, a heated breath escaping. She was thankful for the sunglasses she wore, because her eyes were able to roam freely over every inch of his solid frame undetected. From the dark gray T-shirt that highlighted his muscular cut, to the jeans that clung to his lower half divinely. And he wore the hell out of a black Stetson hat.

She'd learned about this particular headwear after an interesting evening with an intriguing Texan months back. Was this divine creature nearing her car a cowboy, too? The hat he wore cost well over a thousand dollars. Based on the condition of the vehicle he drove, he didn't strike her as someone who would invest that type of money into a headpiece.

You are one good-looking man. Too bad she hated men at the moment. She just wished her brain would send her tingling body the memo. Angered by the fact she found the man drifting toward her so damn attractive, she scowled, then reminded herself that he was the enemy. An incredibly sexy, tempting and alluring enemy, but an enemy nonetheless.

An old saying popped into her head. *Keep your friends close and your enemies even closer.* That just might have worked if Delanie wasn't sure prolonged nearness to him would be dangerous to her mental health.

Enough is enough, Ray Cavanaugh thought when his mother flinched beside him in the passenger's seat for the second time. Apparently, the blaring horn was rattling her nerves, but she was too much of a peacemaker to complain. He, on the other hand...

Ray snatched at the door handle and flung the truck door open. "I'll be right back, Mom." He was out of the vehicle before she could make an attempt to talk him out of it. Usually, he avoided confrontations, especially with a woman wearing a scowl the size of—he glanced down at her front plate—California. But exceptions could be made to almost any rule.

Under different circumstances, he could have found the brown-skinned woman sitting behind the wheel of the fancy car drop-dead gorgeous, even without being able to see her eyes. But under these conditions, he merely found her a nuisance.

Tapping a knuckle against the lightly tinted car window, he performed a cranking motion with his hand. After a beat of hesitation, the window smoothly lowered. He bent at the waist and rested his hands on his thighs. With a heavy sigh, she turned toward him and removed the expensive-looking sunglasses she wore, revealing the most radiant set of hazel eyes he'd ever stared into.

Damn. Up close, she was even more beautiful than he'd first thought. *Stay focused*, he warned himself.

A fruity fragrance wafted from inside the vehicle. *Apple. No, pear.* Didn't matter. He wasn't there to identify the delicious scent or appreciate her appearance. He was there to hopefully talk the impatient woman into giving the horn-play a break. His head was already pounding, and her constant honking was only making it worse. Plus, it was too dang hot for animosity.

"Good afternoon," he said, in the kindest voice he could muster.

"May I help you?" she said.

Ignoring the less than cordial greeting received, he continued, "I know the wait is frustrating, but the horn blowing—"

"I have someplace to be."

We all have someplace to be, but we're not honking our horns like an insane person. Keeping his thoughts to himself, he maintained a sensible tone and said,

"Hopefully, it won't be much longer. But if you don't mind—"

"I've been sitting in the same spot for the past—" she tilted her wrist and eyed the diamond-encrusted timepiece she wore "—half hour."

Ray's jaw tightened, then released. *Unbelievable.* She wasn't the only one who had been waiting. There was a line of cars filled with individuals stuck in the same jam as she was. None of that seemed to matter to her. "We *all* have been held up for the same half hour." *Yet, you're the only one blowing your horn.* Again, to stave off any further animosity, he kept that part to himself. However, he'd lost a few degrees of his cool. "The horn is not going to speed things up, ma'am. If anything, it'll probably slow them down even more." Punishment for her impatience.

He hadn't meant for the words to come out so terse, but the throbbing in his temple was altering his attitude. Her expression hardened, then relaxed slightly. Apparently his words, presence, or both, bothered her. Her plum-painted lips parted slightly. But whatever more-than-likely malicious insult she'd intended to spew was thwarted by her ringing cell phone.

Saved by the bell.

Rolling her eyes away from him, she rudely let the window up in his face. Frozen in place by shock, he simply stared at her through the glass barrier. *Unbelievable.* There was no need for anyone to be this rude. He'd gotten some of the worst news of his life today, but had he approached her in a discourteous manner? No.

A male voice boomed through the cabin of the

vehicle, snagging Ray's attention away from his ill-mannered nemesis.

"Where in the hell are you?" the clearly irritated man asked.

"As of a few months ago, my whereabouts are no longer any of your business," she snapped back in an equally heated tone. "Your bad decision, remember?"

"I'll be damned. As long as I'm giving you my hard-earned money, I'm entitled to know any damn thing about you I want to know."

Like a nosy neighbor, Ray continued to listen as the two went back and forth at one another, each round more vicious than the last. Judging by what he'd heard thus far, the man on the opposite end of the line was her ex-husband and was actively paying her alimony or some other form of monetary compensation he clearly didn't want to shell out. A large sum by the sounds of it. Or at least enough for him to believe he still had a say-so over her life.

Their unpleasant exchange piqued Ray's curiosity. What was their story? Which one had dissolved the marriage and why? Had she been unfaithful? Had he? Thinking about her *your bad decision* comment, Ray would bet money it had been him who'd strayed. Why was she here in Vine Ridge? Was she running from this man? Had he been abusive? The thought tightened something in Ray's chest. He despised cowards who hit women.

When Ms. California slid a razor-sharp glance in Ray's direction, as if she'd just realized he was still there, he flinched. The sour expression on her face translated into *why in hell are you still standing there?*

But while a blazing inferno danced in her leveling gaze, he also saw a hint of sadness. Perhaps she wasn't as hard as she was pretending to be.

Taking his cue, he scurried back to his vehicle, feeling all types of defeated. Hell, beaten and battered pretty much defined the last year of his life. Sliding back behind the wheel of the '55 Chevrolet pickup, he eyed the firecracker through his rearview mirror and inwardly growled.

Most of the residents in Vine Ridge were struggling to make ends meet, and here she was roaring into town in a car that cost as much as most of the homes here, blaring her damn horn like the world was supposed to conform to her needs. *California.* That entitled attitude made sense.

"You look stressed, son. Everything okay?"

Ray dragged his gaze from the mirror and fixed it on his mother. Looking into her dancing gray eyes, his heart thawed completely. "Everything is fine, gorgeous. We'll be home shortly. Are you comfortable?"

After his mother had been diagnosed with chronic kidney disease a year ago, he'd moved back to Vine Ridge to see to her care. While he'd never regretted the move for one second, he'd lost the life he'd built in Oregon. But June Cavanaugh was worth all of the sacrifices he'd made, because she'd always sacrificed for him.

She patted his cheek. "You're a good man, Tank," his mother said, using the nickname his father had given him as a child because of his ferocious appetite. She continued, "You're an even better son, but you fuss over me too much."

"Of course I do. You're the most important girl in my life."

She chuckled, a delicate sound. "That's sad, son. You should have a charming young lady in your life. Someone to love."

"I do have someone to love."

"Besides your dying mother."

His mother's words jarred him. "Don't say that, Mom."

"You heard the doctor. My kidneys are getting worse. Even if by some miracle we did find a perfect donor, the transplant is risky. I'm not sure I even have the energy to go through that."

His mother was the strongest woman he knew, had ever known, so why did it sound like she was giving up? Ray turned away from her. "Doctors don't know everything."

"Look at me." When he did, she continued, "All of us are dying, son. With each breath we take, we get closer to our maker. Some of us are slated to meet the good Lord sooner than others. I'm dying. There are no two ways around it. But I'm okay with that because I'm right with the Lord. I've lived a good life. A great life. A huge reason for that is you."

Ray captured his mother's hand and lifted it to his lips. "I love you."

"I love you, too, my boy. And I need you to be okay with all of this."

Ray's brows furrowed slightly. Was she serious? "I'll never be okay with the idea of losing you. Please don't ask me to be. Please."

Before his mother could respond, California *Steaming* laid on that damn horn again.

June's frail body shifted in her seat. "She sure is an impatient one, isn't she?"

Impatient? His mother was being too kind. The woman wasn't just anxious, she was high-maintenance as hell. And he intended to tell her just that. "I'll be right back."

When he reached for the door handle, his mother rested a thin hand on his arm. "No, son. It'll be fine and so will she."

So will she? They were the ones suffering, not her. Ray sighed, then relaxed against the battered seat. His eyes inadvertently shifted to the rearview mirror again. To think, he'd actually felt sorry for her as he listened to the way her ex had spoken to her. Now, he felt a different kind of pity. Pity for anyone who had to deal with her on an ongoing basis.

The traffic began to move roughly ten minutes later. *Finally*, he thought, pulling forward and tossing a glance over at his mother. Weariness danced on her usually jovial face. He'd give anything to make her okay, even his own life.

"Watch out, son!"

Ray darted his eyes back to the road ahead just in time to see the stopped minivan in front of him. He was forced to slam on the brakes, and they both jolted forward. The sound of screeching tires behind them sent his gaze to the rearview mirror.

A large cloud of white smoke rose from Ms. California's brakes clawing the asphalt, and she was so close to the back of his pickup that he couldn't see the emblem attached to the hood. A beat later, the driver's side door swung open and she bolted out.

Great. He was not in the mood to go another round with this woman. Diverting his attention briefly to his mother, he said, "Are you okay, Mom?"

"Yes. I'm fine."

"I'll be right back," he said, exiting the vehicle a second time.

Ray hadn't been prepared for the full-body view of Ms. California. Tall—five-eight, maybe five-nine, lean with killer curves, and legs that flowed to heaven. Ray chastised himself for his admiring the bristly woman.

Her verbal lashing was immediate. "Where did you get your license, an expired cereal box?"

Ray ignored the insult and strolled past her and out of earshot of his mother—just in case he had to say one or two ungentlemanly things that she wouldn't approve of. Several cars inconvenienced for a second time went around them. He apologized with the toss of a hand.

Ms. California stalked up behind him. "You nearly killed me," she said through what sounded like clenched teeth.

Ray turned, releasing a humorous laugh. "Killed you? We were barely going twenty miles per hour. The worst thing that would have happened is you breaking one of those manicured fingernails. And how does *your* nearly rear-ending *me* put me at fault?"

"Because *you* slammed on the brakes, which meant you weren't paying attention to the vehicle in front of you."

Ray folded his arms across his chest, noticing the slight twitch in Ms. California when her eyes briefly moved to his bicep. The idea of her checking him out would have been flattering had the conditions been less…volatile. "Sooo, I guess that means you weren't paying attention to the vehicle in front of you, either," he said.

The retort definitely didn't sit well with her. Those beautiful hazel eyes turned several shades darker right before narrowing to slits. It wouldn't have surprised him if streams of smoke started bellowing from her ears.

"You better be glad I'm an excellent driver and was able to implement evasive maneuvering," she said.

Evasive maneuvering? Who did she think she was, Tia Norfleet?

Playing devil's advocate, Ray quirked a brow. "Out of curiosity, let's say you had rear-ended me. Other than contacting your insurance company and whining about totaling your overpriced heap of plastic—because you weren't paying attention and were following too closely—what would have happened?"

If she could have shot fire from her eyes, he would have been incinerated right there in the middle of Main Street. A look of bewilderment flashed across her face. Deciding he was too damn exhausted to continue with this ridiculousness, he bowed out. "Enjoy the rest of your day, ma'am." He turned and strolled away.

"So, you're not going to apologize? Why am I not surprised? I can tell you're a Neanderthal by that rusty jalopy you drive."

Ray could handle an assault on himself, but the assault on his truck touched a tender spot. Whipping around, he said, "Look, lady—" He stopped abruptly when Ms. California flinched. He hadn't meant for his tone to be so harsh. Calming, he started again, "Look… I'm—"

Before he could finish his thought, she was walking away.

Despite the fact she'd stepped on his last nerve, his eyes lowered to her ass—perfect in every sense of the word. Something tightened in the pit of his stomach. Lust. Desire. Anger. If it was the latter, it hadn't interfered with his appreciating an attractive woman, and Ms. California fully embodied the term. Too bad her attitude wasn't as appealing as her curvy frame.

She tossed a half glance over her shoulder. Had she been checking to see if he was watching her walk away? No doubt in his mind she was used to men ogling her. It was hard to imagine any man voluntarily losing her. Then again, no it wasn't.

Rolling her eyes, she slid behind the wheel, cranked the engine and sped around him, flicking him the bird.

Nope, it wasn't hard to imagine at all. Again, he pitied the poor sap who had to deal with her on an ongoing basis, thrilled that it wasn't him.

Chapter 2

Between the jerk she'd encountered on Main Street and the conversation with her ex, Delanie was exhausted by the time she finally pulled into the rutted driveway located at 742 Grapevine Lane. *Home sweet home.* Just her luck, the movers hadn't arrived.

Killing the engine, she shook her head. *Loose chickens.* All that time wasted over loose chickens. She actually lived in a place where people hauled livestock in their personal vehicles. Her brother would get such a kick out of this. On second thought, she had better keep this to herself. Especially since she intended to ask—no, beg—Bryan to move here from Atlanta to head the marketing department as soon as things were up and running. And with the recent break off of his engagement, he might be interested in a fresh start, too.

As she stared through the windshield, her heart

raced. Wow. She'd really inherited a freaking vine-yard. Too late for second-guessing her decision to move here now. This was a done deal. Her eyes swept over the white, two-story farmhouse with black shutters, and she blew a heavy sigh. "Can I really do this?"

Why was she doubting herself? Why was she allow-ing Cordell's baseless words to get to her? She could do this on her own. And she would, because she was resilient. Something he would have known had he paid more attention to her and less to his mistress.

Mistress.

Although she and Cordell hadn't been together in over a year, the idea of him cheating on her still hurt like hell. All she'd ever done was love and support him. In return, he'd betrayed her by sleeping with one of the up-and-comers at his talent agency. He hadn't even had the decency to use protection and had got-ten her pregnant.

She hated women who unapologetically slept with married men, hated cheating husbands even more. She thought about her Main Street encounter. Heck, she hated men in general. They were proving far more trou-ble than they were worth.

Scattering her thoughts, her attention moved back to the farmhouse she'd learned she'd be inheriting only six short months ago. Amazingly, the structure was still in pretty decent shape to have sat vacant for the past year. She'd fallen in love with it when she'd viewed pic-tures of it online. She'd fallen in even deeper love with it when her Realtor, Shayna Cavanaugh, had taken an array of digital shots and emailed them to her. None of the photos had done it justice, because sitting here, she'd fallen head over heels.

Her gaze drifted to the acres and acres of bare land. Obviously, the place hadn't been functional for some time. Too bad she wasn't as in love with this. "Picture the possibilities, Delanie. Always picture the possibilities." Something else her mother used to say.

Daydreaming, she envisioned rows and rows of vibrant green vines nearly collapsing under the weight of an abundance of plump and delicious grapes. Yeah, she had this. But she would need help. And lots of it. Maybe Shayna could steer her in the right direction. The woman seemed all-knowing about charming Vine Ridge.

After exiting her vehicle, she ambled across the unpaved, root-battered walkway, nearly losing her balance when she stepped into a dip in the earth. "Gracious." She made a mental note to get quotes on having it, along with the bumpy driveway, paved.

The sight of the oversize front porch already furnished with eight once-white rocking chairs brought a smile back to her face. Not bothered by the likelihood of dirtying her clothing, she eased down into one of the dusty chairs. The aged wood squeaked under the weight. They needed a little TLC, but were still in perfect rocking order.

Closing her eyes, she rocked back and forth, enjoying the warm July breeze that whipped across her face. This moment took her back to her childhood in Greenville, South Carolina. In her head, she could see her mother rocking, hear her humming and crocheting on the front porch of their quaint home, while her father mowed grass. They had so little back then, but she couldn't remember a time she'd been richer.

"There are no worries in the world when you're rocking on the front porch," her mother used to say. Her mother used to say a lot. Now, she wished she'd listened more.

Delanie opened her eyes and focused on the dipping sun. The oranges and reds flowed seamlessly together like an exquisite oil painting. This was her mother's favorite time of day. "I miss you, Mommy. So much. I could really use your wisdom right now."

When her cell phone rang, she blinked away her impending tears and eyed the screen. "Shayna." Just the person she needed to talk to. "Hello."

"Hey, chick. How are you enjoying Vine Ridge so far?"

For the briefest of moments, her thoughts flowed to the man in the rusty pickup truck, then just as quickly shifted away. "There's still a lot to be desired."

"It'll grow on you. I heard you had an interesting introduction to some of the townsfolk. Something about a horn."

That explained how Shayna knew she'd arrived. Delanie planted her face in her hand, her cheeks burning with embarrassment. "News certainly does travel fast around these parts, huh?"

"Oh, honey, you have no idea."

Great.

"So, I was thinking. You're probably going to need *a lot* of help getting that place up and running again. Lucky for you, you know me. And I know just the man for the job," Shayna said.

"You must have read my mind. I was going to ask you for some recommendations. Is he dependable?"

"Yes. Extremely dependable, the best in the vine management business and not too bad to look at, either." Shayna laughed. "Can be a bit stubborn, though. But it's endearing. Trust me, this will be a match made in heaven."

Oh, she'd already experienced *not too bad to look at* earlier. Her thoughts drifted to Mr. Main Street again. The way his veins bulged along his forearms when he'd propped his arms on his thighs. The way he seemed to glide across the air when he'd walked. The way he wore that Stetson hat.

In hindsight, maybe she'd been overly hostile toward him. With so much on her plate—the move, the vineyard, a jerk of an ex—she wasn't herself. Well, there wasn't anything she could do about it now. Maybe one day she'd get the opportunity to apologize.

Coming to her senses, she scolded herself for even noticing anything about him. And she definitely didn't care how *not too bad to look at* Mr. Best in the Vine Management Business was. Men were the enemy, and at this point in her life, tempted her less than a jar of pickled pig feet. Refocusing on the conversation, she said, "Does he have experience with a vineyard this size?"

"Plenty. Before moving back to Vine Ridge to take care of his mother, he operated his own business in Oregon installing grapevines. Plus, he co-owned a winery. Now that sounds like a perfect fit to me."

Delanie experienced a surge of excitement. This was good news. Great news. *Excellent* news, because she hadn't expected things to go so smoothly. This had to be a sign, right? "Shayna, I can't thank you enough. I sensed you were the woman to know."

"Totally, doll. I'm the go-to around here. And no thanks necessary. Just a bottle from your first batch and we'll call it even."

"Several bottles," Delanie countered. A small price to pay for such a big help.

Shayna laughed. "Deal. How about I send Ray over tomorrow?"

Ray. That sounded like the name of a man who knew exactly what he was doing. "That would be great."

"Noonish?"

"Perfect." That meant she could sleep in. When she'd decided to drive from California, she'd underestimated the toll it would take on her. Even though she'd stretched the almost two-day drive into five—stopping to sightsee along the way—she was still exhausted. She groaned when she thought about what she must have looked like to Mr. Main Street. Then again, why did she care?

Delanie and Shayna discussed having lunch once Shayna returned from her Mediterranean cruise and a few generic things about the town, then ended the call. Delanie breathed a sigh of relief. Best in the business *and* ran a winery. Could her luck get any better?

Ray sat at the kitchen table, his arms crossed over his chest. One thing he'd always been able to do was to notice when his cousin Shayna was hiding something from him. She had a tell. Anytime he asked a question, and she responded with, "Huh?" as if she hadn't heard him, it was a dead giveaway.

"What aren't you telling me, Shay?" he asked, knowing for sure she was holding something back about this "perfect opportunity" she'd presented.

"Huh?"

Ray laughed. Yep, a tell. "You're hiding something. Spill it."

"*Okay, okay.* Do you remember the woman you encountered this afternoon? The one who *innocently* kept blowing the horn?"

Oh, did he remember her. "Yeah. Why?"

She bit at the corner of her lip, her eyes turning sympathetic.

The second it hit him what Shayna was implying, Ray stood and left her at the kitchen table alone. "Oh no. *Hell* no," he said in a lowered tone, making sure not to disturb his resting mother.

Shayna spoke in an equally muted tone. "You know you love doing this type of thing."

Well, she had him there. What he didn't enjoy was mingling with over-the-top prima donnas with a sense of entitlement.

"And you could use the distraction," Shayna added.

Had him again. "Yeah, but not the stress. Two minutes with her—"

"Delanie."

Ray eyed Shayna over his shoulder. "What?"

"Her name is Delanie. Delanie Atwater."

Ray tossed up his hands. "*Fine.* Two minutes with *Delanie Atwater* and I was ready to strangle her," he admitted. Metaphorically speaking only, because he would never actually put his hands on a woman. Only a coward did that. Cowards like his biological father. What he didn't admit was the fact he'd thought about her ever since they'd unofficially met in the middle of Main Street. Why were no-good-for-him women always a draw?

Shayna joined him at the sink. Resting a hip against the counter, she said, "Please, cousin. For me. She could really use the help."

Oh, he agreed. She could really use some help all right. Help he wasn't qualified to administer. When Shayna batted those big doe eyes at him, she'd almost caused him to fold. "Are you trying to send me to an early grave? Clearly, you haven't seen the side of this woman—*Delanie Atwater*—" he corrected himself "—I've seen. The woman is vicious. Like a rhumba of rattlesnakes trapped in a burlap sack."

Shayna folded her arms over her chest. "And you came to this conclusion after only several minutes in her presence?"

"Yes."

Her tone turned mushy. "Cut her a little slack. She's going through some things right now."

And he wasn't? Curious, he wondered what exactly Shayna had meant, but didn't bother to ask. It didn't matter. His answer was still no.

"You know how much you love the old Vaughn place. And, who knows, maybe you two will become friends—or lovers," she mumbled under her breath, "and merge vineyards. I know you want to keep yours small, but…" She shrugged. "Who knows what might happen?"

He ignored her *lovers* comment. Mainly because he didn't have the patience for an opposites-attract speech. Mostly because it would take an act of God for him to fall for her. But something she'd said had interested him. "The Vaughn place?"

Shayna couldn't have been referring to the same Vaughn place he'd been trying to secure for over a year. The one that butted up against his seventeen acre ranch. The one he'd been told wasn't for sale.

"Yes. She's the new owner."

Ray growled under his breath, disliking the rude woman even more, because she had something he wanted.

"Old Man Vaughn was her uncle. Her mother's brother. No, her father's. No, I think it was her mother's." She waved her hands through the air. "Or something like that. Anyway, she *really* needs help."

He sighed heavily. "I'm dealing with enough, Shay, without adding one more thing to the mix." He leaned against the counter and stared out the window at the mauve and cobalt horizon.

Shayna ironed a hand over his back. Her tone was tender when she spoke. "Hey. What's up? Everything okay with Auntie?"

He lowered his head, not wanting Shayna to see his distress. "Yes." He sighed. "No. Her kidney function has dropped even more. Dr. Langston says she'll probably have to start dialysis soon."

Just the idea caused Ray's chest to tighten. As frail as his mother already was, how in hell would she be able to handle dialysis? He massaged the stiffness in his neck. If he could trade places with her, he would in a minute.

"I'm sorry, cousin. Had I known, I never would have bothered you with any of this." She hugged an arm around his waist and rested her head against him.

Draping his arm around her shoulders, he said, "It's fine."

Heck, maybe he should do it. Just to take his mind off everything. Giving life to something—even if it was only grapes—had to bring him at least a minimal amount of joy, right?

Something occurred to him, a morally bankrupt thought. This could be his chance to finally get the Vaughn place. With her flawless makeup, manicured nails and privileged attitude, he was sure Ms. California—*Delanie Atwater*—wouldn't last a month. Knowing how to drink wine didn't mean one could produce it. A vineyard was hard work, and something told him she wouldn't know a hard day's work if it showed up on her doorstep.

This could be a win-win situation for him. But could he tolerate her? After only a few minutes with her he'd wanted to banish her to a distant land. For the opportunity to secure the Vaughn property, he could.

"I'll do it."

Shayna reeled back to look at him. "Really?"

He nodded.

"You're the best cousin-brother ever! You're going to make Delanie *sooo* happy."

Somehow, he doubted that.

"She's expecting you tomorrow around noonish."

Ray barked a laugh. "You've already committed me to the job?"

"I know how much you love doing this type of stuff, remember? I was pretty sure you'd say yes." She smirked. "Plus, you get this interesting look on your face when you talk about Delanie. Could be worth exploring." She came up on her tiptoes and placed a kiss on his cheek. "I have to go home and pack. Love you."

"And she is okay with *me* helping her?" he asked.

Shayna made her way to the door. "Um, I didn't exactly tell her who you were. Or that you also owned a vineyard that butted up against hers. Or that we're related. Or that you're filthy rich."

Shayna hadn't told Delanie it was him who would be helping her? For all he knew, he could end up staring down the barrel of a shotgun when he showed up on her doorstep. "Shay—"

"It'll be fine. Trust me. Love you. Give Auntie a kiss for me when she wakes," she said, rushing out.

What in the hell had Shayna gotten him into? And what had she meant by *interesting look*? His brow furrowed. *Interesting look? What kind of interesting look?* "I don't get an interesting look," he mumbled to himself.

The only look Delanie Atwater could draw from him was one of agony, which was exactly what he had a feeling he was setting himself up for. Months of pure anguish. But for those twenty-plus acres, it was worth it.

He hoped.

Chapter 3

Delanie bolted forward and tossed several panicked glances around the room. *What was that?* When it sounded again, she realized there was someone at the front door. She blew a sigh of relief. *The movers.* The ones who should have been there yesterday, but had taken a "wrong turn." *Yeah, right.* They'd probably stopped at a strip club and gotten drunk.

She laughed at herself. *Quit being so cynical, Delanie Claire Atwater.* When had she become so disparaging? Ah! That was easy to answer. When she'd found out her husband was screwing a twenty-year-old via social media. *Ex*-husband, she corrected herself.

Rising from the makeshift bed she'd fashioned on the floor, she grimaced at the stiffness in her joints. She took a moment to stretch her tight muscles. Sleeping in her car would have likely given her a better night's rest. Thankfully, she'd placed the quilt her mother had hand-stitched in the trunk of her vehicle for safekeeping, so she'd at least stayed warm through the night. Comfortable? That was another story.

The movers were early. When she'd spoken to them the day before, they'd told her it would be at least lunchtime before they arrived. It was only eight now. Moving toward the door, she finger-combed her hair and cursed her rough night.

Until she'd attempted to fall asleep, she hadn't realized how creepy the huge house was. The things she'd heard had only been the sounds of the structure settling, but still, it had rattled her nerves. So much so that she'd slept in her clothes and shoes, just in case she needed to make a quick getaway. She made a mental note to contact an alarm company. While she felt safe there, a little extra protection couldn't hurt.

Another round of rapping occurred. *Hold your horses. Geesh.* "Coming," she said in the most cheerful voice she could muster pre-coffee. No use angering them before they'd unloaded her belongings. Oh, how she needed coffee and food. When was the last time she'd eaten?

After the shitty day she'd had yesterday, she definitely needed something strong and dark in her life. *Or wine.* Yeah, wine would do. While it was only eight in the morning in Vine Ridge, it was five in the afternoon somewhere.

Yesterday had been a disaster, but today—a wide smile spread across her face and confidence swelled her chest—today was going to be amazing. *AH-MAZE-*

ZING. She could feel the positive energy seeping through her. Nothing would go wrong today.

Opening the door, the smile instantly slid from her face. Staring into the chiseled mug of Mr. Main Street, she said, *"You."* This wasn't the something strong and dark she needed, but he did have the same warming and perking effect as coffee.

Just as he had the day before, he commanded admiration. The man was obnoxious, rude, pigheaded, sarcastic, but fine as hell. In the midst of lusting over him, something urgent occurred to her. How did he know where she lived?

With that, a bounty of questions flooded her brain: Had he followed her home yesterday? Was he there to harm her? Was she about to become a casualty of delayed road rage? Her mouth went dry, her stomach churned and bile burned the back of her throat.

She desperately wanted to slam the door closed, but her muscles were seized in a painful grip around the knob, and her feet were rooted to the aged hardwood floor. What would she do if he lunged at her? *Die*, she told herself, because no one would hear her scream. And she certainly wouldn't stand a chance against the solidly built man. Her breathing became ragged as fear trickled into every cell in her body.

"What are you doing here?" she managed to choke out.

His clean-shaven face contorted into a tight ball of something. She couldn't determine whether it was the look of a madman or a confused one. When he folded his arms across his chest, her eyes fell to the swell at his bicep. *Magnificent.* Snapping out of her trance, she scolded herself. Was she really checking out the man who was possibly there to do her harm?

Yep. Yep, she was. *Shameless*.

"Shayna sent me," he said dryly.

Delanie's eyes met his hard stare. Several beats of silence passed while her brain rebooted. Finally regaining clarity, and the use of her mouth, she said, "Shayna sent you?" Why would Shayna— Then it dawned on her. "*You're* the vine guy?" *No way would fate play such a cruel trick on me.*

With his expression still set in stone, he said, "Yes."

Clearly, fate hated her. Then again, this more than likely wasn't the work of fate at all. This was probably the workings of the universe. Payback for putting a ripple in its harmony the day before with her sour behavior.

"Shayna said you wouldn't be here until noonish," she said.

He shrugged a solid shoulder. "I had to take Shayna to the airport and decided to swing by. Is now a bad time?"

That's right. Shayna was going on a two-week Mediterranean cruise. "No. Just as good a time as any. I'm just…" *Confused.* She studied him. Obviously, he knew he was coming here to meet her, because he hadn't looked stunned when she'd opened the door. Why in the world would he have ever agreed to help her? She hadn't been the picture of politeness during their initial encounter. And that was putting it mildly. Calling a spade a spade, she'd been a downright witch to him.

Recalling the truck he drove, she reasoned that maybe he needed the money. She had to commend a man who could put a paycheck above his pride. Well, if he were willing to work together, so was she.

"Ray Cavanaugh," he said, sticking out his hand.

Cavanaugh? "Are you and Shayna—"

"Cousins."

Cousins. She'd been leaning toward husband and wife. For some reason, learning they were family gave her unexplainable relief. Why hadn't Shayna mentioned their relation? Delanie didn't give it much thought. Placing her hand into his, a sensation tickled her palm. Her gaze fell to their connection. *What the heck was that?*

"Everything okay?" Ray said, his tone even.

Obviously, he hadn't felt the same surge of energy she had. And why would he have? If his frosty demeanor was any indication, her front porch was the last place he wanted to be. But could she blame him?

Bringing her gaze back to his, she flashed a low-wattage smile. "Yes. Yes, everything's fine." *But not as fine as you.* Had he been this handsome yesterday? *Stop it!* "Um, Shayna didn't mention you two were related when we discussed you." Her eyes rounded. "Not *discussed you* discussed you. When she mentioned— um, recommended you for the job."

Delanie reclaimed the hand still clinging to his and made a fist to subdue the tingling. Ray's magnetism was scrambling her brain, and she hated it.

By the expression on his face, Delanie was sure the man thought she was nuts. Coupled with the scene from yesterday and the fact she'd pretty much insinuated he was a stalker today, he had all the evidence he needed to support the claim.

Yesterday.

Again, her cheeks burned with embarrassment. Now would probably be a good time to apologize for her uncharacteristic behavior. She didn't want to be known around town as the crazy horn lady. Believe it or not, she actually wanted to fit in here.

Ray shrugged one of his solid shoulders. "Maybe she's ashamed of me."

Delanie pushed her brows together. What reason would she have to be ashamed of him? Did he have a scandalous reputation around town? Was he a scoundrel, a playboy? No doubt he'd left plenty of wet panties and broken hearts in his path. Ray's smooth voice brought her back to reality.

"It was a joke," he said.

"A joke?"

He gave one firm nod.

"I see. Usually, when someone tells a joke, it's followed up with a laugh, a smile or some other similar display of amusement. Your severe stone-faced expression threw me off."

Ray's lip twitched as if he were fighting back his amusement. A bout of laughter was just what they needed to break the block of ice between them.

With a tilt of his head, he said, "Let's take a walk," then descended the stairs.

"O-okay."

She trailed Ray off the porch, and they headed toward the vineyard. Grass crunched under their feet as they trudged across her front lawn. A gentle breeze kicked up, floating the scent of Ray's cologne in her direction. Unapologetically, she inhaled a lungful of the masculine fragrance. *Mmm.* He smelled delectable.

Ray didn't seem like such a bad guy. He'd even agreed to help her after the indignant way she'd acted. Of course, it could all be for show. Still, he hadn't deserved the way she'd treated him. Cordell had gotten her so riled up. She rested a hand on Ray's forearm to stop him, but snatched it away when the feel of his warm flesh sent a surge through her entire body.

"What's wrong?" Ray said.

Besides the ridiculous way my body keeps responding to you, nothing. That remained her little secret. Had she seen a hint of concern in his eyes? Briefly lowering her gaze to the ground, she said, "About yesterday... I owe you an apology. I never should have reacted the way I did. There is no excuse for my behavior. I'm sorry."

Ray folded his arms across his chest, and his biceps mushroomed into two impressive mounds that derailed her train of thought. Her eyes slid from one to the other. Realizing how blatantly obvious she was being, she forced her attention back to his face. However, it took her brain a moment to catch up.

"I...um..." She cleared her throat, stealing another quick peek at his arms. "It'd been a really muscular day and—" Her eyes widened. Had she really just said *muscular*? *Ugh.* "Menacing, I meant to say. It'd been a really menacing day. I was exhausted. Still exhausted," she added. "Again, I know that's no excuse for the way I treated you, but I do hope you accept my apology, seeing how we'll be working closely together to bring this place back to life."

Delanie smiled in hopes of triggering a similar reaction from Ray. No such luck. He quietly slid his hands into his pockets and stared at her long and hard with those deep, dark eyes of his. Her skin prickled under his scrutiny. Each silent second that ticked by made her more and more anxious, and aware of him.

When his eyes lowered to her mouth, she swore the devil made her drag the tip of her tongue across her bottom lip. His chiseled jaw flinched slightly. For a second, she imagined him crashing his delicious-looking mouth to hers.

The tingle between her legs jarred her to her senses. *Oh God.* Realizing what she'd just done mortified her. Pulling her bottom lip between her teeth, she shifted her attention away from a tempting Ray Cavanaugh, because there was no telling what other devious things the devil would have her do.

Ray took a step toward her. "You should never allow him to speak to you that way. No matter how much money he's giving you."

Ray's words jarred her. "Excuse me?"

"Your ex-husband. You should have hung up on him."

"How do you—" Apparently, he had overheard a portion of her conversation with Cordell. No wonder he'd lingered at her window for so long. He'd been eavesdropping. Damn hands-free system.

A twinge of anger bubbled up inside her. Who was he to tell her what she should have done? *Just like a man.* But a second later, she wrangled her contempt. Partially because she needed him; mostly because he'd been right. She should have disconnected the call with Cordell.

"With all due respect, Mr. Cavanaugh, I don't see

how my *private* conversation with my husband is any of your business." She pointed toward the vineyard. "Now, if we could just—"

"*Ex*-husband, right?"

Delanie allowed her arm to fall to her side, feeling a bit humiliated by the blunder she'd made, and the fact Ray had called her out on it. But the feeling was short-lived. Grinding her teeth, she shot him a narrow-eyed gaze. Was he intentionally trying to piss her off? Payback from yesterday, maybe?

"Doesn't feel too good when someone keeps pushing your buttons, does it?" He took a step away from her. "I accept your apology, *Delanie Atwater*," he said, continuing toward the vineyard. "And I excuse your reckless driving."

Reckless— Taking a *woosah* moment, she forced a smile. But what she really wanted to do was tell Ray Jackass Cavanaugh to go screw himself. However, she fought the urge. *You get more bees with honey than you do vinegar.* Plus, whether she liked it or not, she needed him.

The best in the business, she reminded herself.

Ray could feel Delanie's angry gaze burning into his back as he walked away, leaving her seething over his words. Now she knew how it felt to be dismissed. It had probably been a first for her.

To be honest, he was surprised she hadn't pounced on him. By the expression on her lovely face, she'd definitely wanted to draw blood. *So fiery*, Ray thought, laughing to himself.

Apparently, it had dawned on Delanie that she

needed him far more than he needed her. Actually, that statement wasn't 100 percent accurate. For a brief moment, he'd needed to kiss her. Especially when she'd glided the tip of her tongue over that suckable bottom lip of hers.

Yep, in that moment of temporary insanity, he'd definitely needed her far more. And something told him she'd needed—or wanted—a little bit of him, too.

"I assume you're not a one-man crew," she said, moving up beside him again. "And that you have the proper equipment. *Work* equipment, I mean," she said.

Ray glanced over at her, never breaking stride. "What other type of equipment would I need besides work equipment?" A rattled expression spread across her face, and he wondered if his words had, in some way, affected her. It could have been the way the sun hit her butter-smooth face, but he thought her cheeks shaded a rosy color.

"None."

Letting her off the hook, he said, "I have a crew, Ms. Atwater. And the proper equipment to satisfy all your needs." Well, maybe not entirely off the hook.

One minute Delanie was there beside him, and the next she was sprawled on the ground.

What the...? Ray knelt next to her. "Are you okay?"

"Does it look like I'm okay? *Ow*," she said, rolling over onto her butt.

"What happened?" Had his words made her knees buckle? He chuckled at the foolish thought. No. This woman was as frigid as an iceberg. She wouldn't melt so easily.

Delanie must have assumed he was laughing at her.

Had her gaze been a blade, he would have been in tiny pieces right now. "What happened?" he asked again, taking a seat next to her.

She brushed debris from her clothing. "I stepped in a hole or something. This entire place is filled with holes or bumps or roots jutting up," she said with a huff. Her eyes canvassed the area. "Stupid ground."

It didn't surprise him for one minute that she would blame the earth for her mishap, instead of simply admitting she should have been watching her step. "Moles," he said.

"What?"

"It was probably a mole hole you stepped in."

"Yeah, well, I'm glad to see you made sure I didn't break anything before you laughed." She slapped her hands over her pants leg, knocking away dirt.

"I wasn't—" He stopped. If he said he wasn't laughing at her, she would want to know why he'd laughed. If he told her he'd been laughing at the idea of his words making her lose balance, it would have sparked a war. "I'm sorry," he said. "Let me help you up?"

"No. I need to sit here a second."

A hint of concern washed over him. "Did you hurt yourself?"

"No." Her tone softened. "Just my pride."

Something that almost resembled a smile curled one corner of her mouth. His eyes fixed on her lips. Man, he bet they were as soft as cotton. Lifting his gaze back to hers, he ignored the slight look of curiosity on her face. "Just let me know when you're ready."

She nodded, then directed her attention to the vineyard. "This place is going to be the death of me, and I've only been here a day."

"Why a vineyard?" Ray asked. She didn't strike him as the get-your-hands-dirty type. Pampered, maybe. Outdoorsy…nope.

A slow smile curled her lips. *"A Walk in the Clouds."*

If she wanted a walk in the clouds, maybe she should have bought an airline. "What does that mean?"

"The Keanu Reeves and Aitana Sánchez-Gijón movie," she said, as if it would make him more familiar.

"Ah. I've never seen it."

"Keanu pretended to be Aitana's husband. She was unwed and pregnant and knew her father would be disappointed. Anyway…her family owned a vineyard."

"Sounds…interesting." Not really, but he didn't want to bash a movie she clearly enjoyed.

"You should watch it. It's a beautiful love story."

Love story? She'd definitely lost him there.

"I've wanted to own a vineyard ever since I saw that movie," she continued.

"Hmm. Must have been a great flick."

Delanie absently crumbled a brittle leaf. "It was. Especially to a thirteen-year-old with humongous dreams. At that age, everything felt possible."

Something distressing lingered behind her words. Ray wanted to ask more questions, delve deeper into her life. Instead, he reminded himself he wasn't there to get to know her; he was there to do a job.

Had he pegged Delanie all wrong? Underneath all those harsh layers, could there actually be a tender heart? A tiny voice whispered yes, but he chose to ignore it. He preferred to continue to view her as the unyielding woman he'd met the day before. That way, he had a fighting chance against this unexplainable attraction he had to her.

Delanie sighed heavily, bringing Ray back to the conversation.

"Don't let this place stress you out," he said. "You're actually in pretty good shape here." He stared out at the acres of earth. "The trellis system is still intact, which is great. I'll go through and check each wood post for stability. We need them to be able to support the vines."

"Okay," she muttered.

"I'll have the soil tested, but I have no doubt that'll be fine, too." This time, a real smile touched her lips, and he fought to keep his eyes from lowering to her mouth again. "Do you plan to use an outside supplier until your vines are producing fruit?"

"I'll more than likely use the year to establish my company."

"What will you do for the next two?"

Her brow furrowed. "The next two?"

He nodded. "It'll take roughly thirty-six months for the vines to produce fruit."

Delanie's back straightened. "Thirty-six months. the internet said I would see fruit in one."

Was she serious? She was relying on a search engine to plan her timeline? Yeah, she really did need his help. "What the internet should have told you is that you'll see vine growth the first year, but no fruit."

Delanie groaned, closed her eyes and allowed her head to fall back.

He should have been giving her some kind of uplifting speech: it's not as long as it seems, quality takes

time, good grapes equal great wine. *Yada, yada, yada.*
Instead, he fantasized about dragging his tongue along
the column of her neck. A sensation stirred below his
waist, reminding him just how long it had been since
he'd had sex.

"He was right. I have no idea what the hell I'm
doing," Delanie said.

Delanie's words forced the thought of making love
to her out of Ray's head. He wasn't sure what *he* Delanie referred to but had an idea it was her ex-husband.
Without having ever met the man, Ray disliked him.
What kind of man would intentionally try to crush
her dreams?

Delanie reminded him of Shayna and how broken she was after her divorce. Feeling a degree of big
brother bravado, he continued, "But I do. If you trust
me with your vineyard, it will thrive beyond your wild-
est dreams."

When Delanie eyed him, something tender twinkled
in her eyes. "You're that good, huh?"

"Great, actually," he said.

Delanie didn't dispute his claim, merely stared at
him as if trying to read his mind. "Well, I guess I'll
just have to be patient and trust you—your skills," she
clarified.

"Patience is good, because it's going to take time.
And money," he said for comic relief. "But we'll get
there. Together. As a team," he added.

"Time and money. Well, thanks to my cheating ex,
I have a lot of both," she said.

It stunned him that she would share a detail so intimate. They had something in common. Unfaithful

spouses. Tamping down the memory of his past life, he refocused on the conversation. "That's a good thing, because I don't come cheap, Ms. Atwater."

"The best rarely do, Mr. Cavanaugh."

Silence fell between them, but their focus on one another remained steadfast. This woman had him experiencing something he hadn't in over a year. Extreme desire. A yearning so powerful it stalled his breathing. But he had a mission. One he couldn't allow to be derailed by yearning.

"Shall we go inside and discuss your fees?" she said.

"Sure."

Standing, he offered her his hand. The second her soft palm connected to his, a surge of electricity shot up his arm, causing him to put a little too much force into the pull. Delanie's warm body slammed against his chest. His free arm wrapped around her waist, holding her snugly in place.

"Oh," she said, her head quickly tilting upward to eye him. "I…I guess I stepped into another mole hole."

Staring down into her cautious eyes, Ray fought the urge to kiss her. Kiss her long. Kiss her hard. Kiss her until they both neared unconsciousness. He wasn't sure what it was about Delanie Atwater that stirred his ravenous hunger, but he craved feasting on her.

After several more seconds of enjoying her soft frame against him, Ray allowed his arm to fall. Surprisingly, Delanie didn't budge. Then, as if her brain had processed she was free to move, she jerked her body away from his, turned and hurried away. He smirked at the glimpse he'd gotten of her beaded nipples pressing against her bra and the fabric of the thin shirt she wore.

The sight was both refreshing and pure torture, all wrapped up into one tight-knit ball of longing. His lips tingled to suckle the taut flesh through her shirt. *Damn.* He had to get this under control. The only thing he should be focused on was doing a great job, not doing Delanie. The more work he did now, the less he would have to do when the property was his. That reminded him, he needed to contact Jessup Ryder, who would help him buy it.

Inside, Ray scrutinized the spacious dwelling. While it was nice, when he took over ownership, he would gut it. Maybe he'd make it a café or possibly a tasting villa.

"I'll be right back. I need to get something to write with," she said.

Ray nodded. When Delanie disappeared into another room, he stood at the window and stared at the several other buildings on the property. Each could easily house overnight accommodations, a gift shop, even a venue for weddings or other events. *Marriage.* He scowled at the thought. Love was a fool's game that he would never play again.

Delanie reentered the room. "I would offer you coffee but I have none. Finding a market is on my to-do list."

"You haven't had breakfast?"

Delanie rested her hand against her stomach. "Oh my God, did you hear my stomach growl?"

Ray chuckled. "No. I just assumed since you said you needed to find the market."

"To answer your question, no, I haven't. After we chat, maybe I'll run into town and find something."

"Grab your things," he said.

Delanie's brows furrowed. "Why?"

"I'm taking you to breakfast. A business meeting," he said, wanting to make sure she knew this was an innocent invitation.

A few seconds ticked by before she said, "Okay."

As he'd stated, this was a business meeting. But Ray had to admit he experienced a great deal of pleasure imagining the things he wanted to do to her. Which should have been his first indication to stay away from this woman.

Chapter 4

The second Delanie and Ray had walked into the Make a Way diner, every set of eyes in the place fixed on them. As if they were some bizarre circus act on display. Even now, nearly a half hour after their arrival, she could still feel their eyes on them. Did they know something about Ray she didn't know? Likely, because she knew less than a little about the man. Everybody had a past. What was his?

"Is your breakfast okay?"

Delanie jerked from the sound of Ray's voice and realized she'd been staring at him. In her defense, he was pretty darn hard to ignore. "Um…yes. It's delicious. Thank you."

"How would you know? You've barely touched any of it."

She dropped her gaze to the bacon, sausage and

cheese omelet on her plate. The one she'd specifically ordered *without* cheese. Just looking at it, she could feel her intestines knotting. "It's a bit more than I'm used to."

That excuse sounded much better than saying *I'm lactose intolerant and would clear this entire restaurant if I ate it*. Since she was probably already known as the crazy horn lady, she didn't bother sending the plate back, adding crazy omelet lady to her title.

"I'm sure Kemp wouldn't mind whipping you up an egg white omelet, quinoa, a spinach salad, maybe."

Ray flashed a half smile, then continued gnawing on the slab of bacon he'd ordered. Had that been some kind of jab? Delanie pushed the plate aside, propped her elbows on the table, then rested her chin against her hands. "That's interesting," she said.

Ray glanced up. "What's that?"

"I was convinced that if you ever smiled, your face would crack. I was wrong."

"I bet that's painful for you, being wrong," he shot back.

Given that Ray was stone-faced 99.9 percent of the time, she couldn't tell if he was mocking her or making another attempt at humor. Given their history, she went with the former. "You don't like me much, do you, Ray?"

Ray placed his fork down and gave her his full attention. Dabbing at his mouth, he said, "I don't know you well enough to make that assessment, Ms. Atwater."

"Based on what you do know, what do you think about me?"

Whether or not he would admit it, she was sure he'd

formed an opinion about her after their initial meeting. No doubt he ranked her right up there with the Wicked Witch of the West. Delanie sounded an evil laugh in her head.

"I don't think about you," he said plainly, returning his attention to his plate.

Instead of consuming the eggs, he pushed them around with his fork. Delanie could have been wrong, but he'd sounded almost defensive in his response. Kind of like someone who's called out on something they know they're guilty of, but refuse to admit any wrongdoing.

Well, that explanation was easier to process than the other possibility—he thought she was the worst person he'd ever encountered and didn't want to say that. The idea saddened her. She really wasn't a bad person; she'd simply had a bad day.

Considering his potential dislike for her brought her to her next question. "Why are you helping me? What's in this for you?"

She wasn't stupid. Even though she was paying him, Ray was using her just as she was using him. She recognized forced kindness when she saw it. He didn't truly want to be there with her; he was tolerating her. But what did she have that Ray could possibly want? Or had Shayna instructed him to play nice?

When the cute, almond-toned waitress sashayed by, flashing Ray a sultry smile, Delanie's imagination took over. Was Ray the town bad boy, sleeping with as many women as he could? It was always the quiet ones. Did he intend for her—the newcomer—to become his next sexual conquest? Well, if so, he was about to be sorely disappointed. No way in hell would she become a notch on his bedpost. Regardless of how tempting the idea of being in his bed was.

"Ray? How are you, sugah?"

Delanie eyed the older woman who'd stopped at their table. The oversize pink hat she wore, with a gigantic white flower affixed to it, made Delanie smile. It reminded her of something her grandmother would have worn, right along with the paisley sundress.

For the first time since they'd met, Delanie witnessed Ray's kissable lips curl into a brilliant smile. This expression was genuine, unlike anything he'd yet to give her.

"Mrs. Madeline."

Ray stood and gave the woman a hug. She wrapped her large arms around him and squeezed him like an orange. The affection in the embrace suggested they were close. Family, maybe? In small towns like this, everyone was family—by blood or by marriage.

"I'm fine. How about you?" Ray asked.

"Fine as frog's hair," she said.

The look on Mrs. Madeline's face shifted from cheerful to solemn.

"How's your mother? I haven't seen her at church lately. I've been meaning to get by there. Me and Lee Earl both."

Ray rubbed at his wrist as if he were trying to wring it dry. His jaw clenched, then released. "She's…good. Yeah, she's fine. Stop by anytime. I'm sure she'll be happy to see you."

"I sure will. I'll make her one of my lemon sour cream pound cakes. She's always loved my cakes." Mrs.

Madeline's gaze slid to Delanie. "Hello. I don't think we've met, sugah."

Delanie stood. "No, we haven't. I've just moved to town. I inherited the vineyard on Grapevine Lane from my uncle." She extended her hand. "Delanie Atwater."

Mrs. Madeline took her hand and cupped it in hers. "Oh, yes. I heard Vine Ridge had a new resident. And just as pretty as you want to be, too. Well, you're going to make a lot of single women in Vine Ridge beyond jealous. They've been trying to snag this one for a long time." She patted Ray's arm. "You have you a fine man here."

When Delanie sent an urgent glance in Ray's direction, he actually looked amused. Why wasn't he as horrified by what the woman had said as she was? "No, we're just colleagues," Delanie made clear, since Ray hadn't seemed pressed to correct Mrs. Madeline. All she needed was for a rumor about her and Ray to burn through town.

Mrs. Madeline gave a warm smile. "Whatever you say, sugah."

Why hadn't Mrs. Madeline believed her? Just because she was having breakfast with Ray didn't mean they were a couple. Men and woman who weren't married or dating ate meals together all the time.

"Well, it was nice meeting you, Deli. I'm sure I'll be seeing a lot more of you."

Ray snickered and Delanie cut her eyes at him. Obviously, he thought Mrs. Madeline butchering her name had been funny. Actually, it was, because that's exactly what her grandmother had, on occasion, called her. Delanie didn't bother correcting the woman.

"Ray, let June know I'll be stopping by soon. You two enjoy the rest of your breakfast date."

Again, Delanie didn't bother correcting her. Obviously, the woman was convinced this was something romantic. Just what she needed, to be labeled Ray's lover.

Mrs. Madeline strolled off, stopping at almost every table she passed and undoubtedly spreading the word about them and their "relationship." Ray eased back down in his seat, but Delanie remained standing, hoping he took it as a signal that she was ready to leave.

"You should at least attempt to eat some of your omelet. When it comes to his food, Kemp can be a little sensitive. And he definitely does not like to see it wasted."

Delanie eyed the mammoth-sized entrée. There was no way she could eat all of that. There was no way she should eat any of it, but it definitely sounded as though she should not offend Kemp. Easing back into her seat, she picked up her fork. *Just eat around the cheese.*

"Because you need me," Ray said.

Her head came up urgently. "Because I need you?"

"You asked why I'm helping you."

Well, he had her there. She did need him. Still, something felt off. Plus, he was a man and men couldn't be trusted. Maybe she was just being paranoid. His only motive for assisting her could just be to help another in need. And a paycheck. Thousand-dollar hats didn't pay for themselves. It could all be just that simple, that innocent.

But her gut told her otherwise. And it was rarely wrong.

* * *

Ray and Delanie rode back to her place in silence. Judging by the questions she'd asked at the diner, she didn't trust him. Understandable. He didn't trust her, either. They barely knew one another. Plus, the last time he'd trusted a woman, it had ended in disaster.

Was it possible she knew he'd tried to purchase her property in the past and was fishing to see if he'd tell her? No. She would have said something. Especially about the two of them being neighbors. Plus, Delanie didn't strike him as someone who could hold something so critical to herself. In case he was wrong, he made a mental note to ask Shayna what exactly she'd told Delanie about his past interest in her vineyard.

A glance in her direction revealed her gaze was still anchored to the passing world outside the window. This more delicate and reserved side of her…he liked. No, he didn't. He didn't like anything about Delanie Atwater, he told himself.

It surprised him she'd agreed to breakfast. Surprised him even more that she'd gotten into his pickup—the one she'd eyed with disdain. Clearly, she preferred traveling in more elaborate vehicles. There was no way for her to know that this truck was priceless to him, or that it had once been owned by Superman. Well, at least to Ray, his father had been a superhero. One who saved him from the villains he'd encountered in foster care.

Ray deadened the memories of his father threatening to creep in, then shifted his thoughts back to Delanie. Why had Mrs. Madeline assumed they'd been on a date? Why hadn't he been the one to correct her? Maybe because her comment about Delanie making a lot of single women in Vine Ridge beyond jealous had stunned him stupid.

Snatching his eyes away from the woman, he focused on the road ahead. "As long as you're okay with everything we discussed, I'll start—"

"I'm not sure you're the right man for the job, Ray."

Since she hadn't given him the courtesy of saying it to his face, he was forced to talk to the back of her head. "Mind if I ask why the change of heart?" She'd been pretty confident about him before. What had happened to alter that? Had it been the Mrs. Madeline thing?

Facing him, she said, "Why are you helping me?"

Hadn't they been over this already? He parted his lips to remind her of his original response, but stopped when Delanie held up her hand.

"And please don't say because I need you. I am tired of men thinking I need them. So, please, give me something else. Give me the truth."

"Because I need you." If he had taken time to run the string of words through his head, Ray was sure he would have decided against them. Unfortunately, they'd escaped before he'd had the chance. And he instantly regretted them. Vulnerability wasn't really his thing.

Faint lines crawled across Delanie's forehead, and confusion radiated on her face. Naturally, the comment piqued her interest, because she shifted toward him and looked as though she were waiting for clarification.

Though the words hadn't come out as intended, if he wanted her to be on board with him doing this project, he had to roll with them. How would he get in her good graces if they didn't spend any time together? More importantly, why did the idea of spending time with her *not* bother him? Twenty-four hours ago, she'd been the last person he'd ever wanted to see again. Now, he was looking forward to seeing more of her.

Staring into her curious eyes, he couldn't keep his brain from processing how damn gorgeous she was. His probing gaze inadvertently lowered to her glossy lips. Big mistake. A myriad of questions raced through his head. Were they as soft as they looked? How would they feel against his? Was she a good kisser?

Snapping out of the foolish stupor, he refocused on the road. He needed to give a plausible explanation, something that would win her over. Something that would convince her he was the right man for her—the job, he corrected himself. Before he could offer her just a nibble of the truth—that working her vineyard would help to take his mind off his mother's health— she spoke.

"You need the money," she said as more of a statement than a question.

Stunned by how delicate her tone was, all he could do was stare for a moment.

"There's nothing to be ashamed of," she said. "We've all been there."

When her eyes lowered to her fiddling fingers, Ray couldn't help but wonder what memory her last statement triggered—*we've all been there.*

"There's no need to be embarrassed," she continued.

She thought he needed the money. He laughed to himself. Money was the last thing he needed. Honestly, he had more of it than he knew what to do with. Choosing to neither confirm nor deny her claim, he eyed the road.

"Whenever you want to start work will be fine," she said, shifting her attention back through the window.

A ping of regret jostled him, followed by shame. He'd always loathed deceitful people—even more so after walking in on his wife and best friend screwing on the kitchen counter. So, why was he becoming one?

Delanie's stomach rumbled, pulling him from his thoughts. Her body stiffened and she rested her hands against her midsection. Moisture glistened on her forehead. Was she suffering from motion sickness?

"Everything okay?" he asked.

"Yes. Fine. Thank you for asking."

Her stomach thunder rumbled again, and she groaned softly.

He arched a brow. "You sure?"

Delanie's placid expression morphed into one of ice. So temperamental, she was. For some reason, her quit-asking-questions scowl made him laugh. But he took his cue.

Several minutes later, they pulled up her driveway. Delanie snatched at the door handle. Man, was she that anxious to get away from him? When the door flung open, she half slid, half fell out of the truck.

"Thank you for breakfast, Ray. I enjoyed it. Enjoy the rest of your day."

"So—"

She slammed the door, sprinted across the yard, darted up the front stairs, fumbled with the door lock and practically fell inside the house. Ray died laughing. If nothing else, Delanie Atwater sure was entertaining, stubborn as a mule with a migraine and tempting as gold bullion.

Chapter 5

It was close to ten in the morning when Delanie cracked open her eyes. God, she was glad to be waking in her own bed and not on the floor. Sitting forward, she stretched for the ceiling, feeling refreshed and renewed. All she needed now was a cup of coffee. She tossed her legs over the side of the bed, pushed to her feet and stretched again before heading downstairs.

After two weeks of arranging, then rearranging, the house was almost how she wanted it. But there were still a few things that needed her attention. Overall, she liked what she'd done with the place. She scrutinized the large family room. The brown-and-cream color scheme worked well, and the furniture she'd chosen gave the space a modern feel, while still honoring its old-time roots.

Continuing into the kitchen, she mentally patted herself on the back. By far, this was her favorite room in the house. White cabinets, wood countertops, white plank ceiling and shelving. What she loved most about the room was the exposed brick wall.

Her Keurig seemed out of place in the rustic room. Maybe she'd order an old-school percolator just for decoration. Taking the first sip from her favorite over-size mug put a smile on her face. Heading for the table, she changed her mind and decided to have her coffee on the porch instead. On the way out of the house, she snagged her cell phone to call Shayna and welcome her back home from her cruise. And to pick several bones with her.

Delanie squinted against the assault of bright light when she opened the front door, then jerked at the sight of Ray's truck in the yard. He hadn't mentioned stopping by. What was he doing here? Better yet, where was he?

From the porch, her eyes swept the property, spotting the black Stetson hat in the distance. What the heck was he doing? She was just about to join him to find out when her cell phone rang. Shayna's name flashed across the screen. Delanie sniggered at the timing.

Answering, she said, "Welcome home! Believe it or not, I was just about to call you."

"Hey, doll," Shayna said, all chipper, like she'd been up for hours. "I am so glad to be back in little ole Vine Ridge. I missed everyone so much."

"I hope you had a great time, at least."

"A blast," she said. "So, I trust everything went well with Ray?"

Delanie shot a glance in Ray's direction. "Yes, it did,

actually." She eased down into one of the rockers. "You neglected to tell me you two were related."

"I know, I know, and I'm sorry. I wasn't trying to be deceitful. I just figured if I told you, you'd think I was trying to push a jackleg cousin on you. I knew once you had an opportunity to chat with him—in a less intense setting—you wouldn't be able to resist him." Shayna snickered. "Resist his expertise, I mean to say."

Delanie read between the lines and couldn't help but wonder what Shayna had up her sleeve. Was she attempting to play matchmaker? If so, Ray wouldn't be the only disappointed Cavanaugh. Ignoring the woman's non-subtle intent, she said, "Ray is extremely knowledgeable. I'm confident we'll get it on. *Along.* I'm confident we'll *get along.*"

Delanie didn't think Shayna would ever stop laughing over her blunder.

Finally sobering, Shayna said, "Is he there now? He said something about stopping by on his way to the farmers market."

Farmers market? Vine Ridge had a farmers market? The town was looking better and better by the minute. "Yes, he's here." Delanie squinted toward the field to see Ray squatting. "Looks like he's checking the posts or something."

"Mr. Thorough," Shayna said.

"Shayna, can I ask you something?"

"Sure, doll."

"When Ray and I went to breakfast the other week, a—"

Shayna squealed into the line, forcing Delanie to pull the phone away from her ear briefly.

"You two went on a *breakfast* date?" Shayna said, squealing again.

"No," Delanie said emphatically. "It was strictly business."

"I see," Shayna said, a hint of disbelief in her tone.

Delanie laughed at her friend. "*Anyway*…a Mrs. Madeline asked Ray about his mother. It seemed to rattle him. Is his mother not well?"

Silence played on the opposite end for a moment, causing Delanie to regret prying. It was none of her business. "I'm sorry, Shayna. I shouldn't have asked."

"No need to apologize. Yes, she's sick. Kidney failure. It's a sensitive subject for Ray, so please don't mention it."

Delanie felt instant sympathy for Ray. No wonder he was tolerating her. He was doing what he had to do. With a chronic illness, the medical bills had to be monstrous. Considering the fact she'd come close to not utilizing his services made her feel awful. "Now it makes sense."

"What makes sense?" Shayna asked.

Delanie hadn't meant to say the words aloud. "Oh… um…why Mrs. Madeline seemed so sad. Don't worry, I won't say anything to him."

"Thank you."

"About this farmers market. How far is it from me?"

"Not far at all. Why don't you tag along with Ray? That way, you'll know how to get there in the future. Ray wouldn't mind at all."

Oh, she had a feeling Ray would mind a whole lot.

The two chatted a couple minutes more before ending the call. Setting her sights on Ray again, she froze when he tossed a hand up in her direction, then started toward her. By the way her stomach fluttered, you would have thought she was sixteen years old and about to kiss the most popular boy in school after dreaming about it for weeks.

While she had dreamed about him several nights—blazing hot and sinful dreams—she wasn't a sixteen-year-old. She was a grown woman. And Ray wasn't the most popular boy in school. He was the enemy…right?

As if sensing Delanie's eyes on him, Ray turned to see her standing on the front porch, looking in his direction. He'd expected her to make an appearance much sooner and tear into him for not calling first to give her a heads-up. Tossing his hand up—in hopes of softening the fiery vixen—he headed toward the house.

"Good morning," Delanie said.

Ray wasn't sure how to take the high-beam smile she flashed him. He tossed a glance over his shoulder to see if someone stood behind him. Surely, such an enchanting display hadn't been meant for him. "Good morning."

"I wasn't expecting you," she said.

"I decided to swing by to take a look at the trellis system and check the condition of the hoses. I hope that's okay."

"Yeah, yeah. Anytime you need to stop by, feel free to do so."

Okay, who was this woman and what had she done with Ms. California? The one thing that hadn't changed, even in night attire: Delanie was still breathtaking. Maybe even more so without the makeup masking her natural beauty.

Behind the dark sunglasses and shadow of his Stetson, he perused her body, starting at the fluffy slippers she wore and working his way up. The baby-blue pajama pants hugged her thick thighs in a magnificent way. When his appreciative gaze climbed higher, it was greeted by her taut nipples, pressing against the thin fabric of her top. A sight that mimicked one from a couple of weeks ago.

He couldn't imagine ever tiring of this sight. And to add to his delight, she wasn't wearing a bra this time. *Damn*. Instantly, his dick stirred. He was a breast man, and Delanie's were perfect—large, perky. But were they real?

"How do they look?"

Ray's eyes shot up to meet hers. "What?"

Delanie smiled. "The trellis system and hoses. How do they look?"

Whew. Ray dragged an imaginary hand across his forehead. He thought she'd caught him checking out those beautiful, perfect breasts. *Focus*. He rested his hands on his hips. "Oh. Oh. Uh, yeah, you're in excellent shape. Condition. They're both in excellent shape and condition."

Those sparkling hazel eyes felt as if they were burning a hole straight to his soul. It was daunting at best, uncomfortable as hell at worse. Delanie folded her arms across her chest as if knowing he'd been eyeing her breasts.

"I should—"

"Would you—"

They both laughed at their attempts to speak at the same time.

"Go ahead," Ray said.

"I was just going to ask if you'd like to come inside for a cup of coffee?"

Okay, now she's offering me coffee? Though he appreciated it, the fact she was being so cordial drew his suspicion. "I better not. I've had three cups already."

"Oh. Okay."

A beat of surprisingly comfortable silence played between them.

"Shayna mentioned there's a farmers market nearby," she said.

Ray nodded. "There is. I'm headed there now. You're more than welcome to tag along."

"I could use some produce. And I love farmers markets." She eyed him with skepticism. "Are you sure you don't mind?"

"Not at all."

A strange look spread across Delanie's face, like his *not at all* response had spooked her. What had that been about? He refused to even speculate. Who knew why women did half the things they did. This woman in particular. Simply thinking about her exhausted him. And he'd done a whole lot of thinking about her.

"Can you give me a few minutes to shower and dress?"

"Sure."

"Thanks. I won't be long."

In his experience with women, *not long* meant no more than five hours, but no less than two. "Okay. I'll just hang out in one of these." He pointed to one of the time- and weather-battered rockers. A good sanding, fresh coat of paint and possibly lubrication for the bearings, and they would be like new.

"You don't have to wait out here. Come on in."

Trailing her inside, Ray unapologetically stared at her ass. It had just the right amount of jiggle, the right amount of fullness and definitely the right amount of appeal. When he visualized taking her from the back, a groan rumbled in his chest. *Business before butts*, he thought, then reminded himself of the mission. Get in Delanie's good graces, not her bed. Though the latter was tempting as hell.

Diverting his attention before his jeans tented, he scrutinized the space, not believing what Delanie had accomplished. The subtle colors and modern decor suited her—rich, but soothing in its own way.

"Make yourself at home. I'll be back shortly."

When Delanie reappeared about half an hour later, Ray was stunned by the sight of her in a black-and-white strapless sundress. Her hair was pulled into a bun at the crown of her head, revealing a neck designed for warm, slow kisses. Maybe this hadn't been such a good idea, after all. The tingle in his briefs confirmed it.

"Ready?" she asked.

Yes, he was. Ready to do all kinds of seductively sweet things to her body. "Yes," he said, forcing his mind away from the countless ways he wanted to please her.

Delanie led the way outside. When the sun kissed her shoulders, her skin shimmered as if they'd been dusted with crushed diamonds. Surprisingly, she hadn't seemed repulsed by his truck this time. Being a gentleman, he opened her door. The flash of leg he caught as she hiked the fabric and lifted herself inside the truck knotted his stomach with an overwhelming need to touch her. What in the hell was happening to him?

Delanie's gentle scent—a mix of almond and vanilla—filled the cabin once he climbed behind the wheel and closed the door. Something told him the fragrance would haunt him endlessly.

The drive to the market was akin to the one to and from the diner—steeped in silence. He guessed he could strike up a conversation. But about what? What could he and Delanie possibly have in common?

"Do they sell homemade pretzels at the market?" Delanie asked. "I could really go for one right now."

Maybe they did have one thing in common. "Some of the best in the county."

Delanie looked as if she were trying to contain her excitement when she spoke. "Really?"

He nodded. "You're in for a treat. There's this beer-battered pretzel that will make your toes curl. It's served with a spicy cheese sauce and stone-ground mustard. I have to get one every time I come. It's—" He stopped when he saw the way Delanie stared at him. "What?"

"You're really passionate about this pretzel."

He chuckled. "I promise, it's worthy of every bit of enthusiasm I'm displaying."

"We'll see."

"Yes, we will," he said. "That spicy cheese sauce is going to blow your mind."

"Yeah, well, if I eat cheese sauce, my mind isn't the

only thing that'll blow." Delanie's eyes widened. "Oh my God. I can't believe I just said that out loud."

"You're lactose intolerant?" he asked. That would explain her mad dash from his truck a few weeks ago.

"Can we not have this conversation?"

"Okay." He trained his eyes forward. For some reason, this made Delanie seem less rigid. "There's nothing wrong with it, you know? Plenty of people have food sensitivities. In fact, I used to be allergic to shrimp. If I ate just one, I'd swell up like a puffer fish." He inflated his cheeks, causing Delanie to laugh. He liked the sound. "As I got older, I built up a tolerance. I still avoid them, though."

"Look at that. We're bonding," she said. Ray wouldn't take it that far. However, this mellower side of Delanie was appealing.

Judging by the number of cars in the lot, Ray was convinced the entire town had chosen today to come to the market. Vine Ridge was known for having one of the best farmers markets in the state. Not only could you get fresh fruit and veggies, but you could get local honey, roasted peanuts and an array of homemade goods, flowers, handcrafts and so much more.

"Here we are," Ray said, pulling into one of the few available spaces. Putting the vehicle in Park, he shifted toward Delanie. "Let's say we meet back here in an hour. Will that give you enough time?"

Delanie's lips parted, then closed. "Oh. Okay."

Noting the uncertain look on her face, he said, "Is that okay?"

"Um, yes. I just thought…" Her words trailed, and she waved her hand through the air. "Never mind. I mean, I just thought we could stroll around together. But I get it."

Ray was sure he would regret asking, but he did anyway. "What do you get?"

"We've already been mistaken for a couple once. You don't want people to talk. Gossip," she said in a whisper. "It doesn't bother me, but these are your people."

Was she serious? After the incident with Mrs. Madeline a few weeks back, she'd looked as if she had wanted to sprint from the diner. And *his people*? Ray released a hearty laugh. "Doesn't bother you, huh?"

Delanie's expression hardened, then softened as if she was forcing herself to be nice to him. What in the heck was going on with her?

"No, it doesn't," she said.

"You nearly bit your tongue in half correcting Mrs. Madeline when she'd made the assumption at the diner."

Her jaw clenched, then released. "I was protecting you," she said, speaking a little less affably than before. "These are—"

"My people," he said, finishing her sentence.

"Exactly."

"You're a part of Vine Ridge now, so that makes them your people, too. You lucked out and landed in one hell of a town, Delanie Atwater. Everything you'll ever want is right here in Vine Ridge, along with anything you'll ever need. All you have to do is ask." Though he had the feeling asking for help wasn't one of her strong suits. And why in the hell was it sounding like he actually wanted her to stay here?

Delanie's expression grew tender and her eyes glossy. For a terrifying moment, he thought she would cry. But she didn't.

"Thank you for saying that," she said. "I like the sound of belonging."

This was the most vulnerable he'd seen her since they'd met. Under those hard layers, he bet a delicate flower existed. This glimpse triggered a feeling he didn't want or welcome. In that moment, he concluded that after today, it was best that he kept his interaction with Delanie to a minimum, because she stirred too much damn longing inside him.

Chapter 6

Standing in line at the farmers market, Delanie felt like a kid who was about to ride a pony, not order a pretzel. While the vendor offered several tasty varieties, she opted for her tried and true—buttery cinnamon sugar with glaze on the side. And though Ray considered trying something new, he stuck with his usual, too.

After what Shayna had shared with Delanie about Ray's mother, she'd vowed to be nothing but kind to him. He was dealing with enough without her attitude. Yes, she could be difficult at times. But what some labeled stubborn, she preferred to call passionate.

"Let's sit for a minute," she said, leading the way to one of several wooden picnic tables.

Instead of sitting across from her, as she'd expected him to do, Ray sat beside her. The heat generated from his close proximity caused a warm sensation to crawl up her spine. While the heat could have been attributed to the August sun, she doubted it.

For the first time since arriving in Vine Ridge, she felt completely at ease. For the first time in months, she wasn't worried about Cordell and whatever new recipe he was cooking up to make her life difficult, and she wasn't worried about whether or not she'd bitten off more than she could chew with the vineyard. For the first time in a long time, she allowed herself to just breathe.

"Next time I'm going to try the garlic cheese one," Ray said, tearing away a piece of the beer-battered pretzel and popping it into his mouth.

"Yeah, right." Ray struck her as a creature of habit, never straying too far beyond the lines. The first bite of the sweet bread earned a gratifying moan from her. "*Mmm*. Oh my God. That's delicious. I should—" She stopped, realizing Ray was staring at her. "What?"

"Don't ever make that sound again," he said with light amusement in his tone.

"*Mmm*. That sound?"

He laughed. "Yeah, that one."

"Why, Ray Cavanaugh? Does it do something to you?"

Obviously, it didn't flow that deep, because his face contorted into a ball. Geesh, she hadn't meant to offend him. When he looked past her, she realized it hadn't been what she'd said that caused the reaction. She followed his stare. "What is it?"

"I thought I saw…" He shook his head, his crinkled features smoothing out. "Nothing." He refocused on her. "Want to try this?"

Ray drew her attention back to him. "Sure. And I guess you're going to want to try some of mine?"

"Of course," he said, reaching for her plate.

In an attempt to keep him from confiscating the pretzel, she reached for it, too. Somehow, Ray ended up holding the tips of her fingers in his hand. Jarred stiff, she didn't pull away, couldn't pull away, even when lightning bolts of sensation exploded up her arm, traveled through her shoulder blades and down her torso, and settled snuggly between her legs.

Finding the tiny amount of strength Ray's touch hadn't zapped away, Delanie inched her hand away without acknowledging what had just occurred. "It's even better with the glaze," she said, pushing the plate toward him, making sure to avoid touching him again.

While ignoring a situation had never worked for her in the past, it would buy her time to figure out what the hell was going on with her. And why Ray was becoming such a fixture in her head and dreams. The answer was obvious, but she refused to acknowledge it. No way was she falling for a man she'd only known a couple of weeks. That kind of thing didn't happen. Especially to her.

On his deck, Ray nursed a mug of steaming hot coffee while staring toward the morning horizon. However, it wasn't the red, orange or yellow streaks that had him lost in thought. It was what lay beyond the forest of his backyard. Or rather, who. *Delanie.*

It had been a little over a week since their trip to the farmers market, and he'd thought about her every single day since. Why in the hell wouldn't she stay out of his head? Since his divorce, he'd avoided this type of nuisance by only enjoying the occasional one-night stand with a nameless willing participant. That had worked for him. What he was experiencing now—this wild attraction to Delanie—not so much.

He slammed his mug down, causing the hot liquid to slosh out and over his fingers and onto the table. "Damn," he said, shaking his hand to cool it off.

"Son?"

Ray glanced up to see his mother. She was getting too good at sneaking up on him. He stood and kissed her on the top of the head. "I didn't hear you coming. You're like a ballerina."

"I'm channeling my youth."

June Cavanaugh had been a dancer for many years. Ray used to love hearing her stories of traveling the world, performing for royalty and dignitaries. When his mother took a seat opposite him, he eased back down into his.

"You seem frustrated," she said. "Does it have anything to do with the Vaughn place? Shayna mentioned it has a new owner. I know how badly you wanted it."

Ray couldn't tell his mother that the source of his torment was the new owner of the Vaughn place, not the property. He could, however, put her mind at ease. She didn't need to exert her energy worrying about him.

"I'm fine, beautiful. Yes, the Vaughn place has a new owner, and I'll be helping the new owner reestablish it as a functioning vineyard."

"That's great, son. Is the new owner someone you'll enjoy working with?"

Yes. And that was part of the problem. Ray had a sneaky suspicion Shayna had told his mother all about Delanie. "I'm hoping for the best. With any project of this magnitude, there's always some pushback." And if history served as an indication, he could expect hurricane-level pushback.

"So, I've been thinking, son. Maybe it's time to explore me moving to an independent-living facility for seniors."

Her words pushed all other thoughts to the back of his mind. "Mom..." It took him a second to find his words. "You're not going to live in some unfamiliar place with a building full of strangers." Why would she even pose something so ridiculous?

June rested a delicate hand atop Ray's. "Tank, your entire life revolves around me. Doctor's appointments. Lab visits. Pharmacy runs. I take up far too much of your time. And now with this new project..." She sighed. "I just don't want you to burn yourself out, son. Like your father. God, I loved that man, but he never knew how to just be."

"Mom, I have upwards of sixty men on this ranch. Sixty men who are all capable of handling anything that arises with the wine production, the horses, the tree crops. Anything. If I never got out of bed, this place would still operate smoothly and efficiently. I set it up this way, so that I could be here for you. The way you've always been there for me. You are *not* going to any facility."

His mother eyed him for a moment before speaking. "What happens when you meet a nice young lady?

You're eventually going to want to settle down and start a family of your own."

Oh, that ship had definitely sailed out to sea and sunk. To appease his worrying mother, he said, "Any woman unable to accept that you are a priority has no chance of securing a position in my life, let alone my heart."

"Son—"

"End of discussion, Mom."

June Cavanaugh's brow shot up, and she displayed the face that had scared Ray straight on many occasions as a youth. But he was a grown man now. The fierce expression only humored him, and reminded him of Delanie, for some odd reason.

"Truce," he declared before his mother's expression translated into words.

Her defiant look softened to something more welcoming. "Only if you promise to *just be* sometimes. You pay the house staff a king's ransom, yet you won't allow them to do anything for me. You have to relinquish some of the control. Accept help."

Ray's shoulders slumped, accepting defeat. "Okay, Mom," he said in an exhausted tone, "I'll let them help. And I'll *just be*."

Whatever that meant.

June stood. "I'll see you inside, son."

Ray nodded. After glancing over his shoulder to make sure his mother had made it in, Ray pulled his cell phone from his pocket and dialed Jessup Ryder.

Jessup owned Ryder's Land Acquisitions in the next town over and had worked to acquire the neighboring vineyard from Old Man Vaughn. While the stubborn grouch never had an interest in selling, maybe his niece would if the price was right. Of course, Ray couldn't approach her with an offer. That was where Jessup came in.

Jessup's deep Southern drawl came over the line. "Ray Cavanaugh. What can I do you for?"

"I have a job for you," Ray said.

"I'm listening."

"You recall the Vaughn place, right?"

"You bet your ass I do. First time in my career I wasn't able to secure a property."

"Well, you may get a second chance," Ray said.

"Go on."

"The place is under new ownership. Old Man Vaughn's niece. I'm not convinced her heart is wholly into running a vineyard."

"Ah. I get it. You'd like me to entice her into selling. Consider it done. I couldn't persuade the old man, but this one should be easy. I have a way with women. Just ask my ex-wife."

Which one? Ray wondered. He had six.

Ray went on to explain to Jessup that his name couldn't be attached to the offer in any way for obvious reasons.

"I'm on it," Jessup said. "I'll need a little time to obtain all the necessary information, then I'll work my magic. Trust me, I'll get her to sell."

Ray was counting on it. Out of sight, out of mind.

After the call ended, Ray leaned forward and rested his elbows on his thighs and lowered his head. Was he going too far? If he had to ask the question, the answer was probably yes.

Chapter 7

Delanie didn't want to sound overly interested in Ray, despite actually being overly interested in him. Was there really anything wrong with being curious about a man who came across as guarded? No. And who better to give her insight on him than one of the few people she was sure had penetrated that hard shell of his. *Shayna*. But she needed to approach the subject gently. The last thing she wanted was to seem too eager to talk about Ray.

"Thank you again for spending your Saturday helping me rummage through all of this mess. I think my long-lost uncle was a hoarder."

"I'm always here to help. I'm free all day and at your disposal. But just know, the first snake I see, Ray and Auntie will be able to hear me scream from here."

Delanie started to ask where in Vine Ridge Ray lived but caught herself. That would seem too eager.

Weeding through what seemed like the hundredth case of mason jars they'd discovered in the barn, she said, "Is Ray always so serious?"

Shayna laughed. "Yes. But only until he warms up to you."

Delanie doubted she would ever see Ray's cozy side. The idea of him warming up to her was downright laughable. "A man as handsome as he is really should smile more often."

"Interested?"

Delanie whipped around to face Shayna so fast she nearly toppled over a box of corks. "Inter— No. God, no." Realizing she hadn't, even to her own ear, sounded convincing, she added, "After my trifling ex, men are far removed from my mind. Besides, I'm probably the last person in this state who would have a chance with your cousin."

An image of Ray filled Delanie's thoughts. The man was like a prize-winning show horse from a royal blood lineage. She gnawed at the corner of her lip when she recalled how good he looked in that damn Stetson.

Another image burned into her head. One of the two of them rolling around in her bed. She'd bet every single dollar she had that Ray was a fantastic lover. The man looked as if he knew his way around the female body.

Delanie jerked when Shayna cleared her throat. "I'm sorry, did you say something?"

Shayna burst into laughter. "Be honest, were you having a naughty fantasy about Ray?"

"No," she said, biting back a smile.

Shayna rested her hands on her hips and gave her the do-you-expect-me-to-believe-that look.

"*Okay, okay.* I find him slightly attractive. Very attractive. Extremely attractive. But so what? I'm sure I'm not the only woman in Vine Ridge who has noticed him."

"No, you're not. However, you are the only woman in Vine Ridge who seems to pique his curiosity."

Delanie's brow arched. "What does that mean?" Had Ray said something to Shayna about her?

Shayna brushed off her words. "Nothing. I'm just running my mouth."

Maybe so, but the look on her face told Delanie there was something to what she'd said. But what? She wanted to delve into Shayna's comment, but considering the way the woman had shut down, she doubted she'd get any more out of her.

Delanie opened her mouth to ask Shayna something generic, but what escaped was, "Why is he still single?"

A half smile, half smirk curled one corner of Shayna's mouth. *Great.* The question definitely suggested that Ray piqued her curiosity, too. He didn't. Or so she told herself. "He seems like a really nice guy and all," she added to thwart any misconceptions brewing in Shayna's head.

"Let's just say you two are victims of the same crime. Vandalized hearts. I won't go into details about his personal business, but I will say you have one thing in common. Trifling ex-spouses."

Ray had been married? Delanie wondered whether it was to someone in Oregon or here in Vine Ridge. Shayna continued, drawing Delanie's attention away from Ray's past.

"There are several women who would love nothing more than to claim the title of Mrs. Cavanaugh, but something tells me their chances have dwindled from small to nonexistent."

Why did Delanie get the feeling Shayna's comment had something to do with her? Ray was not interested in her, and she was not interested in him. It was time to change the subject. "So, do you know anything about utility vehicles? I really would love to get this thing started," Delanie said, kicking one of the tires of the all-terrain vehicle she'd discovered in the barn.

"No, but I know someone who does."

Shayna was definitely the woman to know. "Great. Who?"

Shayna raised a finger, giving Delanie the universal just-a-minute sign, then pressed her cell phone to her ear. Turning her attention back to the several cases of mason jars they'd stacked, Delanie considered the fact that her uncle had been a moonshiner, too.

"Hey, cousin," Shayna said.

Delanie went still. Had Shayna's *someone* been Ray? Of course it was. Turning with urgency, she said, "No, don't—" Shayna flashed that damn finger again, forcing Delanie to swallow her objection.

"So, I'm with *Delanie*."

Why had Shayna said her name like that? All mushy-like. This woman was something else. She certainly wasn't subtle in her attempts.

"There's a utility vehicle she really would like to get running. If you have some free time soon, do you think you can swing by and take a look at it?"

Delanie couldn't explain away the anxiousness she felt waiting for Ray's response.

"Perfect! See you soon."

See you soon. He's coming today? Delanie scrutinized her attire—a pair of leggings and a T-shirt that was a smidge too snug. Luckily, she remembered she wasn't trying to impress Ray. Plus, if she darted into the house to change, it would suggest otherwise. Nope, he would just have to accept seeing her in the dusty outfit. Not that he would care what she wore, because he wasn't interested in her and vice versa.

Shayna ended the call and eyed Delanie. "This sucker will be running in no time."

"I really hate to bother Ray on a Saturday. I'm sure he has other things to do. He's already being such a big help."

"Trust me, if it were a bother, he would have said so."

Truthfully, maybe it wasn't Ray she should have been concerned about. Her body did strange, exhilarating things around him, like react to his scent, warm at his closeness, kick into overdrive when his daunting gaze appraised her. Nope, he wasn't the threat; she was.

To take her mind off her impending arousal doom, she decided to inquire about Shayna's cruise. Delanie had taken a plane, train and automobile, but never a boat. She made a mental note to add it to her bucket list. She would have to live to be two hundred to get through all the things on there already. But what was one more?

"I had the best pastries in France," Shayna swooned. "I gained ten pounds in Italy. Santorini, Greece, was my favorite. Not only was it gorgeous, so were the men."

Delanie had to agree about the men there. She'd attended a destination wedding in Santorini some years back. Narrowing her eyes at Shayna, she said, "Did you really go on that cruise by yourself?"

Shayna laughed. "Yes."

"Mmm-hmm."

"Really, I did. I would liked to have gone with someone, but—" Shayna's expression turned sad "—he's unavailable."

"Married?" Delanie asked.

"A widower. Still clinging to his wife's memory. But I get it. They were high school sweethearts." She shrugged. "Oh well. Guess it isn't meant to be."

Although Shayna had been nonchalant about it, Delanie could tell it affected her, hinting to the fact that Shayna must really like this guy. Delanie didn't press Shayna for the name of her crush. Even if she had told her, Delanie wouldn't have known him since she hadn't met many people in town yet.

"He also has a son, which I'm sure would make things even more difficult. His son would probably hate me because he would think I was trying to take his mother's place."

"Does this guy know you're interested in him?"

Shayna sighed. "Sometimes I think he does, but others… I don't know. He can be just as closed off as Ray. It's no wonder they're such good friends."

So, whoever this mystery man is, he's tight with Ray. Delanie had her first clue. "I'm far from an expert on relationships, but maybe you should—"

Delanie clammed up when Ray popped around the corner. She wasn't sure if it was the fact she hadn't wanted him privy to their conversation that had caused the reaction, or if it was the shock of seeing him in a black T-shirt that hugged him just right, showing off his toned body.

Heat blossomed at her neck and slowly traveled upward, triggering all kinds of inner alarms. At least he wasn't wearing that damn Stetson hat. Instead, he sported a black ball cap pulled low, shadowing his eyes, which made him look all the more daunting. Still, his appearance pressed all of the right buttons.

Her eyes lowered to the dark gray jogger-type pants he wore and all-black tennis shoes. Had they disturbed his workout? Imagining him all wet and glistening with sweat caused her heart to beat a little faster.

"Ladies."

"H-hey, umm…"

"Ray," Shayna said with one of her notorious smirks.

Delanie could feel the fire color her cheeks. If Shayna hadn't been the only friend she had here, she would have reached over and strangled her. She laughed sheepishly. Why was she behaving like a starstruck schoolgirl? It wasn't like this was her first time encountering Ray. Heck, they'd spent almost the entire day together not so long ago. So why was she suddenly struggling? Maybe it was the dream she'd had about him last night. They'd made love in a barn, atop a mound of hay. The encounter had been so lifelike, so fulfilling, she'd been awoken by a powerful orgasm.

Ray wrapped an arm around Shayna's shoulders, pulled her close and jostled her playfully. For a brief second, Delanie pictured herself swaddled in his strong arms, but quickly pushed the intimidating image away and gave her overactive libido a stern warning.

"You better not mess up my hair," Shayna said.

Watching these two reminded her of how Delanie and her brother acted when they were together. Always playful and loving. She missed not having family near.

Shayna glanced down at her watch. "Whoa, look at the time. I'd better get going before I'm late."

Delanie eyed her suspiciously. Get going? Hadn't Shayna told her she was free all day and at her disposal?

"Where are you headed?" Ray asked.

"Huh?" Shayna said.

Ray chuckled, shook his head and moved to the utility vehicle.

Shayna eyed Delanie. "Sorry, doll, I just remembered I needed to run an errand before—" she flipped her wrist to glance at her watch again "—three. It's important." She gave Delanie a sisterly hug, said she'd call her later, tossed a *bye* to Ray and was gone.

Something told Delanie there hadn't really been an errand. Which meant this was a setup. *Sneaky woman.* Joining Ray, who was already bent over scrutinizing the vehicle, she said, "So, do you think there's any hope for it?"

"Well, my mom would say there's always hope."

"And what do you say?"

Ray came to a full stand and stared down at her. "I'll say with any luck, you'll be cruising within the next couple of hours."

"Yay. I've never driven one of these things before. Is it like driving a golf cart? They kinda look similar."

Ray laughed softly. "Yeah, similar. So, do you have a destination in mind when I get this thing running?"

"Yes. I want to check out that huge oak tree in the vineyard. The one with what looks like a fence around it. I've been too lazy to walk there," she said, regretting the words as soon as she'd said them.

"It's a deck," Ray said.

"A deck? That's even better."

"Do you have a thing for trees?"

"Just oak trees." Ray flashed her a quizzical expression. "When I was younger, my mother and I would sit under an old oak tree in our yard for hours, talking, laughing. She'd braid my hair, tease and school me about boys. Some of my fondest memories were made under that tree." Overwhelmed by sadness, Delanie paused a moment, swallowing the painful lump lodged in the back of her throat. "It's hard losing a parent," she said.

"Yeah, it is." Ray pointed over his shoulder. "I need to grab something from my truck. I'll be right back."

When he hurried off, Delanie scolded herself for making the comment about losing a parent. A short time later, Ray reappeared carrying a black-and-yellow nylon bag. When he dropped it to the ground, the contents inside clanked. *Tools*, she told herself.

For the first fifteen minutes or so, Ray paid her little to no mind. However, he occasionally tossed a casual glance in her direction. Perhaps to see if she was still lingering. Yes, she was. Not because she was the least bit interested in what he was doing, but because the flex of his forearms, biceps, shoulders and back muscles each time he yanked or pounded on something held her captive.

"Would you like something to drink? Tea, lemonade, wine. I have an amazing cabernet sauvignon. It's the absolute best."

"Really?" Ray said. "What's the label?"

"Cardinal Oak. My all-time favorite."

Ray paused a moment as if the mention of the name

triggered a memory or something. If so, was it a good or bad one? A second later, he resumed his task.

"Are you familiar with it?" she said.

"I am," was all he offered.

And she left it at that.

Blindly easing down onto one of the old wooden crates she'd come across earlier, Delanie instantly realized she'd made a mistake when the wood made a splintering sound. A shallow breath later, she fell through. *"Yow!"*

Ray dropped the shiny wrench he'd been using and rushed to her.

"I'm okay." When Ray reached for her, she panicked. All she needed was for him to place those large hands on her. Past experience suggested her body couldn't handle full-on contact from him. "I got it. I just need to…" She wiggled, but getting out was a little more difficult than she'd imagined it would be.

"Are you sure you don't need some help?"

"No. I got it."

He shook his head and shrugged. "Okay." He returned to the utility vehicle.

Once she realized she did, in fact, require assistance, she swallowed her I-can-do-all-things-by-myself attitude. "Ray."

"Mmm-hmm," he hummed, never looking in her direction.

Oh, she bet he was loving this. "Actually, I could use a hand, if you don't mind."

He moved back to her in an unhurried manner. "Are you sure? I wouldn't want to impede your progress or anything."

Delanie felt the jab as soon as it had been delivered. She deserved that. Stubbornness—she meant, intense passion—was unfortunately one of her character flaws. "Yes, I'm sure. Will you please help me out of this crate?"

"Absolutely." Ray knelt next to her. "You're lodged in there pretty darn good."

Was he trying to be funny? In a level tone, she said, "Yes, I know this, Ray. Now, if you could please—"

Before she finished her thought, Ray had one arm behind her and the other under her knees. Instinctively, she locked her arms around his neck. His mouth was so close to hers. So very close.

"Are you ready?" he asked.

"Oh, yes." Realizing the sultriness of her voice, she jolted out of the trance his luscious lips held her in. Removing the longing from her tone, she said, "Umm, yes, I'm ready."

In one swift motion, Ray lifted her. Unfortunately, the crate was still attached to her ass, so he had to pump against her several times until it banged to the ground. She prayed the moan she'd hummed had only been in her head. When Ray didn't visibly react, she chose to believe it had been.

"That crate was a little stubborn, huh?" she asked.

When his eyes settled on her mouth, Delanie's heartbeat kicked up several notches. Was he contemplating kissing her? Unfortunately, a blink later, his gaze rose.

"Guess it didn't want to let you go," he said.

For a millisecond, Delanie wondered if they were still talking about the crate.

Chapter 8

Kiss her, fool.

And while he desperately wanted to taste Delanie's tempting mouth, Ray ignored the lustful devil perched on his shoulder urging him to do so, and instead, placed her on her feet. If he held her for one more second, he doubted he'd have the strength to resist devouring her.

Just like the crate, he hadn't wanted to let her go, but knew it was for the best. Business before pleasure. Too bad the statement was becoming less and less of a deterrent. A whole lot of pleasure was all he thought about when he was around Delanie. Plus, she'd felt so damn right in his arms that she almost seemed like an extension of him.

Get yourself together, man.

"Thank you," Delanie said all soft and supple-like.

"I'm sorry if I smell like a barnyard pig. I've been out here working most of the day."

Her gentle words tugged at something inside him. Ignoring the pull, he said, "You don't." And even if she did, he wouldn't have admitted it. Actually, she smelled like a blend of peppermint and lemon. He put some much-needed distance between them before he snatched her back into his arms.

An hour later, the utility vehicle purred to life. While it would need a new battery and tires soon, it was good to go for now. Excitement lit Delanie's face as she celebrated the triumph with applause. Seeing her so elated made laboring over the machine worth it.

"Woo-hoo," she said.

This was the moment he should have said goodbye to her, because just recently he'd vowed to spend less time with her. Instead, he said, "Hop in." It was like he just couldn't stay away.

Delanie stopped mid-clap, visibly stumped by his request.

"You should learn how to properly operate it. It may look like an adult version of one of those battery-powered kiddie cars, but it's not a toy. You could really injure yourself if it's not handled properly."

Had he just given her the speech his dad had given him years ago?

A faint smile curled her lips and she slid in next to him. "You're the type who reads the owner's manual cover to cover, aren't you?"

"What's wrong with that?"

"Nothing."

"Let me guess, you skim a few pages, then label yourself an expert," he said.

"No. *Advanced*, but not expert."

She laughed and so did he.

Okay, this laughing thing was becoming a habit around her. He was fairly certain he didn't like it, and fairly certain he did. That was something else she was causing him to do, talk in doggone riddles.

Delanie's laughter stopped and her lips lifted into a delicate smile. Lord, this woman did too much to him.

"What?" she asked, eyeing him curiously.

"Nothing."

"That expression on your face looked like something to me," she said.

He fixed his mouth to make up some plausible excuse, but decided to give her a little truth to see how she would handle it. "I was just admiring how beautiful your smile is."

"Thank you."

"You're welcome. So, are you ready for your lesson?"

"Yes, Teacher."

For the next several minutes, Ray pointed out the different features and how to use them, showed Delanie how to operate the power cargo box on the back, warned her against the temptation to gun the vehicle, especially on undeveloped ground, and stressed to her the importance of always using the parking brake.

"I learned the parking brake lesson the hard way," he said.

Delanie shifted toward him. "This I gotta hear."

Ray groaned at simply recalling that day. "I failed

to engage the brake and wound up watching my dad's brand-new utility vehicle roll downhill and into the trout pond. I was petrified."

Ray had been sure that when his dad returned home he was going to get a beating. That was what had happened in his prior foster homes when he'd done something wrong. Beaten, sent to bed without dinner, forced to sleep on the floor without bedding or on the back porch with nothing more than a sheet for cover.

His jaw tightened at the memory of the hell he'd gone through growing up in foster care. Because of his inability to conform, he'd been sent to The Cardinal House—a group home for wayward boys. It had been the second best gift he'd ever received. The first had been the Cavanaughs. From the moment he'd entered their small farm home, life had taken on a new meaning and had finally gained value.

"What did your father do?"

Ray chuckled. "Nothing. He simply looked at me and said, 'These things happen, son.' However, something told me he was crying inside."

"He sounds like a very patient man."

"He was. And I miss him every day." Fighting his way through the sadness threatening to consume him, he said, "But anyway…make sure you use the parking brake. And always pay attention to where you're going."

Delanie saluted him. "Aye-aye, captain. Now can we take this puppy for a spin?"

"Let's switch places, so you can get the feel of operating it."

"Since you're already there, how about you drive there, and I drive back," she said.

"Works for me."

On the drive through the vineyard, Delanie closed her eyes and allowed her head to fall back. Ray couldn't help but run his eyes along the column of her neck. He imagined planting tender kisses to her warm, delicate skin, making her squirm and moan underneath him.

His gaze lowered, training on her breasts, threatening to burst out of that snug shirt. They would fit perfectly in his hands. A vision of her crying out in pleasure as he licked, flicked and suckled her taut nipples played in his head.

Something told him none of the sounds she made during foreplay would compare to the ones she would emit when he entered her with slow, steady strokes, savoring every second he spent inside her. The swell in his pants drew his eyes away from her and to his crotch. The dick print along his thigh alarmed him. *Shit.* He adjusted himself before Delanie opened her eyes and witnessed his arousal. How embarrassing would that have been?

Because he was paying more attention to his painful erection than to the path, they hit a dip. Delanie's eyes popped open, and she hooked her arm around his. Uncertainly danced on her face.

"What the heck was that?"

"Sorry," he said. "I hit a dip in the ground."

"Weren't you just stressing the importance of being vigilant when driving this thing?" She flashed a sly grin, then reclaimed her arm.

Ray had assumed Delanie simply wanted to see the tree up close, then return to the house. But when they arrived at the massive oak, she got out and inspected it from all angles, then climbed the three creaky stairs onto the deck and eased down on the built-in seating.

Considering what had happened to her earlier with the crate, he was surprised she wasn't a bit more untrusting of the aged wood. Maybe she was the keep-taking-chances-until-you-get-it-right type. If so, that wouldn't work out well for him. Especially when his acquiring her land hinged on her tucking tail and running.

"Are you just going to sit behind the wheel or join me?" she asked.

The smart thing to do would have been to remain exactly where he was, behind the wheel of the utility vehicle, but common sense tended to evade him when Delanie was involved. Joining her, he took a seat across the deck from her.

Delanie cupped her hands over her mouth and called out, "Hello over there," making it sound as if they were a million miles away from each other. "I don't bite, Ray Cavanaugh. Of course you know that since we rode partially thigh to thigh the entire way here, and I didn't take a chunk out of you."

Ray stretched his long legs out and rested his intertwined fingers in his lap. "How do you know it's you I'm worried about?"

An intrigued expression spread across her face. "Is that your thing? Biting?"

Before he could respond, her phone rang. *Saved by the bell.* But which of them had been in danger, he wondered?

Delanie moved to the utility vehicle where she'd left her phone. Ray couldn't ignore the jiggle of her ass in those stretchy pants she wore. The stir below his waist reminded him of what had happened earlier when he'd lusted over her. Turning away, he allowed himself to appreciate just how breathtaking the vineyard was, even without any vines on the trellises.

When Delanie rejoined him, she took a seat beside him. "I apologize about that."

It was glaringly obvious that the woman who'd walked away a moment ago was not the same woman who returned. Instead of glowing as she had before, her expression looked troubled. He didn't like seeing her this way. "What's wrong?"

She waved his words off. "Nothing. A-OK."

If Ray knew one thing, it was forced happiness. He'd perfected it. "Your ex?"

Delanie tilted her head slightly.

"On the phone," he added. He wasn't sure why he was meddling in her personal business, but he just couldn't help himself.

"That obvious, huh?" She sighed. "He's determined to be *friends*."

"And you? What do you want?"

A beat of silence passed before she said, "Peace." She turned away. "My life the past year has been… hectic. The divorce, the adjustment to single life, the move here. I just want peace."

"Well, you're in the right place for tranquility. Nothing ever happens in Vine Ridge, which is a good thing—great thing, actually."

When she flashed a low-wattage smile, he was tempted to reach over, capture her hand and caress it gently for comfort. It's something his mother would have done. He laughed to himself. Great. He was turning into his parents.

"I'm actually beginning to believe I'm in the right place," she said.

Something intensely sensual played between them. Delanie's lips parted slightly, but not enough to allow words to escape. Maybe a heated breath, which would suggest she definitely felt this burn, too.

As if their connection startled her, she lurched and turned away. "Speaking of being in the right place, are there any car dealerships near here?"

"Several about an hour or so away. Why?"

"I'm thinking about trading my car for something a little less…conspicuous."

So, Ms. California was trying to fit in. It made him smile.

"Maybe I'll get a truck like yours," she said. "Something with character."

"Joleen is an original. There's not another one out there like her."

"Joleen?"

Delanie laughed a sweet sound that made his chest tighten. Seeing her so amused made him chuckle.

She attempted to straighten her face. "I'm sorry. It's just that…"

"It's just that what?" he asked.

"You don't strike me as someone who would name their vehicle. You seem too manly for such a thing."

The way she said *too manly*, all gruff-like, suggested she thought him to be some kind of brute.

She tilted her head to the side and eyed the sky. "I

think I want an SUV. Something small since it's just me. Maybe a hybrid. But I do like Shayna's car."

Ray barked a laugh. "Get out of here. That clown car. I feel like a pretzel every time I ride in that thing."

Delanie bumped him playfully. "You're like eleven feet tall, so I guess you would." She plucked one of the weeds growing up through the deck and tossed it at him. "Giant."

"Ruggedly handsome giant."

"I don't know if I'd go that far."

"Sure you would."

"Okay, maybe I would, but don't let it go to your head."

They shared another fiery exchange, making one thing painfully obvious. Working with this woman—and not kissing her every chance he got—might just be the hardest challenge he'd ever had.

Chapter 9

Delanie had noticed something about Vine Ridge. While the town itself was old—over a hundred years, she'd read—most of the Main Street structures looked brand-new. Entering Downing's Hardware, she felt like she could have easily been in a shop in a larger city. The place had everything one could possibly need.

"Welcome to Downing's," came from an older gentleman sitting on a stool behind the counter, his hands crossed over a rotund belly. He sported a pair of well-worn overalls with a red, white and black long-sleeve plaid shirt underneath. His wiry beard was peppered with gray, but the side strips of hair that remained on his head were jet black. Dye, maybe?

"Hello," Delanie said, finding unusual comfort in the man's deep Southern drawl.

"I'm Lee Earl, owner of this here fine establishment. What can I do you for, pretty lady?"

"A power washer." Delanie figured that after putting it off for a month, she should probably work on the rockers.

"Don't get many requests for power washers. Can order you one, if you like. Mind if I ask what you'll be using it for?"

"I need to clean several rocking chairs."

Lee Earl bellowed with hearty laughter, his large belly jiggling up and down. Delanie bit back a smile. The man reminded her of her grandfather—plump and joyous. The stool he was perched on squeaked, and Delanie was sure it would give way to the pressure and toss the man to the floor. Thankfully, it held.

"You use a power washer, you're liable to blow the paint right off. You might want to consider using a bucket, a rag and a little elbow grease. Unless blowing the paint off is what you're going for. Then still, it would probably be best to use a sander. Those I have."

"I am trying to take the paint off so that I can repaint them. Maybe I'll take your suggestion, though, and use a sander instead."

He pointed toward the back of the store. "Aisle twelve. Buckets and rags on aisle six. Drop cloths on four. You're gonna need two. Sanding gets messy. Oh, and a mask. Aisle eight."

"Thank you."

Delanie browsed aisles, collecting several items she thought she might need—batteries, a hammer, nails, duct tape—then made her way back to the front of the store.

"So, how you liking the old Vaughn place?" He must have witnessed the quizzical expression on Delanie's face, because he said, "Small town, pretty lady. Hear ya quite fond of horns. Not so much of Kemp's omelets." He snickered.

Delanie groaned. "Oh no. Have I been labeled the crazy horn-and-omelet lady? Be honest, I can take it."

He laughed again, and this time Delanie was sure the stool would buckle. It didn't.

"You were until Ray set us all straight. He told us you aren't as bad as you may have seemed when you came barreling into town from *Cal-i-for-nia*." He broke *California* up into all four syllables when he said it.

Delanie's head jerked back. Ray had said something nice about her? Had come to her defense? "Ray... Cavanaugh?" she asked just to make sure.

"Sho'nuff. Coming from Ray, we listened. The Cavanaughs are highly respected around these parts. Lawd, I sho' miss Hank, Ray's father," he clarified. "That man was one of my best friends in the whole world." Lee Earl shook his head as if trying to scatter painful memories.

Delanie was still stuck on the fact that Ray had come to her defense. Maybe he was warming up to her. Well, it sounded good in her head, at least.

"Kinda surprised Ray's helping you with the old Vaughn place. Seeing how—"

Before Lee Earl could finish his thought, the saloon-style doors banged open so forcefully it would have snatched the roar from a lion. Delanie yelped, while Lee Earl rested a hand over his heart. They both eyed the brown-skinned boy who sauntered out like nothing was wrong.

He was young, fourteen, fifteen, if she had to guess, dressed in jeans and a white T-shirt soiled with dirt. He held a strong resemblance to Lee Earl. They had to be related.

"Lawd, Austen, you're going to send me to an early grave. How many times have I told you to be easy with those doors? One day they're gon' fly right off the hinges and knock somebody out cold."

"Sorry, Grandpop."

The lanky young man never broke stride with the handcart he pushed, loaded with merchandise. Lee Earl admired him as if Austen filled him with undeniable pride. With a wide grin on his face, he shook his head, then refocused on her.

"My grandson. He's gon' make something of himself one day. Might even go out to *California* and become a big movie star."

Delanie wanted to tell him that more dreams were lost than found in California, but instead, she smiled. "Anything is possible if the dream is big enough."

"Now, if you really want a power washer, I'll be more than happy to order you one. Could have it here in about two days via the UPS."

Delanie was having the best time just listening to Lee Earl talk. *The* UPS. "No, I think the sander will do."

"Sho'nuff will."

Lee Earl rung up the items. The man definitely wouldn't break any checkout speed records. It was a good thing she was the only shopper in the store. Lee

Earl studied each item, declared, "Good choice," on each, and repeated the price to himself three times before punching it into the register. At this rate, it would be midnight before she got home. She laughed to herself at the idea of it taking him eleven hours to ring her up.

As she was patiently waiting, something he'd said—or had started to say—filtered back into her head. "Mr. Lee Earl, when you said you're surprised Ray's helping me, is it because of his mother being sick?"

Lee Earl's expression grew sad. Placing the triple A batteries down, he shook his head. "June Cavanaugh. Never met a more finer woman in all my days. Heart as huge as the moon. She don't deserve what she's going through."

Seeing the somber expression on his face, Delanie regretted even bringing up Ray's mother. "I'm sorry. I didn't mean to—"

Lee Earl fanned her words off. "You know something, the only reason most of us are still in business is because of that family and their generosity."

Delanie was confused by what Lee Earl had just said. "Generosity?"

"A tornado hit us a little while back. Leveled most of the stores on Main Street. Not many of us carried enough insurance to cover the damage. Ray stepped in. June and Hank sho'nuff raised a fine young man."

Delanie was completely floored by what she'd just heard, but needed to hear more. Like how Ray could afford to help rebuild a town. "How in the world was Ray able to pull off such a task?"

Lee Earl eyed her strangely but a second later,

smiled. "Reckon you ain't been in town long enough to be privy to everyone's business." He chuckled. "I don't like to tell folks' business, so you didn't hear this from me, all right?"

Delanie nodded, eager for him to continue.

"Ray Cavanaugh is the wealthiest man in the county. 'Course, you never would know it. No one around here talks about it, and he's a real humble man. A good man. My son, Austen's father, works at the Cavanaugh ranch."

Cavanaugh ranch? Wealthiest man in the county? Delanie was confused as hell. Her Ray drove a beat-up pickup truck. Definitely not something the wealthiest man in the county would drive. For a moment, she considered there were *two* Ray Cavanaughs in Vine Ridge, but released the ridiculous notion.

"That sure is a gorgeous place, too. That ranch," Lee Earl continued. "'Course, I don't need to tell you that, seeing how you're neighbors and your place is just as nice."

Wait. "Neighbors?" she asked.

Lee Earl tossed her another confused look. "Your properties butt up against one another. Cinnamon Creek separates them, but your vineyard is on one side, his is on the other." He shrugged. "Guess you haven't gotten a chance to do any exploring. Plus, Ray's real private, so I guess that's why he didn't tell you. Anyway…you should get by there if you have the chance. It's a thing to look at."

"Yes, I should." And no better time than the present.

Delanie paid for her items, thanked Lee Earl for all of his assistance and set a destination to the Cavanaugh ranch. The blood boiled hot as lava in her veins. *How dare he play on my sympathies like this. Had me believing he was destitute. All along, he's the wealthiest man in Vine Ridge.* How did he not think she'd find out about this?

Sadness, disappointment, disbelief all filtered through Delanie. How stupid had she been to believe Ray was different from any other man. Men were all liars. This proved it.

Delanie passed her place and continued along the route she'd yet to explore. A deer drank from a creek that looked like if it rose a few more inches, it would swallow the road. One good rain, she thought, and it would be underwater.

She arrived at her destination a short time later. Several of the most gorgeous horses she'd ever seen galloped inside the white fencing that led up the long, paved, tree-lined drive. "Sweet Jesus," she said, eyeing the sprawling property in front of her.

In California, they'd lived in a magnificent home— eight bedrooms, a guest house, pool, tennis court—but all the houses in her neighborhood lacked something. This house had it. Character. If that were even possible.

The white ranch-style home spanned what seemed like a mile in either direction. The pristinely manicured lawn could have easily graced the cover of an exquisite landscapes magazine. Several men walked around the estate, some leading horses, others performing different tasks.

Exiting her vehicle, she stalked to the front door and rang the bell. To her surprise, Ray answered. She hadn't expected that. Neither had she expected the jolt of awareness that rushed through her at the sight of him in a pair of dark denim jeans and a black T-shirt.

Ray didn't appear surprised by her presence. Judging by his darkening gaze and hardened expression, he wasn't overly thrilled to see her. Probably because she'd discovered the truth about him.

"What are you doing here?" he said dryly.

Regrouping, she jabbed a finger at him. "You're a liar, Ray Cavanaugh. You lied to me."

Fine lines crawled across Ray's forehead. "Lied to you? About what?"

"You said you took my job because you needed money. Guess you just happened to forget that you're the wealthiest man in the county."

"How—"

"Or that we're neighbors."

"I—"

"Or that you have your own vineyard, and I assume, produce your own wine, which makes you my competition."

Ray tossed a glance over his shoulder as if to make sure no one was there, then eased out onto the porch, pulling the door closed behind him.

"I didn't lie to you. You took one look at me, my truck, and *assumed* I needed the money."

Replaying things in her head, she grimaced. He was right. But while he hadn't actually told her he was destitute, he hadn't corrected her, either. And that still made him deceitful. "Why did you let me believe it?"

Ray's words were tight when he said, "I didn't let you believe anything. You made that judgment call all on your own. So don't come here—*unannounced*—and go all ballistic on me when you're the reason for your own misconception."

"What about your vineyard and winery? I'm certainly not the reason for you keeping that to yourself. Or maybe I am. What kind of crooked scam are you trying to run on me?" she said.

When the vein pulsed in the center of Ray's forehead, Delanie had a good idea she'd royally pissed him off. His flinty glare hardened, and his nostrils flared. Making a sweeping arm gesture toward her car, he spoke in a deep, pointed tone. "Get back in your vehicle and—"

The door creaked open behind him and Ray clammed up. A thin, petite woman peeped out. His mother, maybe? The two didn't really favor one another, but this had to be June Cavanaugh.

"Son, is everything okay?"

Yep, his mother. While Ray was towering, the woman was barely five feet. Her salt-and-pepper hair was fixed in one thick goddess braid that wrapped from one side of her head to the other. Her features were delicate and kind, but something told Delanie that June Cavanaugh could be stern when she wanted to be.

Delanie noted an instant thaw in Ray when he addressed his mother.

"Mom. I'll be back in in a second," Ray said, his tone far more tender than the one he'd used with Delanie.

Momma Cavanaugh ignored Ray's words and settled a warm gaze on Delanie. "Hello," she said, joining them on the porch.

Switching out of attack mode, Delanie said, "Hello,"

then extended her hand. "I'm Delanie Atwater. It's a pleasure to meet you, Mrs. Cavanaugh."

A wide smile touched Mrs. Cavanaugh's lips. "I know who you are. Call me June, please."

Delanie nodded, but didn't intend to do so. Her mother would roll over in her grave. "I apologize for interrupting your afternoon. I had an urgent matter to discuss with your son." Delanie eyed Ray briefly, then rolled her eyes away.

"You didn't interrupt. Ray and I were just about to watch a movie. Why don't you join us?"

Out of her periphery, Delanie saw Ray's body tense at his mother's request.

"Mom, I'm sure Delanie—Ms. Atwater—has things to do. Isn't that right, Ms. Atwater?"

That hard stare, unyielding expression, commanding stance… Was he attempting to bully her? When his eyes narrowed into a don't-you-dare-accept-my-mother's-invitation stare-slash-scowl, she smirked, then settled her gaze back on Momma Cavanaugh. "Actually, I'm free for the remainder of the afternoon. And I would love to join you."

Delanie eyed Ray just in time to see his jaw muscles flex several times. All signs pointed to him fervently not wanting her there, which made this all the more satisfying.

Momma Cavanaugh threaded her arm through Delanie's and led her inside. The interior of the home was just as immaculate as the outside. High ceilings, large, tastefully decorated rooms. Despite its size, the space felt…homey, warm, filled with love. The feeling was as prominent as the beautiful oil paintings affixed to the walls.

"Mom, may I talk to Ms. Atwater in private for a moment? Business," he added.

Momma Cavanaugh never broke stride. "After the movie, son. I'm sure whatever it is you need to discuss is not too pressing to hold for a couple of hours."

Like any smart man, he didn't challenge his mother, confirming Delanie's first thought… Momma Cavanaugh was not one to be messed with.

Delanie gave Momma Cavanaugh a mental high five for thwarting Ray's plans. She had a strong notion that the conversation he'd wanted to have with her had less to do with business and more to do with him kicking her out of his house. Too bad, because she was staying.

Delanie tossed a glance over her shoulder. Something told her if a drop of water landed on Ray right now, it would evaporate. He'd brought this on himself with his deception. In her opinion, he deserved whatever discomfort he was experiencing. And judging by his heated gaze, anger outweighed unease.

There was something sexy about his displeased expression. A beat later she scolded herself for even noticing. She guessed finding a new vineyard manager would be a must. After today, she doubted Ray would even speak to her, let alone work with her. Not to mention the fact that she didn't want to partner with a liar.

If you lie, you'll steal. It was something her father used to tell her brother every time Bryan got tangled in a web of deceit. Ray couldn't be trusted.

A brief moment of regret and panic filtered into her senses. Maybe she should have declined Momma Cavanaugh's invitation. Why did she always show so much passion when it came to Ray? What was she trying to prove? Whatever it was, it had forced her to shoot her own self in the foot, because now she had to spend the next several hours with the man.

The TV room was far more intimate than the rest of the house. The dim lighting gave the room an air of coziness. There was a jumbo couch with oversize pillows, several recliners and a bar that housed a popcorn and hot dog machine, along with a beverage station. Wow, they were obviously serious about movie time.

They settled on the couch and Momma Cavanaugh pressed Play on the remote.

"I don't remember the name of the movie, but Tank said he heard it's great."

"A Walk in the Clouds," Delanie said, instantly recognizing the opening scene playing on the large screen extending from the ceiling. Her gaze slid to Ray, whose emotionless face gave nothing away.

"Oh no. You've seen it before," Momma Cavanaugh said.

Delanie slid her eyes away from Ray, eyed Momma Cavanaugh and smiled. "Only like a hundred times. It's my favorite movie."

"Really?" Momma Cavanaugh turned toward Ray. "What are the odds?" Facing Delanie again, she said, "Clearly, this moment was meant to be."

Ray scoffed, drawing a look of disapproval from his mother. Delanie bit back a laugh. These two reminded her of her brother and their mother. One look was all it had ever taken for her mother to straighten her brother out.

"Pardon my son, Delanie. He's a skeptic when it comes to destiny."

That didn't surprise her one bit. "If it's meant to be, it'll be," Delanie said automatically. Realizing she'd been staring directly at Ray when she'd said it unnerved her. "Um, it's something my mother used to say."

"Your mother's a smart woman."

"She was," Delanie said, a wave of sadness washing over her. Momma Cavanaugh touched her forearm and gave her a gentle look of understanding.

"Tank, why don't you show Delanie to the bar so that she can fix a plate. I hope you like beef hot dogs."

"I do," Delanie said.

"Good. I'm going to step to the restroom." Momma Cavanaugh addressed Ray. "I trust you will show our guest the usual Cavanaugh hospitality."

Ray's rigid body relaxed as he addressed his mother. "Are you feeling okay?"

Momma Cavanaugh smiled. "As you can see, Delanie, my son loves fussing over me." Facing Ray, she said, "I'm fine. Just have to pee, if that's okay with you?"

This time, Delanie couldn't hold her laughter. Oh, she liked Momma Cavanaugh a lot. She also liked how protective Ray was of her. His love for her was evident. Delanie had always heard you can tell the way a man will treat a woman by the way he treats his mother.

The second Momma Cavanaugh left the room, Ray turned a scathing gaze on Delanie, signaling her to prepare for a fight. On second thought, that was probably what he was expecting, so instead, she decided to kill him with kindness.

"What the hell do you think you're doing?" he said in a muted tone.

"Well, I'm about to fix me a plate, then watch my favorite movie," she said, advancing toward the mahogany-colored bar. "The movie was a great choice, by the way."

Ray blocked her path, causing her body to slam against his. Instinctively, her hands came up in a defensive manner and pressed against his solid chest. The thunderbolt of desire that struck her system caused a puff of air to escape. She needed a moment to catch her breath before she could lift her gaze to meet his.

His eyes weren't so dark now. In fact, they were... accepting. Obviously, some of the electricity she experienced had short-circuited his memory and caused him to forget that just a moment ago he was poised to tear into her.

Delanie had attributed the tingle on her sides to the possible exit site of the bolts, until she realized Ray's large hands rested there. His touch was gentle, and he seemed in no hurry to relinquish his hold on her.

She wasn't sure whether or not he'd intended to peek his tongue out and wet his bottom lip, but he did, and the move sent a warming sensation between her legs. Swallowing hard, she slowly dragged her hands down his chest, then finally allowed them to fall to her sides. The shameless act of copping a feel of him should have mortified her, but it didn't.

Squaring her shoulders and pushing out her chest to mask the fact that he had her knees wobbly, she said, "Could you kindly move out of my path, please. I happen to be starving for your beef." She blinked stupidly several times. "The beef. A hot dog."

The way Ray stared at her—unflinching and hard—she almost thought he would kiss her. Why hadn't the idea of his lips touching hers freaked the hell out of her? Sadly, she was sure she wanted him to cover her mouth with his. This proved it, she was insane. She was craving a man who'd lied to her—well, deceived her, at least.

No, she reasoned. Not insane. Just sexually deprived and starving for affection. She was sure she would have had this reaction to any man. Ray just happened to be the one here at the moment.

As if snapping back to his senses, Ray jerked, then yanked his hands away, brushed past her and left the room. Man, what she wouldn't give for a glass of her favorite cabernet. Scratch that. She needed an entire bottle. Cardinal Oak's smooth taste always soothed her. And she need some serious lulling now.

Delanie stared in the direction Ray had escaped. She wasn't sure what had just happened, but whatever it had been, she knew one thing: the less time she spent alone with Ray, the better. Their connection was far too intense to ignore. Regardless of its potency, ignoring him was exactly what she had to do.

Chapter 10

Inside the kitchen, Ray paced back and forth. He wasn't angry with Delanie. Nope. Not at all. She did what she'd always done—push his buttons. He was furious with his damn self. Why did he keep letting this woman get under his skin, in his head, into his system? And now she had his mother on her side—and Shayna. He didn't stand a chance of ridding himself of Delanie Atwater.

Who in the hell did she think she was showing up unannounced at his home? Maybe that kind of thing flew with her elite friends in California. It didn't work for him. He enjoyed and appreciated his privacy. Why did she think she was entitled to invade it? Especially when she'd done so to accuse him of lying to her. Okay, maybe he had been not so forthcoming with her, but he'd never lied.

Damn that woman. She was already a nuisance, and he hadn't even officially started the job he'd been hired to do. Those supplies had better arrive soon before he changed his mind. A part of him wanted to say to hell with that property, that it wasn't worth the torture of dealing with Delanie. But another part of him whispered that it was—a part he was beginning to hate more than candy corn.

Hell, after today—and her perceived order of events— she probably wanted nothing to do with him anyway. *Good.* Problem solved. She was an intrusion he didn't need. A temptation he didn't want. The often painful reminder that he was all man and still human.

She made him feel things. Things he hadn't felt in years. Things he'd been content not feeling. Their undeniable chemistry clued him in to just how lonely for affection he was.

He stopped moving, rested his palms against the chilly countertop, leaned into them and dipped his head. When her body had butted against his, the intensity of the link had damn near buckled his knees. Staring down into her tender eyes, he'd wanted so badly to smash his mouth to hers that he'd trembled. *Trembled.* That had never happened to him before. *And it had better never happen to me again*, he warned his rebellious body. Not that he had any intentions of ever getting that close to her ever again.

Collecting his thoughts, he rejoined Delanie and his mother. They were both so engrossed in the movie, neither glanced up when he entered the room. His mother had her feet propped on one of the ottomans, while Delanie's were tucked underneath her like she was right at home. Ray grunted to himself. She was awfully cozy in *his* house, on *his* sofa, enjoying herself with *his* mother.

"Come join us, son," his mother said.

As usual, his mother's sweet tone had a pacifying effect. An effortless smile curled his lips when he eyed her, because she looked happier than she had in weeks. Taking her outstretched hand, he eased down next to her.

Sandwiched between him and Delanie, his mother glanced over at Delanie, back at him, then smiled. He ignored what that implied, right along with the satisfied expression on her face. He hated the idea of disappointing his mother, but whatever hopes she had for him and Delanie wouldn't come to fruition.

"Momma Cavanaugh, you're going to need a tissue for this part. It's a tearjerker."

Momma Cavanaugh? What the hell? He sent his mother a pressing look, and she shot him one right back. June Cavanaugh had fallen into Delanie's web. What was it about this woman that immediately pulled everyone in? Shayna, his mother. Him, if he was being absolutely honest.

"Pass me a tissue, son," she said in the most polite voice ever.

"I'll take one, too, please," Delanie said.

Initially, he wanted to toss the box across to her and tell Delanie to get her own damn tissue, but he hadn't been raised to treat women that way. He held the box out for his mother to take one, then pushed it toward Delanie, who confiscated the entire thing.

Several times, he resisted the urge to steal a glimpse of Delanie during the movie: when she laughed at the grandfather and his candy habit, when she gave a mushy moan as they were in the vineyard fanning their arms like butterflies, and especially when she sniffled—which was so many times, he'd lost count.

By the time the flick ended, Delanie and his mother had gone through the entire box of tissues. He'd stared at the screen for almost the full two hours the movie had played, and though his eyes had been glued to the screen, his thoughts had been consumed by Delanie.

"That was one of the best movies I've seen in a very long time. I see why you love it so much, Delanie. Love can influence the most unwavering of hearts," his mother said.

Ray cringed. Why had the statement felt as if it had been directed at him?

June reached for the sky and yawned. "Well, I think I will take me a nap. Delanie, it was such a pleasure meeting you. I do hope to see much more of you."

Ray figured his mother had better get a good look at Delanie now, because it was the last time the woman would be in this house if he had a say. Too bad something told him he didn't.

"It was nice meeting you, as well," Delanie said.

Spare me. Ray stood and walked his mother as far as the hallway.

"Play nice, Tank," she warned before heading toward her bedroom.

"Yes, ma'am." Ray closed his eyes and took a deep breath before returning to the room. He'd expected Delanie to be strapped into her sandals with purse in hand. She wasn't. Which meant she intended to finish what she'd started on his porch. He didn't have the energy or desire to go another round with this woman.

"Can we talk, Ray? Like adults."

Ray shoved his hands into his pants pockets. "Like adults?" He released a humorless laugh. "That's a pretty tall order for you. Are you sure you can handle that? You seem far more comfortable flying off the hinges like a deranged person." Okay, maybe he had just enough reserved energy remaining. But when Delanie lowered her head, as if his words hurt or shamed her, he felt awful.

"You're right. I did judge you. I apologize. I know how it is to be judged and should have never done that to you," she said. A second later, she untucked her legs, slid into her shoes and stood. "Please tell your mother I said thank you again for the hospitality she's shown me. It's hard being in a new place with no family and only one friend."

Damn. It was these tiny glimpses Delanie occasionally flashed of her true self that latched on to Ray like a vise grip, convincing him that under all of those harsher layers she gave way to softness. For the life of him, he couldn't understand why Delanie's words had affected him. But they had. Maybe because he knew firsthand what it was like to feel all alone.

Delanie hadn't been the only one doing the judging. He'd labeled her the second she'd rolled into town. High-maintenance. Mismatched for Vine Ridge. Weak. She'd proved him wrong on all accounts. Turned out, Delanie was probably one of the toughest women he knew. Admittedly, he'd been unfair to her.

"If you have a second, I want to show you something," he said.

Delanie studied him a moment before nodding. "Okay."

They moved in silence out the back of the house

and down the deck stairs, then the bank of stairs on the side of the house that led to his favorite spot on the property. The cellar. His sanctuary.

This was a place of labor, love and passion. Life was perfect inside the confines of this space. Trouble didn't exist. Problems never followed him here. He eyed Delanie. Well, after today, he'd have to alter the latter. But she hadn't followed him; he'd led her here.

Delanie gasped when she walked inside. The reaction brought a smile to his face. The space was awe-inspiring. Dozens of barrels of wine lined the walls. Soft light rained from above. Everything, except the concrete flooring, was made of wood—the walls, the exposed beams overhead, the large bar area where he occasionally entertained, and the large dining area where he often held dinners for his staff.

"Wow! This is…amazing," she said, delicately touching one of the barrels as if handling it too roughly would cause it to crumble.

Ray pointed to one of the retired barrels, now serving as a chair. "Have a seat." Once she'd eased down onto the cushion that had been attached to the top of it, he continued, "Red or white?"

"Red."

A great red was always his first choice, too. He removed one of the black bottles from underneath the bar and placed it down while he retrieved two wine-glasses, making sure the label was visible to Delanie.

"No way," Delanie said, pulling the bottle closer for inspection. "No way." She ran her fingers over the yellow wax seal on the front. "Cardinal Oak…is your brand," she said as more of a statement than a question.

He nodded. "I do recall you saying it was your favorite."

"Which would have been a perfect time for you to tell me you operated a vineyard, bottled your own wine, were my competition," she said.

Ray filled a glass and passed it to her. After pouring himself one, he moved from behind the bar and took a seat alongside her. "I owe you an apology, Delanie," he said. "I should have disclosed the fact that I owned a vineyard and winery. I wasn't trying to run a scam or deceive you. But I get how you could come to that conclusion. I am willing to continue with our arrangement if you are."

Delanie's expression grew somber, and she turned away from him. When she circled the tip of her finger around the rim of her glass, he said, "What is it?"

A beat or two passed before she shifted her body toward him again. "How do I know you won't sabotage my vineyard? I'm your direct competition. Well, not for three years," she said with an eye roll, "but eventually, I will be. That makes me nervous, because you're not going to choose my success over your own."

Ray's eyes slid away and focused on his fingers exploring the stem of his wineglass. "Do you trust me, Delanie?" His gaze met hers. "Not as a person you're getting to know, but as the man you've paid a hell of a lot of money to manage your vineyard?"

"I want to."

"You need to. For this partnership to work—and that's exactly what it is, a partnership because, despite the fact you're paying me, we are working as a team. You need to trust me. I don't do *anything* halfway, Delanie. When I'm in, I'm in. I wouldn't sabotage you. Mainly because

I'm not that type of person. But also because I'm not competition. Or more accurately, you're not competition. You will never produce a wine as fine as mine."

Delanie's head snapped back in what he took to be surprise. Yeah, the confession sounded a bit arrogant, but it was true. Wine making was his passion and for the past several years, vineyards had been his life. He knew how to grow grapes. But not just any grapes. Great grapes. And that was what made for an exceptional vintage.

Delanie barked a laugh. "Ha! Is that a challenge?"

"No. A fact."

"Kinda cocky, wouldn't you say?"

"No. Just confident in my skills and my product."

"Well, if you were to manage my vineyard—taking into account your skills and all—wouldn't my wines taste equally as exquisite as yours?"

"No. Two wines will never taste the same. We're next door, sure, but our grapes can and probably will taste drastically different. The soil and a number of other factors will influence this."

"So, considering your logic, couldn't that mean my wine could possibly taste *better* than yours? Taking into account the soil and those other influencing factors, of course."

Oh, the tenacity of this woman. He shrugged. "I guess anything is possible, Ms. Atwater."

Delanie sighed. "Well, then it's clear. I have no other choice but to allow you to manage my vineyard. I'd be a fool to pass on the services of a man who can produce a wine as fine as Cardinal Oak. But be warned, I'm coming for you, Ray Cavanaugh."

Ray tapped Delanie's glass with his. "Bring it, gorgeous."

Delanie flashed a low-wattage smile and lowered her gaze briefly. Had it been because he'd called her gorgeous? He hadn't taken her as the bashful type.

Over the next several hours, Ray and Delanie talked and laughed like old friends catching up with one another. He would have blamed the wine for his chattiness, but he'd only taken a few sips. He'd shared things like how Portland had been where he'd fallen in love with wine making, while working at his ex-wife's small family vineyard. How he'd taken night classes in enology and viticulture to learn all he could about wine and grapes. How he'd dreamed of one day owning his own winery, and how happy he'd been when it had actually happened. He shared the ups—growing faster than he ever imagined. And the downs—losing most of his first crop to early frost, the second to too much rain, the third to not enough. By the expression on her face, he'd spooked her with all the issues that threatened a vineyard. He could have used this to his advantage. Talked up the less pleasant side of vineyard ownership. Rattled her a bit. Made it more likely that she would sell. Instead, he reassured her that she was in good hands with him. But why?

"So, you were married?" she asked.

Ray laughed to himself. Out of everything he'd told her, this is what she'd chosen to focus on? He nodded, not really keen on the idea of discussing his ex-wife with her or anyone else. "Yes." In an attempt to divert the conversation, he pointed to her almost empty glass.

"I'll get you a refill." He stood, but Delanie's hand blocked his path.

"Another glass and you'll have to carry me out of here."

"In that case—" he eased back down "—no more wine for you."

"Are you insinuating that I'm too heavy to carry?"

Her words were more playful than accusing. Ray tilted his head to the left, then the right, as if appraising her body. "I think I could handle it." In fact, he knew he could. Handle her in ways that would blow her mind.

Delanie pulled her bottom lip between her teeth, and he instantly envied her mouth for getting to taste it. Questions rushed through his head as he stared at her. Ridiculous questions. Like, was she as headstrong inside the bedroom as she was outside? Could she relax enough to even feel the pleasure he was capable of delivering—and yes, he considered himself a top-shelf lover. Would she or could she relinquish control to him?

"We should start over," Delanie said. "A clean slate." Pushing her hand toward him, she said, "Hello, I'm Delanie Claire Atwater. I'm new to Vine Ridge."

Ray eyed her for a moment or two before capturing her hand. It was soft and warm, and fit perfectly inside his. "Nice to meet you, Delanie Claire Atwater. I'm Ray Jude Cavanaugh. Welcome to Vine Ridge. What brings you here?"

"I inherited a vineyard from a long-lost uncle."

The fact that grouchy, grumpy Old Man Vaughn was her uncle explained a lot. Incredulous, stubborn and unwavering were in her bloodline.

Delanie continued, "I have no idea what I'm doing,

but I've obtained the services of an amazing vineyard manager. The best in the business, I keep hearing. We kind of got off on the wrong foot, but I'm confident everything will work out just fine."

"Well, if you ever have questions about anything, don't hesitate to ask. I operate a vineyard and produce my own wines. Maybe you've heard of it. Cardinal Oak."

Delanie scrunched her face and glanced toward the ceiling. "Um, no, I don't believe I have."

They shared a good laugh.

Sobering, Delanie said, "Jude. Your mother's idea? June, Jude."

"Actually, no. It was mine." Ray noticed the confusion on her face. "I didn't have a middle name when my parents adopted me. I wanted one."

Sympathy flashed on her face. "You're adopted."

It was more a statement than question, but he nodded. "Yep."

Her lips parted as if to say more, but was not sure what to say. Most people had a similar reaction when they happened upon his past, so he didn't hold it against her.

Delanie swayed in her seat. "I love this song," she said.

Otis Redding's "These Arms of Mine" poured through the speakers affixed to the walls. "Me, too. It brings back good memories."

"Like what?" Delanie asked.

Damn, she was curious. "My mom and dad used to slow dance in our tiny living room to this song. I miss that."

Delanie stood and held out her hand. "Let's dance."

Ray barked a laugh and playfully pushed her arm away. "I don't dance."

"Sure you do. Everyone dances when they think no one's watching. So, just pretend no one is watching."

He told himself that Delanie wouldn't give up until he gave in, so he released a tortured sound before standing. Truth was, he couldn't pass up the opportunity to hold her in his arms. "I'm not responsible for crushed toes."

"Quit being so dramatic."

Him, dramatic? That was laughable coming from her.

"You can stand closer, Ray. As I told you before, I don't bite."

She wasn't the one he was worried about.

Things were…manageable as they swayed from side to side. It wasn't until Delanie rested her head on his shoulder that they got tricky. Cautiously, he wrapped his arms around her waist, holding her closer to him. The feel of her—warm, soft, relaxed in his arms— set his entire body ablaze. When she spoke, her warm breath tickled his neck.

"See, there's nothing to it." She tilted her chin upward and eyed him. Her tone was tender when she spoke. "You should never miss an opportunity to dance."

It sounded just like something his mother would say. He agreed. At least with not missing opportunities. And with that in mind, he dipped his head and covered her mouth with his. The instant their lips touched, he knew he was in trouble.

Delanie didn't mount a protest. Her soft lips parted

and allowed his tongue full access to explore at will.
And he did, leaving no area of her mouth uncharted.
His hands slowly crawled up her body, coming to rest
on either side of her neck. Deepening the kiss, Delanie moaned into his mouth. That, mixed with his own
ferocious yearning, caused a painful erection.

He wanted her.

Wanted her right then.

Wanted her right there.

Miraculously, his common sense penetrated the fog
of arousal threatening to consume him, reminding him
that Delanie was off-limits. And for good reason. When
he broke their mouths apart, protest danced in her eyes.
Luckily, it didn't travel beyond them and make its way
into words. Maybe she, too, realized how dangerous
this was, had calculated the risks involved.

"You should go, Delanie," he said in a heavy breath.

He prayed she wouldn't object. If her lips touched
his again, there was no way he could muster enough
strength to pull away a second time.

"Okay," she said, barely audible, then hurried from
the room.

Watching her flee was the hardest thing he'd done
in a while. Actually, it wasn't. The hardest thing had
been not tossing her onto the bar and making love to
her. But this was a close second.

The desire to chase after her was akin to fighting
a raging beast determined to break free—exhausting
and painful. He adjusted his wicked erection. Every cell
in his body demanded that he finish what he'd started.
But every ounce of good sense told him letting her go
was for the best.

Chapter 11

Thinking about Ray Cavanaugh was the last thing Delanie wanted to do, but it's exactly what she'd done for the past week and five days—thinking and obsessing. Obsessing over a damn kiss that should have never happened.

How could she have let Ray kiss her like that and done nothing to stop it? How could she have let herself enjoy it so much? She'd been constantly recalling the memory of his mouth against hers since it had happened. Instinctively, she touched her lips. Cordell had never kissed her that way. So thoroughly. So passionately. So completely.

She shook her head to scramble the memory and extinguish the flame igniting in her belly. The same flame that threatened to consume her every time she fantasized about Ray's lips against hers.

"Ugh. Stop it, Delanie! Ray is off-limits. Has to be. I'm his boss. Well, kinda." She fanned her hands through the air. "Doesn't matter. He's off-limits, period." Now, if her body would simply get on board with the notion.

Shifting her attention, she focused on the mound of paperwork scattered across her kitchen table. Unable to sleep, she'd been up since four that morning, electronically submitting this, printing and highlighting that, while trying her damnedest not to think about Ray. It hadn't worked so well for her thus far. Maybe more coffee would help.

She crossed the room and popped another pod into the brewer. As she waited, she lost herself in the events of that evening in Ray's wine cellar. Something had definitely shifted between her and Ray, becoming—dare she say it—undeniable. In his arms, swaying to Otis Redding, he'd felt...comfortable, familiar. Too familiar. Too right. Too good. Too perfect. *Too everything, dammit*. She slammed her hand onto the counter, then shook off the sting.

Leaning a hip against the cabinet, she sighed heavily. She hadn't relocated to Vine Ridge to fall for a man who'd kissed her senseless, then ignored her for nearly two weeks. Unfortunately, that was exactly what was happening. She was falling for Ray. Just a little bit. Still, that little bit was far more than she welcomed.

Wasn't she done with relationships? Hadn't she shunned love? Was this the aftermath of loneliness? Craving a man you knew you shouldn't? Maybe she needed a hobby to keep herself occupied. She could start back doing candles and selling them at the farmers

market. At least until the vineyard was actually producing fruit. Three years? Really? Close to four if she
considered the fact the vines wouldn't be planted until
next spring, several months away.

That seemed like a long time to have to resist Ray.
There had to be a way to ignore their all-consuming
chemistry. *Focus.* That needed to be her ultimate goal,
when she still wasn't 100 percent sure whether or not
she could, or should, trust him.

The *beep, beep, beep* sound of a backing vehicle
snagged her attention. *What...?* Then it dawned on her.
Today was the day Ray and his crew started site preparation for the spring planting. How could she have
forgotten that? Especially since Ray seemed to be the
only thing on her mind lately.

After moving from the kitchen and into the living
room, she peeked out the window to see a large flatbed
truck, with an even larger piece of equipment atop, in
the driveway, along with a dump truck and dozens of
men dressed in T-shirts, jeans and boots.

Ray stood off to the side talking to a gentleman who
held a hard hat tucked under his arm. Ray pointed to
several areas and the man nodded. A short time later,
they shook hands and Ray headed toward the house.

A rush of excitement Delanie couldn't understand
flowed through her. Coming face-to-face with Ray
should have been the last thing she wanted. *That damn
Stetson hat.* Why couldn't he wear a beanie or something far less appealing? A toboggan, maybe. Sadly,
even those generic headpieces would probably look
fantastic on him.

Her eyes studied the hand that ironed up and down

the long-sleeve navy-blue plaid shirt he wore and wished it was her body he was touching. When his long strides stopped, she panicked. Had he seen her spying on him?

Ray cupped his hands around his mouth and called out to someone. A beat later, a tall, handsome brown-skinned man jogged toward him. They spoke a couple of minutes, then both continued toward the house. Ray said something, and the other man bent over in laughter. What had been so hilarious?

Remembering the thin white pajama bottoms she wore, and equally revealing top, she scrambled away from the window and darted upstairs to change. While a pair of jogging pants and a T-shirt would have been more comfortable, she opted for a pair of curve-hugging jeans, a push-up bra and a cozy-fitting T-shirt.

Running her fingers through her hair, she went back downstairs, nearing the door just as the bell rang. She counted to seven, then pulled the door open. Ray's presence hit her like a...she wanted to say semi-truck, but that would have suggested what she'd experienced had been painful. Since it was far from discomfort, she settled on...hit her like a luxurious, feather-filled pillow.

A faint sound rumbled in the chest of the man standing beside Ray, suggesting her choice of attire had been a good one. Though he wasn't the one she'd set out to entice, his response had triggered a reaction in Ray. It was slight, but Delanie saw his jaw clench.

"Ms. Atwater," Ray said.

Ms. Atwater? Guess we're being formal. "Good morning, Mr. Cavanaugh. I hope you're well."

"I am now."

Ray paused, mouth open and face crinkled. Delanie couldn't help but wonder if he'd hinted to the fact that seeing her had made things well. No, she was being ridiculous, again. Something she found herself doing often when it came to Ray Cavanaugh.

Ray straightened his face and cleared his throat. "Just wanted to let you know we're on-site and to introduce you to Walker Downing. He's my lead crewman. If you ever need anything, and I'm not available, Walker can assist you."

Delanie stuck out her hand. "Nice to meet you, Walker."

He shook it firmly. "Same here."

"Downing? Any relation to Mr. Lee Earl at the hardware store?" Delanie recalled him saying his son worked at Ray's ranch.

"My father," Walker said.

Yep, she could see the resemblance. Delanie eyed Ray just in time to see his gaze rise from her and Walker's still joined hands. A hint of displeasure played on his face. Did the sight of another man holding her hand bother him?

Reclaiming her hand, she said, "So, what will you be doing today?"

Ray stared directly in her eyes, but she could tell he was far away. When he didn't respond, Walker stepped in. Once he started talking, Ray snapped out of his trancelike state. What had been going through his mind?

Walker spent the next few minutes telling her about the work that would take place over the next two weeks or so. They would be replacing compromised posts to stabilize the trellis and digging backhoe pits to collect soil samples that would be sent off for analysis. When he started elaborating on the things they would use the results for—plan vine spacing, irrigation and more—her eyes glazed over.

Holding up a hand, she halted him. "I get it. There's a lot to be done. Do whatever you need to do." She eyed Ray. "I trust you. Partner." At least with the work that needed to be done.

The corner of Ray's lip twitched as if he were biting back a smile. Someone called out to Walker and he excused himself, leaving Delanie and Ray there alone.

"A little after seven. You guys get started early, huh?" she said.

"Every ounce of daylight counts."

A brief moment of silence played between them. Ray's phone buzzed inside his pocket, but he didn't answer it. A woman, maybe? Why did she care? She didn't.

Ray pointed over his shoulder. "I better get to it."

"Oh. Hold on one second." She darted into the house, snatched the envelope off the table, then returned to the porch. "I received this." She passed it to Ray, and he removed the letter inside. "It's supposedly from Land and Zoning and says I'm in violation of several codes and ordinances and subject to a ridiculous amount in fines dating back several years."

"Hmm," Ray hummed, his focus still on the pages.

"It looks official, but there's no contact information. Should I be concerned?"

Ray finally glanced up. "No. I'm sure it's some kind

of clerical error. I'll handle it." He returned the letter into its enclosure, then stashed it in his back pocket.

"Thanks for that. If you or your guys need anything, water, a restroom, don't hesitate to ask."

"Thanks, but we should be good."

Ray pointed to the portable toilet. Delanie cringed at the idea of anyone having to use that thing.

Ray turned to leave. In her head, she knew she should have simply let him walk away. But Delanie being Delanie, she had to make things complicated. "The kiss—"

"Was a mistake," he said, turning to face her again. "You hired me to do a job. I crossed the line and jeopardized our working relationship by kissing you. I apologize. It won't happen again."

But what if she wanted it to? What if she wanted him to kiss her senseless again? What if she wanted him to do more than just kiss her? What if she wanted his hands and mouth to explore every inch of her body? What if she wanted him to make her scream his name over and over again? The questions caused unintended arousal, and her nipples tightened in her bra.

Needing to save face, she said, "Good. Because we're associates. We should keep things strictly professional." Her hands sliced horizontally through the air. "What happened between us *cannot* happen again. I wouldn't want it to happen again. And I'm sure you wouldn't want it to happen again, either. Right?" Admittedly, the *right* had sounded a little too desperate.

"Precisely," he said. "It can't happen again. No matter how tempting it is, please, Ms. Atwater, try to keep your lips off of mine."

Delanie sucked in a sharp breath. "My—"

"Gotta go," he said, cutting off her thought, smirking, turning and jogging away.

Delanie folded her arms across her chest, scowled at his back, then laughed. "I can't make any promises, Mr. Cavanaugh," she said, but not loud enough for anyone to hear. Especially Ray.

On his way back to his truck, Ray checked his phone. Jessup. The man undoubtedly had something to do with the letter Delanie had received. Ray knew it was a fake the moment he'd read it. He listened to the message Jessup had left. "Just checking in to let you know the wheels are in motion. I have Scout headed out to the Vaughn place soon to play representative for a very interested party and lay the groundwork for me." Jessup laughed as if something about his words had been funny. "You know he's the best."

Yeah, Ray also knew Scout was a part-time drunk and full-time fool, who talked far too much when he'd been drinking.

"Anyhoo, by this time next week, I'm confident the Vaughn place will be yours."

Why hadn't the man's words excited him? Probably because he recalled the look of worry on Delanie's face when she'd passed him the envelope. *Damn.* What was he doing?

Ray deleted the message. At his truck, he unbuttoned his shirt and tossed it onto the front seat. He'd be much more comfortable in the T-shirt he wore underneath. Especially when the temperature rose and the sun started to beat down on them. When Walker clapped him on the shoulder, he flinched.

Walker laughed. "A little jumpy, aren't we?"

Ray had known Walker for years. He'd been one of the first people he'd clicked with when he'd moved to Vine Ridge as a young'un. While he'd moved away, Walker had stayed, married his high school sweetheart and started a family.

"Man. I see why you're so spellbound. Delanie is several eyefuls. If I wasn't on hiatus, I'd make a play for her. Give you some friendly competition."

Ray laughed a little, ignoring the man's friendly competition remark, because he knew Walker had eyes for only one woman, Shayna. Maybe one day he'd get around to admitting it. Ray wasn't sure if it were Walker's deceased wife or the fact that Shayna was Ray's cousin that kept Walker from pursuing her. In his opinion, the two would make a great couple.

"Spellbound? Ha! You funny, man," Ray said.

Walker leaned to the side and eyed the front porch where Delanie still stood. Ray's gaze followed. Her arms were crossed over her chest, pushing her beautiful breasts even higher. Those skintight jeans she wore were an odd choice for seven in the morning, weren't they? Either way, he was glad he'd gotten the opportunity to experience them. The high had been better than what he'd gotten from the coffee he'd drunk earlier.

Their gazes locked. Even with the distance between them, he could feel that damn draw. The one that made his chest tighten, his heartbeat kick up a notch, his stomach muscles spasm and warning lights go berserk in his head.

"Yep, spellbound," Walker said.

Walker's words drew Ray's trancelike focus away from Delanie. It was the second time in less than thirty minutes she'd held him captive. Once on the porch, again just now. "Whatever. She's just business."

Walker gave a hearty laugh. "Just business, huh?"

"Yes. Just business."

Walker laughed again. "I could possibly believe that had I not witnessed the way the two of you look at each other. All starry-eyed and shit. Hell, just ten minutes ago she had you so mesmerized you couldn't even talk. Which tells me whatever this sorcery is, it's powerful."

That was one thing Ray couldn't deny, the intensity of whatever this was that happened each time he was near Delanie. Walker was right. This felt like some kind of sexy black magic taking hold of him. The only way to break the spell was to distance himself from the caster. Unfortunately, he wasn't sure he could. And that drove him mad.

Chapter 12

Delanie took one look at the image of Cordell on her cell phone screen and tossed it aside. He was the last person she wanted to talk to, especially when she was in such a fantastic mood. She'd be glad when the property they jointly owned in Scottsdale, Arizona, sold so he wouldn't have to contact her with so-called updates. Updates he could easily relay through her attorney.

The chime told her he'd left a message, but she wasn't in any hurry to check it. Her attention slid back to the three outfits spread across her bed, unable to decide what to wear to the Ginger Root, Vine Ridge's watering hole.

What in the heck had she been thinking, letting Shayna talk her into going out? To a bar. In the rain. Well, after a little shy of three months in Vine Ridge, maybe it was time she got out and started meeting people.

With the change of the season, and the temperature dropping at night, she settled on a pair of fitted jeans and a black sweater, then moved to the closet and grabbed the black knee-high boots. Satisfied with the look, she went downstairs. A short time later, Shayna arrived.

The drive to the Ginger Root was a slow one due to the rain falling in sheets. Downpours soothed her, especially at night. "I kissed him," Delanie said before realizing it was coming. At first, she'd been reluctant to share with Shayna something so intimate. But now, for some reason, she needed to get it off her chest. And man, had the confession felt good.

"Kissed who?" Shayna asked.

Eyeing Shayna, Delanie said, "Ray."

Shayna's face lit with excitement. "Shut up! Really?"

"We both agreed it was a mistake and couldn't happen again." Actually, Ray had thought it had been a mistake. For Delanie, something that had felt so right couldn't be wrong.

The elation melted away, and Shayna's face scrunched as if Delanie's words confused her. "Mistake? A blind man can see that you two are attracted to each other. And the chemistry between you two? *Sizzling.*"

"We work together," Delanie said. "Kinda, sorta."

"So, you're just going to ignore the connection? Ignore something that could turn out to be amazing?"

"I'm not even sure I'm ready to date again. And even if I were, Ray seems unavailable. To me, at least.

I just need to focus on my vineyard, not on Ray. I need to ignore him." And their insanely potent chemistry.

Shayna laughed. "I can't wait to see how that works out for you."

When Delanie and Shayna entered the Ginger Root, Delanie was instantly drawn into the rustic establishment. The inside was all cobblestone and aged wood. The earth-tone color scheme made the place warm and welcoming. A live band played on the small stage, and a brown-skinned, heavyset woman sang a beautiful rendition of Dorothy Moore's "Misty Blue." Her voice was so captivating, Delanie stopped dead in her tracks to listen. A second later, she found herself swaying back and forth.

"That's Pearl," Shayna said. "The woman can croon. She used to be a popular singer back in the day. I'm talking Gladys Knight, Aretha Franklin, Patti LaBelle level. Now she owns the Ginger Root. She performs every now and then."

Delanie had grown up with music constantly filling her home. Why had she never heard of Pearl? Had she performed under a stage name? Even so, Delanie doubted she could have forgotten such vocals. "Her voice is amazing," Delanie said.

Once Pearl finished, applause rang out from the thirty or so people in attendance. She performed a graceful bow, thanked everyone for coming out on such a dreadful evening, then sashayed offstage.

"Come on," Shayna said, taking Delanie by the hand and leading her across the room. "I see two familiar faces."

When Delanie realized one of those familiar faces

belonged to Ray, her stomach knotted. But not from how damn good he looked in the black button-down shirt and jeans. It was from the sight of him entertaining some busty woman near the bar.

Was the tightening Delanie felt in the pit of her stomach jealousy? No way. Ray wasn't hers to claim. To envy the woman garnering his attention would have been ridiculous. When the woman tossed her head back in laughter, Delanie had to admit that maybe the scene affected her slightly. But she wouldn't go as far as to label it jealousy. Envy, maybe.

Shayna had stated that Ray wasn't so serious once he warmed up to you. Delanie noted the fact that he appeared pretty chummy with Ms. Laugh-A-Lot. Maybe they'd warmed up to each other a time or two. The thought of the two being intimate bothered Delanie far more than it ever should have. *He's not yours*, she reminded herself.

"Ugh. That heifer is always in his face," Shayna said, cutting through the small crowd blocking their way.

Delanie assumed the heifer Shayna referred to was the woman all over Ray, until she realized Shayna's focus was on someone else. Walker Downing. Was he Shayna's crush?

"Hey, cousin," Shayna said.

Ray turned toward them. "Hey, Sh—"

He stopped abruptly as if Delanie's presence surprised him. The instant their eyes connected, Delanie experienced a ripple of desire that caused her mouth to go dry. Okay, so ignoring him was not a strategy that was going to work for her.

* * *

This explained the sudden surge of heat that had burned through Ray so intensely that sweat lined his forehead. Delanie had entered the building. And he'd thought it had been the cheap beer he'd been nursing while making small talk with Milla. Or was it Missy? It didn't matter, because only one woman had his complete attention now. And he knew her name well.

"Delanie," he said. "Welcome to the Ginger Root."

"Hey," she said, her attention briefly sliding to Milla-Missy.

"I had to practically drag her out of the house," Shayna said. "Bet you're glad you came now, huh? The good singing and all."

When Shayna smirked, Ray had a sneaky suspicion she was hinting at something else.

"How much would you grieve over Shayna if she went missing?" Delanie asked Ray with a hint of amusement in her voice.

Milla-Missy touched Ray's arm, drawing his attention. He'd forgotten the woman was even there. The Delanie Effect, he'd labeled it, had caused every other woman in the room to disappear. Milla-Missy slid a piece of paper into his shirt pocket and then patted it.

"Call me. We can continue our conversation. In private," she said, then ambled off.

"You should probably go after her," Delanie said. "Sounds like you could possibly get lucky tonight."

"Not my type," Ray said.

Delanie scoffed. "Uh-huh."

Ray mused to himself. Was Delanie jealous? Inwardly, the idea made him smile.

"Good evening, ladies," Walker said on approach. "Shayna, would you like to dance?"

"Yes, I would," Shayna said, ambling off with Walker.

Those two, Ray thought. *When are they going to stop playing this game?*

When they were alone, Ray eyed Delanie in silence, contemplating how badly he wanted to kiss her again. So much for absence weaning his desire. He'd better get used to resisting her since it looked like she'd be staying around.

Delanie had declined each offer to sell the property Jessup had made on his behalf, so Ray had told the man to stop trying. Defeated again, Jessup hadn't been too thrilled. But to be honest, Ray was glad she'd held out.

Admittedly, he'd been too unfair to her. It was time he stopped overlooking her strength and tenacity and embrace the fact that she wasn't going anywhere, and he wasn't getting her vineyard. For some strange reason, he was all right with both.

Delanie pointed over her shoulder. "I'm going to grab a table. It was good seeing you."

When she turned to leave, Ray experienced a sense of urgency. "Dance with me," he said, stunning himself.

Delanie faced him again. "I thought you didn't dance."

"Exceptions can be made to any rule."

"Are you sure that's such a good idea?"

"The exception or the dance?"

"Both."

"It's just a dance. But I get it," he said, taking a swig

of his room-temperature beer, then sitting the pungent beverage down.

Delanie folded her arms across her chest and tilted her head to the side slightly. "Get what, exactly?"

"That you can't handle it."

"*It?*"

"Being in my arms."

"Oh. I see," she said. A second later, she grabbed his arm. "Come on," she said, leading him to the dance floor.

The instant her warm body melted against his, he felt lighter. He closed his arms around her, and they swayed to the instrumental of Etta James's "At Last." The song felt so appropriate.

"For the record, Ray Jude Cavanaugh, I'm not that gullible. Your attempt at reverse psychology didn't work."

He loved the way she said his full name, all sexy-like. "So, does that mean you wanted to be in my arms?"

Delanie didn't answer, simply eased her head onto his shoulder. When he tightened his arms around her, he swore he heard her moan. Well, if she was feeling half of what he was experiencing, he understood. He couldn't recall ever feeling so content in his life.

Ray eyed Shayna and Walker across the room and wondered if he and Delanie looked as captivated with each other as those two did.

"You've been avoiding me these past few weeks." She reared back to look at him. "Why?"

"I haven't been avoiding you." Just keeping his distance, because she drew out feelings he wasn't sure he was ready to explore. But the other reason for his absence was the several appointments he'd had to attend with his mother in preparation for her starting dialysis.

"I've only seen you in the vineyard twice. Three times at the most."

Ray arched a brow. "You've been looking for me?"

"No," she said a little too defensively. "I just assumed the vineyard manager would be on-site...managing."

"My guys are professionals, Delanie. They don't need me to hold their hands."

Things went silent between them for a moment, and he could tell Delanie hadn't been satisfied with the answer. "I'll be there more," he said. "If that'll make you happy."

She shrugged a shoulder. "That's not necessary. Like you said, your guys are professionals."

Not wanting to discuss business tonight, he changed the subject. "Why did Shayna have to drag you here?"

"That's a little bit of an exaggeration. It was more like a gentle tug." She laughed softly. "Bars really aren't my thing. However, getting to hear Ms. Pearl sing made venturing out in torrential rain worth it."

"Is that the only thing that made coming here worth it?" he asked.

"What other reason could there be?"

"My amazing dance moves."

Her gorgeous mouth curled into a lazy smile. Ray wanted to taste her mouth so bad he ached. But his desire didn't stop there. He wanted to savor other parts of her, too. Make her scream his name. All the dirty things he wanted to do to her flooded his thoughts and stirred the ferocious hunger she always caused inside him.

"Earth to Ray."

Delanie's delicate voice drew him back to reality. "Did you say something?"

She watched him with suspicious eyes. "What were you daydreaming about?"

The countless ways I want to make you come. Of course, he had sense enough to keep that to himself. Flashing a smile, he shrugged. "Nothing in particular."

By the look on her face, she hadn't believed one single word he'd said.

"What were you saying?" he asked.

"I was asking about Walker," she said.

This garnered all of Ray's attention. "What about him?" He wanted to pretend her inquiry about his good friend didn't bother him, but it did.

"Is he seeing anyone?"

Was she seriously asking him this? "No. You interested?" Instantly, he regretted the bite in his voice. Especially since it made him sound like a jealous suitor. When Delanie stopped moving, he chastised himself for ruining this as-close-to-perfect-as-it-could-get moment.

"You can't just kiss the life out of me one moment, then toss me out on my ass the next. Then get jealous when I ask about another man. And for the record, I wasn't asking out of interest for myself. I was asking for…a friend."

Instead of fleeing his arms, as he'd expected her to do, she started to move again. Well, if she was angry at him, it wasn't enough to force her from his arms. He was grateful for that.

"Look at me, Delanie." When she did, he continued, "I'm sorry for the abrupt way I ended things that night. But it was necessary."

"Because it was a mistake, *right*?"

Ray knew the question had been rhetorical and hinting at what he'd said a while back, so he didn't respond. Staring into her demanding eyes, he was almost compelled to tell her just how wrong she was. Explain that had he not pulled away, he would have poured every ounce of himself into her that night. Confessed that he hadn't been able to stop thinking about her or that damn kiss. Reveal that she affected him in a way no woman ever had.

A clap of thunder and several fingers of lightning interrupted their tender moment. Delanie yelped and pressed herself closer against his chest.

She glanced up at him with much more tender eyes. "Sorry. That startled me." Her gaze diverted from him. "Excuse me for a moment," she said, freed herself and hurried off.

"What…?" Eyeing the direction she'd fled, he saw Shayna urging Delanie in her direction. *Dammit, Shayna.* Several seconds later, they disappeared into the ladies' room. What was that about?

Delanie's absence left Ray feeling empty. How was that even possible? This had to be one of life's mysteries his mother was constantly referencing. He spotted Walker at one of the four-top tables and joined his friend.

"What's up?" Ray said, noting the dazed expression on the man's face.

Walker shook his head. "Nothing much."

Ray didn't believe that for one second, but didn't push. "Okay."

"I think I'm going to ask Shayna out."

"Okay," Ray said again.

"On a date," Walker added.

"I kinda figured that was what you meant."

"Are you okay with that?"

Ray laughed. "I don't think it would matter either way. Shayna's a grown woman. I can't tell her who she can and can't date."

"I know, but she's going to want your blessing. And honestly, I'd like it, too."

Walker sounded as if he were asking for Shayna's hand in marriage. Ray chuckled, then clapped Walker on the shoulder. "Go for it, man. But I have to warn you, if you hurt her..."

"You don't even have to worry about that."

Ray knew he didn't. Walker was a good brother. No doubt he would make Shayna happy.

"So, you and Delanie looked awfully cozy out there on the dance floor. Is that headed somewhere?"

"Trouble," he said. "It's headed straight for trouble."

Chapter 13

Delanie flicked the light switch on and off several times as if doing so would alter the fact she'd lost power over an hour ago. *This damn storm.* She moved back to the sofa and plopped down. Too bad she didn't have any warm arms to snuggle into and fall asleep.

Of course her thoughts went to Ray and how he'd held her on the dance floor the night before at the Ginger Root. She'd felt so protected in his embrace. Her body tingled, recalling how close his mouth had been to hers. "Ugh. Get out of my head, Ray Cavanaugh."

More memories of last night flooded her. How Ray had conveniently cut in when any other man had tried to dance with her. For each intrusion, he'd had an explanation. One was a serial cheater, another a liar, the last a thief. *I'm saving you*, he'd said with a mischievous grin. An even wider smile touched her lips thinking about how he'd escorted them to the car and had offered to follow them to make sure they got home safely during the storm. Such a gentleman.

Deciding she needed a nice, hot shower before calling it a night, she pushed up from the sofa, collected the jar candle and headed for the stairs. The dance of headlights on the ceiling froze her. Who would be visiting her at nine at night?

She crept to the blinds but couldn't see who had pulled into her driveway, thanks to the torrential rain. A car door closed. Several seconds later, heavy footsteps plodded on the front porch. When the doorbell rang, she gasped. Her heart raced as she debated what to do.

"Delanie, it's Ray."

"Ray?" she mumbled to herself, his voice finally penetrating the fog of fear she was lost in. She moved to the door and pulled it open. Under normal light Ray was handsome. By candlelight, the man was majestic. Why did he have to be so damn fine? Tall. Sturdy. Chocolaty.

Knowing he wasn't a serial killer there to slaughter her should have tamed her drumming heart. It didn't. Instead, his presence increased it. The water on his face caused his skin to glisten. The jacket and dark jeans he wore were soaked, along with the boots—mountain, not cowboy.

"What are you doing here?"

"Hello to you, too," he said, flashing a lazy smile.

His smile even looked more brilliant by the flicker of the flame.

Delanie chuckled. "Hey." Then turned serious. "What are you doing here? It's terrible out."

"Are you concerned about my safety?"

"Actually, yes. You're not finished with my work yet. I can't have you drowning on me."

"Oh, that's cold." He shivered. "Almost as chilly as it is standing here soaking wet on your porch."

She stepped aside to allow him entry. He brushed past her, glancing down into her face as he did. Her stomach fluttered. God, she wished her body would stop betraying her every time he was near. *Good grief, you smell so delicious.* A good-smelling man had always been a turn-on for her. *Turn off*, she warned her overactive libido.

"Whoa. Why is it so…seductive in here? Are you expecting company?"

"Ha ha. I'll get you a towel." She went into the downstairs bathroom, grabbed a towel and hurried back to the foyer. "You still haven't said what brought you to my front door on a night like tonight." Not that it mattered. She was just happy that he was there. And so was her yearning body.

"I've been ordered to come and rescue you. Mom thought you might be freaking out alone in this big house without power. She was concerned."

Aww. That was so sweet of Momma Cavanaugh. The dark didn't frighten her. But what lurked in it did. Namely, the sexy beast standing in front of her. "What about you?"

Ray stopped wiping. "What about me, what?"

Delanie folded her arms across her chest. "Were you concerned?"

Ray mimicked her crossed-arm stance. "Actually,

yes. You haven't paid me in full yet. I can't have you scaring yourself to death over here."

She tried unsuccessfully to hold back her laughter. Ray joined in.

When things calmed, Delanie said, "Thank your mother for her concern, but I'm okay. I have a fully charged phone and candles."

Ray's eyes swept the stairs and then the living room. "A lot of candles."

Glass jars lined the stairs, and several jars were scattered through the living room. "Candles are kind of my thing. *Were* my thing. Well, still are, but I haven't made any in a while."

Candle making had been a hobby she'd picked up to pass the time when Cordell was away on a business trip. A way to occupy her.

Ray massaged his jaw. "Huh."

"What does that mean?" Because his *huh*s always meant something.

"Never would have pegged you for a candle maker, that's all."

"Let me guess. You probably thought all I was good at was shopping. Being from California and all."

"Maybe a couple of months ago, yeah. Not now." His eyes narrowed. "I think there's far more to you, Delanie Claire Atwater, than you let show."

In a borrowed Southern accent, she said, "Why, Ray Jude Cavanaugh, I do believe that's the nicest thing you've ever said to me."

"Don't get used to it. I've grown accustomed to our sparring matches."

"Too late. I think I like this gentler side of you.

Makes you seem all cute and cuddly." Like a big ol' sexy teddy bear she'd love to wrap her arms around and squeeze tight. But she kept that part to herself.

"I'm a beast, woman. I don't do cute or cuddly. Now pack a bag."

Delanie's head snapped back and she arched a brow. "Excuse me?"

"I'm in beast mode," Ray said. "Roll with it."

"Okay, *beast*, why would I pack a bag?"

"Because I can't go home without you. My mommy would whup me."

Delanie burst into laughter from the animated expression on Ray's face and the kiddie voice he'd used. She wasn't the only one who'd been unrevealing. Ray had a fun side. Who would have thunk it?

"Aren't we a little too old for sleepovers?"

Something wickedly enticing flashed in Ray's eyes, causing her to gnaw at the corner of her lip. Ray's Adam's apple bobbed as if he'd swallowed, hard.

"Don't do that," he said.

"Do what?"

"Bite at your lip like that."

"Why? Will I cause nerve damage or something?" She laughed, but Ray didn't.

"Because it really makes me want to kiss you. And we've established kissing is off-limits, right?"

Delanie's jaw went slack. Had she heard Ray correctly? Had he just hinted at wanting to kiss her again? Heck, that wasn't a hint. That was a blatant assertion. *Say something, silly. Tell him you vote to revoke the no-kissing rule. Say something—anything—instead of standing here like a wax sculpture.*

"Did I mention we have lights at my house? I have a generator." He tilted his head to the side. "I'll wait for you in the living room, if that's okay."

She nodded, unable to do much else. To hell with lights. How could he be so cool after what he'd just said to her? God, she needed to work on her poker face. No doubt her expression had given away how bewildered she'd been—still was.

After escaping upstairs, she paced back and forth for several minutes. Was she really entertaining leaving with Ray? Going to his house. After what he'd just said. No way. The temptation was too great. She needed to march right back downstairs and tell him she wasn't going anywhere, but thank you for the offer. That's exactly what she would do.

Wait. What if he refused to leave without her? What if he told her he'd stay until the lights came back on? That could be hours. Hours alone with Ray. Nothing but air, mounting lust and opportunity between them.

She shook her head adamantly. *No.* Unashamed to admit it, she was too weak for that kind of lure. All of that sexual pressure… She would crack for sure, and probably beg Ray to screw her right there on the floor. Oh, she was a lady in the streets, but there was a little freak in everyone.

"Are you okay up there?" Ray called out.

"Perfect."

Several more minutes passed as she continued her deliberation. Going to his place might not be such a bad idea, after all. Knowing Momma Cavanaugh was there would tame the horny toad determined to leap on Ray. No way would she ever dream of sleeping with him with his mother under the same roof. Yep, his place it was.

Almost a half hour had passed by the time she headed back downstairs. Ray had taken the liberty of blowing out all the candles except for the one he held.

"This candle smells good," he said.

"Lavender and almond. You can have it, if you like."

"Thank you," he said. "Are you ready?"

"One sec." She moved to the hall closet and retrieved an umbrella. "Now I am."

Ray blew out his candle, then took the small overnight bag from her, reached into his pocket and pulled out a remote. He pressed a button and the engine started. Wow, Joleen had automatic start?

Extinguishing her candle, they headed out. The light from the vehicle illuminated their path. Ray's hand closed over hers, helping to steady the umbrella under the strong wind gusts. Sharing an umbrella should not have felt like foreplay, but it did.

"Whose vehicle is this?" Delanie asked, noticing it wasn't Joleen, but a newer model truck.

"Mine."

"You traded in Joleen?"

"Never. I didn't want to bring her out in this weather, so I drove this one."

"Oh."

Once she was in, Ray jogged around to the driver's side and slid behind the wheel. "Buckle up," he said.

"Yes, sir."

A few seconds later, they were off.

"Damn."

He slammed on the brakes, and she jolted forward, then slammed back against the seat. *"Ow."*

Ray popped the gearshift into Park, unfastened his seat belt and leaned over her. "Are you okay?"

"Yeah. Yeah, I think so. What happened?"

"The road is flooded. It was fine when I first crossed."

She sat forward urgently to see. "Flooded?"

"Yeah. We have to turn around and head back to your place."

"We can't get around it?" Panic laced her words. "You have lights," she said in response to the curious expression on Ray's face.

"I mean, if you're really that determined, we could try to swim across. I'm pretty sure we'd get washed away in the current and drown, though."

"Ha ha. You're just a regular Redd Foxx, aren't you?"

While she'd always liked a good challenge, being water-bound in the house with Ray's tempting ass was cruel and unusual punishment.

Back at Delanie's place, Ray contacted his mother to let her know he was stuck there until morning and to make sure she would be okay. After she'd lectured him on how long she'd taken care of herself without assistance, she told him to enjoy *just being* and ended the call with, *What is meant to be will be.* While he wasn't getting all caught up in the fate rhetoric, he couldn't ignore the fact that that particular stretch of road hadn't flooded in years. *Could—? Nah.* This was not fate, just a fluke.

Ray eyed the stairs, then laughed at how fast Delanie had escaped up them when they'd returned. The rain had given her a chill, she'd claimed, and she wanted to take a hot shower to knock the cold off. *Yeah, right.* She'd fled. Fled from the same craving threatening to consume him. He was sure of it.

His brows furrowed. She sure had been gone a long time. Maybe he should check on her. That would be the gentlemanly thing to do. And he was a gentleman. When he wasn't busy being a beast. He chuckled, recalling Delanie's reaction when he'd made the claim to her.

He hadn't exaggerated. He was a beast. But usually only in the bedroom. He'd chosen *not* to add that part. He'd spooked her enough by the kiss comment.

Ray wasn't sure what had come over him as he'd watched Delanie bite at her lip, but it had prompted him to speak exactly what was on his mind. It had been a brazen move, but it had also been the truth.

Shaking off the tantalizing memory, he stood, then climbed the stairs. He would just peek in on her. Wow, that had sounded really perverted. He'd make sure she hadn't injured herself in the dark. That sounded much better.

Unsure which of the many doors led to Delanie's bedroom, he followed the light radiating from the partially open door. He tapped twice. "Delanie, you okay?" When he didn't get a response, he pushed it open farther.

While the downstairs had looked seductive, this room was pure romance. Several candle jars were strategically placed around the wooden floor, and more on both nightstands. The room was decorated in cream and gold with expensive-looking black furnishings. Its sensual feel suited Delanie to a T.

Realizing she was still in the shower, he turned to leave. Then Delanie moaned his name, stopping him dead in his tracks. He inched closer to the cracked bathroom door and pressed his ear to it.

"*Mmm.* Ray," drifted out. "Yes. Oh God, right there."

To say the idea of Delanie masturbating to the thought of him was arousing was a gross understatement. His dick swelled in his pants and sharp sensations zapped through his entire body. The more she moaned, the greater his need to burst into the room and offer her the real thing.

"Oh God. It feels so… *Ray.*"

Unable to fight it a second more, he pushed the door open and said, "Yes?"

Chapter 14

At the sound of Ray's daunting voice, Delanie screeched, lost her balance and crumbled into the tub, pulling the teal-and-brown embroidered shower curtain down with her. Her elbow caught the edge of the porcelain and shot an agonizing pain up her arm that snatched her breath away. The only saving grace in this moment was the fact the shower curtain covered her exposed body.

When Delanie somewhat recovered from the shock, she opened her eyes to see Ray hovering over her, water pelting the back of his head. More traumatic than the fall, was the fact Ray had heard her moaning his name while masturbating. Was there a word more powerful than *mortified* to express humiliation? If so, she was it.

"You just can't seem to stay on your feet around me," he said with a sexy grin.

"Not the time," she said, adjusting herself to a seated position and holding the curtain in place. "What are you doing creeping around in my bedroom?"

"I came to check on you. You'd been gone for so long that I got worried."

A shadowy smirk played on his face. Yep, he was definitely thinking about what he'd walked in on. Her only option, ignore the elephant in the room. "Well, now that you've discovered that I'm okay, do you mind leaving so that I may finish my shower? Alone, preferably."

"It didn't much sound like you wanted to be alone to me," he said. "Sounded very much like you want me…here."

Being as rebellious as usual, she said, "Yeah, well, maybe you need your ears checked." Inwardly, she groaned. Of all the comebacks that she could have had, that was the first thing to come to mind? *Really, Delanie?*

Ray's eyes lowered to her mouth. "My hearing is excellent. I can hear birds chirping."

It may have been her imagination, but she swore his mouth got closer to hers.

"I can hear horns beeping."

Nope. She wasn't imagining it. She was sure his mouth was nearing her.

"And I sure as hell can hear a woman moaning my name while pleasuring herself."

At a loss for words, instinctively she gnawed at her lip. Without warning and in one swift, fluent move, Ray's hand curled behind her neck and his mouth crushed against hers. Her body tensed, but relaxed a second later, thoroughly enjoying what he was doing to it and her mouth. The delicious kiss numbed the ache in her elbow.

Parting her lips, she gave him full access. He leaned in, causing her to recline until her head rested on the lip of the tub. The shower curtain she'd held to her chin slid down, exposing her right breast. The shock of cold air caused her skin to prickle, which was strange because she was boiling hot.

Before she could put the curtain back in place, Ray bunched it between his fingers and tossed it aside. Her moans apparently motivated him, because he kissed her harder, deeper, wilder. Every inch of her throbbed, craved, begged for his touch.

His free hand went to work again, gliding down her neck, over her collarbone, along her shoulder and resting on her breast. The sensation of his fingertips squeezing made her shiver. Or it could have been the anticipation of where this was headed—hopefully to a place that offered unlimited pleasure and powerful orgasms.

Ray's calloused thumb swiped back and forth over her taut and achy nipple, the friction unbelievably arousing. Obviously deciding he'd spent enough time teasing her breast, his eager hand slid along her rib cage and her stomach and settled between her legs.

Ray circled her clit several times, then slid a finger inside her. Delanie tore her mouth away and sucked in a sharp breath. Instead of searching out her mouth again, he focused his attention on her neck. The combination of his fingers, his tongue and the steady rain of hot water against her skin made her dizzy from sensory overload.

Ray kissed the tender spot beneath her ear, then whispered, "I won't ask if you want me—I can feel that you do." He kissed her lobe. "Instead, I'll ask you how far do you want this to go?"

Just as she garnered enough focus to answer, he applied more pressure to her clit, and his fingers sank deeper inside her. *All the way* danced on the tip of her tongue, but wouldn't take the plunge past her lips. Not because she was having second thoughts, but because the heat, swirl, tingle of an impending orgasm held her vocals hostage.

She clenched Ray's drenched shirt and tugged at the fabric as the quiver in her stomach grew more intense. Then, he stopped.

"No!" she croaked out. "All the way. I want to go all the way." The desperation in her voice should have appalled her. And maybe it would tomorrow. But tonight, this moment, she didn't give a damn about anything, other than what Ray hopefully would do to her.

Ray perched on the edge of the tub, his eyes raking over her naked body. A guttural sound rumbled in his chest. Was that appreciation? She chose to believe it was. He confirmed it a second later.

"Do you know how arousing watching the water roll over your magnificent body is?" he asked.

He reached forward and dragged the finger he'd planted inside her across her bottom lip. Half a second later, he leaned forward and sucked her lip into his mouth.

"Mmm," he hummed. "You taste delicious. But I knew you would."

Before she could respond, he captured her mouth again, doing just as much delightful damage now as he had before. Pulling away urgently, Ray stood, stripped off his shirt and tossed it aside.

A stream of heated air floated over her lips. Ray's chest was a solid mass of ripped muscles, and his arms were crafted to hold someone tight. Tonight, that someone would be her. The thrill sent a jolt between her legs.

Delanie followed the line of black hairs until it disappeared beyond his jeans. Ray unlaced his boots, then kicked out of them. His dark gaze landed on her and pinned her in place. He unbuttoned his jeans, revealing the designer underwear he wore. Hooking his thumbs inside them, he inched them both down his toned frame.

Delanie's eyes rounded at the sight of the most impressive erection she'd ever seen. The length. The girth. The perfect symmetry. Could she handle him? She'd only ever experienced one man, Cordell. Ray was far more well-endowed than he'd been.

When she made a motion to get out of the tub, Ray stopped her.

"Stay there. This is where you started, I want you to finish here. Plus, that water thing…"

Wait. He wanted to… How would they…? "You're kidding, right?"

Ray smirked, removed a condom from his wallet, sheathed himself, then climbed into the tub with her. Well, she had her answer. In one swift motion, he had her turned around and straddled in his lap.

Threading his fingers through her wet locks, he inched her head back and dragged his tongue along the column of her neck. He'd been right about the water thing. The droplets beating against her skin intensified all the pleasurable sensations she was experiencing. But her hair... Well, she just hoped he thought it worth it when he woke up to a lion beside him.

"Lift your hips," Ray said, still exploring her neck with his tongue.

When she did, he probed her opening with the tip of his hardness. Eager to feel all of him inside her, she thrust her hips forward and slid down his shaft. The reward of satisfaction was instant. Her cries filled the room.

"You're greedy," Ray said, pushing her head forward so that their gazes met.

"Hungry," she countered. "And I want to be fed."

Ray attacked her mouth in the most tantalizing manner imaginable. They kissed— Scratch that. They battled. The weapons their tongues. This was the only war they could ever wage and both come out victors.

Delanie's battle cry—a barrage of deep-throated moans and groans—didn't intimidate Ray. It actually seemed to make him more confident. He drew his mouth away, then leaned her back, took one of her aching nipples into his mouth and sucked—hard. The pleasure canceled out the pain.

She closed her eyes and rocked her hips back and forth. She'd just reached a perfect rhythm when Ray wrapped an arm around her waist and somehow maneuvered to a stand with her still connected to him.

"My tongue needs to explore regions of you that it can't get to in the confines of this tub," he said.

After making his way across the waterlogged floor and into the bedroom, Ray placed a hand behind her head and kissed her hard before tossing her onto the bed like a rag doll.

The unexpected move aroused her. Wasting no time, Ray dropped to his knees, spread her legs, gripped her butt cheeks and planted his face in her throbbing core.

"Ray," she cried out.

The heat of his mouth and skill of his tongue brought her to an instant orgasm. Her body bucked and wrenched atop the mattress. She'd finally gotten what she wanted, needed. But now she wanted and needed something else. To feel Ray back inside her.

Using his knee, Ray nudged Delanie's legs farther apart, then effortlessly filled her without having to use his hand for guidance. It was like his dick knew where it belonged. While she'd felt amazing in the tub, this was even better. He delivered long, hard strokes that drew him closer to the edge each time he drove himself into Delanie. And boy was she wet.

With his mouth, he'd made her come pretty hard, but he wanted her to completely shatter when he brought her to another climax. He needed to focus if he were to last long enough to do so. It had been so long. Delanie felt so good.

The sight of her breasts bouncing up and down wreaked havoc on his system. Staring down into her face, witnessing the pleasure he was giving her, ushered him dangerously close to his breaking point. Did she have any idea of the effect she was having on him?

Resting his hands behind her knees, Ray brought Delanie's legs up and together, then pushed them toward her chest. Instantly, he knew he'd made a grave mistake. The new position made her feel even tighter around him. His body shuddered, forcing him to withdraw before he lost control.

Allowing her legs to fall apart, he lowered himself, covering her body with his, and stared into her questioning hazel gaze.

"What's wrong?" she asked.

He pushed a lock of damp hair from her forehead. "It's dangerous mixing business with pleasure. Oftentimes, it's a recipe for disaster. I should have resisted you. But I couldn't."

Delanie laughed softly. "You would have been wasting your energy resisting, Ray. Our chemistry is too potent. This was destined to happen. I knew we would be here the first time we kissed."

She was right. This thing between them was more intense than anything he'd ever experienced. And maybe he'd known it, too, that they would be here.

"Confession," Delanie said. "I've fantasized about being with you more than I care to admit. I just can't seem to keep you out of my head. And I've tried like hell."

Ray arched a brow. "Oh, really? Sooo, what you're telling me—what I'm hearing—is that tonight wasn't your first time alone in the shower with me?"

"If you knew how many times you've made me

come before tonight, your ego wouldn't fit in this room," she said.

"In that case, let's add a few more occurrences to the count."

"Wait, Ray."

Ray reared back and stared into her worried eyes. "What's wrong?"

"If we're doing this—you, me, us—we can't let it get in the way of business. There have to be established boundaries."

Ray kissed the crook of her neck. "Agreed," he said.

"We have to remain professional…" Her words dried up when he kissed the space below her ear.

"Professional," he said. "Always professional."

Delanie moaned as he kissed along her jawline. "So, we're really doing this? You. Me. Us."

Ray pulled back and eyed her again. "I don't think we have much of a choice at this point. So, yeah, we're doing this. You. Me. Us."

Lowering his head, he kissed Delanie, but not in the anxious, raw manner he had before. This time was unhurried and tender. Again, without assistance, he found his way inside her and moved his hips with the same delicate rhythm as the kiss. His mouth caught and swallowed her moans. Her nails scraped along his back but not in a painful way.

Foolishly, he'd gambled on being able to bed Delanie once tonight—just to get her out of his system—then move on. He'd lost big time. The second they'd connected, he'd known there was no going back to the way things used to be. This was no ordinary romp, because this was no ordinary woman.

Delanie's breathing turned to pants and her nails dug into his damp flesh. She was close. So was he. He adjusted her leg, allowing himself to drive deeper. Apparently, he hit the right spot, because Delanie tore her mouth away and screamed his name at the top of her lungs. Two more clumsy strokes and he was a goner, too. He cursed several times in the crook of her neck as the insanely powerful release crippled him temporarily.

Finding the strength to move again, he rolled onto his back, bringing Delanie's soft, warm, quivering body with him. She nestled her head on his shoulder, then kissed the side of his neck.

In a tired tone, she said, "Good night, Ray Jude Cavanaugh. Sweet dreams."

Oh, he had no doubt that he'd have sweeter dreams than he'd ever had. Tightening his arms around her, he kissed her forehead. "Good night, Delanie Claire Atwater. Dream about me."

Yep, he was a goner.

Delanie could tell Ray was restless, because for the past hour, he'd shifted back and forth in the bed. Each time, she'd been on the brink of falling asleep. Her first thought had been that he wasn't used to being in a bed that wasn't his own, but another thought occurred to her.

"You're worried about your mother," she said.

"Yeah." His arms tightened around her. "I'm sorry if I woke you."

"You didn't."

He chuckled. "Liar. You were snoring."

"Was not," she said, swatting him playfully.

"It was cute. You sounded like a low-key grape harvester."

When he made some sputtering sound, she burst into laughter. Calming herself, she said, "If you don't have video, it wasn't me."

Ray chuckled, then went back to rubbing her arm. Delanie lifted her head and eyed him by what was left of the dim candlelight. "It doesn't sound like it's raining too hard now. We can check the road. Maybe the water has receded."

Ray flashed a lazy smile, then lifted his head and pecked her gently on the lips. "We'd better wait until it's light out," he said.

It was three in the morning. Light wouldn't be for another few hours. "Are you sure?"

Ray's smile grew and in one swift move, he had her on her back. Silently, he stared down at her. "I'm sorry," he said.

"Sorry? For what?"

"I should be focused on you, not my mother. I know she's fine. It's just that with her health declining…" His words trailed off. "I'm overprotective."

Delanie cradled his face. "Don't ever apologize for the way you cherish your mother. I think it's endearing."

She'd doted over her own mother the same way, so she understood and would never hold that against him. "Do you want to talk about it? Your mother's health," she said.

Bryan had been her support system when their mother had been diagnosed with heart issues. It had helped to have someone to talk to, instead of keeping everything bottled up. Holding so much inside could be taxing.

Ray rolled off her and sat up in the bed. She followed suit.

"You don't have to," she said, ironing a hand up and down his back. "I just thought—"

"She wants me to be okay with the idea of losing her." He eyed Delanie. "I'm not."

In a tender tone, she said, "No one would be, Ray. Losing a parent is hard. Losing a parent to illness is even harder."

He nodded slowly. "She starts dialysis soon. The doctor says it'll help." He sighed. "I don't know if it will or not, but it has to happen. I guess I'll have to wrap my brain around it. I just don't want her to become a shell of her former self, you know. That woman is everything to me, Delanie. She wanted me when no one else did. Loved me like I was her own flesh and bone."

Ray was as manly a man as she'd ever known, but when he lowered his head and pinched the bridge of his nose, Delanie could see just how helpless he felt. She could feel his pain as potently as if they were physically linked to one another, and her heart ached right along with his.

Delanie didn't know much about dialysis, and by his uncertainty, it appeared Ray didn't, either—or at least, not enough. Reaching over, she retrieved her cell phone from the nightstand.

"What are you doing?" he asked in an exhausted tone.

"Research." Maybe it would help ease his worry if

he knew more about exactly what his mother would be going through. She hoped it would, at least.

An internet search of dialysis yielded several results. Clicking on one of them brought her to a national kidney organization website. Pages and pages of information were available. She spent the next half hour or so reading her findings to Ray.

The website was chock-full of information like what dialysis was—a treatment prescribed when your kidneys could no longer fully perform their job. When it was needed—when about 85 to 90 percent of kidney function had been lost and the patient had a glomerular filtration rate of less than 15 percent. The benefits, the types and how it was performed.

Periodically, he stopped her to ask questions. And she searched until she'd found the answer. He seemed in higher spirits when she mentioned the fact that many patients lived normal lives and often felt much better after starting treatment.

Delanie bookmarked the site for future reference, then replaced her cell phone. Threading her arm through Ray's, she rested her head on his shoulder. "You know you're not in this alone, Mr. Cavanaugh. We're a team, right?"

Ray shifted, placed a finger under her chin, tilted her head back and stared so deep into her eyes, he had to have gotten a glimpse into her soul. What had he seen?

Chapter 15

Delanie hadn't been sure about horseback riding until she climbed onto Rembrandt—Ray's Arabian stallion—behind Ray and wrapped her arms around him. What fear she'd harbored faded instantly. She knew she was in good hands. Ray had a way of always making her feel safe and protected.

"You okay back there?" he asked.

"Yes. Perfect, actually. This is great."

"I'll let you take the reins on the way back," he said.

"Um…no, thank you. I don't think I'm ready for all of that."

Ray turned toward her, leaned back and kissed her cheek. "Come on. You're dating sort of a cowboy. You have to learn how to ride a horse."

"I do know how to ride a horse. A chocolate stallion, in fact. Does that qualify?"

Ray barked a laugh. "Yeah. Yeah, that definitely qualifies. In fact, you could be labeled an expert."

They trotted several miles from the ranch. The scenery along the route was magnificent. Though it was nearing November, the unusually warm October temperature still saw most of the grass springtime green. That, coupled with the rolling hills, reminded her of Ireland, a place she'd always wanted to visit. But until she made it there, this would certainly do.

She rested her head against Ray's back. They'd only been dating a short while, but she was so comfortable with him that it felt like a lifetime. "Do you miss Portland?" she asked.

His body tensed slightly. Maybe because he had an idea where the conversation was headed—his life there. He had to know she'd eventually approach the subject. Tidbits were all he'd ever offered.

"There was nothing left for me there," he said.

He hadn't exactly answered her question. "So, that's a yes?"

He eyed her for a second. "Sometimes. But not for the reason you're thinking."

And how did he know what she was thinking? "What am I thinking?"

Ray chuckled and returned his attention ahead. "If you want to ask me about my ex-wife, Delanie, just do it."

"Okay. Why did you two divorce?"

"I caught her on our kitchen counter with a good friend of ours. Or someone I thought was a good friend."

"Oh my God. The kitchen counter?"

"Yep."

"What did you do?"

"There was nothing to do but leave. So I did and never looked back. I guess I could have smashed his face in, but was a cheating woman really worth going to jail over?"

"No," she said. Neither was a cheating man. But Delanie couldn't guarantee that, had she been placed in that position, she could have simply walked away. In her mind, she wanted to believe she would have kept a level head, but rational wasn't always her strongest quality.

"I'm sorry that happened to you, Ray. I know how it feels to be betrayed by someone you love."

"Yeah, it does suck. But if you ask my mother, God was only preparing me for something better."

It sounded like something Momma Cavanaugh would say. "I like the way your mother thinks," she said.

"My turn," Ray said. "What happened between you and your ex?"

It was a fair question. Plus, she'd opened the door for it. "He had an affair and got his mistress pregnant."

"Damn," Ray said.

"Like you, I left. Honestly, I should have ended my marriage a long, long time ago. Being with Cordell gave me what I thought I wanted."

Cordell had shown her a world she'd never known. Big houses, fancy cars, money. All the things she'd foolishly thought would make her happy.

"And what was that?" Ray asked.

"Money, status, privilege." Delanie experienced a

brief ping of embarrassment by revealing how shallow she'd once been.

"Mmm. Those things tend to come at a pretty high price."

Delanie recalled all the nights she'd spent alone, holidays and special occasions she celebrated without Cordell, the laughter behind her back by so-called friends who knew what was going on but didn't respect her enough to tell her. "Yeah, they do," she said.

"And now?"

"And now?" she echoed absently.

"You said being with him gave you what you *thought* you wanted. Sounds to me like you know exactly what you want now. So tell me. What does Delanie Claire Atwater really want?"

What did she want? It didn't take much thought. "I want simple instead of extravagant. Genuine over forced. I want lazy days cuddled on the sofa, watching movies, eating popcorn and hot dogs."

Ray chuckled. "Okay. What else?"

"I want to browse the farmers market while eating warm pretzels. I want to dance in wine cellars. I want to make love in bathtubs, go horseback riding. I want to kiss and be kissed as if each time will be the last. And I want you, Ray Jude Cavanaugh."

"I'll give you all of those things, Delanie Claire Atwater, and more. I just need to know that you're ready for it."

Despite Ray not being able to see it, she nodded her head. Overwhelmed by unexplainable emotion, she felt a tear trickle down her cheek. When she sniffled,

Ray halted Rembrandt, slid off the horse, then reached up for her.

Vine Ridge and this man were definitely having an effect on her. And she loved it. Even if it scared the hell out of her.

Ray swiped his thumbs across Delanie's cheeks, then cradled her face between his hands. Like most men, he hated to see a woman cry—especially when it was his woman. "Why are you crying?" he asked.

Delanie shrugged. "I don't know." She laughed. "But it's nothing bad."

Ray wrapped her in his arms. "*Whew.* I thought I'd spooked you."

"I don't scare that easily," she said, flashing a confident expression.

"That's a good thing."

Delanie smirked. "And why is that?"

Ray had a good feeling she knew exactly why it was, but he entertained her anyway. He shrugged. "Because I kinda like having you around."

"Huh. Interesting you would say that."

"And why?"

"Because I kinda like being around."

Ray flashed a lazy smile, pecked her gently, then gave her a bear hug. Delanie squealed with laughter, spooking Rembrandt. The horse eyed them as if he didn't know whether to gallop away or return to nibbling grass. He opted for the latter, dismissing their shenanigans.

A vehicle Ray didn't recognize—which was rare—cruised by. He locked eyes with the light-skinned, gray-eyed man behind the wheel. Ray tilted his head in a friendly gesture. Unsmiling, the man mimicked his move.

The man was familiar, but for the life of him, Ray couldn't recall where he'd seen him before. But he knew he had.

Delanie reared back and eyed him. "Thanksgiving," she said.

Dismissing the shiny black Chrysler, he refocused on her. "What about it?"

Her expression turned tender. "It'll be our first holiday together. You do celebrate Thanksgiving, right?"

He chuckled at her please-tell-me-you-do expression. "Yes. But not in the traditional manner." When she arched a brow, he laughed. "Come on. I'll show you."

After returning to the ranch to trade Rembrandt for Joleen, Ray and Delanie headed downtown. Delanie sat nestled against him, her body slightly turned and her gaze out the window. He wondered what innocent or sinful things ran through her mind when she stared off the way she did at times. He draped his free arm around her.

"You comfortable?"

"Oh yeah," she said.

He placed a kiss on the top of her head, then set his gaze ahead. When a vehicle similar to the one he'd seen earlier passed them, he thought about the mystery man. *Where have I seen him before?* He wasn't sure why the fact he couldn't remember bothered him so much, but it did. Usually when something bothered him this much, it never turned out good.

Maybe it was the weasely look in his eyes that screamed up-to-no-damn-good. Instinctively, he wrangled Delanie even closer to him. Was he being paranoid about the man? That certainly was a possibility. However, he didn't think so.

A short time later, they arrived at the Vine Ridge Community Center. The large metal structure served as a meeting and event space, plus housed the town's food pantry. No one in Vine Ridge went hungry.

When they entered the spacious room designated for the food storage, sisters Annie and Fannie Rogers glanced up from the shelves they were organizing. They both stopped what they'd been doing and hurried toward them, wide smiles lighting their faces.

"Hey, Aunt Fannie, Aunt Annie." While they weren't actually any kin to either of his parents, Ray had called them Aunt for as long as he could remember. He hugged each woman, then turned to Delanie. "I'd like you both to meet Delanie Atwater. My beautiful lady."

"No introductions needed. We've heard all about this pretty little thing," Annie said. "Go 'head and beam, honey. I know I would if some handsome man laid claim to me."

Delanie's wide grin grew. "Nice to meet both of you," she said, offering her hand. She yelped when the sisters pulled her into a group hug.

"We hug in Vine Ridge, sugah," Fannie said.

A beat later, they held her at arm's length and scrutinized her from head to toe, turned their gazes on Ray, then brought them back to Delanie.

"June was right," Annie said.

"Yes, she was," Fannie agreed.

"About what?" Delanie asked cautiously.

"Everything," both women said in unison, then cracked up.

Delanie flashed Ray a troubled expression when Fannie and Annie moved away. He draped his arm around her, pulled her close and kissed the side of her head. He didn't know what his mother had said but knew with certainty it was nothing bad, because June Cavanaugh had loved Delanie since the first time she'd met her.

"Don't worry. Whatever my mother said washed you in the brightest light," he whispered.

"How do you know?"

"Because if it hadn't, Aunt Annie would have reached into her bra, pulled out the blade she keeps there and cut you. They don't call her Blade-Toting Annie for nothing."

"What?"

A look of terror spread across Delanie's face that nearly made him burst with amusement. "I'm just kidding…about her cutting you, that is. I would have never allowed that to happen." He kissed her forehead and moved toward Fannie and Annie, pulling her with him.

"Tank, sugah, let June know everything's a go for Thanksgiving," Fannie said, then eyed Delanie. "Will you be serving with us this year? We would love to have you."

"Serving? I don't…"

Delanie eyed him for an explanation. "We serve Thanksgiving dinner here every year. It's like one huge family affair."

"I'd love to be a part," Delanie said.

"Welcome aboard," Fannie said.

"Thank you. But I should warn you, I'm not a great cook."

Annie chuckled. "Honey, no one has cooked for the past several years. Thanks to your handsome beau, all the food is catered in."

"And he keeps the shelves stocked in the place," Fannie said. "Just a blessing, I tell you."

Delanie gave him a look of admiration. "Really?"

"You're a lucky woman," Annie said. "They don't make many men like Tank anymore."

"Stop it, ladies. You're going to swell my head."

The room filled with laughter.

After a quick tour of the building, Ray and Delanie headed out to have dinner with his mother. On the walk to the vehicle, Delanie stopped and glanced up at him. The tenderness he saw in her eyes made him smile. Man, she had a way of soothing him with just a look.

"You are an amazing man, Ray Cavanaugh. All that you do for this town. Just amazing."

The town had done so much for him. "My parents taught me to be a blessing when I can. Fortunately, I can be."

"So can I. I want to help."

"You are helping."

"I mean financially," she said. "I want to help you pay for the catering. That has to be a hefty bill."

"You don't have to do that."

"I want to do it."

Ray knew it was pointless to argue. "Okay. If that'll make you happy."

"You make me happy," she said, then kissed his cheek.

They started moving again.

"What was that about you not being able to cook?" he said.

Delanie burst into laughter. "I didn't say I couldn't cook. I said I'm not a great cook. But don't worry. If you get hungry, I'll buy you a pretzel."

Pretzel. That's where he'd seen the mystery man before. At the farmers market the first time he and Delanie had gone there together. At the picnic table, Ray had spotted the man in the distance and had sworn he'd been taking pictures of them. He'd brushed it off, because at the time, it didn't make sense. Truthfully, it didn't make sense now, either.

Was the man following them? If so, why?

Chapter 16

Delanie couldn't think of a better way to spend a Saturday than hanging with Shayna and Momma Cavanaugh. Actually, she could, but since Ray had driven to the neighboring town that morning to meet with a client, making love to him was not an option. Though tonight she planned to make up for lost time.

"Let me get us more cake," Momma Cavanaugh said, standing.

"I got it," Delanie said.

Momma Cavanaugh placed a delicate hand on Delanie's shoulder. "My dear sweet Delanie, don't you dare turn into my son." She rolled her eyes heavenward. "That man treats me like I'm a porcelain doll poised to break if I even breathe too hard."

Delanie and Shayna both laughed.

"He got it honestly, Auntie," Shayna said. "You

know Uncle Hank always showed the world that his Junie Bee was his priceless jewel."

Momma Cavanaugh smiled so wide Delanie thought the corners of her mouth would crack. She looked as though she were remembering the man she'd loved for so long.

"God, I miss that man," she said.

"What do you miss most about him?" Delanie asked, seeing an opportunity to learn more about Ray through the people who'd raised him.

Momma Cavanaugh eased back down into the chair. "Everything. The way he brought me flowers for no reason. The way he would whisk me off to a movie and dinner. The way we danced together in our tiny living room. He made our small home feel like a mansion." Momma Cavanaugh paused a moment, her expression turning sad. "I miss everything about him, including the sex. Especially the sex."

Delanie's eyes expanded to the size of golf balls. Shayna nearly choked on the sip of tea she'd taken.

Coughing ferociously, Shayna held her hands above her head. "Auntie," she sputtered out.

"What? We're all grown women at this table."

Delanie and Shayna exchanged stunned glances when Momma Cavanaugh stood again and moved across the room to slice up more of the homemade lemon-lime pound cake. It was so good, Delanie swore she could eat the entire thing by herself.

"There's a place a man can take you sexually that will transcend your mind, body and soul. But not just any man will accomplish this. There has to be that bond. It's more than physical. I had that with my Hank."

Momma Cavanaugh rejoined them at the table with a fresh tray of cake. *One more piece couldn't hurt*, Delanie told herself. She needed to work on the sweet tooth she'd recently acquired. That, or start working out more. Start working out, period, she corrected herself.

"The first time Hank and I made love, I swear I nearly blacked out. Don't get me wrong, I'd had plenty of orgasms before him, but nothing like when I was with him. I'd never experienced anything so intense. In that moment, I knew I'd spend forever with him."

"Aww," Delanie and Shayna said in unison.

Delanie couldn't believe she was listening to Ray's mother talk about orgasms. She briefly recalled the first time she and Ray made love. While the things Ray had done to her body had been amazing, she hadn't experienced what Momma Cavanaugh described. But it made sense. She and Ray weren't in love.

Momma Cavanaugh continued, "Hank once told me that every time we connected, he could feel me flowing through his veins, that I was in his DNA. He always knew just what to say."

Shayna reached over and squeezed Momma Cavanaugh's hand. "Anyone who'd ever seen you two together knew you were soul mates, Auntie. What the two of you shared was magical. I want that one day."

Delanie wished she'd been around to witness such prominent love. Like Shayna, she hoped to find that one day, too. An image of Ray played in her head. Maybe she already had.

"Was Mr. Cavanaugh your first love?" Delanie asked.

"Lord, no. When I was young, I fell in love like

leaves fall in autumn. But he was my last, and that's what counts. Hank showed me that all those other times I'd foolishly claimed to be in love were just preparing me for him."

Delanie contemplated Momma Cavanaugh's words.

"Ladies, talking about the love of my life has given me a burst of energy. I feel like painting the town pink. I'm not sure I still have what it takes to paint it red."

Delanie tossed an urgent glance at Shayna, who tossed one right back. Before leaving, Ray had given strict instructions to not allow his mother to overexert herself. Painting the town any color could be considered just that.

"By the look of alarm on both your faces, I'm assuming Tank ordered you two to keep me captive."

Neither Delanie nor Shayna confirmed or denied her allegation.

"I'll take your silence as a yes. Might I remind you two beautiful ladies that I am a grown woman. And while my lovely son thinks he runs things, he doesn't." She clapped her hands together. "Sooo, grab your purses and let's get out of here." She stood and headed out of the room. *"Chop, chop."*

"Yes, ma'am," Delanie and Shayna said in unison and trailed her from the kitchen like two dutiful children.

Watching Momma Cavanaugh sashay along Main Street, greeting passersby and visiting every shop there, Delanie would have sworn the woman was healthy as a horse. Obviously, dialysis was working. Like the article had said, some people felt much better after starting.

After a ridiculous shopping spree, they enjoyed a

late lunch at the diner. As soon as the three of them entered the establishment, they were bombarded by folks happy to see Momma Cavanaugh out and about.

They ended the girls' day out by enjoying hot chocolate and apple spice cake at the bakery. Delanie searched her purse for her cell phone to snap a picture of them. When she didn't find it there, she checked her coat pockets, then her pants pockets, despite already knowing it wasn't in either place. *Shoot.* She must have left it sitting on the table back at the ranch. Clearly, she'd been having so much fun that she'd pushed her cell phone out of her mind. She needed to do that more often.

"Shayna, I left my phone. Do you have yours? I want to snap a picture of us."

Shayna fished hers out of her purse. "Uh-oh."

"What's wrong?" Momma Cavanaugh asked.

"Apparently my phone's been on silent all this time. I have eight missed calls from Ray."

Momma Cavanaugh chuckled. "Lord, I know my boy has probably filed a missing person's report by now."

Instead of calling him, Shayna sent Ray a text that they would be there soon.

The sun was just starting to set when they returned to the ranch. Ray exited the house and headed toward them. The sight of him in the cashmere sweater and slacks sent a warm sensation through Delanie. Life was finally dealing her a winning hand.

Ray wanted to be pissed by the fact Delanie and Shayna had done the very opposite of what he'd asked them to do—make sure his mother didn't overdo it. According to the house staff, they'd left around eleven that morning. It was now going on six in the evening.

But he couldn't be angry. The look of happiness on his mother's face swelled his heart. She always donned the biggest smiles after spending time with those two at the ranch several times a week. And while they'd gone off premises—something they hadn't done before—he knew his mother was in good hands. The Vine Ridge Three, he'd affectionately named them.

Despite his fears, dialysis had been good for his mother. The first couple of weeks had been rough, but once her body had adjusted, she'd become like a new woman. And her medical reports had been impressive. Life was good.

"Ladies," he said. "How much damage did you do?"

"Plenty," his mother said. "You missed out, son. We had one heck of a good time."

He folded his arms across his chest. "It must have been. I haven't been able to get any of you on your cell phones."

"You know I don't tote that contraption," his mother said.

"I didn't realize mine was on silent," Shayna said, removing several bags from the back seat of Delanie's SUV.

Ray neared Delanie and wrapped her in his arms, pecking her gently on the lips. His body reacted instantly to the feel of her. "And you, sweet lady?"

"I think I left mine here," she said.

"Yes, you did." He fished her phone from his pocket. In a low tone, he said, "Your ex called. Several times, actually. I shut it off. The constant ringing was driving me insane." But that wasn't what had really driven him nuts. It was the fact that her ex just couldn't let her go.

Before Delanie could respond, his mother called out to him. "Tank, can you please grab the bags. I'm going inside. It's freezing out here."

"I am right behind you, Auntie," Shayna said.

"You, too, Delanie. You're going to catch your death out here," his mother said.

"I'll be in shortly," Delanie said, her eyes never leaving Ray's.

Ray popped Delanie on the butt. "Go ahead inside, baby. Mom's right. It's freezing out here." He pointed to her phone. "You should probably return his calls. It could be good news about the house," he said, dipping inside to gather the rest of the bags.

"Well, let's just find out together," she said, dialing Cordell and placing the call on speakerphone.

The phone rang several times before there was an answer. "Dammit, Delanie, I've called you a hundred times. Why haven't you been answering your phone?"

Ray didn't like the way Cordell spoke to Delanie, but he kept his cool.

"What's so urgent, Cordell?"

"You're in danger," Cordell said.

The stranger in the Chrysler popped into Ray's head. Had the man been sent to harm Delanie? Had her bastard of an ex-husband placed her in harm's way? Loan sharks? The Mob? A hundred scenarios raced through Ray's head. His stomach knotted at the idea of anything happening to Delanie.

"What are you talking about, Cordell? Danger from what?"

"Not what," Cordell said, "who."

Now Delanie was yelling into the phone. "Quit talking in riddles, Cordell, and tell me what the hell is going on."

When Delanie's hand trembled, Ray took it into his.

"You've fallen prey to a con man by the name of Ray Cavanaugh."

Ray's head jerked back in shock. Him, a con man? What kind of lies was this fool spewing?

"What are you talking about, Cordell? And how do you know about Ray?" she asked. Her face contorted in disapproval. "Are you having me watched, Cordell?"

"It was for your own good, D. You should thank me," Cordell said.

Delanie shook her head. "How much lower can you stoop, Cordell?"

The idea of this weasel having Delanie followed made the blood boil in Ray's veins. Breaking his silence, he said, "Look, man, you need to let go. She's moved on. It's over. Why can't you get that through your head? What the hell is wrong with you?"

"Is that bastard there with you now?" Cordell said, his tone hard and cold. "Ask him about his interest in your vineyard. He's tried on several occasions to acquire it. Ask him about Jessup Ryder and a man they call Scout, who's quite the chatterbox when he's had a little too much liquor. They both work for him."

Apparently, Delanie noticed the confusion on his face and attributed it to guilt, because she took a step back.

"What's he talking about, Ray?" she asked, her tone cautious.

"He's playing you, Delanie," Cordell said, his tone caressing. "He's only using you to get to your vineyard. You can't trust him. He's—"

Delanie disconnected the call, then stared at Ray as if she had no clue how to respond.

"Delanie—" When she held up her hand, he stopped on cue.

"Is it true? Do you want my property?"

Acquiring her property had been his original goal. Not anymore. The only thing he wanted now, the only thing that mattered to him now, was her. "It's not how—"

"Is it true, Ray? A simple yes or no."

Her weary eyes pierced his soul and an overwhelming sense of doom loomed inside him. The hurt present on her face crushed him. What bothered him even more was the fact that he'd caused it. "It's not that simple, Delanie."

"And the letter? The one supposedly from Land and Zoning. Was that you?"

He wanted to say no, that it was all Jessup. Truthfully, he was just as responsible, so he didn't answer.

A single sob escaped from her and a tear slid down her cheek. A trembling hand covered her mouth. Seconds later, she shook her head and walked away from him.

"Delanie, please. Just let me explain."

She stopped and turned to face him. "How can I trust you, Ray? After this. How?"

Knowing he wouldn't get through to her right now, he didn't protest when she slid behind the wheel, slammed the door, cranked the engine and sped away.

Chapter 17

Ray stood at the French doors leading onto the deck and eyed the tree line for only a moment. Enough time to make him feel like shit all over again. Releasing a heavy sigh, he turned away. He jolted when he saw his mother standing there. "Jesus, Mom. You scared me. I need to get you a bell."

"Do I look like a cow to you, son?"

"If you were a little heavier on your feet like a cow, maybe I could hear you sneaking up on me."

Ray scolded himself for the edginess to his tone, and especially the "heavier" comment. If it were up to his mother, she would have preferred having more weight on her. *Get it together, man.* These last couple of days his brain had been on autopilot.

"I'm going to head into town," he said. "Do you need anything?"

"Yes, actually. Delanie gets these amazing chocolate croissants at the bakery. I haven't had one in a few days. Do you mind bringing me a dozen?"

Ray knew his mother well enough to know Delanie's name hadn't come up by coincidence. "Sure. Anything else?"

June seemed to consider his words a moment before saying, "And one of those caramel macchiatos. I really like those things."

Ray laughed. "I don't think they offer that at the bakery, Mom."

A wide smile touched her lips. "They do now. Delanie suggested to Bethel that she add one or two new items on the menu, including the chocolate croissants. Both are a huge hit."

Why didn't it surprise him that Ms. Bethel would listen to Delanie? "Anything else?"

"No, I think that about does it. Be safe."

Ray kissed his mother on the cheek before heading out of the room.

"It's been several days. Maybe you should call her," June said. "I'd like my smiling and happy son back."

Ray stopped. He wanted that man to return, as well. He turned to face his mother. "She's ignoring my calls. Clearly, she doesn't want to hear from me. Frankly, I don't blame her."

"Nonsense. She's hurt. And it's understandable." June gave Ray a look but didn't take her obvious disapproval of what he'd done further than that. "Delanie cares deeply for you, son. I can see it in her eyes every time she looks at you. They dance with happiness. You've stolen her heart, and that's why your actions cut so deeply."

Yeah, well, she'd caged his heart, too. Which was why being without her hurt so damn much. "I betrayed her trust. There's no coming back from that."

"Yes, you did. And maybe she won't forgive you. But you'll never know unless you try." She neared him and rested his hand on her cheek. "Go to her. Make her see that you're not the same man now that you were back then."

"How?"

June smiled. "She has your heart, too. Use that."

On her knees, Delanie scrubbed the kitchen floor as if there were a stain on the wood she just couldn't get out. Truthfully, the blemish wasn't on the floor, it was on her heart. A stubborn stain called Ray Cavanaugh. After a week, the information Cordell had so zealously given her about him still weighed heavily on her mind. What had Ray thought, that he could seduce her into selling her vineyard to him? It just didn't make sense. None of this made sense. But it didn't have to, because she was done with Ray. Absolutely done.

Several hours later, Delanie added fresh water to her ultrasonic diffuser and returned to the living room to relax. She lifted the bottle of frankincense essential oil, but changed her mind and opted for the clove, lemon, cinnamon, eucalyptus and rosemary blend instead.

The spicy-scented oil reminded her of Christmas, her favorite holiday. No doubt, it would put her in a less taxing mood. Almost immediately she felt its calming effects. Still, it wasn't enough to put her completely at ease.

Stretching out on the sofa, she studied the ceiling. How had she not seen right through Ray's deception? The answer troubled her. Because she'd made the mistake of falling for him. She'd been blinded by the attention he'd given her. Her loneliness made her vulnerable, had made her susceptible. The way Ray kissed her, touched her, made love to her, it all felt so…real.

Scattering her thoughts of Ray, she sighed. She'd fallen, but now it was time to pick herself up. The days of a man crippling her were over. First thing tomorrow morning, she'd get on the phone and find a new vineyard manager.

This small setback wouldn't derail her plans. She wouldn't allow it. Regardless of what it took, her dream would still be achieved. Just without Ray. She ignored the twinge of despair she felt.

Her cell phone rang, startling her from the dismal thoughts. Shayna's name scrolled across the screen. Allowing the call to roll into voice mail, she closed her eyes. All she wanted to do was block out the world. At least for a few more days.

When her message indicator sounded, she decided to listen to Shayna's message. "Hey, D. I don't know what's going on but regardless, I want you to know I'm here if you need to talk. I'm neutral. I really miss you, girl. So does Auntie. And so does Ray. Trust me, whatever is going on with you guys has him…not himself. Anyway, please call me. Talk to you soon, I hope."

Delanie deleted the message and tossed the phone aside. Oddly enough, she did believe Shayna would remain neutral, and she was tempted to contact her for a girlfriend chat, but ultimately decided against it. She just didn't have the energy. Plus, regardless of how close they'd become, she was Ray's family, not hers.

Closing her eyes, she inhaled deeply and allowed her mind to go blank.

It was a little past ten that evening when Delanie woke from a nap she hadn't realized she'd needed. Still exhausted, she decided to call it a night. Pushing from the sofa, she headed for the stairs, but stopped when lights filtered through the blinds. She moved to the window and peeped through the slats.

Ray.

What was he doing here at this hour? Heck, what was he doing here at all? Gathering her thoughts, she moved to the door and waited for him to ring the bell. When he did, she flicked the light off and started upstairs. Yes, it had been petty, but warranted, in her opinion.

"I didn't believe in you, Delanie. That was my second mistake," Ray said, obviously unfazed by the darkness.

Delanie stopped, her curiosity earning him a second or two of her time. Standing at the base of the stairs, she waited for him to continue.

"My first mistake was underestimating you. I underestimated your dedication to this venture. I was convinced you wouldn't last two months once you saw all that went into starting a vineyard. I'd predicted you'd give up and return to your posh life. Then I would swoop in and buy your vineyard from you."

Listening to Ray, her heart sank all over again. But

why was he telling her any of this? Did he think it mattered now? The damage had already been done.

"I feel like a complete asshole admitting any of this to you, Delanie. But I want you to know—no, I *need* you to know the truth."

The truth? As if he were able to tell it. Deciding she'd had enough, she started up the stairs again.

"I didn't believe in you, Delanie Claire Atwater, but I sure as hell believe in you now. You're a remarkable woman. Resilient. Determined. And you make me... better. Woman, you make me better."

Despite wanting to believe he was anything but genuine, she couldn't, because she could hear the sincerity in his voice. Backtracking to the door, she parted her lips to tell him to just leave her alone, but the words wouldn't come. Did she want him to stay or go? Why was she so torn?

"I'm proud of you, Delanie. So proud of you."

The declaration softened her. Other than her father, no man had ever said those words to her. *Damn you, Ray Cavanaugh.*

"And if you're thinking about giving up, because of me, I won't let you."

Delanie tilted her head and shot a narrow-eyed scowl at the door. *Won't let me?* This nearly broke her silence, but she remained tight-lipped.

"If you want another vineyard manager, I'll help you find one. Just don't quit, Delanie. You've come too far."

Oh, he was good. Sounding like he actually cared. Was she supposed to swing the door open and leap into his strong arms all because he believed in her...now?

Because he wanted her to believe he cared whether or not she succeeded? Because he was proud of her?

For some foolish reason, the latter clung to her and was as annoying as an off-key choir singer. The words replayed over and over in her head. *I'm proud of you.* Why was she even contemplating opening the door?

Just walk away, she silently urged him.

"Say something, Delanie. I know you're there. I know because I can feel you. I can feel you," he repeated in little more than a whisper. "Everywhere."

Delanie didn't need him to explain what he'd meant, because she could feel him, too. Like a forceful energy that grew more intense the closer she got to the door. How was this even possible? *Don't fall for any more of his deceit,* she told herself.

"Just let me know you've heard me, Delanie. That's all I ask."

Her hand rose and hovered over the handle. A part of her wanted to fling the door open, but another part needed it to stay closed.

"Delanie, please."

It sounded like Ray rested his palm against the door. As if beyond her control, her hand flattened against it, too. Maybe it was all in her head, but the surge of energy that raced up her arm felt real.

"Thank you," he said. "Baby, I don't want to spend Thanksgiving without you. I don't want to spend another second without you. And if you knew how hard any of that was for me to admit…" His words trailed off.

She waited for him to say more, but he didn't. A beat later, she heard him pad across the porch. Fisting her hand to her chest, she considered that fate wasn't done with them. That might have explained why she opened the door.

Stepping out of view, she waited for him to respond to the unspoken invitation. Several seconds later, he entered, pushing the door closed behind him. For some reason, the move alarmed her. Or it could have been the way her stomach knotted, cheeks heated and breathing hitched at the sight of him.

No, it was the door thing, she chose to believe.

Under Ray's scrutiny, she wished she wore more than an oversize T-shirt. And a bra would have been extremely helpful, as well. Forcing the most unpleasant frown she could muster, she crossed her arms over her chest. Unfortunately, the move caused her breasts to swell, so she dropped her arms to her sides.

"I miss you so much," he said.

Honestly, she missed him, too, but that changed nothing. Standing there staring at the man she'd actually imagined a future with, she had to know one thing. "Was any of this real?" She detested the vulnerability present in her voice. If ever there was a time she needed to sound strong, stand strong, this was that moment.

"All of it was real. All of it *is* real," he said, moving closer to her.

Of all the men in the world, this one should have been the last one able to arouse her, but he did. And she hated it. Standing her ground, she warded off the quiver his closeness provoked. The nearer he got, the hotter the room grew. When his manly scent filled her nostrils, she swallowed hard and demanded her body tame itself.

"My feelings for you are real," he continued. "And whether you admit it or deny it, you have feelings for me, too."

"Even if that were the case—" she shrugged "—what does that change?" She shook her head. "Nothing, because the fact still remains that whether or not you abandoned your scheme, you had been okay with it at one point. That says so much about your character. I trusted you, Ray. Do you have any idea how difficult that was for me? To open myself up to you?"

Ray spoke with conviction when he said, "You can still trust me. And I think you know that. Otherwise—" he jabbed a finger in the opposite direction "—you would have never opened that door."

"Now I realize that was a mistake," she said.

"Why? Does my being here force you to admit to yourself how much you miss me, too?"

His assessment angered her. Mainly because it was true, but she would never admit that. "No. It forces me to recall that the man I allowed into my life, into my bed—" and sadly, into her heart "—was only there to con me."

Obviously, being labeled a con man didn't sit well with Ray, because his jaw clenched and released several times. The relaxed expression he'd worn moments earlier tensed and the corner of his left eye twitched.

"When I kiss you, does it feel like a con?" He paused. "Or does it feel like a man trying his best to consume the woman who fills him to the brim? *Hmm?*"

Delanie didn't respond, but her silence didn't keep Ray from pushing forward.

"When I touch you, does it feel like I'm deceiving you?"

Ray took another step toward her and her breath hitched. Why was he so damn close? And why couldn't she just ignore him? How was it she could still experience such a draw to him? She wanted to hate him, so why couldn't she? Too many unanswered questions.

Ray cocked a brow. "Does it feel like I'm deceiving you, Delanie? Or does it feel like I'm trying to learn every inch of your body?"

Her heart rate increased and slammed against her rib cage. Why was she allowing him to affect her this way? Doing the only thing she felt she could do, she pointed toward the door. "You should go."

Ignoring her, Ray rested his hands on her waist and pulled her flush against him. His eyes lowered to her mouth, then slowly rose to meet hers again. In her head, she shoved him away. In reality, his touch paralyzed her.

"When I make love to you, does anything about it feel forced? Fake? No, it doesn't," he answered for her. "It should feel like a man pouring a part of his soul into a woman he's crazy about."

Ray's head tilted forward and his mouth drew closer and closer to hers. Still, she couldn't move. If he thought he could simply walk in here and make everything all right with a few well-thought-out lines he'd probably spent the past several days perfecting, he had another think coming. And if he even considered kissing her, she'd bite his bottom lip off.

Ray stopped, but his lips were so close to hers, she could feel the heat escaping past them. *Pull away,* she urged herself. *Eliminate this foolish temptation to taste him.* It was as though she stood outside her body, watching herself succumb to Ray's charm.

"Let me back in," he said. "I'm not here to hurt you, Delanie. I'm here to help you heal. The same way you're helping me."

Stunned by his words, all she could do was stare at him. The emotion in his eyes was so raw, so intense, her eyes clouded with tears. When she attempted to blink them away, they rolled down her cheeks. Ray kissed the wetness, scooped her into his arms and climbed the stairs.

By the time they reached the top, Delanie had come to her senses. She protested. "Stop."

And he did.

In the stillness, Delanie could hear her mother's voice as clearly as if the woman were standing next to her. *Eyes are never silent. They usually speak louder than words and oftentimes are the most truest form of communication.* Staring into Ray's, she looked past what she saw on the surface and delved deeper, searching.

What she saw contradicted what she wanted to believe—that Ray was a bad guy. Believing he was should have made things easier, should have made him easier to walk away from. Oh, how wrong she'd been.

"Don't give up on me," he said.

The way he eyed her… She couldn't recall the last time a man looked at her this way. Her heart did a double-tap in her chest, and her mother's voice sounded again… *Trust your instincts.*

And so she did.

Leaning forward, she kissed Ray in a way that was so urgent, so intense, it scared her. A soothing feeling coursed through her, and she experienced a sense of unexplainable relief. Instantly, she felt lighter, freer, happier, whole again.

Apparently believing he couldn't make the short walk to her bedroom, he lowered to the floor, blanketing her body with his. Thankfully, the hallway was carpeted. However, if it weren't, she doubted she would have felt the chill anyway. Her body was boiling hot.

Ray reared his head back and eyed her silently. A beat later, he dipped forward and dragged the tip of his tongue across her lower lip, then captured her mouth again. The kiss was so raw and passionate it made her dizzy.

Stone-hard, his erection pressed into her core, causing a sensation to spark all through her body. Anticipation. Want. Need. Delanie wasn't sure which was the most powerful of the three. All she knew was they each threatened to rob her of her sanity.

Ray snatched his mouth away and Delanie shamelessly sought his lips.

"I want to taste you," he said.

Exhibiting the same level of urgency as before, he didn't bother removing her underwear. He simply shoved them to the side and buried his face between her legs. The magnificent way he worked his tongue forced her to scream his name.

As if he'd deemed the amount of pleasure he was dispensing inadequate, he curved a finger inside her and worked it slowly. Fire swirled in her belly, igniting every cell in her body. Her arm jutted out and her hand tightened around one of the stair balusters.

Dangerously close to tipping over the edge, Ray suckled her, sending her body careening out of control. Her pleasure cries tore through the house. The orgasm struck with so much force she snatched the baluster completely free from the handrail and landing tread. Discarding the broken component, she rode this ferocious wave of ecstasy.

When her cries calmed to whimpers, he ended his delicious manipulation, removed her panties and tossed them aside. A second later, he returned to her center, placing a single kiss to her sensitive nub. The sensation it caused made her shiver.

As he kissed his way up her torso, lifting her shirt along the way, tiny bolts of electricity sparked through her. After taking time to pleasure her breasts, he made his way to her mouth—licking and nipping along the way.

Against her eager lips, he said, "All I needed was a taste. I can leave a happy and satisfied man now."

"You're not going anywhere, Ray Cavanaugh," she said breathlessly. "Not until you finish what you started."

He kissed one corner of her mouth. "And what have I started?"

"An inferno."

"Mmm," he hummed, kissing the opposite side of her mouth. "And what would extinguish it?"

"You inside me," she said without hesitation.

Ray flashed a mischievous smirk. "I can give you what you want."

"Good."

He placed a tender peck to her lips. "But not until you admit you missed me, too."

Really? Was he really ransoming the dick?

He came up on his knees and removed his shirt. The sight of his chiseled chest reminded her that he held all the leverage. When he unfastened his pants and pushed them tantalizingly low on his hips—but not enough to reveal the one thing she wanted most in the world at this moment—she couldn't get the words out fast enough.

"I missed you. More and more every day. I missed you like crazy."

Ray nodded slowly, then stood. In a teasing fashion, he undressed in a slow, arousing manner. It made her long for him even more. Had that been his plan? Yes, she reasoned, when she noticed the roguish smile on his face.

To say this man's body—and assets—were merely impressive would be like calling the Notre-Dame de Paris a simple building. Both would have been an insult. Ray removed a condom from his wallet, sheathed himself, then returned between her legs. Dipping his head, he kissed her deeply and entered her slowly. Her hands explored his warm body as he glided in and out of her with precise strokes.

The feels—all of them—were so decadently divine, they momentarily snatched her breath away. Their moans mixed and mingled. Obviously, he was experiencing just as much pleasure as she.

"I've never felt anything like this before," he said.

At first, Delanie assumed he was speaking of what they were doing; but when he stared down into her face, and she glanced into his eyes, she understood his words meant so much more. He sealed his mouth over hers again and hungrily claimed her. The speed and force of his stroke increased, causing pressure from another orgasm to build inside her. She had a feeling he was reaching his breaking point as well, because a guttural sound rumbled in his chest.

Several strokes later he teetered over, pulling her with him. Their symphony of delight echoed throughout the large space. Ray collapsed down next to her.

Lifting the broken baluster, he chuckled. "What happened here?"

Delanie nestled close to him. "You. You happened." He wrapped her in his strong arms, and she felt right at home.

Like Ray, she'd never felt anything like this, either. It both thrilled and frightened her. The fear stemmed from the tiny voice chirping in the back of her head, asking an urgent question: *Can you trust this man?*

God, she hoped so. But the only things she could trust for sure were her instincts and they favored him. Plus, she'd tried to walk away from him. Fate had led her right back. *Everything means something*, her mother used to say. If that were true, what did her inability to walk away from Ray mean?

Chapter 18

Delanie stood off to the side, observing the crowd who'd all shown up for Vine Ridge's annual Thanksgiving feast. The chatter and laughter swirling around her made her smile and appreciate being part of the camaraderie.

Before the attendees sat to enjoy a bountiful spread—turkey, ham, dressing and numerous other Thanksgiving staples—Momma Cavanaugh had asked everyone in attendance to name something they were thankful for. Many had placed her and Ray at the top of their list. It was obvious they'd both come to mean a lot to the town.

Delanie couldn't recall experiencing a Thanksgiving filled with so much love and gratitude since her childhood. The aromas wafting through the air, the smiling faces, they reminded her of her mother's kitchen during the holidays. It also made her long to see her brother.

Until this very moment, she hadn't realized just how much she'd missed the feel of family. In California, holidays were not like this. The dinners she and Cordell had attended were all shrouded in pretense. Instead of representing a time to be thankful, they had been an opportunity to brag and boast. But the good cheer being displayed in this room was genuine.

"Speech, speech!" someone called out, drawing Delanie from her thoughts. Someone had given Ray a mic that he passionately tried to return. The room cheered for him to say a few words, as if he'd been chosen as their leader. They loved Ray Cavanaugh. And while she wanted to dispute it, so did she.

"Okay, okay," Ray said, tapping down the air with his hands.

He draped an arm around his mother's shoulders and drew her close to him. Delanie absolutely loved how good he was to Momma Cavanaugh. Even with so much going on, he'd made it a point to check on her throughout the night to make sure she had everything she'd needed.

Momma Cavanaugh had had a rough day at dialysis earlier in the week when her blood pressure dropped from having too much fluid removed from her blood. Like Ray, Delanie and Shayna both had fussed over Momma Cavanaugh, too. Especially when they found her doing anything that could possibly overexert her.

Ray spoke into the microphone, his commanding voice booming through the room. "Echoing what I said earlier, I'm happy that all of you chose to celebrate with us. I have a lot to be grateful for, especially this year."

When Ray's gaze landed on her, Delanie's heart

pounded a little harder. The way he eyed her caused her skin to prickle.

"So much," he said. Turning back to the crowd, he said, "There's plenty of food still remaining. Eat, drink, eat some more."

Everyone, including Delanie, clapped as if he'd given the speech of a lifetime. He made his way across the room and wrapped her in his arms. The fact that he freely and openly showed her affection made her feel proud. This wasn't the stern man she'd met months ago. He was a gentle creature who showed her at every opportunity that he cared about her, even if he hadn't confessed his feelings.

"It's a beautiful sight to see, huh?" he said, kissing her gently.

"Yes, it is. It's amazing. You're amazing." She placed a palm against his chest. "Your heart is so tender, so huge. You are a beautiful soul, Ray Jude Cavanaugh, and I'm thankful for you."

Ray stared deep into Delanie's eyes. "I l—"

"Smile for the camera, you two," Shayna said, cutting Ray off.

Delanie couldn't help but wonder what he had been about to say to her. Was it what she thought? That he loved her? They both turned toward Shayna and donned huge smiles. The woman snapped what seemed like a hundred pictures before moving on.

Before Delanie and Ray could pick up where they left off, someone summoned him. Giving him a peck, she sent him on his way, then retreated to the bathroom. After relieving her full bladder, she washed her hands and headed back to the festivities.

When she pulled the bathroom door open, Ray was there, leaning against the wall like the sexiest statue she'd ever laid eyes on. Silently, he held out his hand, and she took it without hesitation. Her curiosity rose when he guided her in the opposite direction from where they should have been heading.

"Where are you taking me?"

He led her into a small office, closed the door, pressed her back against it and captured her mouth in the most primal kiss he'd given her all night. If she hadn't wanted him already, she certainly did after the way he ravished her mouth.

When they finally came up for air, their chests heaved.

"What did I do to deserve that?" she asked breathlessly.

"Looking so damn hot in this outfit."

When she'd chosen the tattered jeans and pumpkin-colored sweater cardigan set, comfort had been her goal, not looking hot, which is why she'd paired it with the flat leopard-print shoes and not stilettos.

"Thank you," she said.

"You're welcome."

Ray took a step back, his gaze running the full length of her body. Something daunting flashed in his eyes that made her nipples peak. Damn him for this effect he had on her.

"Take it off."

"Take...what off?"

"All of it."

"Excuse me?"

"Oh, I think you both heard and understood me well," he said.

Yes, she had. "You are insane, Ray, if you think I'm undressing with a hundred people practically next door. And we're definitely not having sex," she said in an unnecessary whisper.

"You're not going to take it off?" he said, meshing his body against hers again.

She exhaled a slow, steady breath when his hands rested on her butt and squeezed. "Are you trying to get me banished from town, Ray Cavanaugh? What if someone catches us? Or worse, what if they hear you? You know how loud you can get when we're in the throes of passion. I'm not going to risk it." Regardless of what tantalizing tactics he used, she would stand her ground.

"Are you sure about this?"

Those warm, soft lips peppered kisses to the crook of her neck, and she whimpered. But he wasn't going to break her. "Y-yes, I am." *Kinda.*

"Absolutely sure?" he asked.

His large hands crawled up her body and cupped her breasts. The pads of his thumbs smoothed back and forth over her now sensitive and achy nipples. Still, she stood firm. Weak in the knees, but firm.

"Uh-huh." *Mostly.*

"Well, what if I ask you nicely?" he said, kissing his way to her mouth and claiming it once more.

Lord, this man can kiss. "Not even then," she managed to say against their joined mouths.

Ray pulled away and kissed the tip of her nose. "Damn, baby. You're tough on a brother."

The roguish grin on his face foreshadowed trouble. Ray kissed a trail down her body as he lowered to his knees. Her womanhood became instantly aware of his close proximity.

"What if I got down on my knees and…"

When he unfastened her pants, she did nothing to stop him.

"…begged."

Without waiting for her response, he lowered her pants, along with her panties. His soft lips pressed against her mound, and her legs wobbled. "Please," he said, kissing her again. "Please," he repeated.

Delanie was fairly certain she would black out from the buildup of arousal expanding inside her. And when he guided his tongue between her wet folds and teased her clit with the tip, she nearly toppled over.

Then he stopped, sending her body into panic mode.

Returning to a full stand, Ray cupped her chin in his hand and pecked her gently.

"I'm going to have you, Delanie Claire. Right here. Right now. But you know this already."

Cocky bastard.

Close to her mouth, he continued, "What you don't know is that I'm going to die if I don't."

Well, that changed things. She couldn't be responsible for the loss of a life. Especially this life.

Shoving her hands into his chest sent Ray playfully stumbling backward a couple of steps. She kicked out of her shoes, then stepped from her pants. Ray's hungry eyes consumed her whole. The intensity in his stare aroused her even more.

"Keep going," he said, caressing his stubbled jaw.

She couldn't recall ever wanting anyone the way she wanted Ray right now, how she always wanted him. On the edge of delirium, her heart banged inside her chest. Her body throbbed, pounded, thumped, pulsed, vibrated, ached. All for him. Only him.

Removing the sweater set, she stood before him in the state she'd first resisted.

"Your body is a testimony to God's great ability and wisdom."

He always knew just the right thing to say, and he'd just given her the holy grail of compliments.

In a swift move, he snatched her into his arms, carried her to the sofa and placed her down. Had she been in her right frame of mind, she would have mounted a protest against the frayed piece of furniture. But at the present moment, its dilapidated state didn't faze her.

Ray dropped back to his knees and captured her core with the urgency of a man on a mission. Her orgasm came in record time, slamming her around like one of those metal pinballs. While he'd given her pleasure, she wanted more. He made her gluttonous when it came to intimacy, because he was so damn good at satisfying her. His ultimate goal always seemed to be her ultimate gratification.

Ray came out of his pants, then tore into the condom he'd removed from his wallet.

"I'm on the pill now," she said.

Ray froze as if a million loaded guns had been pointed at him. "We...don't need to use this?" he asked.

She shook her head. "Only if you want to. And if you do, I understand. I won't be offended."

Ray hurled the foil across the room before she'd released the last syllable, then blanketed her body with his. "Remind me to get that before we leave. Probably shouldn't leave it lying around."

"Probably not," she said, pulling his mouth to hers. "Make love to me, Ray. Insane, passionate, untamed—"

Ray drove into her with urgency. All types of mind-boggling sensations shot through her, causing her to cry out. Ray covered her mouth with his.

"Shh," he hissed against her lips, releasing several guttural sounds of his own.

"Shh," she mocked him.

Their lovemaking was the rawest, most intense episode they'd had thus far. Ray didn't hold back, and she welcomed his enthusiasm in giving her exactly what she'd asked for. Clearly, they'd both stopped caring about whether or not anyone heard them because moans, groans, whimpers and cries bounced off the walls of the room. Delanie chose to believe they were far enough away from the crowd not to be exposed.

Ray came inside her and she swore she could feel his energy invade every cell in her body. They'd come together plenty of times before, and while she'd felt all of the sensations she typically experienced when he brought her to a climax, something was different. This time embodied far more than just a release.

In the midst of this pleasure storm, she recalled something Momma Cavanaugh had said a while back. *There's a place a man can take you sexually that will transcend your mind, body and soul. But not just any man will accomplish this.* Delanie understood now.

Ray gathered her in his arms. "That was…" He released a hard breath. "I have no words for what that was."

Placing a hand on his cheek, she stared into his eyes. "No man has ever made me feel the way you make me feel. Not just sexually. Though you make me feel pretty damn good in that way, too."

"I do what I can," he said.

"I haven't looked forward to Christmas in a long time, but I'm so looking forward to spending this Christmas with you. I'm crazy about you, Ray Jude Cavanaugh. And I hope you know that. Don't say anything. I don't want to get all emotional and have to do my walk of shame with red, puffy eyes."

Ray didn't say a word, simply turned his head and kissed her palm. It truly wasn't necessary for him to reciprocate her sentiment. She didn't need words, because his actions told his story. And his tale suggested he cared about her, too.

The second they reentered the room, Shayna bombarded them, her lips spread wide enough to fit a saucer.

"Where have you two been?" A second later, she fanned the words off. "Never mind. Judging by the glow on both your faces, your response would probably be TMI."

Definitely too much information, Delanie thought. "What's up?" she said.

"You're going to be sooo excited," Shayna said, taking Delanie's hand and pulling her across the room.

Delanie glanced over her shoulder for Ray. Instead of following them, he stood chatting with Walker, a bemused look on his face. When he eyed her, his puzzled expression turned to a troubled one. What was Walker saying to him? And why did she get the impression it had something to do with her?

"Surprise!"

Delanie turned with urgency and gasped, slapping her hand over her mouth to conceal the scream. Her eyes grew big in disbelief, then cloudy with tears. She flung her arms around her brother's neck and held him so tight she doubted he could breathe.

"Hey, sis," Bryan said in a strained voice.

Delanie held him at arm's length and scrutinized him just as their mother used to do when he'd come home from school or playing outside or spending the night with a friend. He hadn't changed much. A little more muscular than she remembered from the last time she'd seen him, ten long months ago.

"Oh my God, Bryan. What are you doing here?" She pulled him into another tight hug, promising herself she would never go this long without seeing him again.

"Welcome to Vine Ridge, Bryan. I'm glad you made it here okay," Ray said.

Delanie jerked away and eyed Ray, utterly confused. "Why does it sound like the two of you know each other?" she asked, looking from Ray to Bryan, then back to Ray.

Ray smiled. "Because we do. Sorta."

Shayna spent the next several minutes telling her how Ray had orchestrated this elaborate plan to get Bryan here, because he knew how much Delanie missed him. *To make your Thanksgiving perfect*, Ray had said.

And he had.

She'd never been more in love with Ray than she was at that moment. And she'd almost confessed it, but they'd already had enough excitement for one evening. "Thank you. Thank you, both," she said, eyeing Shayna.

While Bryan would have to leave tomorrow because of a work deadline, she was thankful for the time she would have with him.

For the next hour, Delanie doted on her brother, telling everyone who would listen about his success as a marketing executive in Atlanta. When Bryan garnered the attention of several of Vine Ridge's single ladies, Delanie went to find Ray.

After a short search, she finally located him standing out in the cold, staring into the darkness. Bundled up with his hands shoved into his pockets, he looked to be in deep concentration.

"A nickel for your thoughts," she said, wrapping her arms around him from behind and resting her cheek against his chilly coat.

"Hey, beautiful. Just came out to get a little fresh air. Everything okay?"

"It is with me, but not with you," she said. "Something's bothering you. Does it have anything to do with what you and Walker were discussing earlier? I saw you two talking."

Ray tensed in her arms and she knew it did. Reaching around, he positioned her in front of him, then encased her in his arms, kissing her gently on the lips. When he pulled away, he stared into her eyes.

"What is it?" Whatever Walker had said to him clearly had him bothered.

"Your ex-husband's in town," he said plainly.

Her brows shot up. "You invited him, too?"

While she got the impression Ray hadn't wanted to laugh, he did.

"No. I definitely had nothing to do with that one."

"Then what is he doing here?" When she realized how silly the question had been, she waved it off. One thing was for sure, if Cordell was in Vine Ridge, nothing good could stem from the visit. "Wait. How do you know it's Cordell?"

"Walker's sister runs the B and B. A Cordell Atwater checked in a little over an hour ago. He hasn't tried to reach out to you?"

"No, he hasn't."

Ray flashed a look she couldn't quite decipher. Either surprise or skepticism. This situation had the makings of a true disaster. Just like Cordell to find some way to spoil her happiness.

"I don't—"

The door banged open behind them, cutting Ray off midthought. Walker rushed out, his face riddled with concern. Something was wrong.

"Ray, it's your mom."

Chapter 19

Watching his mother sleep, Ray leaned forward, rested his elbows on his thighs, intertwined his fingers and thanked God for the hundredth time in the past hour. When he had rushed into the room to see her on the floor, it had scared the hell out of him. A leg cramp that had made her lose her balance.

Thankfully, she hadn't broken any bones. She was just a bit battered and bruised. But because of her pre-existing health conditions, her doctor had admitted her as a precaution. Plus, she'd been mildly dehydrated. She hadn't liked the idea of staying another night but didn't make too much of a fuss.

"Tank?"

He glanced up, pasting a wide smile on his face. Seeing his mother in this hospital bed broke his heart, but he knew it was for the best. "Hey, beautiful."

"You're still here? I thought I told you to go home and get some rest. I'll be A-OK. I'm in capable hands."

"I will when Delanie and Shayna return." He sent them both home after being there all night alongside him. "They should be back here soon."

June inched up in the bed. "What time is it?"

"A little after two in the afternoon. Why? Do you have some place to be?" Ray chuckled.

"No," she said in a long, drawn out breath. "The girls and I were supposed to do some Christmas shopping today. Guess that's not happening."

"No, it's not," he said. "You have to take it easy, Mom. *Just be.*"

June rolled her eyes at her son when he used her words against her.

Ray took his mother's hand. "I know you don't want to be here, and I don't want you here, either. But it is what it is. The only thing you should be focused on is getting better," Ray said. "As an incentive, when you're feeling better, I'll send you ladies on a shopping spree that rivals all shopping sprees."

She scoffed. "I feel fine. It was only a leg cramp. Can't I just eat a banana and go home?"

Ray wished it were that simple. "You know you can't have bananas."

"I can't have anything. Bananas, oranges, potatoes, spinach, tomatoes. I have to limit meat, eggs, dairy. This body is slowly becoming my prison. Sometimes I wish..."

Her words trailed off, and Ray was grateful she hadn't finished her thought, though he had a feeling about what she'd wanted to say. If he could change places with her, he would have in a heartbeat.

Before he could give her a pep talk, Shayna entered the room.

"Hey, family," Shayna said, kissing the top of Ray's head, then moving to the bed and inching in with June. "Hey, Auntie," she said, nestling close to her. "How are you feeling?"

"Fair to middling," June said.

"Where's Delanie?" she asked, taking the words right out of Ray's mouth.

"She'll be here shortly." Shayna eyed Ray. "You should go home and get some rest. I promise I won't leave this pretty lady's side."

Taking Shay up on her offer and promising to return soon, Ray headed home. But instead of going straight there, he decided to make a pit stop first.

After getting her brother off to the airport, Delanie stopped by the B and B before she headed to the hospital. She took a deep breath before knocking on the door to Cordell's room. Since he'd been in town twenty-four hours and still hadn't reached out to her, she decided to take the first step.

"Delanie?"

Cordell looked stunned by her presence. Brushing past him, she said, "What are you doing in Vine Ridge, Cordell?"

Cordell's shoulders fell like a man defeated. Closing the door, he kept his back to her instead of turning.

"Why are you here, Cordell?" Delanie repeated, and this time her voice got deeper.

He whipped around. "I don't know, Delanie." He washed a hand over his head. "I don't know. I just needed to see you. I woke up Thanksgiving morning to an empty bed and a barren house…" He massaged the back of his neck. "Once I was here, I was afraid to contact you, especially after the last time we spoke."

"Well, you've seen me. Now what?"

"I've made a lot of mistakes, Delanie."

"Like having me followed? Like breaking your vows? Like having a baby out of wedlock?"

He lowered his head. "Yes."

"You're here for absolution. Is that it? Well, congratulations, Cordell. You have it. I forgive you for all the pain you've ever caused me." She moved to the door and snatched it open.

"I forgive you, too," he said.

Delanie stopped, pushed the door semiclosed and faced Cordell. "You forgive *me*? Forgive me for what?"

"I know about you and Simon. He told me."

Delanie's stomach knotted at the mention of Cordell's best friend.

"I've known since it happened. As hurt and angry as I was about it, I didn't want to lose you. So, instead of confronting you, I sought payback. I did what I did, because you—"

Delanie jabbed a finger at him. "Payback? For what? Don't you dare fix your mouth to put *your* affair on me. You did it because you *wanted* to do it."

"You don't think you sleeping with my best friend was enough to push me to irrational thinking? You were my world."

Delanie forced her brows together. "*Wait, wait, wait.*

Sleeping with your best friend? What are you talking about? I never slept with Simon."

"He told me everything, Delanie."

"He told you lies. Simon tried to force himself on me the night of your birthday party. He groped me, tried to kiss me. Stuck his hand up my skirt and tried to rip off my panties. He told me I should give him some of my brown sugar, because you were giving yours to every woman you could. Foolish me, I didn't believe him. Until I learned you'd fathered a child."

"Delanie—" Cordell's words caught. He ran a hand down his face. Through clenched teeth, he said, "Why didn't you tell me Simon did that to you?"

"Would you have believed me? Simon could never do any wrong in your eyes. He had an affair—it was his wife's fault for gaining weight. He got a DUI—it was a setup by a rival production company. He was your *best friend*."

"But you were my wife!"

Delanie jerked at the strength in Cordell's voice.

"Shit," he mumbled to himself. "I'm sorry. I didn't mean to startle you. He lied to me, cost me everything," Cordell said more to himself than to Delanie. "Our divorce was a mistake."

"Yes," Delanie said.

Cordell's face lit with hope. He moved to the door and pushed it closed. "Come home with me, Delanie. Abandon this ridiculous idea of opening a vineyard and come home. We can start over."

Delanie shook her head. "No. While it was a mistake for you, because you sacrificed a good thing, it wasn't one for me, Cordell. When I arrived in Vine Ridge, I was lost, broken. Because of you. Then I met someone who believed in me. Believed in me," she repeated.

Cordell's face soured, but he remained quiet.

"For the first time in a long time, I'm happy. Vine Ridge is where I found myself. It's where my home is." An image of Ray flashed in her head. "It's where my heart is. I'm not going anywhere. Goodbye, Cordell." She turned and started away.

"Delanie."

Stopping, she tossed him a glance over her shoulder.

"Not that it matters now, but before Lorna, I swear, *swear* I had never been unfaithful to you. Ever." He sighed. "I'm glad you found happiness. You deserve it."

Yes, she did.

In her vehicle, Delanie phoned Shayna after her call to Ray went straight to voice mail. When Shayna informed her he'd gone home to get some rest, she detoured and headed to the ranch instead of the hospital. She couldn't wait another minute to tell Ray she loved him unequivocally. Hopefully, he felt the same way.

When someone had closed the door at the B and B, it hadn't mattered. Ray had heard enough anyway. Delanie thought her divorce had been a mistake. One she was obviously open to fixing.

Ray hurled himself behind the wheel of Joleen, cranked the engine and sped off. The entire drive to the ranch he kicked himself for ever allowing himself to fall in love with Delanie. He struck the steering wheel, then cursed the pain that shot up his arm. He'd been doing just damn fine before Delanie had come into his life. Now look at him.

When he arrived home, he stretched out on the sofa, closed his eyes and draped his arm over his forehead. The conversation he'd heard between Delanie and her ex played on repeat in his head. What Delanie had gone through at the hands of Cordell's best friend made him wish slimy Simon was standing in front of him right now, so he could pulverize the lowlife bum.

Clearing his mind, he drifted off. When he woke a couple of hours later, he spotted Delanie asleep in the chair across from him. When had she arrived, and why hadn't she woken him?

Approaching her gingerly, he brushed a stray hair from her face, then stood and admired her for a long time. He knew what he had to do, but this moment only made it that much more difficult. He loved this woman. Loved her like he'd never loved another, not even his ex-wife.

He pulled the ottoman closer to her chair, eased down and shook her gently. "Delanie."

She stirred, then opened her eyes. A soft smile curled her lips. "Hey." A troubled look spread across her face. "What's wrong?" She sat up urgently. "Is your mother okay?"

"She's fine."

Delanie blew a sigh of relief. "Thank God."

He eyed her a moment, trying to build up to the conversation they needed to have. "I'm going to fix a drink. Would you like one?" he asked, stalling.

"I'll have what you're having."

Ray stood and moved toward the bar. With his back to her, he said, "Did your brother get off okay?"

"Yeah, he did. Thank you again for flying him here. That was extremely thoughtful of you."

"You're welcome." Filling the glasses, he said, "You weren't with Shay when she came to the hospital earlier. Was there a hang-up at the airport?"

"I…" Her words trailed. "I swung by home and got tied up with stuff there."

"Ah," was all he said.

As small as Vine Ridge was, she had to at least assume someone had seen her at the B and B. Yet, she'd chosen to lie to him. Unfocused, he spilled the rum he'd been pouring. "Damn."

"Ray, are you sure everything's okay with your mom? You seem…distracted."

He glanced over his shoulder. "I would tell you if it wasn't, Delanie. I wouldn't hide anything from you."

A hesitant smile curled her lips. "Okay."

Returning to where Delanie lounged, he passed her the glass, then eased back onto the ottoman in front of her. He decided to be a little more direct. "Still no word from your ex?"

"Um…" Delanie's eyes lowered briefly. "No." She gave a nervous laugh. "But that's a good thing, right?"

"Right." *Damn.* He'd given her a second chance to come clean and still, she'd lied.

Lifting her glass, Delanie took a long swig. Ray downed the contents of his. It did little to dull the sting of her deception. So much for a relationship built on truth and honesty.

For a brief moment, he hesitated making his next move. But when he recalled what he'd heard at the B and B and Delanie lying to him now, he pushed forward. He would break his own heart before she could. Would that make things easier on him? Honestly, he doubted it. "We need to talk," he said in a low, reserved tone.

She planted her feet on the floor. "Okay."

Ray lowered his head and fixed his eyes on his feet. "My mom…" His words trailed off. "Her health…" He stopped again and massaged the back of his neck. "I need to focus on making sure she's getting the care she needs. You deserve someone who can give you their undivided attention. I can't do that right now."

Worry lines crawled across Delanie's forehead. "Ray, are you breaking up with me?"

He remained silent.

Delanie rested her hand under his chin and lifted his head. A warm smile spread across her face. "Ray Cavanaugh, I admire you for wanting to protect me from what you obviously believe is too much of a burden on me," she said, "but you don't have to protect me, because I want to be here. I'm in this with you. All the way. I love your mother, as much as if she were my own. And I l—"

Ray cut in before Delanie could finish her sentence. Before she could say what he thought she'd been about to say, *I love you*. Because you didn't lie to the one you loved.

"I can't do this…" His exhausted tone faded. With his thoughts so jumbled, he wasn't sure if he was talking to Delanie or himself. "This is best for the both of us."

Delanie's hand fell to her lap, expression laced with confusion. "I'm so lost right now, Ray. We have something here. Something good. Great. You want to end it? Just like that? With no real explanation."

"My mother's health is explanation enough, Delanie. It's stressful enough. It's a private matter and needs my full attention."

"Private matter?" Visibly confused, she said, "Are you trying to say I'm not in your inner circle, that you don't trust me?"

He ignored the question because he wasn't sure whether he did or not. His mind was all over the place. "I don't have time for games."

"*Games?* Is that what I am to you, Ray, a game? Is that the only thing our relationship has been to you?"

Again, he remained silent, giving what could be construed as legitimacy to her claims.

Unable to stomach the pain he saw in her eyes, he turned away. Delanie was quiet for a while, but Ray could feel her eyes penetrating him. Then she stood and moved away without uttering a word. Still, he couldn't bring himself to look at her, especially to watch her leave. Despite it all, he loved her. He loved her so damn much it hurt.

Her footsteps stopped. A couple of seconds passed before she spoke. "The next time you end a relationship, be man enough to look her in the eyes."

With that she was gone, taking with her his heart and any happiness he could ever hope to have.

The following week crawled by. Seven days without Delanie felt akin to an eternity for Ray. She had become such an intricate part of his life that it wasn't as easy as he'd thought it should have been purging her from his system. But he had to. For his own good and for everyone's around him. Admittedly, he'd been a grouch since they broke up. No one around him deserved to suffer for his mistake—falling in love.

"Hey. You okay?" Shayna asked, walking into the kitchen where Ray was preparing lunch for her and his mother.

"Perfect. Why do you ask?"

"I'm not the best cook, but I'm pretty sure you're supposed to take the sausages out of the packaging before placing them into the pan."

"Damn," he said. "With Mom's recovery, I've been preoccupied."

"Are you sure that's all it is?"

No doubt Shayna was hinting about his breakup with Delanie. Until now, Shayna hadn't broached the subject with him and he hadn't with her. However, he was sure she'd gotten all the details she'd needed from Delanie. Those two had grown as close as sisters.

"When does she leave?" he asked, allowing himself one inquiry about Delanie.

"Who?"

Ray shot Shayna a look and she shot him one right back.

"Delanie," he said, his tone more gruff than he would have liked.

Shayna rested her hands on her hips. "Where is she going?"

Why in the hell was Shayna acting so clueless? "Back to California, I suppose."

"Who told you Delanie was moving back to California?"

So he had been right. She was leaving. "Doesn't matter. And you know what else, it doesn't matter when she's leaving."

Shayna patted him on the back. "You should check your sources, cousin. Delanie's not leaving Vine Ridge. Especially when—" She stopped abruptly, as if realizing she was about to say too much.

"Especially when what?"

"Especially when she's put so much work into the vineyard. The one thing I've learned about Delanie is the woman doesn't give up easily. Especially on someone—I mean, something, she loves." Shayna pointed over her shoulder. "I'm going to check on Auntie."

A blink later she escaped the room. Ray couldn't figure out if her words had been support for Delanie or a jab at him. He washed a hand down his face. If Delanie wasn't returning to California, did that mean she wasn't reconciling with her ex?

Chapter 20

Christmas was supposed to fill everyone with goodwill and cheer. Not Ray. It was a week until the joyous day and instead of celebrating along with everyone else inside the Ginger Root, he wanted to torch every piece of decoration in the building. He didn't care one iota about the impending holiday. In fact, he hadn't cared about much lately.

Walker elbowed him, then head-pointed toward the entrance. At the sight of Delanie, something vicious struck him deep in the gut. As always, when their eyes locked, the electricity nearly short-circuited his system. A moment later, she broke their connection, freeing him from her hold, but not the self-inflicted pain of losing her.

Instead of joining him and Walker as they would have normally done, Delanie and Shayna secured a table at the opposite side of the room. As hard as he tried, Ray couldn't keep his eyes off her. And when Jagger Crane pulled her onto the dance floor, Ray's fingers wrapped around his beer bottle so tightly his knuckles hurt.

Ray tipped the bottle to his lips and took a long swig. With every sway, Ray's jaw clenched tighter and tighter. The mere idea of Delanie being in another man's arms made his blood boil. Actually *seeing* it nearly sent him into a rage. He slammed the bottle down on the table with so much force it echoed through the space.

Walker jolted. "Damn, man. You okay?" he asked.

Delanie's gaze settled in his direction, a concerned expression on her face. Ray scooted his chair back with so much force, it tipped over. A second later, he banged through the doors of the Ginger Root.

Walker called out to him. "Ray, man, wait up."

"Can you get a ride home with Shayna?" Ray said over his shoulder.

"You dropped her, man. You don't get to be angry when someone else picks her up," Walker said.

Ray's hands balled into tight fists. Walker was right, but he didn't want to hear the man's logic. Not now. Not when it felt like his world was collapsing around him. Not when he could hardly breathe. At his truck, he struck the hood with an open hand, then pressed both palms flat against the icy surface and leaned forward.

"Do you love her?" Walker asked.

Ray glanced at him briefly, then looked away. "More than love her," he said in an exhausted tone.

"Then fix this."

Ray released a humorless laugh, then dropped his head. *How?*

* * *

Initially, Delanie hadn't wanted to venture out tonight for the same reason she hadn't wanted to go to the Ginger Root several days back. Fear of running into Ray. Thankfully, her luck had been better tonight. She hadn't seen or felt Ray anywhere.

While she had enjoyed her outing at the Main Street festival visiting the shops all decked out and festive for the holiday, sipping on peppermint hot chocolate, listening to the carolers by the twenty-foot-tall decorated tree in the square, it still didn't feel like Christmas. Not as the most wonderful time of the year should have felt. In fact, it felt downright depressing.

She stared out into the darkness as Shayna drove her home. An image of Ray at the Ginger Root filtered into her thoughts. She'd done her best to ignore him. A near impossible task, because his presence had been so damn potent. Selfishly, she'd wanted to make him jealous by dancing with another man. But when he'd stormed out of the building, she experienced a ping of regret.

Delanie sighed to herself. A few weeks ago, she'd pegged this to be the best Christmas she'd had in years. Now it was on tap to be the worst. Unfortunately, she was ending the year just as she'd started it. Alone. Well, not exactly. She glanced over at Shayna behind the wheel. Even though Delanie and Ray were no longer together, Shayna and Delanie's friendship hadn't changed. Delanie was grateful for that.

"Thank you, Shayna."

"Don't sweat it, doll. It's easier to find parking for

my car than it is for your SUV. Plus, I don't get towed when I park someplace I'm not supposed to."

Which is exactly what the risk-taking woman had done. The space had clearly been marked Tow Away Zone, yet Shayna's car had still been there three hours later when they'd returned.

"Not for driving," Delanie said. "Well, that, too, but mostly for being you. You're a great friend."

Something tender flashed on Shayna's face. "I love you, too, girl."

A short time later, they pulled into Delanie's driveway. She squinted at the utility vehicle, positive she hadn't left it there.

Shayna killed the engine. "Come on," she said. "We're running a little behind schedule."

Puzzled, Delanie said, "Behind schedule? What does—"

Shayna closed the door before Delanie could finish her thought.

"—that mean?"

After a moment or two of confusion-induced paralysis, Delanie joined Shayna, who was now positioned behind the wheel of the utility vehicle.

"Shayna, what is going on?"

"You'll see. Get in."

Delanie did as instructed. Bryan had told her he had to fly to Japan for business. Had that been a ruse just to surprise her again? No. He would have definitely met her in the house, not the vineyard, which is where they were headed.

Delanie gasped when the huge oak tree lit up with what seemed like a thousand clear, sparkling lights.

"What…?" She eyed Shayna, who was grinning from ear to ear. Had Shayna done this for her? To cheer her up?

As they got closer, Delanie's mouth went slack. In addition to the lights, hundreds of teal and silver ornaments hung from the branches. The deck was littered with red, white and pink poinsettias, and dozens of wrapped packages sat at the base of the tree. When they came to a stop, Delanie nearly toppled over her own feet getting out of the utility vehicle for a closer inspection.

"I really hope you still consider me a great friend after tonight," Shayna said.

Why wouldn't she? Delanie turned just in time to see Shayna driving away in the opposite direction. *What the heck?* "Shayna!"

"Sorry, doll. I had to choose sides this one time," she called out in an elevated tone.

"Where are you going? You can't just leave me here all alone."

"You're never alone in Vine Ridge," a masculine voice said from behind Delanie.

An instant warmth washed over Delanie. She whipped around to see Ray stepping from behind the massive trunk of the tree. The Stetson was what first caught her eye, and it lowered her defenses. *"Ray."* His name came out in a pant, and she felt a twinge of embarrassment. Clearing her throat, she squared her shoulders to appear far more confident than she actually was.

While that might have been true, that you were never alone in Vine Ridge, she had felt pretty lonely lately.

And it was all because of him. What did he think, that this elaborate setup would make her forget he'd broke her heart?

"What is going on?" she asked plainly, trying to ignore all the emotions crashing around inside her. How could she still miss him so much?

Ray interlocked his glove-covered fingers. "Do you remember the first time we met? On Main Street?"

Delanie sighed. "Ray, I don't have time for a hundred questions. It's late and I'm freezing. I assume you've told Shayna not to come back until you've given her some kind of signal, right? Well, just say what you have to say so that I can leave." And he'd better make it quick. She didn't like the idea of having to hike back to the house, but she would.

Ray removed his coat and draped it around her shoulders. Her body quaked at his nearness. "You're going to catch pneumonia," she said, scolding herself for showing concern for the man who'd dumped her. While she kind of understood why, it had hurt. Still hurt. Why hadn't he believed he could tend to his mother and love her at the same time?

"Answer the question," he said, removing his scarf and wrapping it around her neck.

Ray's scent saturated both the wool coat and scarf, forcing her to realize just how much she'd missed it. "Yes, Ray, I remember." It hadn't been one of her best moments.

Looking into her eyes, he said, "Do you regret that day?"

She wanted to say yes, but it would have been a lie. "No."

Ray's lips curled into a lazy smile. "Me neither. That day changed my life, because it was the day you barreled into it." He studied her for a moment. "I have lied to you, Delanie. My first and my last time doing so."

Delanie's brow bunched. *Lied to her? About what?*

"The day we broke up—"

"Don't you mean the day you dumped me?" Delanie asked. Dropped her flat without even the respect or courtesy of looking her in the eyes while doing so. "I mean, if we're being honest, that's what—"

In a swift motion, Ray held her face between his hands and positioned his mouth dangerously close to hers. "Delanie—" He stopped abruptly, his jaw muscles tensing as if fighting against words or will. Strain was evident on his face. The man was intense, had always been intense, but this...this was something else. Something that resembled torture. Several beats of tension-filled silence ticked by before Ray allowed his hands to fall, and he took a step back.

"The day things ended between us," he continued, "I'd gone to the B and B to talk to your ex. I wanted him to know he'd had his chance and blown it. That you were mine now, and I wasn't letting you go. Not without a fight."

Delanie was confused. If Ray had gone to the B and B to fight for her, why had he let her go?

"You were there," he said. "I overheard you agree with him that your divorce had been a mistake. I felt..." He blew a heavy breath and a stream of heated air floated between them. "I don't know what I felt, because I've never felt anything so paralyzing before in my life." Worry lines creased his forehead. "Then when I asked if you had spoken to your ex, you lied to me."

"I was *protecting* you. You were already going through so much. I didn't want to add to your stress. So when you asked me, yes, I lied. But it was for your own good."

Now it made sense. Their breakup had nothing to do with his mother and everything to do with fear. Ray had assumed he was losing her?

Whatever conclusion he'd jumped to, over a conversation he'd partially heard, hadn't given him the right to hurt her this way. "Is that all?" she said. "Is that everything you needed to say, Ray? I really would like to leave now."

"No, it's not." He reclaimed the space close to her he'd surrendered earlier. "I love you, Delanie Claire Atwater."

Ray's chest rose and fell as if saying those words was the hardest thing he'd ever done.

"You don't love me, Ray."

"I do, Delanie. I love you more than I ever imagined was possible for me."

"You don't love me," she screamed out. "If you did, we wouldn't be here right now. You wouldn't be fighting for something you never should have destroyed. If you loved me, you would have trusted what we had. If you loved me, you wouldn't have broken my heart." She swiped a hand across her chilly cheek, surprised that her tear hadn't frozen on her face. Ray attempted to comfort her, but she pushed him away. "If you loved me, Ray Cavanaugh, you would have simply talked to me and I would have told you that there had been a but."

Ray's brow furrowed. "A but? What does that mean?"

Delanie hugged her arms to her chest and looked away from him, batting back more tears. "You only heard a snippet of the conversation, Ray. Yes, I told Cordell that the divorce was a mistake. But I also told him it was a mistake for him, not for me. That Vine Ridge is my home now. That my heart is here." She eyed him again. "My heart is here, because you are here. I love you, Ray Jude Cavanaugh. *You*, not Cordell."

"I didn't…" Ray's words trailed off, confusion playing on his face.

Delanie could have spent the next hour, day, month making him pay for walking away from her, but she would have only been making herself suffer, too. Hadn't she done enough of that? "It shouldn't have taken you so long to come for me," she said.

"I'm here now. Completely," he said.

Delanie studied the man before her, a good man. "So am I."

Ray grabbed her into his arms and held her so tightly a puff of air escaped. They stayed this way for several minutes. She closed her eyes and savored the feel, warmth, scent of him.

Ray reared back and stared into her eyes. "I love you so much." A second later, he kissed her with enough heat and passion to ignite the entire vineyard. Her moans of delight filled the nighttime silence. When he ended their connection, they both panted for air.

"Was this your idea?" she asked, glancing up at the lighted oak tree.

Ray led her onto the deck. "Yes. I wanted to make up for ruining your Christmas."

"It's not Christmas yet," she said, spinning to see everything. She nearly fell flat on her ass when she completed the circle to see Ray down on one knee. Gasping, she slapped both hands over her mouth. "What are you doing, Ray?" As if it weren't obvious.

"I didn't think I was capable of ever falling in love again. Then you came along and proved me all-the-way wrong. I've never loved a woman the way I love you, Delanie, and I know I never will. You're it for me, baby. My fate-driven destiny. And I want to spend my life with you."

"Why? Why do you love me? Why do you want to spend your life with me?" Delanie wasn't sure what had prompted the questions, but now she really wanted to hear the answers.

"Because you're nothing short of amazing. You have accepted me at my best and my worst, through perfection and flaws. You stand beside me. You're my strength, woman. I smile because of you, laugh because of you. Baby, I breathe because of you. Deep, cleansing breaths. You allow me to just be."

Delanie flashed a low-wattage smile, tears stinging her eyes.

"I love you for so many reasons, Delanie, including for your courage. Especially for your courage."

"My courage?"

"When you arrived in Vine Ridge, you had been broken by love. Still, somehow, you had the courage to love me, even when I was unlovable. I want to spend eternity kissing you, making love to you, slow dancing with you, loving you. Delanie Claire Atwater, will you marry me?"

Delanie eyed the huge diamond Ray presented to her. Rational thinking told her to question everything. What they'd gone through. The short time they'd been together. Her unsuccessful past with love. But as usual, her mother's voice chimed in at just the right moment. *The heart knows what the brain can sometimes not figure out.*

"Don't doubt my love for you, Delanie. I will move glaciers for you, woman. Be my forever Christmas gift. Be my—"

Delanie placed a finger over his lips. *"Shh."* Holding his face between her hands, she smiled, a tear rolling down her cheek. "Yes."

Ray slid the icy ring onto her finger, pulled her into his arms, and kissed her hard and long. The thought that she'd get to experience love-highs like this for the rest of her life filled her with overwhelming joy. Their connection came to an abrupt halt with Delanie pulling away.

"The Lighted Oak," she said.

Ray flashed a perplexed look.

"The name of my vineyard. The Lighted Oak."

"I love it, and I love you," he said.

"I love you, too."

Their lips touched again, and Delanie knew now more than ever that she'd made the best decision of her life.

Epilogue

Delanie ironed a hand up and down Ray's arm, giving him time to gather himself before they had to enter the brick building in front of them. She knew how hard this was for him, but she would make sure he got through it. "Let's go, baby," she said gently.

"I can't do it, Delanie. I can't go in there and see my mom—" He stopped, his hand tightening around hers.

"Yes, you can," she said.

Inside the exquisite facility, Delanie bellowed in laughter at the sight of Momma Cavanaugh leading the conga line inside Jasmine Springs, an independent senior living community, twirling the ends of the royal blue boa around her neck.

Ray gasped. "What kind of horse and pony show are they running around here?"

Delanie was laughing so hard that she wasn't able to keep Ray from intervening in his mother's fun.

"Mom!"

Momma Cavanaugh smiled when Ray approached, but never broke the line. "Oh, hey, son. Wanna join in? It's loads of fun."

Ray marched alongside her. "No, I don't want to join in. What are you doing?"

"Conga!" she sang out.

"Conga!" the twenty or so other seniors in the room echoed, then cheered.

Ray and Delanie had married in a beautiful ceremony by the oak tree at dusk on what was now *their* property, but had postponed their honeymoon when, by some great blessing, a perfect kidney match had come available for Momma Cavanaugh.

While they'd been told the surgery was extremely high-risk, Momma Cavanaugh had opted to go ahead with the procedure. *Because I wanted to be here for my grandbabies*, she'd said, then had winked at them as a way of saying *hint-hint*.

By the grace of God, the surgery had been performed without a hitch, and Momma Cavanaugh made a full recovery.

Ray and Delanie had finally carved out some time for a honeymoon, a week in Ireland. But when they'd returned, Momma Cavanaugh had moved into her new home a short drive from Vine Ridge. Both Delanie and Ray had begged her to return to the ranch, but she'd been adamant about staying here. When Delanie had realized how happy Momma Cavanaugh was, she'd accepted her absence.

Ray, on the other hand… Delanie shook her head at her husband.

"Mom, you should be resting."

"Son, my surgery was months ago. I feel brand-new. Now join us or get out of the way. Conga!"

"Conga!" the room cheered.

Ray stopped and rested his hands on his hips. Delanie came to stand beside him, wrapped her arm around his waist and rested her head against him. He draped an arm over her shoulders.

"As much as I hate to admit it, she does seem happy here." He sighed. "I don't think she's coming home."

"I don't think she is, either," Delanie said.

Ray rubbed his hand up and down her arm. "We have to let her go."

"Yep, we do." She glanced up at him. "Think you're going to be able to handle that?"

His brows shot up. "Me?" He barked a laugh. "Ha! I do recall you being the one who suggested we swoop in like thieves in the night and kidnap her."

Delanie laughed. "I don't recall that conversation. That's my story and I'm sticking to it. Plus, we're talking about you, not me."

Ray stared deep into her eyes. "I'm going to be A-OK, Mrs. Cavanaugh. I've got you."

* * * * *

SPECIAL EXCERPT FROM

HARLEQUIN®

KIMANI™
ROMANCE

Completely captivated by his new employee, André Thorn is about to break his "never mix business with pleasure" rule. But amateur photographer Susan Dewhurst is concealing her true identity. Although she's falling for the House of Thorn scion, she can't reveal the secret that could jeopardize far more than her job at the flagship New York store. Amid André's growing suspicions and an imminent media scandal, does love stand a chance?

Read on for a sneak peek at
Love in New York,
the next exciting installment in the
House of Thorn series by Shirley Hailstock!

As she turned to find her way through the crowd, she came up short against the white-shirted chest of another man.

"Excuse me," she said, looking up. André Thorn stood in front of her.

"Well," he said. "This time there isn't a waiter carrying a tray of champagne."

"I apologized for that," she said, anger coming to her aid. She was already angry with Fred and had been expecting this sword to drop all day. Unprepared to have it fall when she thought she was safe, her sarcasm was stronger than she'd expected it to be. "Please excuse me."

She moved to go around him, but he stepped sideways, blocking her escape.

"Let me buy you a drink?"

Susan's sanity came back to her. This was the president of the company for which she worked. Susan forgot that she could leave and get another job. She knew what it was to be an employee and to be the owner of a business.

"I think I've had enough to drink," she said. "I'm ready to go home."

"So you're going to escape my presence the way you did at the wedding?"

Her head came up to stare at him. Instead of seeing a reprimand in his eyes, she was greeted with a smile.

A devastating smile.

It churned her insides, not the way Fred had, but with need and the fact that it had been a long time since she'd met a man with as much sexual magnetism as André Thorn. No wonder he fit the bill as a playboy.

"I guess I am," Susan finally said. From the corner of her eye, she saw Fred sliding out of the booth. He should know who André Thorn was, but if he planned to put his arm around her in front of another man, he would be making a mistake. "Excuse me," she said and hurried away.

Susan stood in front of the bathroom mirrors. She freshened makeup that didn't need to be, stalling for time. Why had she reacted to André Thorn that way? Embarrassment, she rationalized. She'd run into him at her friend Ryder's wedding. Judging from where he'd sat in the church, he must know Ryder's bride, Melanie. He would. Frowning at her reflection, she chided herself for the unbidden thought. It was a total accident that she'd slipped and tipped the waiter's tray filled with champagne glasses. André had reached for her, and the comedy of flying glasses and fumbling hands and feet would have made her laugh if it happened in a movie. But it had happened to her—to them. And there was nothing funny about it.

Too embarrassed to do anything but apologize and leave, Susan had rushed away to try to remove the splashes that had hit her dress and shoes. She hadn't returned.

She'd never expected to see the man again, so their eyes connecting across the orientation room had been a total surprise, but the recognition was instant. And now she had to return to the bar where he was. Snapping her purse closed, she went back to her group.

Don't miss Love in New York
by Shirley Hailstock, available July 2019
wherever Harlequin® Kimani Romance™
books and ebooks are sold.